The Messenger of Eshra
Cyndi Hughes

Enjoy !! CKH

Journal One

Ayden rested her small frame between the gnarled roots of the cottonwood tree. The hot summer day wrapped her in warmth as she snuggled into it.

Softly caressing the etched leather cover of her book, she sighed. It was time for her to rest. Time for her to pen her thoughts.

She opened the book, reached in her pack and produced her favorite pencil and poised her fingers around it. With the lead touching the blank page, she began.

I do not confidently remember when it first started for me? I'm sure Eleea could tell you, if he were asked. But he isn't one to dwell on those kinds of questions. He would consider it to be irrelevant.

"Frivolous thinking wasting precious time which should be spent in the here and now," he would say.

Anyways, I already know, for him, the important start was when I finally listened. When I finally started to hear what he wanted me to hear. When I began to learn, and accept what he wanted me to do.

To look at him, a person wouldn't think he had such immense emotional power. He brought life to my feelings in a way I could never have imagined. He taught me how to manage my emotions and my preconceived attitudes. It was one of the most frustrating experiences of my relationship with him.

And yet, isn't this the place where a person learns the most: When confronted with uncomfortable and frustrating predicaments, one has to define how they will handle the situation with grace and confidence. And, sometimes humility.

Now, as I sit with my thoughts, I could not imagine life without him. Life without his guidance. Where would I be if it wasn't for him?

Some average kid wandering around wondering how to navigate my mediocre adolescent world of unpredictable circumstances.

The richness of my life and all I have experienced directly relates to what I thought was my happenstance meeting of Eleea. His planned intervention to save me... I know now, was not happenstance at all.

Chapter One

"What can I do, Eleea? I am just a child. I don't know anything about survival on my own," Ayden whimpered as she brushed back the auburn locks rippling in the wind across her right eye and cheek. She looked away from him and deliberately focused on the end of the dirt road. Ayden pretended she could see something approaching as she kept her eyes locked on the distant marker reading Grinnell Road.

"Plus," she stated emphatically, "it is just plain scary, and I might add not very responsible, to even think about going on some type of trip not knowing anything about where I am going! There's no map to Google. No Wikipedia search to teach me about the unknown surroundings. It is just too dangerous for a child of my age to go into the unknown," she concluded.

"I will be with you. You will not be alone," Eleea soothingly chided with words of encouragement.

Ayden lifted her chin and steadied her stare. "What if I forget how to listen? What then? Then you will just be a bird, a little chickadee, flying around me chirping!" She apprehensively stated.

"I'm too young. This is wrong!" Ayden aggressively determined as she stomped her favorite sneaker of white, chartreuse and turquoise causing dust to fly around her firmly planted foot.

"Ayden, you are the Messenger. You will not fail. I won't let you," Eleea quickly countered.

She looked into Eleea's eyes as he focused on her. She tried to contain her fear. She thought, "What was it about his eyes? How could he always convince me I should cross over into the unknown? The eerie unfamiliar?"

Those eyes. From a distance, they looked like any other eye of a chickadee or for that matter any bird's eye. Yet, when he got close, and he looked at her with such intensity, it was mesmerizing. It was like looking across the horizon as the morning proclaimed its entry for the new day.

Vibrant hues of orange, brown, and purple, with a hint of blueish sky interlaced within the vivid colors as they danced with the clouds, announcing the entrance of the yellowish-orange glow of the sun as it crested over the mountains.

The hope she sensed from gazing into his eyes, his precious soul, always embraced her with trust and warmth. He projected his inner core into her heart as he transfixed on her. Strength and beauty soared through his spirit into hers when he looked at her.

It wasn't she inevitably always allowed him to persuade her to agree to his plans for her future, and his. It was her need to prove what he desired her to accomplish was not totally impossible.

Her need to hope her world of adolescence was more than just a rite of passage every child must traverse on the road to adulthood. It was the desire to believe her life...her existence...had purpose. To believe in miracles where sheer determination could overcome any odds.

Up to this point of daily living, her life had been anything but eventful. Full of family discord and anger, and teenage angst. Constant fighting between her parents coupled with her uncomfortable body image and always being ridiculed by her dad. Who had plenty to say about how she was a disappointment to him?

Her desire to prove she was more than what her dad felt about her fueled her
desperate need to help others and to help herself. To fulfill a soul's longing for acceptance and love was at the root of all her decisions.

Ayden was only fourteen, how else was she supposed to think? She wanted to be accepted by Eleea. She wanted to be loved by him too. Not in the man versus woman relational sense, but in the respect and, 'I honor you,' sense.

"Eleea, I have to think about what you are asking me to do. I can't give you an answer right now," she impatiently told him.

Soon it would be summer with tourists flooding all the beautiful surroundings of her little town, known as East Glacier, nestled in the bosom of the great glaciers. The slow-moving lifestyle the slightly less than four hundred locals relished throughout the off season would once again be accelerated into a fast-moving grind of trying to accommodate whatever new whim the latest guest or traveler demanded.

Or the constant concern of the townsfolk echoing in the kids' ears to watch out for each other as the thousands of vehicles and foreigners infiltrated their turf wanting to experience Glacier National Park.

But, right now Ayden needed to get to her first class and couldn't allow her mind to fret about what Eleea needed her to do. "I promise you; I will seriously have an answer for you by the end of the school year," Ayden finally cajoled him.

"Ayden, I trust you to make the right decision. It's just, time is of the essence, and souls are at stake," Eleea softly replied.

"You know, Eleea, you are beginning to sound a lot like my teachers! It's all about how important their assignment is and why I need to put them first in my study schedule," Ayden pouted as she spoke.

"Before you found me, you had no idea how to accomplish what you needed. So, in my humble opinion, time is not of the essence. Time is what you make of it," Ayden replied smugly.

Eleea lowered his eyes as Ayden stood there telling him why she was not in a hurry. She knew he was disappointed, but he would never say it to her. He never told her she had to do anything. He only showed her through examples and stories of why she needed to do it.

His story telling was amazing. It felt like the trees swayed as the wind gently rustled their leaves in a spring breeze when he spoke of times past. But she didn't have time to hear his stories or to wonder if he was emotionally hurt.

She only had enough time to catch the school bus. Ayden hurriedly picked up her backpack without looking at Eleea to avoid feeling remorse for her curt answer. She left him and started to run to the bus stop.

It was her last year in middle school. Not only did she have to complete the end of the year requirements, she also had to decide if she wanted to apply for the summer advancement course in English.

"Yuk! Sometimes the thought of not trying hard in school sounded appealing. Then no one would expect so damn much from me," she thought as she scowled.

Always having to push to do better than the last assignment seemed so demeaning. She was only as good as her last great score.

It felt like she was a caged hamster in the running wheel. No matter how hard she tried, she would still be running in circles going nowhere. Never reaching beyond the confines of the wheel.

Deborah was already waiting for Ayden and she could see she was not pleased with her tardiness, again. "What is it with you," Deborah demanded with her arms folded across her chest.

"Ayden, I am feeling like more and more this friendship of ours means less and less to you," she quizzically blurted out with a hint of fear in her voice.

Ayden rested her greenish hazel eyes upon her friend. Deborah's hair was the color of winter wheat. Naturally highlighted in beautiful hues of gold, blond and tiny streaks of adobe brown.

Deborah loved her bouncy hair to just touch below her shoulders, when she didn't have it in its inevitable loose braid with her forehead completely covered in bangs. She claimed she had to keep it out of her way by not falling around her face if she was to do her best thinking.

"Thinking," Ayden's left side of her lip curled slightly as she sarcastically remembered hundreds of past moments with Deborah and her thinking.

Deborah had an eidetic memory. She devoured and flawlessly remembered anything and everything she read, watched or heard.

"How could it possibly matter to have her hair tucked away in a discombobulated mess behind her head when she never forgets. And, therefore does not have to really work to remember or think," Ayden frustratingly thought.

It was Deborah's idea to call each other by the first letter of their names. "Our friendship needs to stay uncomplicated," Deborah declared one day. "I propose a simple syntax of our own linguistic and mutual understanding by using the initial of our first name to address each other."

Oh! How Ayden desired to tell her everything knowing it would be so much easier on their friendship. "Only if she knew about Eleea," Ayden lamented in heartbroken silence. "If she knew about Eleea then there would be no more awkward moments of Deborah feeling the strife and self-doubt about their bond with each other."

Bound to silence and secrecy was the order, though. She was not allowed to speak of this other world which needed a young child who could speak to a bird.

Truly, if Deborah knew what Ayden was keeping from her; her world of scientific theory and rational reasoning would send her into overtime conjecture. Causing her to probably admit herself to a psychiatric ward.

No, the knowledge of what Ayden was to do in the near future, even if it was limited like a fledgling bird taking its first flight from the nest, had to stay a secret.

"'D,'" Ayden said in a gentle tone, as if she were talking to a baby rabbit who had unluckily jumped into her path and was frozen with fear by the presence of a human.

"'We have known each other since we were ten years old when you moved here. You are the only true friend I have ever known. I value everything about you," Ayden tenderly told her.

"You are my sanctuary against the storms of my life. You know that, 'D,'" Ayden appealed to her. "What would I have done," Ayden stated candidly, "if you had not come to live in my town? With my parents always fighting. Especially when my dad is drinking?"

"It's just, I am really confused about who I am right now," Ayden sheepishly lied. "Please give me some space to come to terms with my confusion and know in your heart I will always depend on your friendship to keep me sane," she begged her.

Deborah zeroed in on Ayden with her penetrating piercing blue eyes. Ayden knew all too well from past experiences if Deborah cocked her head to the right, she was in for one of Deborah's theoretical classroom lectures. And, sure enough there went her head.

"OK, 'A', but I feel the need to do some explaining here," she instructed. "I want to take you back to a day when you and I decided to go for a picnic," she continued. "It was my first summer living here and I knew nothing about the outdoors. Well, not nothing because you do realize I was extremely versed in the history, landscape and indigenous species of this region. I researched it before we moved here, you know," Deborah declared.

"You knew book knowledge. But you knew nothing about living in this environment," Ayden correctly reminded her.

"Anyways," Deborah continued as if Ayden hadn't spoken, "It was a beautiful day with no clouds in the sky and we were laughing and walking up the mountain trail to the falls. I had just taken the backpack with the food in it from you as you were tiring, remember?" Deborah inquired.

Ayden silently rolled her eyes as she tried to maintain her school-girl-esque demeanor. She felt as if she were listening to one of her classroom teachers give the next empirical instructions to a boring assignment.

Deborah continued, ignoring Ayden's attempt to hide her dismay. "I reached around to put the pack through my right arm and as I was getting ready to put my left arm into the pack, I lost my balance and began to steady myself on the boulder next to the trail."

"Really 'D'," Ayden interrupted, "How could I forget that day. If I had not immediately reacted and grabbed for you, you would have been bitten by a rattlesnake," she expressed in frustration.

Ayden replayed the whole event in her mind as Deborah continued her latest persuasive speech which was intended to convince Ayden to do what Deborah desired. The way she had seized Deborah's forearm with her hand had become their signature shake when they wanted to bind their decisions of trust to any new situation which required total agreement.

Ayden had clutched Deborah's right forearm with her right hand which caused Deborah to instinctually grab Ayden's right forearm with her right hand. It had turned into a unique handshake because it had come from a moment in their young lives when danger needed to be averted.

If Ayden had just reached for Deborah's hand and not the forearm it would not have created a strong hold. By grasping her forearm, she was able to propel her away from danger without Deborah's fingers slipping through Ayden's fingers.

The symbolism of the clasp of the arms with their hands had become a defining moment in their young relationship.

The power behind the handshake was more than just an emotional attachment of
danger narrowly escaped. It was the message of strength it possessed in the hearts of the girls. And, neither one of the girls were 'girly girls' who wanted to use something like a 'pinky swear promise' to bind their hearts' decisions.

So, it became an emotional bond they used when they needed to speak without words. Proclaiming, "I trust you deeply with every secret, fear and dream I have."

"'D,'" Ayden continued, "you do not need to tell me in detail the importance of that day. I was there, remember?" she irritably expressed her impatience.

Ayden knew she needed to stop Deborah's train of thought from wrecking, but her mind was already exhausted from quieting Eleea's. Relief flashed across her face as the bus rounded the corner. Deborah wouldn't be able to finish her demanding plan to get her to confess she wasn't hiding anything from her.

"Ayden," Deborah's speech became hurried as she and Ayden stared down the road at the fast-approaching bus.

"I want you to meet me after dinner tonight so we can finally discuss our situation. I want you to shake on a promise you are not hiding anything important from me. I have asked mom for a sleep over and she is expecting you tonight at our house. Don't say no, cuz your mom already has agreed to you spending the whole weekend with us," Deborah quickly finished.

"What! No one asked me if I wanted to go on a sleep over! When did it become customary in your family to make decisions for me and go behind my back to ask my mom for permission?" Ayden spewed at Deborah.

Ayden's mind raced with feelings of helplessness. First Eleea demanded she do what he wanted, now Deborah had her future planned. She had no real say with either one of them because they both felt they had her best interests in mind.

"Their best interests in mind is more like it!" Ayden surprisingly spoke audibly.

Deborah's head snapped back to Ayden like a fixed drone. "What do you mean, 'their best interests?'

"YOU! My mom! Your mom!" Ayden deftly expressed before Deborah found out the truth of her thoughts.

"All of you think you can tell me what my best interests are without even asking me how I feel about it. It is just plain rude and wrong!" Ayden defiantly expressed and then slumped her shoulders in defeat.

"Whatever, 'D'," Ayden half-heartedly stated, as she kept her eyes on the approaching vehicle. "I'll see you after dinner tonight."

The girls took their usual seats on the bus and rode in silence. Ayden walked through the day in a dazed fog.

Her mind swirled with possible scenarios of what would happen when she was left alone with Deborah at the end of the day. "Maybe," Ayden conspired in her mind, "I could feign sickness."

Feign was Ayden's newest favorite word. Feign: 'the choice to make up a story or an excuse which wasn't true; to fabricate or invent a false scenario.' It reminded her of the word 'fiend' which was an evil word and behavior of trying to deceive someone.

"So, there goes that idea out the window," she thought, "I don't like it when someone lies to me and I don't want to make a habit to lie to others. And, I definitely do not want to be looked at as an evil person.

"Once a person starts to tell 'white lies'," Ayden continued thinking, mindlessly ignoring her required school tasks. "They then start down the slippery slope of justifying those lies and then the lies become more frequent and get bigger.

"Soon the person doesn't remember what was fabrication and what was truth. They become duped by their own lies. Tragic to sell yourself and your honor for the easy way out with lies," Ayden determined.

"No," Ayden breathed as she straightened her shoulders back. "I need to face the facts and honor our friendship. I will have to tell her I can't tell her, and then try to convince her we still have a strong friendship," Ayden finally decided.

"What a mess Eleea has created for me!" Ayden exhaled as she closed her eyes, covering her face with her hands.

Journal Two

Ayden perused what she had written. Lifting her eyes, she tried to rationalize her thoughts.

She never wanted to be looked at like a selfish brat or like a person who only cared about using someone for their own personal gain. Nor, did she wish to be viewed as weak by anyone.

Life is not easy, she wrote. Crazy twists and turns can make you feel out of control. And, feeling out of control can cause you to revert back to old habits to try and gain back a sense of control.

Whether it be the use of familiar white lies, exerted anger to look like you are powerful or the silence of not letting anyone know you need help. It didn't matter.

All three habits were harmful to me. I feigned confidence, when I felt like screaming. I spewed angry words when I felt cornered. I kept quiet when others tried to get me to talk about what was bothering me.

Even though I tried to avoid lying to others, I had to finally come to terms with those 'white lies' because they were me.

I constantly lied to myself to avoid breaking down in tears. Even though I hated anger, it would rear its ugly head when I felt overwhelmed. And, even though my motto had always been no one was ever going to see me vulnerable, I was exposed all of the time.

All three behaviors, what I thought were positive coping skills, were viewed by others as a selfish little girl who was trying to manipulate everyone around her. And, what I thought were strengths, were really weaknesses.

Fear was the constant thread which ran through each problem of trying to stay in control of my environment.

They say, "the first step to change is to recognize what is wrong."

Now, I had to recognize fear had ruled my life. I had to learn how to use fear to make me a person who didn't have to react negatively.

I had to learn to positively propel myself out of its' hold and come out on the other side.

With the power to break its deathly grip on me.

Chapter Two

Eleea had a working knowledge of the land of Eshra. It was his land and his home. He loved Eshra.

But this journey he was asking Ayden to take with him would lead to terrain he had never seen before. Territory he had no familiarity with. It would be dangerous and pitted with serious known and unknown enemies.

"Why did she have to be so young, and a girl of all things," he thought to himself.

He knew it was not his choice, only his purpose to complete the mission. He had been sent to find the messenger. And, he found her. But, what a fluke in how he discovered her.

From a bird's point of view, humans were a curious sort. Always bustling around unaware about how they were being perceived by other creatures. Acting as if they owned the universe and the universe only revolved around them for their own desired purposes. Especially young children who had not yet learned how to help others by giving from their hearts and souls.

Granted, not all humans were unaware. He had seen some who truly understood the laws of nature. Living in East Glacier surrounded by the Park had shown him a side of humans which pleased him. Respect for the land, what it had to offer and an appreciation for the animals who called it home.

Eleea was sure the people who grew up in the region held this respect through a deeper connection they had with their ancestry. Forged within the traditions of an ancient people who sojourned across this world was an unspoken truth of how they didn't own the land. But how they shared the land with all nature. Together they helped each other, and together, their mutual respect allowed them to sustain life for both of them.

"Yet, if it had not been for foolish human behavior," Eleea reminded himself, he would never have found Ayden. What a peculiar girl wrestling with boys? She definitely didn't fit the mold of a young girl. She loved getting into mischief and dirt.

"I guess," he reflected, "one could say she lived to explore her surroundings and explore her abilities, even if it was fighting."

And, there she was rolling in the grass pummeling her opponent. A line of juvenile males yelling and encouraging the ruckus. All of them waiting for their turn to take her on.

At the time, Eleea thought, "Well, at least our nest is not built yet, so I don't have to worry about babies in it. They would have been so nervous from all the uproar."

He watched in subtle amusement; hoping all of them would soon tire and leave the area so he could relax.

That was when it happened. The boy tried to get the upper advantage on Ayden. He pulled her hoodie off her back and aggressively ripped her jacket downward to the ground as she struggled to stand. She fell backwards, and the back of her neck and her lower back became exposed.

The oblong form of the dark brown mark started at the base of her hairline where it distinctly showed the regal head of a bird with a long neck and a beak which stretched several inches away from its head. The huge section of slightly lighter brown followed her spine, curved in a graceful stance of the bird with its wings at rest.

Granted, humans called it a birthmark. But, Eleea knew, from legend spoken for hundreds of years this was no birthmark. To an untrained eye it would look like a blotched mess of discolored skin. To him, there was no doubt it was the mark he sought since he arrived.

At first, Eleea thought his eyes tricked him. He actually had felt defeated and frustrated in his endless search for it.

How long had he pursued after it? Every male adult who came and went in this country was researched meticulously. He knew the prophecy, or so he thought he knew it. A human from this world would be the messenger.

A human found in the area surrounding the East Glaciers was where the prophecy said he would be found. He would be the one to secure order to his world as well as to Eshra; Eleea's world. He was needed for the survival of both their worlds.

Shock was an understatement when Eleea realized it was a girl and not a man who would fulfill the prophecy.

When he first started his search, he was so determined it would be someone who was a true warrior. One who would be able to fight. Who would be strong physically, mentally, and spiritually; and who could lead?

Then, as time went on with no prospects. He had to widen his exploration to any male who came to the land.

But now, this could not be. Now he had to play the role of nursemaid to this young life. To convince a child to do the right thing; to look beyond her selfish, childish mindset? And, he was not allowed to tell her to do it, she had to make the decision on her own volition.

"What a spiraling nightmare of horrors!" Eleea lamented as he exhaustively thought about the past attempts to find the messenger and the future trials with Ayden.

This girl who he had watched several times from his tree with her best friend, Deborah. How could it be her? He was not prepared to reason with a child.

Yet, there it was. The mark which proved she was the one. He almost fell off his perch when he saw it on her back.

The memory of the prophesy's words was etched into his soul:

"Upon the back deliverance comes. At rest the crane stands, head held high."

Granted it wasn't a professional looking canvas like a painting on her back. Eleea knew it would only carry the resemblance of the majestic bird.

A birthmark down the back exhibiting the full stature of the crane. It is what lore told him to search for in the messenger. What he didn't expect is it would be so prominently depicted on her spine. There was no denying this was the mark he had looked for years to find.

The boy who took off her hoodie stood and stared at Ayden's back. "Hey! Guys look at this!" He yelled.

"Ayden what is wrong with you!? Your back has some ugly marks on it!" He grabbed her shirt and pulled it lower down her back to reveal the whole mark.

Ayden quickly thrust her body to get loose from the hold the boy named Travis had on her, and stood up. She torqued her body in a semi round-house kick and planted her foot in Travis' chest. Even though he was one year younger than her, he was twice her size and he quickly lost his balance and fell to the ground.

He looked up at her with a menacing smirk. "Ayden's full of crap," he started to chant as he backed far enough away from her foot.

Quickly standing, Travis got all but one of the other kids to join him in his chant as he danced around her singing, "Ayden is full of crappppp! Ayden is full of crapppp!"

Ayden's body took a rigid stance as she squared off her approach against Travis. Staring at him, fists with thumbs on the outside, she began her descent.

Only taking four steps, she reached him and planted her feet equally to gain solid ground and not lose her balance. She put one forceful fist under his jaw, sending him reeling down the grassy knoll. Lowering her hands, she stared at the rest of them with a look of fire in her eyes.

The boys carefully backed away from her and went after Travis. All except a boy named Nick, who did not join the others in song.

He looked at Ayden with eyes of deep compassion as he quietly walked away from her and the boys. Ayden repositioned her hoodie, and slowly walked home, alone.

Eleea pondered for weeks on how to approach not only Ayden, but the Council back in Eshra to tell them the messenger had been found.

He tried to convince himself the mark didn't mean she was the one with the right mark. But, deep within his spirit, he knew. Reluctantly knew, she was the one prophesied about.

He kept close watch of her every move to decipher what made her so special? What made her destined to save all of them?

Day in and day out he observed Ayden and her interactions from everything with family, friends, animals, to daily home and school responsibilities. She didn't seem to be extraordinary in anything she was doing. Just an average human living in her given environment. No profound skills she could use to fight or to run to get herself out of a dangerous predicament.

Sure, she took classes with her friend for martial arts; but that was just kids play.

Sure, she knocked Travis down in a moment of anger and embarrassment. Not real combat readiness, though.

Yes, she seemed to have common sense. And she definitely had a kind heart towards animals and her friend, Deborah.

"Just an ordinary girl. A girl! "Of all the stupid unpredictable moments in the history of our worlds," Eleea thought as he slumped on his perched limb.

Eleea rested his head on his chest; begging sleep to overtake him. He wanted this whole Ayden mess to just go away. Deep in his thoughts on this early night before the humans' big holiday to celebrate what they called Easter; he just wanted to rest in peace.

He had become very familiar with the fights between Ayden's parents when her dad had too much to drink. He witnessed several such occasions of violence in Ayden's household.

As the familiarity of anger increased, it became normal fair where alcohol wasn't needed for a fight to start. But this night would prove to be a defining moment in Ayden's life...and in his.

He had been spending a good amount of time staking out Ayden's home to try and figure out how to break the silence and begin to speak to her. The window in the front room of her house was cracked open to allow a spring breeze to enter in, and he could hear and see the family's interactions.

What he heard and saw this fateful evening caused his heart to bleed with pain for this child who had no idea she was so desperately needed by all of them.

Ayden was rocking in the rocker with her legs folded under her, eating an apple. Eleea could sense her mood to be heavy as, once again, her parents anger escalated through their speech.

Her mom started to leave the room, telling her husband he didn't need to be so angry all of the time. For whatever reason, this statement triggered something in her dad and he grabbed her mom's arm and started beating the woman in the face and head. The force of this man's full-blown rage as he kept hitting her startled Eleea.

Suddenly, Eleea saw the flash of the apple pass by the dad as Ayden stood and shouted, "Bastard! Leave her alone!"

After observing the power of her father's rage, Eleea expected Ayden to run away from her dad once she spoke. But she just stood there, waiting.

Her dad approached her with his open hand flying across her face. She continued to stand her ground as his other hand reached for his belt and he proceeded to beat her and beat her and beat her with the belt.

Every inch of her body, except the face of course, connected with the leather of the forceful strap. With each strike, he would viciously say to her, "You ...think you... are ...such a...love...child! Do...you?"

Ayden never spoke as she fell to her knees under the pressure of the strikes to her body. She never raised her voice in pain.

She just soundlessly took the slashing rips to her skin with silent dignity. In her own way, she stood her ground even though it was obvious she had lost control of her bodily functions and had soiled her jeans.

Eleea watched intently as her father drunkenly stumbled away from her body. To leave her on the floor like a bag of garbage.

He observed her mother approach her when Ayden began to stand. Innocently thinking he would see her mother lift Ayden to her breast to comfort her as any mother would.

His heart sank even deeper in despair while he watched her mother grab Ayden by the hair and start to shake it and pull it, telling her, "Don't you ever speak to your father that way again!"

Eleea wanted to scream, "Stop!" He desperately wanted to take flight to help this young girl who had been emotionally destroyed in a matter of twenty minutes by those who were supposed to protect her and love her.

The cries which whimpered from Ayden's throat as her mother continued to pull her hair resonated in Eleea's ears. The haunting sound Ayden made pierced the inner core of his soul.

"What have I just witnessed?" He shockingly asked himself. "How could any person behave with such hate towards another? Where did this evil come from?"

His emotions went numb as he waited outside the front room window when the house went dark. All he could think about was how to help Ayden.

"Where was she?" he wondered. The house was shrouded in complete silence.

Eleea patiently clung to the tree branch straining to hear any sound, any movement from Ayden. The minutes turned to an hour as he replayed the night's events.

His heart spoke loudly, reprimanding him for his preconceived notions about Ayden. He had been misguided by his prejudiced and judgmental attitudes concerning her.

This child, who struggled to maintain her composure humbled him with shame for ever doubting who she was.

He needed to know she was OK. "Please Ayden," he silently begged her, "Show yourself. I need to know you are alive. I need to know If you need medical care?"

Then he saw her. The hour was late. She quietly slipped through the screen door to sit on the porch.

The porch was situated the farthest away from her parents' bedroom. It gave her the private refuge Eleea had seen Ayden use before to retreat to when there was chaos in the home.

She ran her fingers across her scalp and as she did clumps of hair landed into her hand and fell to the floor. The full moon illuminated her legs and arms and he saw the red raised welts where the belt had met her skin. She was alone in her pain and sorrow.

Eleea knew instinctually, he needed to be with her in this moment. He flew down from the tree to the handrail nearest her seat. Softly he began to chirp, hoping she would hear his song of strength and love for her.

Her silence, her lack of tears, and her eyes of sorrow engulfed his soul. He continued with his soothing serenade, waiting for her to hear his voice. A good amount of time went by before she finally spoke.

"Chickadee, you should be in bed with your family," she softly said, as she gazed at him with pure innocence. But I thank you for spending time with me right now," she continued, "I needed you tonight, and you have filled my heart with hope. Your song sings to my heart, chickadee."

Eleea continued his slow melodic chant as he ever so softly eased into speech. "Ayden, my child, I need you and you need me," he began. "Reach deep into your soul and hear my words," he encouraged her.

"You know chickadee, this is Easter morning," she stated. "I don't know if you have ever heard the importance of this holiday, but it is a big one for a lot of us humans," she explained.

"You see, Jesus came to earth thousands of years ago to bring a message of hope and salvation to the people. Some high-up high-fluent guys didn't like what he was doing. He was taking away their coerced income from the people of the time. Cuz, you see, he was telling them the truth. By explaining to the people these guys were selfishly using them. So, the guys had him crucified to shut him up. He was severely beaten before he died, you know?"

"Kind of ironic, huh! Not to say I was beaten as bad as he was, mind you. But it does give me a whole new meaning about this day, now," Ayden softly said.

Ayden placed her chin in the cup of her hand as she rested her elbow on her knee. She looked at Eleea intently and said, "What did you say your name was, chickadee?"

"Eleea," Eleea responded.

"Well, Eleea that is a very unique name," Ayden stated. "Kind of flows off your tongue when you say it. "E-Lee-Ah. Kind of like 'Julia' but with an E," Ayden matter-of-factly continued.

"Do you celebrate any holidays Eleea," she asked?

"How perfect," Eleea thought. He had wanted to start explaining to Ayden about his world and expose her to its' history. He couldn't come up with a good start, and now, she opened the door for him.

"Ayden," Eleea began, *"There was a time, long, long ago in a world where people lived side by side with animals of all sorts and they were able to speak with these animals. Animal and man respected each other.*

They worked together to help each other live a life with more abundance for each of them. There was no need to have a value system to determine whose work was the most important as they all lived harmoniously out of a mutual trust and understanding they needed each other.

No one felt their skill or gift was better than another's." He stopped speaking to look at Ayden. He wanted to make sure he had not lost her in her own thoughts and she was still listening.

Ayden spoke up when she realized Eleea was silent, "It must have been wonderful to be able to talk to the animals and not fear them, or even disregard them as if they were not there."

Then she curiously asked, "What was the land like? Did it look like, you know, Glacier where nature is just so beautiful?"

"Oh, the beauty of the land," Eleea dreamily expressed. "Ayden, it was the most magnificent setting of movement and color. As you moved amongst the flowers and the grass, they swayed in unison with you. There was a sense of freedom and one of belonging when you were with them."

"Natural walkways were formed by them so that no one trampled over them. The plants, flowers, trees, and grass were responsible for all the paths. There were no man-made trails because there was no need to make them. The correct ones had already been made," he explained.

"Each plant, each tree, and each flower had its own way of showing forth its iridescent light," Eleea reminisced. "Even the plant world didn't try to outshine each other, Ayden. They worked together to create a tapestry of light versus shadow showcasing their playfulness and rhythm of creativity," Eleea continued to interpret.

"But, back to your original question of whether I celebrate any holidays," Eleea reminded himself and Ayden.

"We don't really have special days to commemorate specific events like yours for this person, Jesus," Eleea conveyed and continued. "We celebrate all life, as all of it is important and should be honored."

"Without respect for that which is alive, one loses part of their soul," Eleea reverently told Ayden.

Abruptly, Ayden interjected in a troubled voice, "Does this mean, for you, my world is evil because we use animals for food?"

"No, child," Eleea calmingly stated, "Even I take a life when I eat a seed or an insect. It has to do with honoring what you eat as precious. Realizing its' life was given for you to survive. Just as you have domesticated animals for food, so, too, do we in my world."

"So, to truly answer your first question," Eleea pressed on. "There are no holidays celebrated in my world. But we do have festivals which revolve around our moon."

"The moon rises in the evening just as it does here in your world. But, in our world, the moon has a distinct image of a feather belonging to a majestic crane on its surface which can only be seen one night each month on a full moon."

"Then once a year at our new year in July, when the moon is full, you can see the full image of our magnificent crane. Every fourth month we have a day festival when the illumination of the moon is at its brightest and you can see the feather at its clearest. But, on our New Year festival, when the full image is seen, we have a week-long festival," Eleea stopped speaking as he could see Ayden was having difficulty keeping her eyes open.

"Eleea," Ayden began, "I am feeling very tired right now. I have to go inside and go to bed. Will I see you again?"

"Yes, Ayden," he gently said, "You will see me again. Go to bed now and sleep peacefully. And, have sweet dreams my child."

Ayden rose from her chair in a sleepy stupor as she walked away from Eleea and entered her home.

"Good job," Eleea told himself, feeling pretty confident this first meeting had gone well. Actually, it had gone better than he hoped. She didn't get hysterical. She didn't run away and she listened.

He reviewed the day's happenings as he flew towards home. He had gone from perturbed he had to reach the heart of a child to help him. To horror at watching this child's heart crushed by those who were supposed to love her and protect her. To reaching from the depths of his heart to comfort a child who, now more than ever, he needed to help as much as he needed her to help all who lived in their two worlds.

"What a turn of events," he whispered out loud as he flew. This monumental point in time, these past few hours, would forever become the binding thread to interlace Ayden's and Eleea's hearts together. It would be his constant reminder to never quickly judge a person; especially Ayden.

Their new life together, their future, would bring power to their hearts. And, respect to those who were lucky enough to experience their journey.

Journal Three

Ayden set her pencil in the crevasse of the book spine and closed the book. Bringing her knees to her chest, she wrapped her arms around them.

She lazily focused her eyes on the river next to the tree where she sat. The water silently rested as it glimmered like a mirror from the sun's rays. Each plant, each intimate piece of life near its' bank flawlessly reflected perfectly on top of the water. Deep in thought, she replayed the first night she met Eleea.

"A chickadee of all things," she whispered. "His perfect little body of maybe a fourth of a pound, if he was lucky," she chuckled to herself, "was designed like an artist's masterpiece. His slightly large head donned the blackest little cap which surrounded his eyes and tapered off his back and ended right where his spine attached to his wings.

White feathers defined the cheekbone area from the black; almost appearing like he was wearing a bib tied with white ribbon around his neck. The black base, looked like the foundation of a pyramid at the top of his chest, which then rose to a pointed peak leading to his beak; with the rest of his chest sporting the white feathers. Shades of grey, white and black mixed with a little brown covered the rest of his body.

Eleea was a proud breed; not prideful...but proud. When his chest protruded out in a stance of determination intermingled with his words of wisdom, he seemed so much larger than his total body length of five and half inches."

"Truly," Ayden thought, "Eleea has been more of a father, a parent, to me than my own flesh and blood. Strange how unplanned moments in time cause one to redefine one's own existence," Ayden mused.

She opened the book to write: No matter how hard you try to forget the bad...you won't! It may filter down to the far recesses of your mind, to sit in the sediment of your desired forget-fullness.

But, then a smell, a song, a familiar word will jolt it forward like a roller coaster descending down the track bringing it to the forefront of your raw emotions; causing you to relive the pain.

All of us have had those defining traumas where we have felt hopeless and defeated. Instead of working so hard to forget those painful events, embrace them for the good you find in them.

Don't let it define you as a failure...as a nothing...or as a person who is only a victim.

Forgive, accepting you won't forget. And, let the person who inflicted the harm stay the one responsible for the heinous act they choose to perform.

Use those experiences to find the good about yourself. Such as:

"You determined to survive."

"You found strength to learn how not to act towards others."

And, "You developed compassion from your experiences, for those who, also, had been horribly harmed."

"Painful events, no matter how hurtful, like being beat with a belt, can reveal something good.

If not for that night," Ayden wrote, "I would never, so easily, have accepted a chickadee freely talking to me."

Chapter Three

Ayden increasingly felt like life was being drained from her. She had no freedom in her home. She was afraid all of the time.

She had no clue what would set her dad off to become angry and possibly physically hurt her again. Let alone, wondering if her mom would readily join in on the attack when her dad started.

She walked around her home sequestered and empty. She didn't dare speak freely about anything for fear they would blitz her with more retaliation.

She had no freedom to talk to her best friend. If she told Deborah about her ability to magically speak to a bird, she would break trust with Eleea and be told by Deborah she was crazy.

If she told Deborah about her being beat with a belt and having her hair pulled out? Well, that was just not going to happen. She didn't need anyone pitifully feeling sorry for her. It just seemed any way she turned, she would anger or disappoint someone.

Spending the weekend at Deborah's was bittersweet for Ayden. Bitter, she had to be honest with Deborah, and, yet, not betray Eleea's confidence. Sweet, because Ayden adored Deborah's family.

Her parents, Graycie and Robert Laverson, were full of respect for each other, and for their only child. The dignity they showed in all they did, from their jobs to their interactions with everyone was very different than her family.

Ayden felt special being around them because she knew they accepted her and loved her. She had become their second daughter; especially after she saved Deborah from the rattlesnake.

Graycie took a job as a visiting professor for the University of Montana out of Missoula four years ago. This is how the family ended up in East Glacier. The family decided to stay. Wth Graycie becoming a permanent adjunct professor who spoke to her students over the internet.

She was a doctor of something where she studied all aspects of the plants, flowers, trees, and bugs of the region. All technical stuff which was far out of Ayden's realm of reasoning. Deborah seemed to understand what her mom was, though, and had professed she would study one day to be a botanist like her mom.

Robert had made wise choices with on-line trading which allowed the family to have financial freedom. He invested most of his money into land and businesses around Glacier and Seattle, Washington.

During the summer, he hosted aspiring artists and taught them how to use water color and pencil to paint the landscapes and wildlife around Glacier.

The only solace Ayden had about the weekend; was she didn't have to go to their house until after dinner. Which meant it was closer to nighttime and she could fall asleep quickly and avoid talking to Deborah. The plan was for Ayden to call Deborah after dinner for her mom to come get Ayden and her clothes.

But, as it goes, the best laid plans do not always mature. Ayden's dad had the day off from his job as an auto mechanic at the local garage and he was well on his way to a drunken rage by the time she got home from school.

Her mom was in her typical foxhole, her bedroom. Trying to avoid the inevitable confrontation when dad decided he needed to flex his, which Ayden had coined, 'coward-power' over her mom.

Ayden knew all too well from recent past experience since he had passed the threshold of only seeing her as a child and now, she was seen as an extension of her mother, she was not safe. So, she succumbed to the only plan she could. She called Deborah to have her mom come get her before dinner.

Ayden was in her room, filling her backpack with clothes when her dad walked into her room. She kept her eyes down to avoid any chance of him seeing her fearful with his presence in her room. Or any chance he felt his authority was being questioned by her looking straight at him.

"Where do you think, you are going!" He demanded.

Ayden timidly stated, still keeping her eyes away from looking at him, "Mom said it was OK for me to spend the weekend at Deborah's."

"Your mom does not say what goes on in this house!" Her dad's alcohol-breath declared.

"It is about time you realize who you need to respect! Your ugly back shouldn't have affected your brain. But who knows with you! The stupid things I have seen you do must be because of that filth you carry around every day," he yelled as he stumbled closer to her.

Ayden carefully zipped her bag shut as she walked determinedly around her bed, away from her dad's out-stretched hand. She reached the door where her dad tripped as he lunged towards her, and fell on the floor.

Her mom stepped in between her and her dad as she exited her room stating in a fearful voice, "Ayden, Graycie and Deborah are in the living room, waiting for you."

She grabbed her coat, nodded to her mom and went to greet her friends. She hurriedly guided them out the front door of her home to avoid any exposure to what her dad might say to them.

Sitting in the back seat of Graycie's car, she let out a silent sigh of relief, thankful her dad was unable to show his alcohol-induced rage to them.

Everything went well up throughout the meal as Graycie wanted Deborah and Ayden to help her make it. Graycie loved perusing food blogs and was always coming up with new recipes she tweaked to her family's liking.

Tonight, it was pizza minus the sauce and the meat. Potatoes sliced thin surrounded the bed of mozzarella on the pizza crust; finished with virgin olive oil, dill and freshly grated parmesan.

The pizza would be served with a green salad full of several vegetables. Side sauces accompanied the meal and would serve for dressing or dip. Your choice of ranch, marinara, garlic infused with other spices in olive oil or Italian. It was beyond delicious! No one even missed the meat not being on it.

That's just one of the things Ayden loved about this family. They were not afraid to try new things where they enjoyed the process all the way through to the end results. She was full and happy as they cleaned up the kitchen after dinner.

Just as the last of the dishes were being put into the cupboard, the call came in. Robert belonged to the volunteer fire department and he had to leave to help with a fire.

Graycie asked Deborah and Ayden to help her in the greenhouse she used for research. "Which was unusual," Ayden thought, since she usually liked to spend her time alone there. It was always looked at as Graycie's time to relax and commune with whatever she had going on at that particular time. From past experience, after they ate, Deborah and Ayden got to do their own thing for the rest of the evening.

"But, no big deal," Ayden continued her thoughts, "We'd just spend time with Graycie and do our stuff later. Actually, it is a much-needed escape to prolong the inevitable talk Deborah wants to have with me," she silently breathed.

Ayden noticed Graycie seemed agitated and unfocused as she tried to tell the girls what she was doing. Her cell phone was on the work table and she kept picking it up to look at it.

They had been in the greenhouse about forty-five minutes when Graycie took her ringing phone and stepped outside. Ayden looked up to the sky as Graycie opened the door and saw a large plume of smoke rising from the west.

"Wow!" she exclaimed to Deborah, "It must be a big brush fire this time. I hope the whole tourist season isn't going to be full of fires like it was two years ago. Remember all of the firefighters and planes with water buckets?" She asked.

Thinking back to that summer, the girls weren't allowed to venture off into the mountains for fear they would be surrounded by fire. It was extremely dry and no one knew where the next spark would ignite an uncontrollable blaze.

What a boring summer it had been; and a summer of fear for all who had to combat the flames. And, because the forests and meadows were engulfed in fire, the wild animals came closer to the town hoping to survive the deadly inferno and smoke.

The wildlife was beautiful and, yet, dangerous at the same time. They needed food and water, and clean air to breathe. But they were still unpredictable and they all had to be on guard to avoid being attacked.

The grey air had surrounded all of them for days and days with no sun able to penetrate the atmosphere making it overwhelmingly dreary.

Graycie came back in and by the look on her face they knew something had happened. Ayden's first thoughts went to Robert, "Did he get hurt?" She worried as she went to Graycie's side.

"Ayden," Graycie's voice cracked, "Girls would you come with me into the house."

Deborah came by Ayden's side as they silently grabbed each other's hands and walked behind Graycie. The girls sat down in the living room on the edge of the couch with great anticipation waiting for Graycie to speak.

Graycie sat on the coffee table right in front of them. She took Ayden's hands in hers. She looked at her with eyes full of sorrow as she stated, "Ayden, honey, there was a fire at your house. By the time the firemen got there the bottom floor was engulfed in flames. Ayden, your father didn't make it."

Ayden looked at Graycie, not sure she was truly saying what she had just said. Her mind started to race with totally irrational thoughts. "Did my dad intentionally start the fire? Was my mom beaten by him and he accidentally killed her so he started the fire?"

Graycie continued, "Ayden, your mom is badly injured, but alive. They have air-lifted her to Missoula. She will be at St Patrick's Hospital. Robert has a friend who has a Cessna and is waiting to take you to Missoula. Robert is on his way home to get you so he can fly with you."

Graycie took a deep breath as she stood up and pulled Ayden to her in a warm hug. She hurriedly grabbed Deborah and the three of them stood there clinging to each other.

She lifted Ayden's chin as she looked into her eyes and stated, "Deborah and I will drive to Missoula. It takes approximately three hours to get there from here. Don't you worry about anything, Ayden. We are here for you and we won't leave you. Robert is in the driveway. Go with him, and know we are right behind you," Graycie reassured her.

Ayden wanted to cry but she was so emotionally stunned by what was happening, she couldn't. She had never really cried for herself before. It was easy to cry for others and their pain. Whether it be emotional or physical, it was easy to cry for them. But it was never easy to cry for herself.

She was afraid if she started, she would never quit. Therefore, she determined she could not entertain the act to allow herself to emotionally break down and wallow in tears of self-reflection or pity. She managed to hold herself together even with Graycie's hug, and resolved to not lose her composure as she got into the car with Robert.

Ayden stared straight ahead while Robert drove and talked nonstop. All she could think about was, "How did this happen?"

Robert knew she had never flown before and he prepared her for the bumpy ride of a small airplane. As he explained it, "OK, Ayden, a little plane is not like sitting comfortably in a car and driving. You need to tell me if you are getting cold so we can adjust the temperature for you, because it can get really cold high up in the atmosphere.

"Here is some gum to help with your ears popping. It won't be a long ride, but it may get jumpy with lots of turbulence if the wind is heavy; which it usually is going over the mountains into Missoula. In case you start to feel sick, I have medicine for you to take right now. It's the non-drowsy kind so you won't get sleepy," he comforted her.

Ayden started to feel crazy because he was talking so fast. It finally dawned on her he was trying to keep her mind off of why they were driving to the airport to begin with. Her mom was knocking on death's door.

He must have sensed she was dwelling on her mom because he stated, "She's going to be alright, Ayden. I know she will be fine."

Ayden knew the tone of voice he was using all too well. When an adult in her family spoke with that tone it was to promise without truly following through on the promise.

It was used to pacify her for the moment. Not that Robert was trying to pacify her and discount her like she was used to. She knew he was scared and was trying to make her feel better.

Ayden just had this gut-retching sense her mom was not going to be living very much longer. Hopefully, she would get to see her in time to say good-bye to her.

When they arrived at the hospital, her mom was in the intensive care unit; she had severe smoke inhalation. Even with the oxygen mask covering her nose and chin, Ayden saw the familiar disturbing marks of a beating around her face. But, no one mentioned those marks as another medical issue.

The doctors only spoke to Robert in a hushed tone to avoid her overhearing them talk. Ayden felt uncomfortable for them when they would quickly glance at her and try to give her a half-reassured smile. Which, to her, meant this was another clue her mother would not survive.

She was allowed to see her mom for only short spurts of a few minutes because she was heavily drugged and surrounded with monitors. Reddish marks along her upper arms started to form, outlining the fingers of a man who supposedly loved her on their wedding day.

Ayden tried to angrily smirk as she watched her mom. She thought about a man's love leaving his imprint on her. But the pain she felt for this woman who never knew true love left her empty and sad rather than angry.

Being fourteen, she was so unaware of how to handle a crisis of this magnitude. Ayden gave continuous silent thanks for Robert and Graycie and the ability to make everything look so easy. From having a car ready for them at the Missoula airport, to the motel room, to the food and clothes for her; they did it all.

Everyday Ayden spent time with her mom. On the third day of the hospital vigil, her mom was still unable to speak. She would look at Ayden with those hollow eyes of what Ayden assumed was supposed to be love, but seemed more like sorrow or regret.

Ayden, the dutiful daughter, stayed as long as the nurses would let her. And then, would leave to be with the reassuring love of Deborah and her family.

At times, her guilt seemed to swallow her because she was guarded happy when she was away from the hospital. Being around Deborah's family was a stark change from her own. They surrounded her with love and care continuously. She had never felt this type of unconditional love from her own family.

Graycie and Robert sat Ayden down in their hotel room on the fourth day of the hospital ritual, to have a "serious talk" with her.

"Ayden," Graycie began, "your mom wrote me a note yesterday. She has asked me to bring her our personal attorney so she can sign legal documents to make Robert and I your legal guardians. I need to know from you if you are OK with this decision?"

Ayden defiantly rolled her eyes and stood up from where she was sitting. Putting her hands on her hips, she started, "OK, Graycie, let's be totally honest here. You know and I know mom is going to die. I am never going to hear her voice again. And now she is telling you instead of me what she wants to happen to me?"

"Don't you guys think it's about time you treat me with some respect and give me the right to be told by her and the doctors what she wants! I'm not trying to be difficult, really. It's just at fourteen I have been thrust into an adult situation and I'm just a little tired of everyone treating me like a child!" Ayden demanded.

"Ayden you are totally right," Robert quickly chimed in, "You have become a young adult because of this. But I ask you to give us the freedom to help you weather this storm. We know we will make mistakes and not do everything right. But we need for you to understand is because you are not legally of age to make your own decisions we have to act on your behalf. Would you give Graycie and I the honor to be your legal guardians with the understanding we will consult you at all times about what you want and need?"

Eleea stopped what he was doing to look at her. "Yes, Lora," he said, "It is just as beautiful as you."

Lora sweetly chirped at him and continued singing.

It was his job to make sure the nest was ready for Lora to pass the eggs. Which meant he had been busily pulling thin strips of bark from the young trees to place in the hollow of the nest he found.

It was by Deborah's home, and he was busily padding the bottom and sides of it. He added feathers and any other soft materials he could find to make it befitting for the love of his life. He was determined to make sure the nest would be comfortable and it would pass the test of not being predator accessible.

"What a beautiful soul she is," Eleea thought as he affectionately gazed at her.

Whenever she was with him, the world seemed right. It brought him great pleasure to listen to her sing nearby while he worked.

Eleea felt confident the nursery was prepared to nurture and protect the young birds it would soon hold. He leapt back to admire his finished handiwork when he heard the sirens and saw the smoke rising from the direction of Ayden's home.

He turned to Lora, who quickly told him, "Go! Now!" She already knew what he feared. Ayden could be in trouble and he needed to get to her.

Eleea felt his heart pump so hard he thought it would explode as he flew in the direction of the smoke. When he rounded the corner leading to Ayden's street, he saw her home surrounded with men fighting the blaze.

Horror struck him as he frantically flew around the burning building in search for Ayden.

Several times he circled looking for her auburn hair to no avail.

Eleea risked his life by flying into the smoke-filled rooms through the blown-out windows caused by the extreme flame, hoping he could reach Ayden. Panic set in as he realized she was nowhere to be found.

Exhausted and choking from the deadly fumes, he decided to perch in the evergreen closest to the fire truck to regain control of his thoughts. He listened to the men below.

"How many people are in the house?" One man yelled.

Another responded, "It's the Phillips' family. There are only three of them. The parents and the child."

A third man shouted, "Their child isn't in the home. She is spending the weekend at my house with my daughter, Deborah."

Eleea caught himself as he started to lose his balance. He slumped against the tree limb when he heard the man say Ayden was safe.

He watched as Ayden's father's lifeless body was carried to the side of the road away from the smoldering home. Overhead he heard the sound of the whirling blades as the mercy flight helicopter lowered itself to land in the middle of the street. Men were carrying Ayden's mother on a stretcher towards the helicopter.

Deborah's father turned to the people who jumped off the helicopter, yelling, "I have a plane ready to bring her daughter to the hospital, we will be close behind you!" He then got into the sheriff's car and sped away.

"The child is safe," Eleea repeated over and over again to himself as he began his flight back to Lora.

Instantaneously, his heart panicked when he thought about Ayden's future. He had to know if Ayden was returning to East Glacier or what was going to happen to her.

He was sure he could find his answers at Deborah's home. He swiftly turned in flight away from his nest, and headed to Deborah's.

He perched in the Douglas fir next to Deborah's room, knowing she always had her window open.

Her mother entered, and sat Deborah on the bed next to her. She began, "Deborah, Ayden's mom is clinging to life right now, she took in a lot of smoke to her lungs. You need to pack enough clothes for you and Ayden as we will probably be in Missoula for at least two or three days. Any more time spent there we can find a laundromat, or buy new clothes."

Graycie continued, "If her mother should pass, we need to be there for Ayden; we can't lose her too. She has no other family since her parents have no known relatives they have ever talked about. Your dad's and my plan is to become her legal guardians, but you need to keep silent about this as we do not want to alarm her while she is struggling with her mom's condition. And, I need to know from you if it is OK, should Ayden come to live with us?"

Deborah grabbed her mom's hands and said, "Mom! Ayden is my best friend, I love her. I would do anything to protect her and take care of her. Of course, I am fine with her always being in our home; it is the right thing to do. And, mom, you and I both know our family has been more of a family to Ayden than her own. I don't mean to sound cold and heartless, but Ayden can finally be free from all of the anger she has lived with," Deborah finished.

Deborah's mom put her arm around her child and quietly said, "I know, honey, I know."

Eleea's heart felt safe as he flew to Lora's side. Now, all he needed to do was concentrate on his family.

"The Eshra Council will have to wait. Besides, they have waited for years to hear if the Messenger has been found. A few more weeks will not make that big of a difference," he said to himself. "My immediate attention has to be in the here and now with my mate and children who soon will hatch," Eleea stated out loud.

For any bird family, or for that matter any part of nature, this time of year was extremely busy. With the entrance of spring, new life emerged in all of its' glory. This was the season where hope began anew.

"How appropriate," Eleea determined, "With spring in the air, Ayden would be given a new birth too. By living with Deborah and her family, she would be safe, now."

"The reality of her situation is horribly sad, and it looks like it will become even sadder with the passing of her mother. She will need time to come to terms with it. But, living with Deborah's family would give her the freedom to be safe from beatings," Eleea determined.

Journal Five

    Ayden's eyes traveled across the river to the far side as she dreamily rested her gaze on the driftwood protruding out of the water. Beautiful green moss flowed along the log. Anchored near it were little yellow lotus lily flowers touching the gentle surface of the river.

    "Funny," Ayden thought. "Even the log has a purpose to help other life-forms survive. If it were not for the log slowing the flow of the river and creating a little pocket of protection around the bank, those tiny little yellow flowers would not be able to stay in place. She once again picked up her pencil to expound on her new revelation.

    No one goes through life alone. Survival dictates you will need help to make it in this world. I needed my parents in order to survive as a baby and a young child. My parents taught me through, mostly, negative behavior. But their lessons still formed me in how I would react; whether it was a positive reaction or a negative one.

    I did not know there were other ways to deal with uncomfortable situations except through anger, hitting, or silence. So, I was on a path to repeat the same pattern. And so, on this path, my heart would have remained damaged.

    I was lucky enough to be exposed to others who didn't react the same way my parents did. By watching them, I learned new positive ways to act.

    I still had to walk through my dysfunction of negative behavior to finally begin to change to positive behavior. I had to get uncomfortable with my bad behavior and how it made me feel ugly before I could begin to change to positive behavior.

    This true-life altering change only happened because I looked at myself and decided to be honest about what I didn't want.

    I didn't want to be angry anymore. I had to admit I was wrong in how I reacted to uncomfortable situations.

    Once I started to realize I needed to change: That's when my heart truly started to heal.

Chapter Five

Ayden said her last goodbyes to her mother, who had lapsed into a coma. She insisted she wanted to be with her mom when they pulled the plugs and shut off the monitors keeping her alive.

But she was only given a partial privilege to her request. She had to stand outside the room in order to not hear any sounds her mother might make when she expired. "Lame," Ayden thought, "but, adults will be adults."

Before they left Missoula, Graycie and Deborah took her shopping for bedroom furniture, linen, and clothes. Which at the time, Ayden felt it was way too much money being spent on her?

Upon their return to East Glacier, Ayden, again, sensed the uncomfortable pressure of attention on her. The whole town surrounded her with love, gifts and words of encouragement.

A double funeral was Ayden's decision. She didn't think she could handle two
 ceremonies. It was just too much drama and emotion. Besides, "they pretty much died together, therefore they should have a funeral together," she told everyone.

Another decision she made was to have their remains cremated. She wanted to take their ashes and set them free in the mountains of Glacier.

On the day of the funeral, Ayden wore most of her hair back behind her ears. Usually, her hair was cut to fall in a freestyle bounce of different layers; parted on the left side with her bangs partially covering the right side of her forehead like a half moon.

She chose to wear a yellow ribbon around her head, with a small bow tied just above her left ear in honor of her mother's favorite color. The ribbon complimented her thick reddish-brown hair as it layered down the back of her shoulders.

After the funeral, Ayden was, again, showered with gifts. And, again, she felt overwhelmed with the thoughtfulness of the towns' people.

"It's not that I am unappreciative for what all these people have given me," Ayden whispered to Graycie and Deborah during the reception, "It's just, I feel so guilty!" "All of this food, all of these gifts. I don't deserve any of this," she insecurely expressed.

Graycie put her arm around Ayden's waist and said, "Honey, it's OK to feel

overwhelmed and guilty. What you are experiencing is normal emotions in a very abnormal set of circumstances. I promise you this will get easier as time goes on."

Ayden looked into Graycie's eyes knowing she would find strength there, just as she had found it already numerous times in the past days. And, once again, she mustered the tenacity to face all of the people who were there for her. With a determined nod to Graycie and Deborah, Ayden straightened her stance and walked tall into the reception room of well-wishers.

Slowly the crowd dispersed, with a few lingering behind to talk with Graycie and Robert. While others, including Deborah, busied themselves by cleaning up.

Since everyone was occupied inside the reception hall, Ayden ceased upon the chance to disappear. Finally, able to enjoy the lack of attention on her, she effortlessly exited out the back door of the building without being seen.

Juggling her milk and plate she positioned herself on the wooden stairs. Her favorite pie was huckleberry and she finally could not resist eating a piece made by the town's best baker, Mrs. Martin.

Thankful she didn't have to talk to anyone, she relaxed her body and mind to enjoy each morsel she put in her mouth. Engrossed in her bounty of goodness, she did not notice a figure approach from around the large fir tree which naturally shaded the steps.

Startled to see anyone, Ayden almost missed her mouth as she took a bite and jerked forward to salvage it. Staring at Nick, she wanted to be perturbed at his presence, but instead she put her fork on the plate and placed the plate next to her on the step.

Nick was a nice kid. She had several classes with him over the years, and he shyly stayed to himself, most of the time. His parents owned a gift shop and he was always helping them.

There were times, though, when his quick wit made her laugh. He very rarely allowed anyone to see this side of him. Standing well over five feet, he had coal black hair which almost shimmered purple if the sun hit it right. His immaculate braid lay down his back to the center of his shoulder blades.

Ayden knew Nick well enough to know he was having difficulty starting the conversation. She sensed he needed to tell her something. So, she determined she would have to be the one to break his silence.

"Well, Nick," Ayden's voice pierced the awkward air. "How've ya been?"

"Ayden," Nick stumbled to say. He cleared his throat and tried to stand a little taller. "Ayden, I want to tell you how sorry I am for...for...I am so sorry, Ayden." Nick lowered his eyes as his body slightly slouched. Pushing the dirt around with his shoe, he, again, stood taller and lifted his eyes to Ayden.

He began again, "I know I had no right to be on your property, even after the fire. But I just knew I was looking for something special. Something that could not stay lost. I was supposed to find this for you." Nick hesitantly pulled his hand out of his pocket.

Ayden could see his hand was tightly holding onto what he found. Slowly, he opened his hand and placed a charred sterling silver bracelet chain with a feather shaped charm locket in the palm of her out reached hand.

Ayden closed her hand around the bracelet and admiringly looked at Nick. "Nick, don't you ever feel wrong about trying to help another," she comfortingly said to him. She stood up, walked down the steps, and gave him a hug.

Which obviously was too much for Nick to handle in one day, because he hurriedly hugged her back while he mumbled something. When he was safely out of reach of Ayden, he stated, "Gotta go, Ayden. I'll see you around." And he disappeared in the same direction he had appeared.

Over the next several weeks, Ayden was thankful everyone started to move forward with life. The focus was not so directly on her and her loss as they all started to get into the groove of her living in her new home.

Graycie felt it was important for Ayden to have her own space. Robert's artist room was transformed into Ayden's private bedroom.

Then, because Graycie was so deeply aware of everyone's emotional stability, she felt Deborah needed to have a bedroom overhaul too. Deborah's new bedroom was adjacent to Ayden's.

"So, you girls can have your own area, but can also be close to each other when you need it," Graycie determined.

Carpenters were hired to knock out a wall for the girls' rooms to be open to each other, yet designed with each girl having their privacy, if need be. A spacious bathroom emerged on the other side of the rooms. Perfectly designed for two growing girls to share.

Ayden loved her room. She decided she wanted her bed to be against the large plate glass window where the two side windows could crank open to allow air to flow into the room acting kind of like a head and foot board.

Looking up to the sky as she lay there gave her a sense of being in the outdoors as she fell asleep. At night, she would lay in bed, look out her window and watch the moon and stars as they moved across the sky. It was peaceful energy for her to stare off into the cosmos and wonder what she would do with her life since it had abruptly changed.

One of the things Graycie and Robert made for her to help with her "calmness," as they called it, and that she just adored was a flower box which fit outside her bedroom window.

She got to go to the store in Missoula to pick the plants she wanted to grow in it. Ferns, catnip which is a mint type plant, little purple flowers when matured looked like the old-fashioned European castles where trails of greenery grew and climbed up the stones of the building.

Deborah also had a flower box outside her window, and true to her heart she had arnica plants which were native to Montana, and all other sorts of plants which could be ground into mush for some type of healing concoction. Deborah was crazy about the natural plant properties to help a human body.

Ayden loved it that Deborah had her own flower box because it meant she wouldn't think Ayden was being treated special by her parents or she was being left out of their love.

She worried about this very point all of the time, "Did Deborah feel like she was ignored by her parents. And, did Deborah feel like Ayden was intruding on her home?" Every time Ayden tried to explore this fear with Deborah, Deborah would sit her down and go into one of her long speeches about human behavior.

Such as, "'A,'" head cocked to the right, of course, "*there is nothing to worry about when it comes to you and me. You have always been an extension of me. Just because you live here in my home, which is now your home too, doesn't mean I am viewed any less in my parents' eyes.*"

"*There was this woman who was a poet, Maya Angelou is her name, and she is famous for this statement, 'You make family as you make friends.' "Therefore," Deborah* continued, "*It is imperative for you to come to the understanding we were first friends and now we are family. And, there is enough love to go around in this family where none of us will feel like we are being forgotten. Got it?*"

Ayden came to her own conclusion of, if Deborah wasn't worried about feeling left out then she should stop worrying about it. Plus, she was not a big fan of Deborah's long drawn out explanations over the subject.

Life in Deborah's home was so very energetic. No more fights, no more yelling, and no more fear she may get beat again. Yet, her guilt would at times cripple her.

She questioned herself, "What if I had stayed home instead of ran away to safety at Deborah's that horrible night? Maybe I could have saved my mom and even my dad from the fire!"

Guilt would then turn into anger as she brooded about how stupid her dad was. Smoking while lying on the couch where his lit cigarette landed. And, being so drunk his bottle of vodka fell over and helped to ignite the flames which finally consumed the house. At least, this was the final report by the investigators of the fire.

From guilt to anger to depression it seemed like she was constantly being tossed around with these ugly emotions trying to suffocate her.

It was just another weekend, close to the end of the school year, and Ayden lay restless on her bed. Not knowing what to do with all the phantom emotions swirling around her head and heart.

She couldn't stop her mind from racing. She didn't want to bother Graycie who was out in the greenhouse. Nor, did she wish to speak to Deborah who was immersed in her books on the natural healing effects of the latest plants she was studying.

She, really didn't want to talk to anyone about how she was feeling. She just wanted the feelings to disappear and stop resurfacing. Deep in her thoughts, Ayden turned her head from looking out her window to see Robert pop his head into her bedroom.

Gesturing for permission to step in, he plopped down on her oversized bean bag chair by her desk.

"You know Ayden," he nonchalantly stated, "I've been waiting for the right time to talk with you about all that has happened in the last month or so. Now seems to be a good time."

"I grew up in Seattle, you know," Robert began. "When I was your age I had, a best friend named Andy. I loved that guy."

"He and I would always find ways to get into the craziest predicaments. This one time he wanted me to go with him, on our bikes, to a side of the city which was considered 'the seedier side.' Ya know what I mean? The bad side of town where people could get a little unconventional in their lifestyles and decisions."

"Well, anyways, I felt very uncomfortable about going down there as I knew it could be really really dangerous. So, I tried to talk Andy out of it and convince him to stay with me at my house. But he was determined to go and I let him go, by himself." Robert sadly explained.

"About four or five hours later Andy's parents came to our house and asked if we had seen Andy. They couldn't find him. I told them where he went and they and the police went to search for him down there."

"They found him in an alley. Dead. Supposedly it was a hit and run from a vehicle. I never believed them. I let my young mind wander with scenarios of what happened to him and what he felt as he was dying. It was a horrible time of my life," Robert revealed.

"The overwhelming guilt I felt because I allowed him to go there by himself was eating me up inside. Unexpectedly, I felt emotions of guilt and anger and then terrible depression would surround me," Robert stated.

"One day, a long time after Andy died, Andy's dad came and took me for a drive. He wanted to talk to me about Andy. He explained to me it was not my fault Andy went down there by himself. Andy had made a decision on his own and his decision took his life." Robert expressed as he looked away from Ayden with sadness in his eyes.

"Andy's dad continued to explain to me the whole process of grief. First there is guilt a person wasn't there to stop the tragedy. Then comes anger over the person not making the right decisions. On to depression because the loss is just so deep in your heart. Sometimes a person goes through denial of not believing this horrible thing has happened. Then, finally, comes acceptance where you resolve the grief and realize your own life is important with purpose and you have to let go of the sorrow over the loss. Not that you forget. But you no longer dwell on the what if's of how you should have been there to stop it." Robert told her.

"The greatest thing Andy's dad told me I could do to honor Andy's life was to become the best person I could be. And to make my life matter for those whom I loved. And most importantly to love myself like Andy loved me."

"I turned to Andy's dad and cried and cried and cried. It was the best moment in my life for healing my heart." Robert smiled at Ayden as he explained.

"Ayden, I pass on this message to you, love yourself and reach out to others and love them like they love you and help them the best way you can. Make your life matter for yourself and others." Robert tenderly told her.

Ayden could feel her emotions burst in her heart as Robert talked. Unable to control them anymore, Ayden felt the tears begin to fall like a spring rain storm down her face.

She sobbed uncontrollably as Robert moved over to her side and placed his arms around her, and put her head into his chest. Both of their bodies rocked back and forth as they cried together.

Journal Six*

Ayden respectfully set her book down next to her, and stood up to stretch. Leaning back to crack her spine, she intently looked at the branches of the tree and then at the trunk which so kindly had been keeping her comfortable.

"Eleea is right," she clearly thought as she replayed his voice in her mind. Sitting back down, she picked up her pencil.

"Always remember, Ayden," Eleea instructed her, "Life is to be respected. From a branch on this tree, here, to the light which shows forth from the rays of the sun...all of it has purpose and meaning.

It takes light for this branch to grow. It takes water and the ground's nutrients for it to become strong. Nothing in nature, in our worlds, truly happens by chance. There is purpose, Ayden; there is meaning," he expressed emphatically.

"And, do not become confused and defeated about purpose and meaning by life's circumstances of evil. Do not let those events destroy your heart, Ayden," Eleea passionately communicated.

"Remind yourself when life seems horribly wrong, how very valuable you are. Remind yourself you are here for a purpose, and there is meaning in what you do!" Eleea ardently requested of her.

"You will not always have the answers to your most pressing questions right away. Sometimes, it may take days or even years for answers to surface. And, while you are waiting for those answers, continue to strive to be the best you can be. Look for the purpose and meaning in your life," Eleea encouraged her.

"Keep your mind open to hear with your heart, Ayden. When you listen to your heart, you will hear your instincts. Trust your instincts. If something feels oddly uncomfortable, or strangely too good to be true: Listen. Stay alert, lest you miss your heart speaking to you, telling you to get to safety," he cautioned her.

"And lastly, my child," Eleea tenderly stated, "just as this branch I sit on is dependent on this tree for survival, so, too are we all dependent on you."

Chapter Six

Eleea kept close watch over Ayden during her move to Deborah's home. He didn't hassle her with words, he only sang to her while she dealt with all of the changes. Each night and morning he perched outside her window and sang to her.

One thing he was pleasantly thankful for was his home being in the same area as Deborah's home. Behind Deborah's house was the forest with a stream and all of the beauty of Glacier.

Deborah's parents owned the land, but decided to keep it as natural as possible. And as luck would have it, he and Lora had chosen this area for their nest. From his home, he could see Ayden's window and watch her while she slept. It provided him great relief to be so close to her.

There were three eggs in the nest, ready to hatch within the next few days. Which kept Eleea and Lora vigilant to make sure they stayed warm. They were quite the team he mused as he took time to sing to Ayden.

While he sang, Ayden began to hum along with him. He had never heard her voice in song, it was beautiful and natural. He began to test her pitch and her ability to follow his lead. She easily hummed along beside him which made him think about how he would feel when he started to teach his own children to sing.

He was overjoyed with this unexpected trait of Ayden's. This child constantly amazed him with her depth of character. Whatever she was presented with, she seemed to rise to the challenge; right down to being able to sing.

Lora had taken her own initiative to introduce herself to Ayden. Shortly after the funeral, she plucked a single chicory flower and laid it on the windowsill where Ayden was looking out from the open window. Ayden picked up the blue wheel-shaped prize and placed the stem behind her ear. The little flower looked perfect peeking out of her hair.

Eleea never really knew what the girls talked about since he was egg sitting each time they were together. What he did know, was they had become dear friends.

Evidenced by their constant, what he called, 'girl giggling' and the hours they spent together. Lora would lightly perch on Ayden's shoulder as soon as they were clear from the house and deep into the woods by the water they would go.

It was getting close to the time for Ayden to give Eleea the answer he had been waiting for. To say she would take on the responsibility to follow him to Eshra and fulfill the prophecy.

He didn't know if his anticipation for her answer was the reason he felt so edgy or if it was the children would soon be emerging out of their shells. He just knew he felt uneasy.

Ayden had stayed home while the rest of her family took a drive along the Going to the Sun Road, as it had just completely opened. Ayden was outside tending to her flower box and Eleea was busily gathering food. It was a beautiful late spring day.

While Ayden and he worked, she explained to him the allure of this road. The road generally was covered in snowpack which made it inaccessible by vehicles until the road crews removed all of the snow.

Traveling the Sun Road before the tourist season was in full swing was common for the locals to partake in. It was less crowded and less dangerous with fewer vehicles on the road.

Ayden scholarly informed Eleea how the construction of the road took eleven years to complete, 1932 being the year it was finished. Its highest elevation was at 6,646 feet with a narrow winding road which was barely able to accommodate two vehicles on it side by side.

And, it was now considered an engineering marvel, being listed on their National Historic Landmark register. She continued to inform him the road was fifty miles long and connected East Glacier to West Glacier.

Eleea enjoyed listening to Ayden speak proudly about her land. It reminded him of his pride for his own land. He lit on the flower box to watch her more closely.

"Ayden, have you given any more thought to when you will be ready to travel to Eshra," he asked her.

Ayden stopped what she was doing and looked at him. "Eleea, I know you want me to go with you and Lora and your children to Eshra. I just don't quite get this prophecy thing," she stated with confusion.

"I mean," Ayden brushed her hair back as she gazed past him. "I really have nothing here in this world holding me back. But, really, what can I do? I'm a child with an ugly birthmark. It's your prophecy, not mine, Eleea."

"Ayden, it is deeper than just words spoken as prophecy" Eleea tenderly expressed. "I was sent to find the messenger. The only way I could find the messenger was through the words of a prophecy. It guided me on what to look for in my quest. Someone with the mark of the crane on their back was foretold long ago would save our worlds. Your mark is our very foundation to survival, Ayden."

"Here, let me tell you the whole prophecy. And listen with your heart, Ayden. Not your mind," Eleea encouraged her as he stood on the ledge of the flower box and lifted his head like a sergeant ready to give his walking orders to the troops.

"Cross to the East.
Send the seeker to the mighty glaciers.
There his search will see the one.
Upon the back deliverance comes.
At rest the crane stands,
Head held high.
When the morning sun kisses the day,
The messenger enters through.
Prepared to take flight.
Riding the winds to the mountains,
Where the dead tree stands,
A fight ensues.
The stirring sound rings
Throughout the lands.
And, once again the wings of the crane,
Bring the light of day."

"You, Ayden, have been chosen. For whatever reason, I cannot explain. It is you who will bring the light of day to our worlds. It is your presence in Eshra which will ignite our worlds and stop the darkness creeping into our worlds," Eleea said with reverence.

"OK, Eleea," Ayden stated with pent-up frustration as she continued, "We cross over to Eshra, we travel to the dead trees, and this crane takes flight? Exactly what does that have to do with me?" Ayden questioned him.

"You, Ayden, are the Messenger," Eleea stated. "It is your voice which must be heard in Eshra. The prophecy says we have to travel to a specific spot in order for your voice to ring throughout the lands," Eleea explained.

"I apologize for not being able to give you more solid information to help you understand more clearly," Eleea said with a bit of anxiety.

"But, in my heart, Ayden, I know you are the one. The one I have sought for years to find. And, Ayden, it has been my greatest honor to be the one who brings you to your destiny to fulfill the prophecy. And, my hope is you will trust me to take you to Eshra," Eleea finished with deep respect.

"Fine, Eleea," Ayden exasperatedly expressed. "I will go with you when the time is right. But I still do not get it. For all of you to put your hope into a child? It just goes beyond any rational understanding for me," Ayden stated with lingering doubt.

Before she could continue her next statement, Lora, who was in the nest with the eggs, screeched in terror.

Eleea's head jerked in her direction to see an oversized Merlin hawk attack the nest with his claws. The hawk continued to pull at the top of the tree opening with the immense strength of his legs and mouth.

Lora flew at the hawk and began to attack him, going after the hawk's eyes. The hawk repeatedly tore at the nest, while he flapped his wings to keep Lora away from him.

Eleea sprung into flight reaching the hawk. Who had grabbed one of the eggs in his talons, then let it go, causing it to drop to the ground. Lora flew down to try and save the egg from its fall, but it was futile.

Eleea zoomed in to stand between the hawk and the nest, but the Merlin's wings bashed him against the bark of the tree. The hawk quickly grabbed the second egg and repeated his first deathly act.

Eleea came in above on the hawk's blind side and was able to take his left eye out with his claws clamping down on his head and his beak drilling into his eye. Lora came in from the other side and tried to do the same.

The hawk grabbed Lora's neck in his claws and flew up away from Eleea with her in his death grip. With his one good eye, he looked at Eleea, and for a brief second Lora's and Eleea's eyes connected.

In that moment Eleea heard her heart as it reached his soul telling him she loved him and, then, she said, "Live on Eleea. Fulfill your destiny and protect Ayden!"

His eyes flashed back to the hawk who was still staring at him. With a look of disdain and a smile forming in his eye, the hawk snapped Lora's neck letting her fall from his clutches.

Eleea heard Ayden scream as she ran to the bottom of the tree where she caught Lora in her hands. Ayden kept screaming in horror as she fell to her knees gently holding Lora.

The hawk's cackling caws were deafening as he flew away into the horizon.

Eleea reached Ayden and Lora, knowing Lora was expelling her last breaths.

"Ayden!" he cried out, "Put her on the ground next to the eggs." As Ayden gently laid her down, Eleea blew his breath over all of them. He then put his body over Lora and his children, and spread his wings to cover them.

Quietly he said to Lora, "We will meet again, my love. Back to Eshra all of you go!" He lifted his wings back against his body and their ashes took flight in the wind.

Ayden's voice howled in terror as she screamed, "Eleea where is she. Oh! My, God! Where is she, Eleea?" Ayden's sobs were piercing as she tried to catch her breath, choking on her tears. Her whole body was heaving as she wailed in deep sorrow.

Instinct told Eleea to fly to the nest; there was no time to grieve. He discovered the lone egg in their home.

"Ayden!" he screamed, "There is one egg left. I need your help."

Ayden immediately forgot her pain and tears. She sprung to her feet and stated, "Eleea you stay with the egg and keep it warm. I will be right back."

Eleea watched as Ayden ran to the shed and came out with a ladder and a bag. She placed the ladder at the base of the tree and dumped the contents of the bag on the ground.

She proceeded to climb up to the limb next to the nest. Placing a jute string rope over the limb she made a pulley system for a tiny bucket to be lifted up and down from the tree.

As she worked, she told Eleea, "I will bring you food. Do not leave this egg."

She ran back to the house and then again ran back to the tree. Eleea watched as she took small worms from a baggy and put them in the bucket.

"Eleea," she directed, "These are mealy worms from Graycie's greenhouse. She is using them for some type of research she is conducting. I'm sure she won't miss a few worms. I will bring these to you three times a day. Is that OK, or do you need them more than three times a day? Plus, I will shell sunflower seeds for you, OK? And I will put small amounts of water in the bucket for you too, so you can stay put and save your baby."

The whole time she talked she worked out the kinks of the pulley system to make sure it would reach him.

Eleea thought, "What a beautiful child she is! What care and confidence she possesses in the midst of crisis?" His heart was overwhelmed with deep love and appreciation for her.

"Ayden," Eleea spoke, "I don't even know if this egg will hatch."

She stopped his speech by putting her finger in the air, gesturing him to stop. "Eleea, this egg will live!" Ayden authoritatively said.

Her voice held strong determination. Eleea knew right then, she would not permit him to speak otherwise, so he allowed her the right to believe.

As the hours turned into days, Eleea's heart was inconsolably heavy for Lora and this lone egg he sat on to keep warm. He doubted even if he could have gathered food, he would not have tried. Helpless sorrow covered him in a black hole of despair as each day passed.

If it hadn't been for Ayden keeping watch over him and taking care of his every need Eleea didn't know what he would have done. Not being able to leave the nest gave him hours of time to think about what was ahead of him and how important Ayden had become to him. He had wanted to protect her and help her. And, now, it was she who was doing the protecting and helping.

The past days of egg sitting seemed like an eternity; not being able to leave the egg for fear it would not survive. Even the fear it was too late and the egg was already dead was something he could not bear to think about. This was Lora's and his only baby and he desperately wanted it to live.

He watched as Ayden slipped outside her home before anyone else woke to bring him more food. Concentrating on Ayden's approach, he felt his belly move. At first, he thought his leg had slipped and caused the movement. Then he heard the egg crack and the wonderful sound of a little peep.

"Ayden!" Eleea screamed, "the egg is hatching!" He quickly lifted his body to the side to help this little creature emerge from its shell. "It's a girl Ayden! It's a girl!" Eleea cried out with joy.

Ayden started to cry, and Eleea could tell from her voice, they were tears of happiness. Both of them needed to see new life right now. Especially since they had experienced so much sorrow in the past several weeks.

"What are you going to name her, Eleea?" Ayden questioned him.

"Well," Eleea said, "it is usually up to the female to name the young."

Ayden blurted out, "Can I name her, I'm female?"

Eleea looked at Ayden and said, "I would be honored to have you name her, Ayden."

"OK," Ayden began, "I have been thinking about this for two days. I knew you'd let me name her and I knew in my heart it was going to be a girl; one which would be just like Lora. So, I want to name her Elora. She has the first letter of your name and all of Lora's name. It is a perfect name for a brave little one who has already overcome great odds to live," she said triumphantly.

"Elora," Eleea repeated, "That is a fine name, Ayden. Elora it is."

"And, one more thing Eleea," Ayden hesitantly continued, "I am ready to go with you to Eshra. When you and Elora are ready, I am too."

Journal Seven

Ayden welled with tears as her mind replayed the last moments of Lora's life. She unraveled the turquoise bandana from around her wrist and wiped her eyes dry.

"How to tell someone about Lora," she pondered. "A life so perfectly precious, cut short by evil," she bereaved.

Meeting Lora, Ayden began to write. Was, well it was enlightening. I knew I could talk to Eleea, but I had no idea I could speak with other animals who came from Eshra.

The tiny little blue flower she brought me, as her entrance into my life was just so her. Matter of fact in her nature and no pretense she had to formally introduce herself.

It felt like Lora and I had known each other since the beginning of time. I could tell her things I would no way of dreamt of telling Deborah or Eleea. I never had to worry I was disappointing her or I was wrong for how I felt.

Lora became my sounding board. My young heart was so full of rage and confusion.

She would softly sing to me as we walked and sat by the stream. I would mouth off about everything and everybody who wanted to control me and she would listen and sing.

And, every now and then...she would gently nudge my neck with her head as if caressing my hurt and sorrow away. I loved her.

Her little chickadee body held more love and insight in its small frame than most humans could ever possess. She sacrificed her life for Eleea...and for her only child.

When she told Eleea to "Live on," and to fulfill his destiny...they were such powerful words. Then, instead of thinking of her egg, she told him to protect me. Me! How was it I was so important? That she valued me so deeply? I would have done anything to save her and the other two eggs.

Yet, here I sit and she is gone. Rather than wallow in regret, Lora would push me to look for the light. To see how I could turn my latest circumstance into a positive return of goodness.

She would never accept her death to be used as a crutch to avoid growing.

She would giggle in my ear and ask me, "What can we learn from this, Ayden? I know there is some beauty in your heart just waiting to rise up and tell you what to do.

"Think about it," she would push me. "Just as this stream continues to flow, so does life continue to change. The beauty of this water brings life...but it can also bring death.

Just like the dragonfly, laying there, who accidentally took a sharp wrong turn, and got caught by a gust of strong wind. He plummeted into the quick current where, now, his life is suddenly over.

Are you going to stop striving to be a better, a stronger you because you feel disappointed by life's ugly turns?"

That was Lora, always the perpetual optimist.

"She will always live on in my heart!" Ayden stated out loud as she wrote the words.

And, I know, now, her life lives on through Elora. Another precious soul, who carries her mom's beauty and her father's strength in her own heart.

Chapter Seven

It had been a crazy, long, spring for Ayden. With the chaotic dramatic emotions and changes over the last three months, she was thankful the end of the school year had finally arrived.

The summer was, "to be one of rest," as Graycie put it.

She had decided Deborah and Ayden needed to take time to enjoy their freedom and each other. But, true to Graycie's love for learning, she had already enrolled the girls in their third year of Tae Kwan Do classes which had begun last weekend.

Ayden felt the ache of her muscles as she practiced her moves on the grass. Taking martial arts was something she had always enjoyed. She took to the training like a nursing pup took to its mother's belly.

Deborah lay on her back while Ayden practiced. She really had no interest in learning how to defend herself. Her mind was more about how to create the next great herbal concoction or to explain the last great fact she had just learned.

Her and Ayden were exact opposites, in most ways. Maybe this was why they had become the best of friends.

They complimented each other. Where one was physically skilled, the other was intellectually skilled. Where one was mechanically savvy the other was geographically savvy. Together they maneuvered through any obstacle in front of them with deft efficiency.

Ayden slid in next to Deborah, enjoying the smell of the grass as she lay on her stomach and crossed her arms to hold her head.

"'D'," she started, "I want you to know how much I appreciate you. Without you and your family, I wouldn't have made it through these past months. I thank you for loving me."

Ayden continued, "If anything should happen to me, I want you to remember how much I love you and how important you are to your parents. And, how important you are to me."

"What I mean is, you have a beautiful mind and heart which is a unique combination amongst most people. Not very many people can claim intelligence, common sense, and compassion, and you have all of it. You are a very beautiful friend and I will always love you."

"Ayden!" Deborah declared, "You're not sick or anything, are you? You're making it sound like you are going to die or leave town and you have to say your last good-byes. Please! Stop scaring me!" Deborah exclaimed as she sat up.

"No, no, no," Ayden quickly calmed her, "I'm not trying to scare you. It's just look at what has happened to me. I have lost my parents and none of us had a chance to say our last goodbyes, really. And, I just didn't ever want it to happen to you and me. I want you to know how special you are."

"OK, 'A'," Deborah exhaled, "I agree with what you say and copy it right back at ya. I love you and thank you for your love."

"Whew," Ayden thought as she smiled at Deborah "I almost blew it trying to tell her how much I cared for her without letting her know I would be leaving her soon to go with Eleea."

That evening, Ayden sat on her bed with her head by the open window waiting for Eleea to fly down to see her like he did every evening since Elora had hatched. This was their time to talk about all they needed to do. And, of course, talk about how Elora was doing with her chick training.

"Eleea," Ayden whispered as he landed on her windowsill, "Just like Elora needs training, I need training too. How am I going to be able to succeed when I have no idea what I am doing?"

"Ayden, once we get to Eshra we will travel to the depths of the forest where it is safe and where we will meet up with others who will help us with all we need to learn. There we will stay until you are properly prepared to go on further," Eleea whispered back.

"Ya know Eleea, is it going to be OK for me to pack things I want to take with me? I mean there are certain survival things I want to pack. And what about clothes? Won't I need clothes to change into? Seriously, I want to be properly prepared here, before I go with you there!" Ayden quietly shouted.

"Ayden, I really don't know what to tell you. I have never done this journey before, either! Let alone bring someone from this world to my world!" Eleea quietly shouted back.

"The best thing I can tell you is," he paused for a second, "is to trust your own instincts, first. Then, think about the burden of having to carry everything long distances. What will you be able to carry without becoming tired too quickly? This is all I can tell you, Ayden. Pack wisely," Eleea advised.

The next day, Deborah and Ayden were walking home from Tae Kwan Do practice when Ayden decided to pose the question about survival kits to Deborah. "'D'," Ayden coyly started, "you know how our instructor says we need to be prepared for whatever comes our way and to be able to defend ourselves? Well, what do you think about having a survival bag so when we go on our nature hikes, we are prepared? Things like, ya know, rope, fire starter flint, knives, and what else do you think we need?" she pressed on.

Deborah totally bought into her question by saying, "Yeah! We do need to be prepared for the unknown. Officially, 'A', it is known as an emergency preparedness pack."

Deborah reached into her pocket, pulled out a small notebook with a short pencil in the spiral binding. "Baggies to hold water would be a good idea," she stated as she quickly started to write.

Deborah was on a mission to make the most outstanding survival pack anyone could imagine. This is where she shined. Those small details most people saw as insignificant, she proved them to be detrimental to a successful project. By the time they reached the house Deborah had the whole bag designed with everything it should hold.

"She is so-o-o-o cute," Ayden smiled to herself as she looked at Deborah's list. "And, she has no idea I just set her up to help me." "Well," Ayden thought, "That's one less problem I have to solve before I go. Now, on to the next."

Because she was a minor when her parents died, she was given a social security income determined by what her parents were paid in their jobs. So, she had money which went into a trust fund for her with some of it to be given to Deborah's parents for her care.

And, because Graycie and Robert are who they are, all the money which was supposed to be used for her care went directly to her to be put in a college fund and with some of it to use as she wanted.

Ayden loved wearing bandanas when she didn't feel like fixing her hair and she wanted new ones to take with her on the journey. She found a website showing all sorts of colors to choose from and she ordered twelve of them.

"Besides," she convinced herself, "I might have to tie them all together for some odd reason while I'm away, right?" There were also ones with a non-traditional bandana design showing the constellations of each star with small glittery thread sewed into the fabric. So, she bought twelve different colors of those for Deborah.

Anytime Ayden bought something, she made sure she bought for Deborah too; it was her heart to always include her. It helped her feel like she was paying Deborah's parents back for living with them.

Then she found on another website lightweight colored camouflage pants which zipped off at the knee to become shorts. One had her favorite greens: chartreuse, hunter, fern green; mixed in patterns of leaves and different browns of tree bark and limbs. And, for Deborah there was another camouflage mix of yellows, browns, reds, and oranges with the same tree and bark limbs of her favorite colors.

"Yep," she thought, "things are going pretty smoothly," as she rummaged around in the garage. She mentally checked off her list of supplies she had acquired for the trip. Survival backpack, bandanas and camouflage pants.

"What else do I need?" She wondered, as you looked around.

Robert was meticulous about keeping everything organized, and the garage was no exception. All she needed to make a fishing trip successful was right in front of her. Fishing line, hooks, sinkers, lures, and a break down pole; "excellent," she told herself, "this will fit nicely into the backpack."

He even had extra pepper spray which all residents who lived in bear country had several cans strategically located throughout their homes. "It wouldn't hurt to put this in the pack, too," she determined.

Ayden took thirty dollars she had saved and secretly put it in Robert's fishing vest pocket. She knew Robert would have told her to just take the items she put in the survival bag, but she didn't want to explain to him her reasoning. Nor did she feel it was right to always expect she could take without giving in return.

A couple of days later, Ayden sat in her favorite restaurant, Bitterroot Cafe, waiting for Deborah and Graycie, who were getting their hair cut down the street. Sipping on her coke, she saw Nick enter and take a seat at the soda fountain bar.

She watched as he placed his order; noticing he still seemed to be uncomfortable in his own skin. She observed him struggle to place his hands and arms in a comfortable resting position while he waited. He didn't know if he should rest his elbows on the counter or fold his arms across his chest as he repeatedly tried each position several times.

She got up from the booth where she was sitting and went over to him. "Nick," she said.

Nick jumped off his seat, acting like he was ready to bolt out of the restaurant.

Ayden, slipped into the seat beside him and stated, "Nick, it's just me, why don't you come sit with me over there," gesturing to her seat which held privacy from gossipy ears at the bar.

Nick hesitantly turned his head to see where Ayden was pointing. Shyly, he said, "OK, Ayden."

Silence ensued while Nick accepted his meal from the waitress. He slowly chewed each bite, as if he was trying to prolong the meal to avoid any conversation.

Ayden placed her arms on the table and locked her hands on each elbow. She decided she would begin her conversation with him by appealing to his, already proven 'locket' desire to take care of others.

"Nick, I need your help," Ayden earnestly said.

Nick stopped eating, put his hamburger on his plate, raised his eyes to her and slightly leaned forward. "What do you need, Ayden?" he quizzically inquired.

"Well, Nick," Ayden eased into her newly hatched plan. "I have had a lot happen to me with my parents passing, ya know? And, I have had a lot of time to think about loss. Loss of parents, friends, and all that goes with it. Not that I have lost any friends," she quickly interjected so he wouldn't read too much into her request like Deborah did a few days earlier.

"It has caused me to seriously think about all the people I love, she purposefully continued. "And, not that anything is going to happen to me. I don't have any foreboding doom I am feeling, but what if something totally unexpected did happen? Something like what happened to my mom and dad," she encouragingly led Nick.

"I would want to know someone like Deborah, who is my best friend, was not left alone if I wasn't there," she cautiously said.

Ayden expelled air as she sighed deeply, saying, "Nick, bottom line, I trust you. You have a really good heart. There is no one else in this town besides Deborah's parents who could be there for Deborah, but you. I want you to promise me, if anything ever happened to me, you would be there for Deborah and forge a strong friendship with her. That you would stop feeling uncomfortable about stepping on people's toes, or, or feeling like you are not important to others. I want you to realize how valuable your heart is and take the leap to open up and be there for another. And, I know when you finally do, do this, you will see your true worth not only to others, but to yourself too," Ayden tenderly pressed his heart as she stared into his eyes.

Nick stared back at Ayden in silence for about a minute. Without taking his eyes off of her. He finally said, "I promise you I will be there for Deborah. I promise," he said again as he determinedly focused his gaze on Ayden, "I will be there for you too, if you ever need me, Ayden."

Ayden averted her stare, feeling a sudden tenseness about their locked eyes. Quickly, she said, "Good! We got that settled. Now, let's enjoy the food. I think I will order some huckleberry ice cream. You, know they carry Wilcoxson's ice cream here? And to seal our deal, I will pay for yours."

As she finished her statement, Deborah and Graycie came through the door and sat down with them to join in the meal.

Happy she had time to speak to Nick alone. And, relieved they were interrupted; not having to spend any more private time together. Ayden tried to enjoy the small talk surrounding the table.

Journal Eight

Ayden intimately traced the raised etching of her journal with her hand. Beautifully crafted leather displayed smooth boulders rising up the sides and meeting half-way in the middle of the book.

Midnight blue sky colored most of the top and halfway down with a smudged blend of blue and white on the outer top right corner. From across the center to the end of the book the same blue and white trickled downward as if an artist had taken their paintbrush and dripped it over the canvas. It looked like a waterfall in motion.

A quarter of the way down, slightly off center, sat two smaller rocks situated on the ledge as the water began to flow. Standing tall, right after the rocks, in the center of the book, stood a majestic white crane.

Tall greenish-yellow grass anchored around the stones and rose around the crane's feet. Hints of midnight blue defined the bird's body and wings, and a sliver of goldish yellow formed its beak and legs.

Opening the book, Ayden took pencil in hand to once again reveal her heart. When you are young, you are not aware of others judging you. Most of your positive memories about yourself revolve around interactions with your family. Or at least this is how I would assume it should be.

For me, I learned at a very early age I was "damaged." I was not like other kids. My father would either make fun of me or chastise my mom for not properly hiding my back.

As I grew, and started to play with kids in the neighborhood, I learned very quickly if my back was seen, I would get teased or ridiculed.

My safety was to keep it covered. I became extremely creative on how to avoid a chance mishap of exposure. A scarf around my neck, a hoodie even when it was sweltering hot outside, or a t-shirt for wadding.

Swimming was not an option for fear the wet shirt would cling to my body or the shirt would rise above my swimsuit top in the water. It hurt getting teased and made fun of because I had an ugly birthmark. From the age of seven or eight, I did everything I could to keep my secret hidden.

Maybe this is why I excelled at martial arts? I had to fight to protect myself. To view this mark as a good thing was not something I was prepared to believe. No one had ever made me feel special because I had a huge birthmark from my neck down to the middle of my back.

Chapter Eight

Eleea rested on the limb above the nest watching the horizon as the sun set. It was one of those beautiful displays of color which filled the eyes with a panorama of three-dimensional shapes and contours. Allowing the eyes to form boundaries around the mountain peaks and trees as the sun showed forth its most radiant energy of pigments without having to look through a prism to see it.

Eleea's mind wandered to Eshra, as it always did when he was at rest. "The sunsets there were so much more vivid and full of life compared to this world," he reminisced. He loved Eshra and all of its wonder and he missed its splendor. Which made him excited and full of anticipation he would soon be returning there.

"Luckily," he thought, "the Council dispatched a runner to Ayden's world to find out why he had not returned to present his findings." Phum had arrived unexpectedly while Eleea was foraging near the stream. Eleea looked up startled to see him running, actually jumping high over the tall grass, towards him.

"Phum!" Eleea yelled. "Phum, my friend. What a joy it is to see you," Eleea happily expressed.

"Eleea," Phum stated as he arrived near the bird. "The Council sent me. They are concerned you have not returned to speak to them."

Eleea breathed a small sigh of despair as he sat back on his legs and looked at Phum. Phum's breed were trusted couriers of his world. Quick on their feet, they could easily traverse any obstacle to reach their intended goal. Small enough to slip into unknown areas, they strategically were able to listen without being seen.

Phum's unusual coloring made him even more rare. His black coat afforded him the ability to blend into the night. He was highly respected in Eshra and equally trusted to succeed in his missions.

"Phum," Eleea began, "Give the Council my apologies, but I could not return due to unforeseen events."

For the next hour Eleea explained what had shaped his decision to not return to Eshra. From first finding the messenger, to learning it was a child and a girl and to all of the complications surrounding it.

He then went into detail about all of the deaths and the impact they had on him. Finishing, he concluded with all of the past events were the reasons he could not address the Council himself.

"A child?" Phum stated in disbelief. "Surely, Eleea, the loss of Lora must have skewed your ability to see the prophecy clearly." Phum sat back on his haunches and lifted his back foot to scratch his chin with his claw.

"We can't bring a child over, Eleea!" He finally exclaimed. "By the Crane, what has gotten into you," he continued.

"You were sent here to secure our future! And, now you nonchalantly tell me I have to go back to our Council and give them the news, with a straight face mind you, that you are bringing a child who is a girl over to save us!"

Phum continued his rant, "I may look small and easily led because I am a squirrel. But, let me tell you, Eleea, my size is enormous compared to you! Just what do you think the Council is going to do to me when I return with your revelation of hope?"

"Huh! No, I am not going home. You and I," Phum with an air of petrification in his voice stated, "You and I", he continued, "we will just stay right here and try to figure this thing out. We, will...we will wait... wait until the Council sends someone else to come and get us...I just can't return with this news and expect to be respected by those who are depending on us."

Eleea knew better than to interrupt Phum when he was motor-mouthing his feelings. He also knew he could convince Phum to see what he already knew to be the truth about Ayden. He just had to give Phum the space and time to decompress and stop worrying about always having to look perfect to others.

For the next couple days, Eleea tried to avoid engaging Phum in any type of conversation; hoping he would freely explore the town of East Glacier. He knew Phum's desire to learn the culture of Ayden's world would keep him entertained and out of Eleea's way of training the girls.

On his third day of exploration, Eleea found Phum laid out flat, relaxing, waiting for him on a branch far above his nest. Eleea looked up and nodded to Phum in a friendly gesture of, "how you doing."

Phum acrobatically jumped the branches down to Eleea, stating, "I've been waiting for you to wake, Eleea. Did you know humans stare into windows that show other worlds? They're everywhere!" he excitedly explained.

"Big box windows, handheld windows, even huge windows where they all sit and watch in a very large dark room. The windows are called screens...and the craziest things happen in these worlds. I do like the music, though. They have so many more instruments than we do in our world," Phum eagerly continued.

Eleea inwardly smiled at Phum's innocence and newly acquired knowledge. He was truly a rare gem, who loved to learn about everything. Not that he got each study of what he learned right, though.

"Perception can be a fickle thing," Eleea reminded himself. "Just because one sees something, like 'a world in a window' it doesn't make it real."

But, Eleea determined he would have to address this confusion with Phum when it presented itself. Right now, it was time for Phum to meet Ayden. Eleea excused himself and flew to Ayden's windowsill.

Shortly after Eleea spoke to Ayden, she emerged from her home and slowly
approached the tree where Eleea and Phum were talking. Eleea had already explained to her the latest dilemma about Phum's reluctance to accept her as the messenger. He had instructed her on how to arrive in their presence, and to wait for Eleea to introduce her to the reluctant comrade.

"Ayden, I would like you to meet Phum," Eleea began. "Phum, this is Ayden. What I want you to do is show the mark of the prophecy on your back before either of you say anything to each other."

Ayden obediently took her hoodie off and turned her back to them for Phum to see the full effect. She had timidly chosen a sports bra as her under garment to make sure the fullest version of the birthmark could be seen.

Phum gasped as he fixed his eyes on her back. Slowly he spoke: *"Upon the back deliverance comes. At rest the crane stands, Head held high."*

Phum turned to Eleea and reverently said, "I will return immediately to Eshra, Eleea. There is no need for anymore dialogue. The Council must to be told you have found the messenger."

Phum nodded to Ayden and quickly climbed the trees and was soon out of sight.

With the Phum distraction eliminated, Eleea determined the days he had left, in Ayden's world, would continue to follow his meticulous timeline. Keeping the girls separated, was his choice from the beginning.

It secured for him fewer interruptions. He couldn't afford for the girls to flitter off task with silly girl stuff.

Elora's training was going well, just like her mother, her mind was quick. She took to flight with ease and she was a delight as she easily learned to talk. Her young mind brought forth a thirst for knowledge which Eleea found refreshing.

Each morning and evening they spent time in the nest as Eleea shared stories from his and Lora's past. He explained the history of the world she was born into and that of Eshra. And, he tried to answer all of her insatiable questions.

Throughout the rest of the time it was physical training. How to dart from danger, or where to find the best supply of food. As well as learning to listen to one's surroundings to know how to react correctly.

Likewise, Ayden's training also included Eleea teaching her about how to discern her environment to protect herself and to expand her understanding of compassion and self-worth.

Through story telling he tried to get her to see a different way of approaching difficult situations. Ayden was quick to react with frustration, which he knew came from living in a volatile home with her parents.

She was never allowed the freedom to mature with good self-esteem. And, she doubted herself continuously. Even though she had agreed to cross over, she constantly questioned the validity of the prophecy and her role in it.

Yet, the most exciting part of returning to Eshra for Eleea was Elora and Ayden traveling with him. The two of them would experience Eshra for the first time together. And he was looking forward to watching their awe of the land.

"Yes, their days were full of joyful activity. "But," he sorrowfully thought, "my joy would be so much fuller if Lora could have shared these moments with me."

He knew all about the grieving process by proxy of listening to Deborah expound her psychology onto Ayden. Generally, it takes eighteen months to process all of the stages of grief.

And, during that time one would pass through the stages of anger, denial, guilt, and depression repeatedly depending on the severity of the heart's loss. Finally, one's passage through time and emotions would rest in acceptance at what happened and with what had been lost.

"It's just not easy to categorize these stages with understanding and acceptance when it is so personal to have to deal with the pain of it," he agonized.

Both Elora and Ayden had been training with Eleea for weeks. But the day had come for their first training together. Eleea was beyond nervous thinking about the difficulty of handling two young girls and trying to keep them on track.

"Elora, today we will meet with Ayden to begin the planning process to cross over to the other side," Eleea told her.

"I need you to stay focused and keep your questions to a minimum," he advised his daughter.

"Father," Elora expressed, "How else am I to learn if I don't ask questions? Especially since Ayden and I have not had time to speak directly with each other. You have only trained us both through your eyes, Father," Elora stated.

"Neither one of us has been allowed to be around each other to talk or to learn through each other's eyes," she excitedly chirruped.

"And, now, you ask me to keep focused and silent when I am to officially meet Ayden for the first time? Watching her from a distance and hearing you tell me about her is totally different than a face to face meeting," she continued to inform him. "This is the female who saved my life, Father," Elora passionately spoke. "Already, before I meet her, I have deep feelings for her."

"Yes, child," Eleea agreed, "But remember, you will have plenty of time to speak with her once we reach the other side. All of us need to stay focused to ensure a safe entry into Eshra."

Eleea planned the girl's first meeting to be in the meadow where the mighty Glaciers overlooked the landscape. One lone sage tree stood tall, amidst the grassy terrain of bear grass, glacier lilies, and wildflowers of the region.

He wanted the girls to become familiar with this tree as it would be the meeting point for all of them. He knew if they all got separated on the day of entry the girls would know to look for the tree and would be able to get to it if they could not find him.

Eleea needed to drill into the girl's mind the importance of timing through song. He had already been preparing them for some time through humming along with him. But it was a major leap to go from the humming to the singing, and his anxiety was heightened.

Eleea and Elora did not have to wait long for Ayden to arrive at the tree. And now that they were all together, Eleea was anxious to begin the lessons.

"OK girls, what I want both of you to understand, is what it takes to make the leap to the other side," Eleea began his instructions.

"Ayden," Elora interrupted Eleea's training, "What do you think about the color purple? Father says when we get to Eshra some animals opt to wear clothes or just accessorize with small things like a scarf. I'm thinking of going with a purple bandana. What do you think?"

"Bandana!" Ayden exclaimed. "I love bandanas! Matter of fact I have some packed to go and one of them is this lilac purple which would be just perfect. I could size it down to fit you."

"What are you thinking," Ayden continued, "around the neck or around the head?"

"Girls!" Eleea yelled, breaking up their girl moment. "We are not here to discuss what color or style is the perfect fashion statement! Pay attention!" He shrieked.

"Both of you need to know how to cross over, or there won't be any purple, red, green, or whatever other color your little heart's desire to wear!" Eleea exclaimed.

The girls simultaneously jumped into submission at the sternness of Eleea's voice. Neither of them had ever heard him raise his voice to them. He was always the calm one with insurmountable patience.

Eleea ruffled his feathers as if he was brushing off the morning dew from his wings. Pushing his chest out and clearing his throat, he began, "When the sun kisses the day is when the leap will be made."

"Both of you will take your cue from my lead. We will start with humming. Then as we are humming, I want both of you to focus on the lowest point between the two mountains. The cradle of those two mountains is our focal point," he told them.

It is imperative," Eleea continued, "for the two of you keep your eyes directly in the cradle of those two mountains. Because when the sun begins its ascent, it will first be seen in the cradle and we will only have a few seconds to be in sync with our singing. This will be the final moment where we will begin our descent into Eshra."

Eleea kept the girls regimented for days. Bringing them to the tree to practice their humming.

He knew the more they practiced, the better chance they would have to fall into a comfortable pattern which guaranteed all of them making it over without complications.

Time was short, now, and Eleea was feeling the pressure of his responsibility to bring the messenger to her destiny.

Journal Nine

A light southerly breeze began to rustle the pages on Ayden's book as it lay open next to her. She stood up to get the full effect of the wind as she turned her head to let it cool her face.

Ayden walked down to the river, with bent knees she steadied herself at the edge of the riverbank as she cupped her hand to reach into the clear water. Lifting her hand to her mouth, she let the cool water flow down her throat.

Ayden steadied her gaze, while she listened to all of the sounds of river life. In the distance, upriver, she could see two lone limbs resembling a cross. She thought about the death of her parents and the events which surrounded it. Returning to the tree, she opened the book again.

I don't know what to say about my parents. There were so many things I did not understand and so many things they kept secret so I couldn't understand.

It was a family who knew not how to love; who only knew anger. What an empty existence to raise a child in. This was my home environment.

What they showed to the world was different, though. My father was the life of the party at social gatherings, always joking and kind to everyone. The towns people loved him to come to their events.

Whereas my mom was quiet and polite; always the dutiful partner. Even in her job at the convenience store which was attached to the garage where my dad worked, she was quiet and respectful.

I have sorrow for them. Sorrow in the truth of how they could have been so much more than they were.

I am embarrassed, though, because my dad was a thief. I had lost count of the memories of where I thought he had brought something home under the illusion a friend had given it to him. Only to find out years later, through my mom's anger, it was all stolen.

I hated what he did. I wondered how many stolen items were from the tourists' cars he worked on? He was deceptive.

I hated my mother lying for him by not immediately confronting him for stealing. I hated my mother was weak and allowed him to beat her and me. I hated he beat me. I hated she beat me.

Hated them? No, what I hated was their actions...their choices.

Hate for a human is a worthless emotion. It sucks the life out of you. Dwelling on hate paralyzes your ability to walk out of the wrong it created.

If they would have only allowed themselves the freedom to walk out of their wrongs and mistakes...to see how they were hurting each other and me. Unfortunately, the past cannot be changed. And sadly, their future will never be.

But my past does not have to be my future. Their legacy for me is to learn from their mistakes and not repeat them in my own life.

To try to remember those brief moments when they did do right and build on those memories as good. Discard the bad as their problem and their loss.

And to work hard to overcome. To build my own memories through those whom love me and respect me.

And, most importantly, to build memories through the power to finally love myself. All of myself!

Chapter Nine

Ayden felt the urgency of her time left in her world. She knew all of the instructions she and Elora received from Eleea meant the day to leave would be soon.

Before she left, she wanted to do one final memorial to her parents. And, this involved their ashes riding the winds of Glacier.

Ayden explained to Deborah and her parents what she wanted. Everyone felt comfortable with her doing this on her own.

Each understood this was her way of finally saying good-bye to her parents. She planned it for the next morning as the dawn broke through the day.

Her heart was heavy as she laid her head on her pillow. She wasn't sure she wanted to be alone. Yet she felt she needed to honor her parents by herself, with no interruptions. She even told Eleea he could not come with her.

Early in the morning, Ayden rose quietly as she did not want to wake anyone or to worry about the off chance of having to make small talk. She wanted her thoughts to be steady without the drama of another's emotions.

The sun was just rising over the mountains as she began her trek to the top of the small hill past the meadow. With her phone set on shuffle, she listened to several songs as she began her trek. From 'Dust in The Wind' by Kansas to Fleetwood Mac and Journey, the songs continuously helped her climb to the top of the hill as she gave herself permission to let the tears fall freely down her cheeks.

Ayden kept a steady pace; which was easy to do by not having to adjust for a heavy pack. The only thing in the backpack were two boxes containing the ashes of her parents, the bracelet Nick had found in the rubble of her home, a bottle of water and the required bear spray Robert insisted she take.

At times, she would have to stop to let her eyes refocus from the blinding tears. Her sleeves of her hoodie were full from wiping her face and nose.

As she walked, her mind drifted to all of the good times she had with her parents. From their laughter, to their love of Glacier, and to all of the things they did right in raising her.

She loved East Glacier. Her parents could have taken more lucrative jobs in a bigger city, but they chose to stay in the small town where, "kids were safe." Both her parents loved to listen to classic rock; and she too enjoyed it.

Her mom's laugh could be contagious, at times. When she was very young, her mom would lift her up and tell her how beautiful she was. Tell her she was brought into this world through a special love.

And then her mom would freely laugh in a tender manner. She would put her down and lift her chin to look into her eyes. Saying, "Ayden don't you ever forget you were made out of pure love."

When Ayden turned twelve her mom gave her a bracelet which held a beautifully engraved locket shaped like a feather. She told Ayden she was given the locket by someone very important as she opened it to reveal a small picture of her and Ayden as a baby.

Ayden's painful memories were washed clean through her tears of sorrow as she continued to climb. When she reached the top of the hill, she sat down and took her backpack off. Ayden took out each box and set them on her lap.

"This is all that is left of my parents," she contemplated with pure sorrow. As she stared at them, she wondered if she should say a prayer while she let the ashes fall into the wind. Once again, the tears flowed freely.

"Oh Brother!" she thought, "This is a lot harder than I thought it would be." She began to focus on the song playing in her ears and her heart. "The songs made her realize not only were her tears for her loss, but for the loss of what could have been for her parents if they had lived. And if they had changed their hearts.

Ayden thought back to the funeral service where the pastor had quoted a Bible verse: "Ashes to ashes, dust to dust, we are returned to the earth from whence we came."

She opened the boxes as she rose to her feet. And allowed the wind to catch the ashes.

Ayden determinedly said out loud, *"We may be dust in the wind, and we may return to the earth from where we came, but our soul lives on through those whom we loved and touched on this earth.*

Good will always outweigh bad and I vow to carry this truth forward: As long as I take a breath on this earth, I will fight for righteousness; I will seek peace where it can be found; I will not be afraid to confront danger, including evil.

And I will keep those whom I choose to love close to my heart. I will not let the bad prevail in my heart or my life! I will look for the purpose and meaning in any situation and carry its light in my heart!"

When she had spoken the last word, a powerful gust blew directly at her and picked up the final ashes. As she watched them leave their box, they rode the wind.

Ayden placed the boxes in the pack, and pulled out the locket. Opening it, she focused on the portrait inside for a long time.

The picture was the only thing salvaged from the fire that held any importance to her. She took the locket off of the bracelet chain and attached it to the inside zipper on her backpack.

Ayden sat back down on the little hill and stared at the locket. She intimately caressed it as she looked at the landscape and mountains in front of her. She, then, allowed herself one last good cry before she started for home.

Journal Ten

Ayden put her head back as she rested it against the trunk of the tree and closed her eyes. Her heart overflowed with emotion, as she thought about how she had to learn to accept all that was happening around her. And to fully accept her decision to cross over to Eshra.

I was closer to fifteen than fourteen when I finally made the choice to follow Eleea, she wrote. But, I was still a child full of fear and self-doubt.

My young mind could not totally comprehend what was being asked of me. I wanted so desperately to do the right thing for everyone. I didn't think about any of the consequences of my actions. And, how it would affect those around me, long term anyways.

The short of it, I felt I could quickly take care of the situation, secure everyone's feelings, and return to a 'normal' life. I did not expect the whole effect would so drastically change me.

From the moment, I told Eleea I would go with him, I put into motion a strong case of manipulation to make sure Deborah was safe from my decisions. I did not want her to be left without answers, but I couldn't let her know the truth, either.

At times, I felt so very ugly inside for lying and manipulating. I questioned my motives, constantly. "Was I any better than my parents, who kept secrets from me? Who would rather lie to me than speak a truthful word?

Plus, what could I really do once we got to Eshra? I was just a kid. I had no working knowledge of how to manage a crisis, to survive on my own, or to even help others make it out of danger.

Deborah's parents helped me get through my mom's stay while in Missoula and after. Then they took me in to have a home with them.

Deborah was always there so I wasn't alone. I knew she protected me from getting teased because of my birthmark. And, the only time I protected someone from danger was when Deborah almost got bit by the rattlesnake.

I was foolish. A silly little girl who had a lot to learn. I had to learn that choices, of any nature, had a cause and effect on me. And, on those who depended on me.

Chapter Ten

It was the part of night where the girls separated to spend quiet time in their rooms before bed. Deborah's intuition was on high alert, and she was having difficulty falling asleep.

She knew something was up, but she just couldn't put her finger on it. She wanted to talk to Ayden, but she knew Ayden would blow her off and not tell her.

"Ayden is hiding something and I need to find out what it is," she resolved. "She keeps slipping away to the meadow. And, I know it is more than grief over her parents," she frantically thought.

"So, Deborah," she said to herself, "Let's analyze what is going on with Ayden? If you look at each suspicious fact you should be able to surmise what she is doing," Deborah schooled herself.

Suspicious Fact One: Ayden leaves to the meadow every morning.

Suspicious Fact Two: Ayden is humming all of the time now.

Suspicious Fact Three: Ayden is acting overly sweet to me, always wanting me to know she loves me and appreciates me.

Suspicious Fact Four: Ayden is obsessed with the survival backpack; making sure it is properly packed.

Suspicious Fact Five: I hear Ayden whispering every night, like she is talking to someone.

Suspicious Fact Six: When I talk about what we should do this summer Ayden acts like it won't happen. She won't even join me in planning for it.

Suspicious Fact Seven: She's becoming more and more excited.

Suspicious Fact Eight: She's giving me some of her favorite belongings to keep.

"OH, good Lord!" Deborah silently screamed. "She's preparing to kill herself! She's losing her mind. Talking to herself and she wants to die to feel happy. I just know it. She is gonna go deep into the woods and end her life!"

"That's it," Deborah concluded, "I will have to watch her every second she is awake. And, I will have to follow her everywhere so she doesn't do something stupid! If I say anything to mom or dad, they will send her away to Missoula for inpatient counseling. Nope, the only way to help Ayden is by staying close to her. Close enough without alerting her I am watching over her," Deborah finally determined.

"OK," Deborah calculated, "I have got to be prepared to follow her tomorrow morning. This is when she secretly goes to the meadow."

Deborah hurriedly dug through her clothes to find the perfect ninja outfit for her mission. The black and grey bandanas Ayden had given her would help. She decided to use one around her head to hide her long blond hair, while the another one would serve as a facial cover.

"There," she thought as she looked at herself in the mirror, "Only my eyes and forehead show through, now. But they still look pretty white, and they will stand out in the dark." Deborah found black artist chalk in her dad's art supplies and used it as eye shadow above and below her eyes and across her forehead.

She took several more of the bandanas and placed them in the pockets of her pants. "Just in case I need them," she determined. Black tights and t-shirt under her camouflaged pants finished the look. She was set for her intervention with Ayden.

Deborah set her alarm clock for 4:30 a.m., believing she would have plenty of time to watch for Ayden's departure to the meadow.

"Well it didn't really matter if I set my alarm," she thought, "since all I am doing is tossing and turning and now it is 4:00 a.m."

Her heart jumped; she heard a noise come from Ayden's room. "She's already awake!" she silently breathed.

Quietly she eased out of her bed, to put her clothes and shoes on. She rolled her hair into a tight bun and placed the black bandana around her head and tied it firmly. The other scarf she tied over her nose and mouth. She had kept the black chalk on so she wouldn't have to do it the morning; and she was ready.

While she dressed, though, Deborah would periodically stop to listen intently to see if Ayden was still moving around her room.

Which caused her stress level to increase and rise higher and higher. She kept thinking Ayden had already left and she would deliberately stop what she was doing to listen for Ayden's movements.

A shadow flashed across her window and she knew it had to be Ayden leaving for the meadow. She waited for two long grueling minutes before she slipped out her window to follow.

Deborah could see Ayden fifty yards ahead of her when her eyes finally focused to the outside darkness. Even though the moon was full, and the stars were bright like recessed lights throughout a room, it still was difficult to step cautiously in the unknown turf while Deborah tried to hurry.

She stayed far enough away so Ayden didn't know she was being followed, and yet close enough to see her. Which began to confuse her as to why Ayden was dressed in her camouflage and had the survival backpack.

Deborah quietly spoke to herself, "Maybe she isn't trying to kill herself. Maybe she is running away from home. Why does she want to run away? Is she that unhappy living with us? Well, when I finally figure this out, she has a lot of explaining to do!" Deborah comforted herself.

Ayden slowed her pace as she reached the meadow by the sage tree and stopped. Suddenly, she turned to look behind her. Deborah was already crouched down when she saw Ayden start to turn, which caused her to instantly lay flat.

She waited until Ayden turned back and then began to inch her body forward in a small steady movement. Almost like a caterpillar would move its body forward.

Deborah could hear Ayden's voice speak to someone, but she could not see the person; nor could she clearly hear the conversation as Ayden's face was towards the mountains in front of her.

Plus, those damn birds muffled the sound with their cheery morning chirping. Which irritated her to no end that they were the cause of her confusion to not be able to hear the people Ayden was talking to.

Deborah wanted to move faster, but she dared not make any more noise than what the slow movement was already making.

"Thankfully," she told herself, "the grass is wet from the morning dew and I don't have to worry about dry grass or twigs breaking under the weight of my body and making noise."

At approximately ten feet away from Ayden, Deborah heard Ayden start to sing. "Hey! She has one beautiful voice," she mused.

"How come I never knew this before? She never told me she could sing," Deborah lamented to herself.

Suddenly the ground under her began to tremble. Almost like a bounce that was musically choreographed to Ta Dum Ta Dum Ta Dum. Slowly the bounce became more intense.

Deborah, took her eyes off of Ayden, looked around her and saw the grass and the sage tree swaying ever so slightly to the Ta Dum.

Then, she noticed Ayden had a bird on each of her shoulders and they were both chirping like they were in unison with Ayden's singing.

"Something is not normal here!" Deborah cried under her breath. As their voices became louder, and more beautifully in sync with the chanting, Deborah caught her mouth from releasing a scream.

"Oh Lord!" She silently screamed, "My mind is tricking me! I'm beginning to think those birds are chanting with Ayden. Crap! Those birds have made Ayden crazy and now they are trying to suck me into their craziness! What do I do? WHAT DO I DO?"

Deborah lifted her body up and began to move closer to Ayden. She didn't know if she should run to Ayden or run away from her.

She found the swaying motion had become stronger and it was incredibly hard for her to not sway with it. The vibration of the ground seemed to increase as their song became louder.

Deborah's mind began to race at the same pace as the vibrations. She felt her heart would bounce out of her chest as her breathing seemed to keep beat with the ground under her.

Deborah looked to the mountains, knowing the sun would soon emerge. She hoped the light of the sun and its brightness would stop all of the chaos she was experiencing.

Deborah's body, by now, was bouncing and swaying to the rhythm of Ayden's singing when she felt the grass begin to ripple across the meadow.

As each ripple progressed away from Deborah's body, another ripple would start. Everything was working together as if it was one body in fluid motion. Deborah didn't know if she should cry, scream or laugh uncontrollably; she had never before fathomed anything like this.

Her fear increased as the singing reached a crescendo where Ayden's voice was joined by a choir of other voices. It sounded like a Gregorian chant. So absolutely gorgeous to hear that Deborah felt chills run down her spine. Just as the chant reached an unbelievable high pitch, the ground's movement changed.

Deborah started to panic thinking it had to be an earthquake moving directly towards Ayden. Not only was the ground trembling in Ayden's direction, but the ripples had increased in speed like they were building up pressure.

Deborah jumped to her feet and began to run to Ayden as the sun crested over the mountains. She lunged forward and grabbed Ayden's waist when she felt the flowers start to swirl.

Thousands of petals of different types began from the ground up, moving towards the sky, twisting and turning in a visual display of unity as they magnificently showed forth their brilliance in color from the rays of the morning sun and engulfed Ayden, the birds and Deborah in their dance.

The force of Deborah's body as it tackled Ayden caused both girls to fall and roll down the small hill as Deborah held on to Ayden tightly. Ayden screamed and Deborah matched her with her own screams.

The girls stopped rolling and looked at each other in astonishment. Each began to talk simultaneously and neither one could understand what the other said.

Elora broke the confusion when she said to Deborah, "Hey pretty lady, are you OK? You have black all over your face."

Deborah did a crab crawl away from Elora, and said, "OH Sweet Jesus! I have totally lost my mind! I am hearing voices and it is in the form of a bird's voice!" She started to cry uncontrollably.

Ayden quickly came to Deborah's side, soothingly saying to her, "'D', you are OK. You're not hearing voices. The birds really can talk and you can really understand them. You are OK."

Dead silence ensued as Deborah and Ayden held hands and just stared at each other.

Eleea started to pace back and forth on the log next to Ayden, visibly upset. "How in this world did this happen!" He exclaimed. "Everything was planned so perfectly. And, now I have to deal with her!"

Ayden patted Deborah's leg in a reassuring manner and turned to Eleea. stating, "It's OK, Eleea, we will work through this."

"What do you mean we can work through this," Eleea blurted. "She is in Eshra, our world, not your world, Ayden!"

"World!" Deborah screamed. "Are you guys trying to tell me I am not in America? Where the hell am I!"

Ayden walked half way back to Deborah, then half way back to Eleea not wanting to leave either one alone with their own thoughts. Finally, she decided Deborah needed her more since Eleea already knew where he was.

"Deborah," Ayden began as she took her hand in hers, "We are not in America. But we are also not in our home town anymore. This world is called Eshra and it is Eleea's world. We went through a point of entry into another world when we were chanting and singing in the meadow. Because you grabbed on to me as we entered, you are now with us in this other world, Deborah."

"Oh, sweet Lord of all things rational!" Deborah cried as tears, again, started to run down her face.

She jumped up and away from Ayden and began to wring her hands as she spoke, "This is not rational nor is it plausible to be in what you call another world. There is no substantiated evidence there is an alternate universe in any science book I have ever read!"

Eleea flew to Ayden's shoulder stating, "We have all got to move quickly and leave the area. It is not safe for us to stay here. Deborah, I promise you, we will explain everything to you, but right now we have to get to the woods and to our safe home. There is too much danger for us out in the open and I need to keep us moving to safety."

Ayden offered her arm to Deborah with their signature handshake. Elora flew to Ayden's left shoulder and everyone began to walk.

Eleea directed their path, with a whisper, as he said, "we need to go quickly and silently."

When they reached the first of the trees which lead deep into the forest a horseman appeared from behind the forest covering. "Eleea, my dear friend, it is so good to see you, and to see all is well with you and your family," a man dressed in buckskin pants and a loose cream cotton smock said.

"Nadab my friend, thank you for meeting us," Eleea responded back.

The man pulled out a long smock, beautifully embroidered with a crane depicted on the back of the shirt, and motioned to Ayden to put it on over her clothes. He then turned to his personal pack, where he always carried extra clothing. He gestured to Deborah and had her put on a similar pair of pants and smock like he wore. He cinched Deborah's pants with a leather rope to keep them on her hips, and then took Ayden's backpack and put it inside a bag on his horse.

He reached into another bag attached to the horse's saddle. In his hand, he held two round wooden charms. He put his finger to his lips, and whispered to the girls, "Put this in your hand and blow on it." The girls did as they were directed. Immediately, as they breathed on them, a form of a beautiful red fox appeared on the disks.

The man took the medallions and strung a piece of leather through the holes in the top of them and tied the two ends together. He handed them to a black squirrel and stated, "You know where to place these, Phum."

The black squirrel hung them around his neck. He nodded in agreement, and took off in the same direction from where the girls had entered into Eshra.

The man reached for Ayden's hand. She took it and he lifted her up on to the horse. He then jumped on behind her and reached his arm to Deborah and pulled her up to the horse behind him.

He took two intricately woven blankets full of color and geometric designs from his saddle bag and placed one over Ayden's lap and wrapped each leg, making sure her shoes were covered and then did the same for Deborah. Eleea perched on Nadab's shoulder, while Elora stayed close to Ayden.

The man's horse was a large multi-colored stallion with a gradation of blends from soft gray to brilliant black intermingled in a pattern which looked like soft clouds whimsically crossing the sky. He was covered in an elaborate tribal designed bridal and blanket which matched the colors of his coat.

Ayden had a front row seat to all the beautiful patterns of flowers, foliage and trees with their tri-colored moss on the trunks, mixed with vines climbing and twirling around the bark as they rode deeper into the woods.

The visions that played across her eyes as they rode seemed to be more intense since no one was allowed to talk. She wanted to soak in all she could about this new world she felt, already, blessed to be a part of.

Deborah's mind was full of confusion as she tried to decipher her new surroundings. Their travel was well into hours, already, and she still wanted to cry out of fear. And, because Ayden had not told her anything about this land called Eshra. Or her ability to talk to birds.

She felt sad more than betrayed by Ayden's silence about where they were. She watched as the black squirrel caught up with them and traversed the limbs ahead of them. Her sorrow was deep as she thought about Ayden's reluctance to tell her the truth.

Then, she began to rationalize the whole experience in her forced silence. "I doubt, if it was me in Ayden's shoes, it would have been easy for me to tell her what I knew. These types of experiences are not normal. And sometimes you just have to accept the unknown and move forward as you continue your research for answers. Poor Ayden she must have felt so alone not being able to say anything to me," Deborah sadly concluded.

After several more hours of travel where it led them deeper and higher into the mountains the small caravan stopped in front of a massive tree. Nadab first helped Deborah down from the horse and then lifted Ayden to the ground.

He jumped off the horse and stood in front of the tree with his arms outstretched and palms facing outward. Slowly he brought his hands together in front of him, placed his palms together and raised his thumbs to touch the middle of his forehead.

As he lowered his head to his chest, he slowly lifted his hands, still together, and then sliced the air downward and the tree split open in front of them. Nadab quickly turned around to the travelers and ushered them through the open tree.

Once all were inside, the tree closed its doorway. A sigh of relief was audibly heard coming from Nadab and Eleea.

Nadab turned to Eleea, and stated, "What happened? How is it another has come with you, Elora and the Messenger?"

Eleea responded with frustration, "I do not know how this happened. Everything was planned with great care and now it has all been compromised. My fear is we will have to abort the mission or someone will have to take the girl back through the entry from whence she came."

Nadab rubbed his forehead as if trying to massage a headache and said, "Eleea, you know it is too dangerous to go back to the point of entry so soon after one has entered. No, we will have to keep the other one here, under guard, while the mission is completed."

Deborah and Ayden, both, intently listened from the shadows as Eleea and Nadab planned their fate.

Finally, Deborah had enough of being talked about in the third person. She walked into the middle of Nadab's and Eleea's conversation and stated, "I have had just about enough of you two! I am not to be looked at as someone who cannot make my own decisions, nor am I to be looked at as someone who has to be guarded!"

"We have been traveling for hours, in what seems to be a land neither Ayden and I have ever been in before. Although, I might add this land sure does seem to be a lot like the land we came from. The forest and the sky do appear to look like areas around Glacier. Except for this tree which opened up into this grand entrance," Deborah concluded.

Anyways, I doubt there is an easy answer to your dilemma. And Ayden and I are tired, not to mention hungry. Maybe the wisest thing to do right now is to find some food and a place to rest. What do you think boys?" Deborah finished.

Elora flew to Deborah's shoulder saying, "Good job pretty lady. I'm with you."

Journal Eleven

Deborah crossing over with us made my journey so much easier. I know, at first, it was scary for her. But I secretly gave thanks for it. She was someone I was familiar with; not someone from Eshra.

I, now, was not alone in a strange world. I had my best friend beside me. And, I was so relieved I didn't have to lie to her anymore. Plus, when we got back to our world, I didn't have to keep Eshra a secret either.

The freedom of being able to be honest is exhilarating. Especially when it is towards someone you love and care about. It has to do with being respectful with self and another.

I understand the whole dignity and respect thing. Show dignity to others and, generally, you will receive respect back. Always try to be decent with others. Don't be a jerk for just the sake of being hateful.

Sure, all of us have had those experiences that turn us. That make us hurt so deeply inside we want to lash out. A problem can develop, though, if we don't look past the hurt.

Yes, it may be necessary to attack, verbally, to protect yourself. And, even physically, if someone is trying to seriously harm you.

But, to daily live in a mindset where you constantly are looking for a fight is deeply harmful to your psyche. You stop growing as a positive human being when you let anger and hurt control you.

One summer, Deborah's dad had an art student who spent the summer training in East Glacier. She was a counselor for troubled youth.

Deborah and I spent an afternoon with her while she practiced what she learned from Robert. While she worked on her canvas, she told us a story about a youth who lived in a group home. He had to leave this home to go to a juvenile prison. This is how she explained it:

"This child was not a bad kid. It was the laws at the time that were bad. And rules were rules. He had developed a strong bond with the group home houseparents and their child. They all loved each other.

About two weeks before he was to go, things changed. He became extremely distant and verbally combative. By the time he left, everyone in the home was relieved to see him leave. And, yet, very sad for the loss of what was before."

The counselor had learned about the whole situation after the child was out of the home. She sat the family down to explain to them why he had changed.

"Loss creates strange emotions of hurt. Anger, fear, combativeness, depression you name it; any emotion can be triggered when a person senses a loss. This child knew he was leaving and had to stop his hurt," she told them.

"He chose anger. Anger is a secondary emotion. Most people do not understand it is a masking emotion.

Before you feel angry, you feel hurt, embarrassed or scared; which are initial emotions. This child was deeply hurt over his inevitable loss of this family.

So, he made sure they didn't like him. He used anger to avoid the pain of feeling sad. And, therefore he was able to avoid his true emotions of hurt and sorrow by reacting in anger and combativeness.

The family would then start to dislike his behavior and it would be easier for him to leave angry. Because they were all mad, no one would break down in tears over losing each other," she explained.

"Negative anger stunts growth. It keeps a person stuck in a vicious cycle of reacting in negative ways," she continued to teach them.

"Most people don't know when they feel the anger emotion rise, they need to look at a root cause like hurt, embarrassment or fear to find the true foundation of the emotional reaction."

Her explanation of anger always stayed with me. By recognizing your true emotion of hurt, embarrassment or fear, you can, sometimes, avoid reacting without dignity and respect.

Chapter Eleven

A young man approached Nadab, greeted him and took his horse down a hallway in the opposite direction where Eleea and Nadab started to lead the girls.

The tree was massive on the inside. Everywhere were turns and easements which flowed upwards and downwards to other hallways and rooms. Be that it was a late in the night, the girls saw no other residents of the tree as they walked with their guides.

Eventually, several floors above from where they entered the tree, Nadab and Eleea escorted them into a large bedroom with three beds. Lovely as it was, the girls really did not care to assess their surroundings. Food and sleep was the only goal on their minds.

Eleea made sure dinner was brought as they settled into their room. A middle-aged man, who carried the food, set their table with utensils and other niceties and then smiled at the girls as he left.

The girls were told by Eleea they would share the bedroom while living at the tree. He explained to them his nest was just outside their room where he and Elora would reside.

He got Elora settled for the evening after she ate with the girls, and double checked all three were sleeping before he left to find Nadab's workshop.

"We must meet with the Council tonight, Nadab," Eleea urgently requested as he flew into Nadab's shop.

"Yes," Nadab began, "the Council is aware you are here and have need to talk with them. I was waiting for you, so we could go together."

Eleea flew to Nadab's shoulder and they began to walk the corridors of the Great Tree. The council room was nestled deep in one of the tree's upper branches.

Only if a person knew where they were going could one find it, as it was hidden from view by most who passed by.

To enter the room took a special series of actions to release the latch of the door. Nadab reached for a vine which twisted around a banister. He untangled the vine from the root and lifted the vine upwards and placed the uppermost tip of it on a section of the main tree trunk.

Magically, the vine flattened and became part of the trunk, with only its outline showing through. Nadab then used his index finger to touch the trunk and followed the vine down to the middle of it. He traced a circle with his finger and a latch appeared. Nadab turned the latch and they entered a large room.

Carved benches and chairs protruded out of the structure of the tree and surrounded the circular room. Several wooden and stone engraved perches of varying sizes stood in between the benches and chairs.

The wood floor was magnificently shiny, as if it had numerous coats of resin on it to keep its natural brilliance. All of the different carvings seemed to accent the floor as they followed the same grain of the wood, giving the illusion it was one massive floor design.

Each bench, chair, and perch had someone sitting on it. Whether it be human or
animal, the room was full.

From the center of the room, looking north, there was a lighted path which lead to a massive dark rich blue lapis lazuli boulder where the tree had grown halfway around it as it stood alone and faced the rest of the room. Out of this boulder was a carved chair with arm rests and perches on the top of each side. The back of the chair curved slightly in and far above the chair was a brilliant blueish green beryl stone radiating light in a star like pattern. Nadab took his seat in the lapis chair, while Eleea flew to the left lapis rock perch.

Facing the Council, Eleea began, "All of us here know the prophecy." He turned to look at the squirrel who was sitting to the left of him and said, "I am indebted to Phum to have come to you before I arrived to let you know I had found the messenger. I ask for your forgiveness I, myself, did not come to tell you, but unforeseen circumstances did not allow me to leave my young uncared for."

Gethsemane, on the right side of Nadab, was perched on a brilliant sapphire stand hand crafted in the shape of a feather. A noble golden eagle with plumage which magnified his stature as he stood tall with eyes that seemed to pierce one's soul began to speak, "Eleea. All here bare your sorrow in losing Lora. And, we are all thankful you and your travel companions have made it here safely. But, there is grave concern this child known as Ayden, can truly be the one foretold of. And, now her friend, Deborah has also come with her."

"I too was very confused at first," Eleea retorted back, "but I have seen Ayden in battle. She does not cower when in danger. She stands her ground. The courage I have seen in her is way beyond that of a child."

Eleea stopped his speech and sighed as he looked down. He then raised his eyes as his chest protruded out and said, *"It is not our providence to choose the one, Gethsemane. It is only our place to accept the one who was chosen,"* Eleea finished.

"Wisely spoken," Gethsemane expressed as he paused for several minutes and continued. "Then for the next several months she will need to be trained in our ways. It is our responsibility to give her as many tools as we can to keep her from danger as she approaches her destiny. And, as far as her friend is concerned, I will take on the personal responsibility to determine what we will do with her," Gethsemane stated.

A white fox raised his paw, saying, "During this time of observation, Gethsemane, all of us need to be assured she is our answer. If she falters and seems too young, then we need to reassess our decision tonight."

Another slightly smaller white fox with tinges of red highlighting the tips of her fur who sat next to the first one said, "All of us need to take heed to Eleea's words and his mission. He was sent to find the messenger. He has searched for years. We all know and trust him. He did not take this task lightly and he would not return to us with a half-hearted, 'maybe she is the one.' It is not our decision to choose. It must be our decision to accept, not only her, but the magic and prophecy of Eshra."

"Thank you, Marjome and Bardol for voicing your concerns and wisdom," Gethsemane said. "All of us here, feel the passion both of you feel for our future. This community has been given a great privilege to be the ones responsible for the Messenger to successfully achieve her prophecy. It will take all of us to vigilantly watch and direct her instructors to secure victory."

"Let us not forget," Nadab said as he raised his hand and stood. "Her friend is just as important to her as we all here are to each other. Do not quickly put your personal emotions into play and discount her friend as a nuisance or someone to be discarded. Just as Marjome has said, remember, 'the magic and prophecy of Eshra.' She also entered our world with magic surrounding her."

"Agreed, Nadab," Gethsemane stated. "Therefore, do not let Deborah know she may or may not accompany Ayden when the time comes. We will search for Deborah's skills and allow her to train where her skills take her," Gethsemane informed the listeners.

The Council acknowledged Gethsemane's decision and the meeting broke into the members speaking with each other in groups. Many crowded around Eleea to give him their condolences and regards.

Ayden woke the next morning to the singing of Elora. She opened one eye which caused Elora to jump on her pillow joyfully mixing singing with words.

"Ayden," she chirped, "you have got to get up and see this place. It is the most beautiful home I have ever seen!"

"And, and Deborah has already been up for hours. She's pretty, but kinda boring, ya know? She has been reading these old books for hours and she won't talk to me. I've been singing to you for over thirty minutes to get you to wake up and talk with me."

"Slow down, Elora," Ayden affectionately told her, "I'm up now and I will spend time with you. But, I have got to figure out what is going on first, OK?"

Ayden dressed in the clothes she found laid out for her at the end of the bed. Cotton pants intricately embroidered along the outer seam of the pant with a drawstring belt. A pullover top with a scooped neck and the same intricate broidery. Leather boots which fit slightly above her ankle with leather flaps that folded down in the front in a V-shape to expose the leather strips of the shoelaces.

After dressing, Ayden noticed the beautiful ornate bed she had slept in. Huge diamond willow trees, stripped and stained perfectly, were made into the head and foot boards with the same trees used for the four posts which raised the bed up off the floor approximately twenty-four inches.

She had never seen diamond willows cut and used as posts and head boards. All of the diamond willow she had ever seen were the ones people bought for an extremely outrageous price from the Glacier gift shops to use as walking sticks when they hiked.

The bedding was beyond beautiful. Rich colored sea blue green silk covered the thick fluffy down used on the inside of the blanket and pillows.

"It was the most luxurious sleep I have ever had," Ayden silently spoke to herself as she caressed the pillow with her hand and thought back to the night before when she crawled into bed and was surrounded in the deep feeling of peace and safety.

"What would you like to talk about, Elora?" Ayden asked as she started to make her bed.

Before she could finish her statement, Elora was in full swing chattering about all she had seen since being in Eshra. How much fun it was for her to be able to talk freely to every human she came into contact with and all of the animals she had met were just as nice as the humans.

She explained in the other world her father had kept a tight grip on her and she didn't really get to explore. But here she had the freedom to go wherever she wanted and it was just exhilarating to not have to worry about her father looking for her.

Ayden felt exhausted listening to Elora talk as fast as she was flitting around, but knew it was good for Elora to feel validated by her. The minute a break came into the conversation, Ayden quickly interjected, "OK Elora, now it is time for you to show me where Deborah is."

Elora directed her through the grand hallways of what could be considered a castle within an enormous tree. Ayden noticed the massive finished woodwork throughout the whole structure was filled with carved plants, trees, animals and people as if it all was telling a story as they walked past it.

Pillars seemed to be growing out of the walls, almost like they were the tree's roots. They passed several small rooms, well at least small compared to the main meeting rooms she had also seen as they walked.

Each room was designed with finely handcrafted furniture and beautifully ornate rugs. Uniquely designed pottery filled with the most gorgeous flowers and plants she had ever seen rested against paintings which seemed to come to life as one passed by them. The theme of peace and protection throughout the tree was constant as she maneuvered through the halls.

Deborah was sitting at a long table stacked with several books around her when Ayden finally saw her. She lifted her head when she heard Ayden and Elora enter the room.

"'A'," Deborah began, "You will not believe what I have been doing. These books are full of detailed information about the plant life and its properties of this region. This world is absolutely fascinating when it comes to the ability to use plants to derive drugs and potions to help a person survive here. It'll take me months to digest all of this information."

"That's great 'D'," Ayden started, "But I don't think we will have months in this place for you to do that."

Eleea had flown into the room as the girls were talking and interrupted. "Actually Ayden, we will be right here for at least two months before we are able to move forward with the mission."

"How can that be, Eleea," Ayden asked nervously, "What about returning home before the end of summer and the beginning of the school year? Deborah has to return. Her parents will be so worried about her!"

Eleea responded, "I neglected to explain to you how we would keep Deborah's parents from worrying about you two, Ayden. Do you remember blowing on those amulets last night? Well, your breath brought forth the image of the Red Fox. Do you remember?" Eleea asked the girls.

Both girls nodded in agreement to Eleea's request.

"The Red Fox is considered in our world to be a shape shifter," Eleea started to explain. "What this means, is this," Eleea continued. "Your breath brought forth his image which allowed him to take on your shapes. All the thoughts and experiences you have ever had, he could feel and know from your breath. He, now, knows each of you intimately,"

Eleea continued to elaborate. "He knows your personalities and how to act like you. He looks just like you. He will walk in your place, in your world, as if it is you doing it. No one will know the difference. Because you are still there, every day." Eleea soothingly explained to them.

"When Phum took the amulets from Nadab, he ran them back to your pillows. He placed them inside the pillowcase so the magic would work." Eleea expressed.

"When you return, you will take the amulet and breath on it again. Every experience the Red Fox had while you were gone, will enter your mind and soul. You will know each conversation, meal, meeting, etc. he had in your place." Eleea confidently told the girls.

"OK, hold up, Eleea," Deborah stated. "First, awesome! I love foxes, and how cool is that! We have foxes acting as us. In Japan, they are called Kitsune. Second, what happens if the amulets get lost because my mom decides to wash our pillowcases?"

"That won't happen, Deborah," Eleea assured her. "The amulet is hidden by magic in your pillowcase and cannot be found or removed until you ask for it to come forth. Then, it will appear for you to breath on it where you will immediately receive its knowledge of what happened while you were away." Eleea finished.

Ayden listened intently to Eleea's explanation as she became more and more agitated. Finally, she shouted, "I hadn't planned on us being here for months or even years, Eleea! How could you even think about asking someone to stay here for years? How could you conveniently," Ayden raised her hands in the air, and gestured with two fingers from each hand, "neglect" to tell me I had to stay here forever!" She continued to shout.

Deborah joined in the conversation by saying, "Hey! It's really no big deal, Ayden. We need to look at this as a very cool experiment. We will get to learn a whole slew of new activities here and when we return home, we won't have been missed by anyone. And, bonus, we will have gained a ton more knowledge. This is definitely the most exciting adventure I have ever been on!"

"No, no, no, no it is not OK Deborah," Ayden said with determination. "'D' this isn't some afternoon outing like taking a hike up the trail. We will, from what Eleea seems to think, be gone for a very long time. I am just not too sure I am comfortable with this plan. I can accept you are excited and everything. But, seriously!"

Ayden's heart and mind began to swirl with anticipation about the unknown. She liked to be in control of her surroundings and this new twist caused her a great deal of fear.

Deborah gently patted her arm in reassurance that all was well.

"You have no idea, 'D' what this is all about. The real reason we are here," Ayden blurted out as she moved her arm away from Deborah.

"Do not agree just because you get to learn some great new knowledge from books!" Ayden stood up and yelled. "They want me to be a messenger to deliver a message somewhere in Eshra to stop the darkness. And, let's be honest! Anytime the word darkness is used as something that has to be stopped, there is a danger attached to accomplishing it," Ayden frustratingly claimed.

"It would seem to me all of these people and animals of Eshra are pretty nonchalant about me doing it and not concerned about any consequence that may come from it. This has gotten just a little scarier for me than I planned. I am just not sure this is such a good idea to be here," Ayden claimed as she sat back down.

"OK, I get it, 'A", Deborah proclaimed. "I get that you are scared of the unknown. I get that you are concerned about being gone for too long from our home. I get that there is something scary to this whole plan. But, for the next two months or so we will be safe in this home. This tree. So, how about we learn and enjoy our time here for now. Then, after our time is up we can decide if we continue on with the 'Eshra Plan', Deborah pleaded.

Ayden realized there was no reasoning with Deborah who was way too excited about learning. Looking at Eleea, she impatiently stated, "What is the plan now, Eleea?"

"Well," Eleea began, "We will stay here until you have had time to learn the ways of this land, learning everything from customs to skills you will need to know to protect yourself and survive here. Then we will need to travel two mountain ranges to reach the depths of the inner most center of the land. This is where everything will become challenging," he said.

"But, for right now, all you need to focus on is your training here. I do not want to overwhelm you with too much information. I just want you to become comfortable in your new surroundings and to be free to learn," Eleea gingerly stated as to not upset Ayden anymore.

"What about Deborah?" Ayden pressed Eleea to answer. "Will she be allowed to go with me when we leave here if I decide to go on? Because I just want to set the record straight right now. If she is not allowed to go with me, then I will not continue and you guys can just send us home right now."

"Ayden," Eleea said, trying to stay calm, "It is dangerous to ask Deborah to sacrifice her life to go with us."

"Oh No you don't, Eleea!" Ayden quickly fought back, "Do not try and manipulate us with words and emotions! I expect more respect from you than this!"

"And," Ayden continued, "is it not you and Lora who drilled into me out of every uncomfortable situation, good can be found. There is a reason for when unexpected things happen and I need to turn it into good and not dwell on the bad?"

"Therefore, since you see Deborah as a bad mistake," Ayden elaborated, "don't you think maybe you need to see the good in it. And, how do you know, maybe there was a bigger reason for Deborah coming with us. Something you and I don't know about. I believe there is a bigger purpose for Deborah falling through the entry with us and I promise you we will find out she will be invaluable to us if we move forward on this quest."

"Fine Ayden," Eleea compromised, "Deborah will be trained with you. But, I do want you to know my deepest honest reaction is it is dangerous and I am concerned about her safety."

Deborah pushed her chair back and walked over to Ayden, slapped her lightheartedly on the back and stated, "Nicely done, 'A'. You presented your case with skill. I'm proud of you!"

Turning to Eleea, Deborah gave him a confident nod and said, "Eleea I will not let you down. I understand your concern and I appreciate the fact you want to protect me. And, I promise you I will be an adept student."

Journal Twelve

Ayden lifted her head to get a better view of the geese in their 'V' shape pattern move across the sky. It reminded her of one of Eleea's stories on how to overcome a difficult situation.

"Ayden, he would begin, "Once, back in Eshra, when I was young, I heard a story about a family struggle. They wanted to begin their flight to the north as they did every year in the spring.

Ah! springtime in Eshra. The morning dew rests on the leaves like a fresh nectar just waiting for its recipient to partake of its goodness. The first drop touches your tongue like liquid honey. Yet, not overpoweringly sweet like honey. And, of course it is not sticky, because it is water. No, it is an elixir with the power to rejuvenate your inner core. Not only did it quench your thirst, it healed your soul. Of course, it is just plain simple water but, the taste left you rejuvenated.

But I digress. Back to the family. They were arguing about what to do with one of the elders of their group. They were sure he would not make the long flight with them.

Should they let him try? Should they leave him behind? None of them could agree on a plan. They argued for days out of earshot of this elder or so they thought.

One day in the middle of their discord, the elder stepped forward. He said to them, 'The disrespect I have witnessed has left me sad. All of you talk of me as if I am already dead. You feel you can freely speak of me, assuming all of you have the right to what you say. And, you believe I am far enough away to not hear you. Where did any of you learn, it was perfectly acceptable to speak of another's fate without the respect of asking the one you speak about, what they feel, or think, or wish to happen?

I know I never took you as young goslings and left you with no thought. If I remember your growing years, I kept you close as I trained you and asked you to speak your heart to me when you were confused by our ways.

Then, I would sit with you and help you to understand, so you could move forward. Move forward to freely gain strength spiritually and physically. For each of you I was there to encourage you and to strengthen you.

Where, my children, is this same respect for me? Yes, I am weak but, is it not my choice if I stay or go? If I should expire on the journey, well, I will be doing that which I love. Rest in this, if I should die, then I do so with joy in my soul because I was with all of you.'

Ayden, it was the most eloquent speech about the right to be respected. And as legend has it, this is where geese of all breeds learned to make a 'V' shape in their flight pattern.

The lead goose sets the pace. Those who flank him sound the call to help all the rest stay strong. The elderly and the weak fly deep inside the pattern where the momentum of the outside wings creates a wind tunnel of movement where they are lifted up to continue their flight with less stress on their bodies," Eleea stated.

"Out of conflict, out of a difficult situation these beautiful geese found strength through honesty, respect, and working together to solve their dilemma.

Point being, Ayden, we are not alone when difficult situations arise. We need each other to help each other and to carry each other through the winds of our difficult times," Eleea explained.

Chapter Twelve

Eleea found Nadab in the blacksmith barn forging a blade for a handheld knife. This was Nadab's gift, to perfectly design the right tool to the right person. The recipient of Nadab's carefully crafted work knew immediately the piece they were presented with would become part of their arsenal and their personality.

Nadab would observe and listen to a person or, at times, he could just sense before he got to know them, what he had to make for them. And, as gifts go, Nadab's natural talent automatically forged magic into each one he made for someone.

The unique thing about this gift of his, was no one knew what type of magic would emerge from the weapon or tool, not even Nadab. Whoever received the gift would one day be using it and the magic would show itself.

"Is this a new weapon for you?" Eleea asked.

Nadab continued working as he looked up at Eleea, and said, "No, Eleea, this is Deborah's weapon. I know you are not happy about her going with Ayden. And, at first, I wasn't liking the idea either. But several days have passed since they arrived and I have come to believe she is here by design. She will need to be prepared for this journey. I felt this overwhelming drive to complete her knife first, before I started on Ayden's weapon."

Nadab placed the glowing blade against the anvil and began to pound it into shape. Meticulously he examined it and then quenched it in oil where it sizzled and smoked.

While looking for imperfections, he told Eleea, "I have this immense desire to make sure her weapon is made with great detail and care. I don't know how to explain it, Eleea. This weapon is going to be extremely important one day. My whole focus is to make sure the magical gift it will possess when it is finished will be perfect."

Eleea watched him work for a while longer, and then flew away to leave him alone with his craft. Discouraged by the thought of Deborah being in harm's way with the journey and now a weapon was too much for him to think about.

He flew to the outer edges of the tree community to where he and Lora used to nest. Here he let his mind reminisce of happier times.

As sleep drifted into his soul, his mind began to soar in flight with Lora beside him. Throughout the Great Tree they flew in unison exploring and observing all below them. Simultaneously they landed on the back of Nadab's chair in the council room.

Lora turned to him with her eyes glowing like a twinkling star and said, "Eleea, my precious Eleea, rest your heart. This burden you feel you must carry closes your mind. Trust in Eshra, Eleea. Trust in Eshra."

Eleea woke frantically calling Lora's name, wishing it had not been a dream. He once again whispered, "Lora." Then, he pondered her words as he repeated them, "Trust in Eshra."

When Nadab was engrossed in designing a new weapon all time seemed to slip away. He would spend hours and hours developing the right angle or carving the perfect handle.

He took into account the personality of the future owner by gearing each detail to their most intricate psyche. Observation of the person and how they interacted with their environment and the people and animals around them was Nadab's first clues on how a weapon should look for the person or animal. He instinctually felt the presence of the individual and forged in their identity as he worked the materials.

Each gift he made was bound to the user's soul where when its special quality was needed, it would appear. Naturally, the designed gift could be used for daily activity, but if there was danger or crisis, the tool would rise to the occasion.

Nadab had worked through the night on Deborah's gift, right down to the beautifully carved handle. Vines and flowers of all sorts of plants intimately wrapped around the ancient myrtle wood.

Natural earth pigments were mixed to create the vivid colors of the flowers and the different shades of green and brown for the vines and stems. The butt of the knife was a pestle which could be used to grind herbs for use in the making of potions, etc.

The blade itself was etched from the base to the tip with a majestic oak tree on one side and on the other side Nadab wrote along the spine of the knife in small letters:

"Within each seed a soul emerges to live... protect these souls."

He moved to the fireplace, holding the knife in the light of the flames, admiring the curves and coloring of the base. He marveled as he watched the blade's etched tree shine with brilliance and style.

It almost looked as if it was swaying in a summer breeze as the fire's light danced across it. And, for one last time, he caressed each part of the knife to make sure it was finished and ready to be given to its new owner.

Satisfied, he placed it in its specially made leather case next to the wooden mortar bowl which matched the handle of the knife, minus the colors. And, then he placed it in the carved box which matched the tree on the blade and had Deborah's name carved at the bottom of the box.

Days later Nadab decided to start on Ayden's gift. He was troubled because he could not determine if it should be a knife, a sword, a piece of body armor, or some type of tool. He had never known such conflict over making something for someone.

He had always felt a certain pull to one type of weapon over another. But not this time. He was totally at a loss on what to do.

Finally, he told himself, "I will go spend time with Ayden to help me understand her better and find out what she likes and dislikes."

Ayden was in the courtyard practicing her martial arts when Nadab arrived to sit and watch her. She was engrossed in her practice of moving around the whole yard when her eyes caught Nadab sitting there.

"Ayden, may I speak with you? Join me on the bench, please," Nadab asked.

Ayden slowly finished her last stance and dropped her arms and walked in the direction of Nadab. As she walked towards him, she recognized how quickly her heart felt trust for him. Thinking about her feelings, she analyzed him.

This man stood tall at over six foot. His sideburns showed most of the grey which was mixed in with his black hair where it touched his shoulders. A black scarf folded like a headband, lay across his forehead and behind his ears to keep his hair neatly away from his face and to pull his hair off his neck, where it was tied. His hands were weathered and strong, while his face still looked kind and young.

Just by listening to him talk, one could sense he had a tender heart which constantly showed great care for others' needs and feelings. He was the type of man Ayden had only known in Robert Laverson, Deborah's dad, before. One who was kind, strong and trustworthy. She sat next to him on the bench, curious to know what he needed from her.

"I want to create a unique weapon for you, but I am having great difficulty in deciphering exactly what type of weapon it should be," Nadab expressed frustratingly. "Usually, when I start to crush metal and shape it, I get a vision of the soul of the weapon, which directs me to which way to go with it. With you, I start to forge and I go blank with no plan. Would you please tell me about yourself? What you cherish and what causes you to be proud?" Nadab asked her.

"Well, let's see," Ayden thought out loud as she looked at Nadab, "I cherish my friendships, honesty and beautiful scenery. Where I come from is the most gorgeous natural beauty one could ever be surrounded by. The sunrises and sunsets can take your breath away when you look at them. And, I love the moon. I don't know why, but I have always loved to watch the moon at night with the stars. It just calms me."

"As far as what makes me proud," Ayden thought for a few seconds before answering, "Deborah makes me proud. She is a wonderful person with a huge heart where she always looks to help others. Her vast knowledge is just amazing. You know, she has a photographic memory. How can a person retain so much information?" Ayden asked rhetorically.

"I wish I was as intelligent as her. Sometimes I feel so stupid and worthless." Ayden closed her eyes and shook her head like she was trying to shake off something from her body.

She looked at Nadab and said, "Sorry, sometimes I get lost in my thoughts and blurt them out for all to hear."

"Now, where were we? Oh! Yah! Pride. Basically, I have pride for others and their skills and knowledge. I love it when others are happy. But for me, I can't really give you any examples of what I am proud of about myself. Sorry, Nadab." Ayden apologized.

Nadab grasped her hand and said, "No, do not be sorry Ayden. You have given me a lot of good information to work with."

He squeezed her hand and intently looked into her eyes saying, "Child, one day you will know what it is to be proud for who you are and what you have accomplished. But, I tell you now, I sense a deep pride already within your soul. Not one of useless haughty pride. But, one of dignity and power. It burns with great intensity; so, great I have not known another who has such a presence as you."

Nadab started to stand up to leave, saying, "I bid you good-bye for now my, dear friend."

Ayden hesitantly touched Nadab's arm to stop him from leaving, stating, "Nadab, may I ask you a few questions?"

Nadab sat back down and said, "Of course Ayden, I would be proud to answer your questions."

"I was, I was wondering about the night we met you," she began. "You told Eleea you were glad all was well with him and his family. Why did you say that? Why did you call all of us family?"

"Ayden, first let me explain our worlds to you." Nadab stated. *"The sun is slowly dying, causing this world to soon be shrouded in darkness. The sun is able to still shine, but it is not as bright as it used to be. Once our world succumbs to darkness, then it will happen to your world, too.*

"Legend tells us someone will come to our world, a messenger, who will restore the sun to its natural brilliance. And, as a result, restore order to our worlds. You see, if this world is not restored, soon, then your world will begin to experience the same effects this world is experiencing. Both worlds need each other to live," Nadab explained.

"Second, because this world is becoming darker and darker, there is grave danger for anyone walking around without protection. When you and your friend entered with Eleea and Elora, you were all exposed to danger. By me saying to Eleea all was well with his family, I was protecting you and Deborah," Nadab told her.

"Unknown forces exist out there. And no one can be sure where the danger will come from. Many ears and eyes, those who follow evil, surround the darkness. And, all of us have to be hyper-vigilant we do not alert this evil to attack us. Because you and Deborah were foreign here, you were vulnerable to being attacked. I tried to divert attention from your entry by saying you were family."

"Lastly, by us staying quiet until we reached the tree; and by having you dress in our garb of the land, and covering your shoes with a blanket it allowed us continued protection. As we traveled, anyone who was watching and listening could have harmed you. They would have taken notice if you or Deborah started to talk and ask us questions about the land. They would have immediately known you were not from here and would have alerted others who might want to physically harm you. It was imperative for all of us to stay quiet."

"Thank you, Nadab, for being completely honest with me," Ayden stated.

"One last question, though." Ayden lifted her eyes to Nadab's eyes, seeking an answer from him, and timidly asked, "Do you know who this messenger is?"

Nadab fixed his eyes on her as he stood. He faced her and put his hands on her arms to help her stand to face him, saying with deep determination,

"The prophecy has come to life and has come to Eshra, Ayden. *You are the Messenger.*"

Journal Thirteen

Destiny. What is it really? Ayden thought as she used her pencil to trace the dirt near the trunk of the tree. Is it determined or is it by chance? I guess it is a mixture of both. We are born into our life without being able to make the choice. So, this is determined.

We are raised in a way that is not our choice. So, this is determined. Not until we are exposed to others outside of our immediate world, do we see things differently. So, this is the beginning of chance.

All of us, eventually, make choices which determine our path. Where it will lead us. Learning to make wise choices is the crux of destiny.

I believe in order for a true destiny to feel it is worth the fight, one has to make mistakes. Mistakes, big and small, are not failures. Mistakes help you to see the importance of how you may need to change the way you viewed something. Or the way you reacted incorrectly to a situation. And how you want to handle it better the next time.

Destiny starts with a predetermined set of circumstances...this is true. But, along the way, time and experience bring very real choices.

And, you have to give yourself the freedom to stop and assess it. Which way do you want to go? Which way does your heart tell you to follow?

I guess, what I am trying to say is this: Destiny is not the end of your journey.

Destiny is a course of travel you take which helps you learn about life and others. It helps you find out about yourself and what you desire for yourself.

Destiny gives you purpose to live.

Chapter Thirteen

The Great Tree where everyone lived housed a vast community of people and animals. As Ayden watched all of the activity throughout the tree, she saw it as a small town, like East Glacier was a small town.

Except, everyone enjoyed being together and intimately knew each other. Everybody had their own specialty or skill they shared to help everyone else.

The girls quickly developed a routine of training each day. First, they spent time together in the morning while they ate breakfast in the main kitchen. Then they separated for their individual lessons, and would regroup for the teaching of the customs and history of Eshra during lunch. Followed by more individual training, and then dinner. They spent the evening together in their room, where each would tell the other everything they had learned and done throughout the day.

Deborah immensely enjoyed her new-found love of all plant's native to the region. She learned what it took to make different healing potions and other concoctions.

Which she considered the greatest gift she had ever received. To have the means to create along with the books to teach her the ways of old-time herb botany and lore was beyond her wildest dreams; she was ecstatic. Each day she spent hours in the garden and the adjoining laboratory.

Shamgar, a man, was one of her mentors who taught her how to cultivate a seedling into a sturdy living plant. Whereas Yabinith, another human, taught her the importance of mixology, or the properties of how to administer the correct amounts of ingredients to get the desired outcome needed.

Shamgar and Yabinith were a married couple whose best friend was Nekoh, a lynx, who did everything with them. Just in a different sense, of course, because he had paws.

Nekoh spoke to Shamgar and Yabinith constantly about what to do and how it should be done. It was as if there was one like-mind in three bodies. They flowed together in thought and action whenever they were in the same room.

Deborah loved having Nekoh always around. Whenever she was reading or just concentrating, he would wind in and out of her legs or lay close to her hands so she could scratch his coat.

He especially loved to be scratched on the top of his head. He would hold his head perfectly still with a slight lift for her to rub the crown of it.

The other thing she loved about Nekoh was he was mischievous. He lived to tease and, sometimes, annoy others.

It was the cat in him where he would toy with his prey; and he loved to toy with others. For example, her pencil had a small feather attached to the top of it which drove Nekoh crazy when she would write. He would bat at it with his paw and she would deliberately move it away from his paw so he would miss it. But, when she wanted to be left alone to take notes, he would attack her pencil or her. And, when she would finally get frustrated with him, he would lay on his back with all four legs in the air. Where he would look at her with those deep amber, innocent eyes which always caused her to rub his tummy.

One day while she was studying, she asked the three of them about the prophecy. "I know Ayden is the chosen one because of the mark on her back," Deborah stated.

"What can you guys tell me about this prophecy? And about the 'Eshra Plan' (a term she had coined with Ayden when they first arrived)," she asked.

"Well, Deborah," Shamgar began, "the prophecy tells us the messenger has to come to our world to stop the darkness for both of our worlds. She is a messenger because she has to speak at the Dead Trees which are over two mountain ranges away. You will have to travel to these trees and it will take many days to get there."

"Whatever Ayden has to speak to release the Great Crane none of us know exactly what it is supposed to be. What we do know is the light of the Great Crane will be set free to reign again in our worlds once she speaks. As prophecies go, you do not always get the full picture from a prophecy. You just go with it, and it will reveal itself the closer you get to its destiny." Shamgar explained.

"It is a matter of faith, Deborah," Yabinith stated. "We believe in the prophecy, and we believe Ayden is our answer."

"It is more than just mere words, Deborah," Nekoh continued Shamgar's and Yabinith's explanation. "This prophecy is like a plant who was first started from a seed. A seed nurtured and cultivated into a magnificent tree. Like the tree we live in. This prophecy is a life force. It provides all of us with hope and a future," he finished.

Deborah looked at the three of them and said, "Well, not that I totally understand your faith and hope. I do understand I have been given a gift to learn from you three. And, I believe it was not by chance I came over with Ayden. I am here, as you would say, by destiny's choice. It is my job to learn all I can from you to help Ayden. Whether Ayden decides to go or stay, I have been given a gift. And, whatever Ayden decides, I stand with her," she concluded as she smiled at them and went back to her studies.

Ayden did most of her training in the courtyard with Abner. Eleea usually stayed close by to give his input on how he thought she should be trained.

Abner was a man who did not get too excited about anything, not even with Eleea's constant interruptions. What both of them seemed to agree on the most, though, was the need for Ayden to be aware of her surroundings at all times. To listen not only with her ears but with her heart.

Abner took Ayden to the extreme basics of physical learning. Constantly bringing her to a sweat while doing the same thing over and over again. From running in place to full blown martial arts performances she continuously moved around the courtyard.

Except for when she had to sit perfectly still. The hardest part of her training was to sit in one spot and be quiet. It drove her crazy to just sit there and not talk.

She was supposed to keep her eyes closed, but it was, almost, always impossible to do. Ayden would sit silently, and then, it would start with a slight lift of her left eyelid. Slowly, the right lid would raise so both eyes were open slits.

She was not allowed to move her head, so she could only see what was in front of her. Most of the time she would just admire the shrubbery, the perfectly manicured grass, or the serene pond with its waterfall. She would trace each detail of the different foliage and how it wound around each other in perfect symmetry throughout the courtyard.

She had hours of time already spent admiring the formation of the leaves and stems. As well as the beautiful stones throughout the structure.

At other times, she was able to watch Abner as he practiced his martial arts or watch him interact with Eleea and Gethsemane. Gethsemane would spar with Abner, and it amazed her as she watched them perform.

The skill and grace each possessed was like watching a fast action movie. Although, when she was supposed to have her eyes closed, Ayden noticed she had to be careful not to flinch when their sparring got too intense. And, if she flinched, they would both stop what they were doing and look at her, as if scolding her.

Ayden's and Deborah's lunch hour were used to learn about the culture and customs of Eshra. Their main teacher, for the most part, was Gethsemane.

Gethsemane, felt he needed to be sure they were well informed about how to walk
around Eshra when away from the Great Tree.

He would set up scenarios where the girls had to pretend they were walking into a town or meeting someone on the road. They were instructed to discern if they should openly talk or be cautious with the person or animal. He would raise his wings and spread them out. When his wings returned to his sides, a new imagery would appear of a full city or road where they would have to walk into it and interact with whatever Gethsemane placed in the scene.

The cover story of why the girls were traveling Eshra was they were doing a rite of passage enlightenment journey. Something all teenagers did around the age of fourteen in Eshra.

Their journey was to find out what they could learn from their environment to make their life, and their clan's life more productive. They were descendants of the Glacier clan. Whereas they came from the foot of the glaciers where for generations their families had lived and survived.

Even though most enlightenment journeys were short in nature, the girls were considered to be chosen by the spiritual leader of their clan, Nadab, to travel great distances to gather plant life, document the terrain they traveled, and to learn from those whose path they crossed.

It actually was not far-fetched for the girls to be from this clan as many of the tree people were originally glacier clan descendants. Just by living in the tree, the girls were already exposed to the mannerisms and the ways of the people they were to represent.

At each meal, the girls were taught to give thanks for the food presented to them. Placing their hands together they would lift them to their forehead and then to their chest, silently giving thanks for the food.

The food mainly consisted of some type of stew, whether it be an oat-based breakfast, a vegetable styled soup, or a meat pie. Each meal was served with a sweet or savory freshly baked bread and a variety of fruits and other delicious desserts.

The eating utensils were made from a high-quality wood, and each person had their own specially designed fork combo spoon and knife. Eating in inns, people's homes, or in the wilderness while on the road, the girls would be expected to use their own utensils.

And, while using these utensils, the onlookers would be acutely aware of where the girls were originally from. And, would be able to determine their status in their clan by how intricate and well made the cutlery was.

One afternoon when the girls met for a late lunch due to both of them having worked extra hard during the morning, Gethsemane visibly showed excitement when the girls greeted each other.

Deborah and Ayden both seemed emotional and were particularly relieved to be together. As they entered the room, they both instinctually grabbed each other's right forearm for their traditional handshake of trust.

Gethsemane flew down from his perch onto the chair next to them, stating, "Girls, where did you learn this handshake?"

They turned to him and both began to talk about the day when the rattlesnake tried to bite Deborah. Slowing down, they then took turns filling in the story.

Gethsemane listened intently to every detail they gave, and then spoke, "This handshake is very unusual. It is not known by many in this land." Gethsemane informed them, and continued:

"Many years ago, this gesture was used by those close to the Great Crane. As you both know, at the new year in July when the moon is full and the crane's full body is seen, we have a week of celebration in this world. The feather resides there each full moon, and is considered sacred. But the new year brings the full crane into view.

What you don't know is the Great Crane is spiritually linked to the sun. The sun has importance also and is considered sacred. But, for our purposes here, the crane is my focus to help you understand our world.

The reason for the need of a messenger is because the sun, needs the crane to bring true balance to the night in order to stop the sun from increasingly becoming dimmer and dimmer.

This phenomenon has taken thousands of years to happen, causing most who live in Eshra to have no comprehension as to why it is happening. They just go about their daily activities as if nothing is strange or abnormal.

But, if the sun completely died, well, then our worlds would cease to exist. The Great Crane protects both of our worlds from becoming extinct." Gethsemane explained.

"You, Ayden, for whatever reason have been chosen to bring light back to the sun," Gethsemane stated emphatically.

"None of us know why you were chosen, nor do we know how you are supposed to accomplish your mission. We only know, through the prophecy, which direction we are to send you to accomplish your goal. And, as a result, the Council made a decision to help you become properly prepared for whatever danger or task you will be presented with while you travel. Yet, it would seem there is a much deeper reason you were chosen; something we are not aware of yet. The fact you two use this handshake is extremely intriguing," Gethsemane stated and then stopped talking and nodded respectfully to Lydia when she entered the room.

Lydia was Nadab's wife and was the girl's other instructor during their meals. She was holding several folded clothes in her hands, stating, "I have finished the girls' clothing. Let's see how they fit, shall we?"

Ayden and Deborah looked at their outfits, admiring the detail woven into them. They went into the changing room and came back out in their new attire.

Deborah's and Ayden's pants were designed after the camouflage pants they wore into Eshra; but did not have the multi-colored patterns as the camouflage. Instead they were made from a unique sturdy cotton-like material which was dyed a greenish tan brown. A color Lydia told them would blend into any type of natural environment they would come across.

A beautiful belt made from leather fit around the waist of the pant, and the legs could zip off to make shorts. No zipper was used, though. Magic was in place with these pant legs.

Lydia explained all they had to do was act like they wanted to unzip the pant and it would automatically unzip. The pants had several pockets along the legs, back, and, of course, the side.

Their shirts wrapped around the frame of their body as they pulled them over their head. They were also made of some type of cotton and were colored a warm light orangish red for Deborah. And, Ayden's shirt was colored a beautiful greenish blue turquoise.

Each girl had an open smock which went over the shirt and had a hood attached. The smocks were a linen type material which showed off their femininity. Yet, were fashioned to be functional in wear and in the environment.

And, as Lydia's special gift went, the clothes she created possessed an ability to stay warm or cool and to keep the person who wore them dry and comfortable. Lydia stood back with pride in her eyes as the girls modeled their new outfits.

Not only was she proud of what she had designed, but she was proud of these two young women who had unexpectedly come into her life and she had grown to love ever so deeply.

The girls ran to her on each side and hugged her. Throughout the girls' stay at the Great Tree, Lydia would mention to them all of the time, "you are the girls I never had. I am very proud to be part of your lives."

Gethsemane broke into the girl's special moment by saying, "Lydia would you bring two hand mirrors here, please." He then turned to Ayden and said, "Ayden do you know the importance of the mark on your back?"

Ayden quickly turned to look at Gethsemane and then at Deborah and Lydia. With trepidation, she answered, "No, I am not sure what you mean Gethsemane? I was born with this mark. And to be quite honest, I have always been embarrassed by it."

"My child," Gethsemane softly spoke, "This mark is one of great beauty. One of power and integrity. You have been blessed with a gift. You have been chosen by this mark on your back. Here, let me show you what this mark stands for."

Lydia held one mirror for Ayden to see and gave the other mirror to Deborah for her to place it so Ayden could see her mark on the middle of her back. Her new shirt somehow allowed the birthmark to be visibly seen.

Gethsemane raised his wing and used the tip of it like a finger. He traced the birthmark outline as he explained to Ayden what it represented.

"There is a prophecy which has passed through the generations, giving all of us hope for a brighter tomorrow," Gethsemane raised his wings out from his sides to emphatically say, *"literally a brighter tomorrow.*

Because it has to do with the sun being brought back to its glory. As the prophecy states a messenger will come to bring back the Great Crane. We do not know what this messenger will say, we only know a fight will occur and the messenger has to be prepared for battle.

We also know, through the prophecy the messenger has to travel over two mountain ranges to where the Dead Trees are, as this is where the fight will happen. Even though the prophecy seems to be vague, and I have to be honest, everyone I am acquainted with felt the messenger would be an adult, and a male.

It came as quite a blow to all of us the prophecy talked about a young girl. But, as Eleea so eloquently stated several nights ago, 'It is not our providence to choose the one. It is only our place to accept the one who was chosen."

"With this being said," Gethsemane continued, "The prophecy also gave us a symbol, a sign, to show us who we were looking for to bring it to fruition. You, Ayden, are our sign, our symbol. And it is because of your birthmark we are so sure you are the messenger."

Ayden began to stir uncomfortably as she looked at the mark. With furrowed brows, she shook her head in doubt.

"It is just an ugly birthmark, Gethsemane! It isn't anything cool or prophetic, really it isn't. And, yes, I know Eleea told me I was the messenger and I agreed to this information. But I had no idea I would have to fight not only for my life, but for the life of all who would be with me. This is scary and I do not know if I am the true messenger. I think you guys have gotten it all wrong!" She proclaimed.

Ayden's heart began pounding faster and she could feel her cheeks begin to flush. Her eyes pleaded with Gethsemane to tell her he was wrong.

Gethsemane placed his wing tip under her chin and steadied her head to look into his eyes. Eyes of power, yet warmth, seemed to settle her soul as she stared at them.

"Hear what the whole prophecy says, Ayden," Gethsemane encouraged her as he let his wing leave her chin and sweep the air as he spoke:

Cross to the East.
Send the seeker to the mighty glaciers.
There his search will see the one
Upon the back deliverance comes.
At rest the crane stands
Head held high.
When the morning sun kisses the day
The messenger enters through
Prepared to take flight.
Riding the winds to the mountains
Where the dead tree stands
A fight ensues.
The stirring sound rings
Throughout the lands
And once again the wings of the Crane
Bring the light of day.

"You Ayden, carry the mark of the crane. Your birthmark is the prophecy of the one who will fight to restore the Great Crane."

"Already eight of the sixteen stanzas of the prophecy have come to maturation because of you," Gethsemane passionately spoke. "It is not just an ugly birthmark as you see it, Ayden. It is a beautiful mark of divine prophecy. All of us are gravely indebted to you. Without you, none of us will survive," he finished.

Ayden's body slumped into the chair. Deborah came over to her and kneeled down to look in her eyes as she took Ayden's arm, the girls instinctually grasped each other in their familiar handshake of trust.

Deborah, holding on to her arm, said, "'A', I promise you I will be with you all of the way. You do not have to do this alone. I am just as afraid as you are, but we will overcome together, OK?"

Ayden looked at Deborah, shook her head in agreement. And then placed her forehead on Deborah's shoulder.

Journal Fourteen

Could anything, really, prepare me to follow a prophecy? People think kids are irrational! Have the adults looked at their line of reality, lately? I looked pretty sane, at fourteen, in comparison.

Sure, any training is a good thing. It teaches you new skills and hones your old ones. But, seriously, how do you train for the unknown?

No one knew what was exactly going to happen...pure conjecture on how to interpret the prophecy. A bunch of words formed in a somewhat poetic style to tell you what you have to do for the prophecy to be fulfilled.

Crazy, if you ask me! It just does not make common sense to follow whimsical words.

In reality, it is a vague treasure map, so to speak. No real direction...just go forward and wait to see what it reveals.

And, yet, this is exactly what I was supposed to do. What all of us planned to do. Everyone was to put their trust in me and follow me into the unknown.

And, because they thought they knew the right direction to go all of us were to just blindly follow.

It was an understatement for me to say I was scared and confused.

Chapter Fourteen

The girls were bubbling with excitement as the week-long festival had arrived. They would be released from their past fifty days of rigorous training to enjoy the new year and full moon celebration.

Elora was just as excited because she got to spend time with the girls and didn't have to share them with their trainers. Even though she too had been bird training, her schedule had been a lot more flexible.

Which filled her with lots of free time to just watch the girls train. But rules stated she could not interrupt their instructors, so she watched in utter bored silence when she wasn't training.

The three of them spent the first three days around all of the activities. They taste tested several different foods, watched all of the beautiful decorations come together, played new games and received little gifts just like they would have gotten at their carnivals back home. They even got to ride different contraptions which jolted them around in furious circles or others which swung them high into the courtyard.

On the fourth day, Deborah announced she wanted to spend time in the plant lab and rest there, alone. Ayden turned to Elora saying, "Hey! Do you think you could give me a 'private' tour of all the hidden areas of the Tree, Elora?"

"Absolutely, Ayden!" Elora said excitedly. "It should be simple as most everyone is at the festival. We will be able to dart in and out without them seeing us. And, even Father is busy with mission stuff right now. So, he won't become alarmed wondering where we are," she happily concluded.

Elora guided Ayden down hallways and levels until they were close to the entrance where they first entered the Great Tree. She quickly flew behind an extremely large root which seemed to be part of the tree's wall.

But, upon closer inspection, there was a hidden entrance behind the root to a room full of hundreds of items on the tables, shelves and walls. Most had sediment of dust on them, as if they had not been touched in decades.

One particular item, a strange cloth like material book with two wooden rods on the front of it to open and close the book, had no dust on it.

Ayden walked over to the book, unlatched the rods and opened it. The first page, in beautiful script, said, "The Messenger of Eshra." Her throat choked as her hands started to tremble while she turned the page.

Reading, she continued to turn the pages while tears began to form in her eyes. It was her story from East Glacier to now, with several authors penning their thoughts, observations and experiences with her. She looked up from the book to realize Elora had been softly singing to her the whole time.

"I wanted you to know," Elora began. "I wanted you to see, Ayden, how very important you are to all of us," she reverently continued. "This room, this book contains the history, the lore, and the treasures of the people of Eshra."

"You, Ayden, are a treasure of Eshra. What you have agreed to do. To continue on your quest with all of us helping you, is a great treasure of this land," Elora softly stated.

"Elora," Ayden expressed with combined fear and frustration. "Elora, I have not made my final decision if I will go forward or not."

"Yes, Ayden, you have," Elora fervently explained. "When we crossed over to Eshra, your true decision was already made. All this fear, all of your second guessing...it is nothing more than mind games to keep you confused. Listen to your heart, Ayden. What has it always told you?" Elora asked her.

Ayden looked at Elora with a new sense of awe at her determined intelligence into her soul. "Elora, yes I still have the fear of the unknown. Yes, I am totally confused with why it has to be me. But, deep down you are right. I knew when I crossed, I would fulfill this mission."

"Even if I stayed confused, I would follow it through. So, yes, we will go forward. No matter how I feel, we will go forward." Ayden sat down on the bench nearest the book and stared off into the empty space as Elora flew to her shoulder and rubbed her head on Ayden's neck.

Deborah sat in the corner on the floor of the plant lab totally engrossed in a book on plants which healed deep wounds. Suddenly, Yabinith came in with three other women and quickly gathered dried plants and ground spices from the shelves. They left just as quickly as they entered, not seeing Deborah.

Stealthily, Deborah followed the women down a hallway adjacent to the kitchen area; making sure she stayed hidden from them. A room with several makeshift beds, separated by sheets which hung from the ceiling to keep each bed privately held animals who were wounded.

Yabinith called out to a worker, asking for more cayenne pepper as she stood over an enormous bear. She separated his fur from his neck to reach his skin and dumped a generous amount of pepper into the wound. Closing the wound, she placed honey all around it and put a plant leaf over it. She checked his wellbeing by putting the palm of her hand on his forehead. Nodding at him and smiling as he looked at her, she moved on to her next patient, a dog.

She assessed the coyote's wound on his left back paw, smeared honey all over it and wrapped it with cloth. Next, she moved to a hawk whose wing was broken. Gently she lifted it off of his body and took a thin board from the person who was waiting to hand it to her and placed it under the wing. Taking the second piece of wood, she spread a powder on it and then placed it securely on top of the wing; binding both pieces with cord. Up and down the rows Yabinith tended to her wards.

Deborah counted seven beds with various degrees of wounds by the occupants in them. Two rams, a bear, a dog, a hawk, a fox and a crow needed medical care.

Her brow wrinkled as she tried to understand this serious consequence of battle that must have taken place outside of the Great Tree. She pushed her body back against a wall where two hanging blankets slightly opened to create a curtain for her to see out of.

On the far side of the room by the kitchen a gust of air caught one side of the blanket. Deborah held on to the blanket to keep from being seen as Gethsemane's wings landed him on the left side of the bear.

"Fergal, tell me what happened?" Gethsemane asked.

The bear lifted his left arm and rested it on his bed as he lifted himself to speak to Gethsemane. "We were at the meadow close to the ocean when we were ambushed," he stated.

"Ten wolves came out of nowhere and surrounded us. The only way we could avoid all being killed was for me to shield the others as they tried to escape behind me. When I started to be attacked by the wolves, the rest came to my rescue. They refused my request to run and save themselves," he stated as he tired of holding himself up and laid back down.

Fergal looked off into the distance and continued. "The wolves were beyond anything I have ever seen before. The anger and death in their eyes were incredibly intense. They had no fear and only desired to kill."

"Staggel and Wynard flew around me and attacked the wolves from behind. All of them came at me with incredible force. Wynard was killed instantly when one of them broke his neck. Staggel's wing was crushed under the weight of another. Hamgar lifted two of them up off of the ground with his horns and tossed them far down the ravine. One sunk his teeth into my neck and I felt life quickly leaving my body."

"But before I passed out to wake here at the Great Tree," he stopped and intently looked at Gethsemane. "I saw, Gethsemane. I saw the Great Crane. At least I think I saw the Great Crane. But then I saw this woman with huge wings and then there was smoke everywhere and we could no longer see the wolves. We were in the air, all of us including Wynard. We were flying on huge wings, Gethsemane. And, then I passed out." he forlornly finished.

"Rest, Fergal," Gethsemane said as he patted the bear with his wing. "The Great Crane returned you to us, today. We are forever thankful for his watch over us and for him sending those who can help us. No other wounds amongst you will cause death."

"As with you, my heart aches for the loss of Wynard. You did not fail in your mission, my friend. What you have told me is of great value. And, I thank you for your sacrifice as with the others who journeyed with you." Gethsemane stated as he took flight and left the room through the kitchen.

Deborah quietly eased her way back to the plant lab. Sitting on the floor, she started to cry. "I do not like death," she said. "I do not like evil and hate," she continued. "What is it about these dead trees and why is it we have to go to them?" She questioned.

Finally, after several minutes of sitting she wiped her eyes, and stated, "Well, whatever it is out there at those trees, Ayden cannot go without me. She needs me for this 'Eshra Plan' to work and no one is going to stop me!"

"And, the last thing is to not let Ayden know about this. She's already scared and doesn't need me adding to her fear. Plus, if I even breathe to anyone, I have doubt and fear, they won't let me go with Ayden. I have got to keep this to myself to protect both of us," Deborah resolved as tears began to flow again.

Eleea flew into the room to see Deborah wiping her tears. "Child, what is causing you such great sorrow," he tenderly asked.

"Eleea," Deborah began. "Eleea, I know you do not want me to go with all of you. But I have to go, Eleea. I have to go," she pleaded.

"I know very little about how you and Ayden met, or how Elora lost her mom. And, you know me well enough to know I am most comfortable with knowing everything. Learning everything I can. I just feel so very overwhelmed right now. Could you talk to me and teach me what you know?" Deborah pleaded.

Eleea looked at Deborah realizing she was right on all accounts. She needed to go. Gethsemane was right to say she would go, and she needed to know about the past, the East Glacier past.

He lit on her knee saying, "Yes, Deborah it is time for you to hear the story of how I became the seeker and how I found Ayden."

Eleea began with the words of the prophecy and how the Council determined it should be he who was sent. He then explained the endless years of searching and who he thought it should be and how baffled he was when he found out it was Ayden.

Eleea deliberately left out the beating Ayden received from her parents by only saying he spoke to her on her porch late one night. He then described the death of Lora and how Elora got her name.

"Deborah, it was no accident you arrived in Eshra like you did," Eleea explained. "Just as others who have come to know you, here, and believe you are where you're supposed to be," Eleea sighed and pushed his chest out. "I too, believe the success of this mission is dependent on you being with us."

Deborah started to cry again. "Thank you, Eleea," she said through her tears. Eleea flew to her neck and rubbed his head on her saying, "all will be well, Deborah. All will be well."

"I just have one more question, Eleea," Deborah quietly expressed as she wiped her tears away. "How, how did Lora and your babies become ash when you sent them back to Eshra?"

"Deborah, all who are given the privilege to travel to your world know the danger of possibly losing their life there. Lora could have, in her final breath, sent herself to Eshra. Instead, she used her final words to speak to me. It was my duty to make sure her and our eggs returned by breathing over them, covering them with my body and telling them to return. All who cross over know they can send themselves and others back, through magic of course, if they were to die. Our breath, our words, carry magic for specific instances as these. By me professing they needed to return to Eshra, it gave them flight to return through their ashes," Eleea solemnly told her.

"Eleea, I am so very sorry for your loss," Deborah stated as tears, again, trickled down her face.

"Deborah, my friend," Eleea began. "I thank you for your heart, child. Just as I have watched Ayden in East Glacier, so too have I watched you. Your friendship, your love you so freely share has not gone unnoticed. For this prophecy to be successful, it will take both of you to accomplish it. With all the rest of us who go, we will all succeed because of you two. Take heart, child, the beauty of your soul will bring all of us great joy," Eleea profoundly claimed as he began to sing to her.

Deborah smiled at Eleea as she let her heart hear his song.

The rise of anticipation from everyone who lived in the Great Tree was huge for the final day of the celebration. The girls had lazily wandered around the Great Tree while preparations were being made for the large banquet to be held with everyone in attendance.

By mid-afternoon Lydia corralled the girls back to their room. She ordered them to take a nap as the nighttime performance would last late into the evening and she wanted them rested. After Lydia left the room, the girls were hard pressed to try and sleep.

Ayden pretended to fall asleep and waited quietly until Elora and Deborah were breathing peacefully. Carefully she inched off her bed and looked at Deborah to make sure she didn't stir. Huddled next to Deborah's head was Elora, snuggled in tightly with her wing covering her head.

Cautiously, Ayden opened the door a small crack and checked to see if anyone was in the hall. She squeezed her body out of the door opening and headed to the wardrobe room.

Once inside the room, she looked for a disguise to hide her appearance. Her whole purpose was to walk around the Great Tree to see how others acted rather than reacted to who she was to them.

It was not that she didn't appreciation their kindness towards her; it was she just wanted to feel normal again. Although, she handled the attention better than she did when it was her parent's funeral. She still felt somewhat self-conscious with any interaction she had with animal or man as it was one of reverence. Not one of just an ordinary person.

She found a hooded vest and a smock to put under it. Next, she put on a pair of weathered pants made for a man and added a leather belt to them. A pair of tall boots gave her the freedom to tuck the long pants inside to look as if the pants fit her appropriately. She checked her attire in the mirror, and placed the hood on her head before she, again, looked to see if anyone was in the hall.

Ayden followed the corridors down to the main festival room. Carefully she kept her eyes slightly lowered when someone passed her by. A short friendly nod to them seemed to help her avoid detection.

Once she entered the main festival area, she was able to walk more freely in and out of the booths as they were being taken down to make room for the banquet. Everywhere she walked people and animal were happily enjoying their work and chatted openly about the night's events.

The heightened anticipation showed in their speech as they talked about the messenger leaving on the quest. Some were supportive, while others voiced their concern about the lack of ability for a child to stop this figure named Choran from destroying both worlds.

Ayden felt somewhat queasy at the unknown prospect of this creature they so easily spoke of and the glaring fact no one had mentioned this important detail to her while she trained.

She decided she urgently needed to speak with Nadab. The one man she could trust in this world to not hide information from her. Nadab's workshop was deeper in the tree on another floor, and she had to coyly traverse around many people who busily had arms full of items for the banquet setup.

She stopped at the entrance to Nadab's workshop. Hesitantly she held her hand in the position to knock. Before she could make the first rasp, she realized she could hear voices.

She put her hand back down and leaned her head forward to eaves drop on the conversation. Something eerily familiar stirred in her heart.

She thought she recognized the person who was playfully bantering with Nadab,
but she couldn't put a face to the voice. The two seemed joyous at their fun teasing which suggested they had known each other for a very long time.

Ayden's mind grew with uneasiness as she tried to decipher how she knew this person who was so friendly with Nadab. She pushed her body closer to try and learn his identity. And as she moved forward, she lost her balance and fell into the room, landing on the floor.

Startled, Nadab and his friend rushed to her side to help her. Each took an arm to lift her to her feet.

Nadab exclaimed as they set her upright, "Man, what is this nonsense where you linger outside my door and do not respect my shop. Tell me who you are and what your business is with me!"

Ayden lifted her head and lowered her hoodie. As she did, she gasped in unbelief. Tears began to flow down her cheeks as she stared at the person who was with Nadab.

Nadab looked at her and said, "My child, what is troubling you where you needed to find me today. Here, sit on the bench and help me to understand your tears."

Ayden refused to sit and tried to choke back the tears as she spoke, "Nadab. Nadab, I trusted you and now I don't know who to trust. Or who to believe. "What the hell is Nick doing here," she screamed as her voice cracked. "I am truly scared right now and I think I just want to go home," she continued through her sobs.

Nick looked at Ayden, then he looked at Nadab as he tried to decide which person he should speak to first. Nadab, in his wisdom, nodded to Nick to address Ayden.

"Ayden," Nick began. "Ayden, this is my Uncle Nadab," he revealed. "I know this is all very confusing for you. But you must believe me, I was sworn to silence. I could not let anyone in our world know about this world. And, I am equally as confused as you, as to why you are here. And, to see you know my uncle."

Ayden stopped him from further speech by raising her hand to him as she stated with harsh accusation, "How could you not know about me and this, this, this prophecy, Nick? How could you keep it secret when Eleea was with me every day in our world for well over three months? she asked with angry confusion.

Nadab stepped forward and stood between the two of them stating, "Ayden, Nickalli, let me be the one to clear your confusion and answer your questions. Both of you take a seat on the bench and give me the honor to help you come to terms with your new-found knowledge."

Nadab led the two of them to their seats, and then he pulled up a chair to sit in front of them. He looked at them, and began, "Nick's real name is Nickalli Lawliet. He has the same last name as I do. His father is my brother."

"Ayden, do you not think it strange no one mentioned my last name to you since you have been here? It is because we knew you would become confused and troubled by this information. It had nothing to do with withholding truth from you. It had to do with protection for all who are involved in both worlds," he stated.

"Just as we protected you, Ayden," Nadab continued to explain, "we needed to protect Nickalli. Eleea was instructed to show great care to avoid being seen by Nickalli when he was with you. To put such a great burden on my nephew, if he knew the truth, would have been cruel. Plus, our worlds are full of evil eyes and ears. Neither one of you were prepared to deal with such evil on your own."

Ayden interrupted stating, "Nadab. I still don't understand. He has seen the mark on my back. If Nick is from this world, first, then how would he not know about the prophecy?"

"It is because, Ayden," Nadab sadly began, "Nickalli's parents do not hold the same value to this world as they do to yours. They wished for Nickalli to grow up without the lore of our world."

"This is why he was called Nick and not Nickalli as they knew he would not be understood with a name like his in your world. They worried he may have been teased. Even though they could cross over to our world as they desired, they usually only come once a year for the largest festival celebration in July when he is not in school."

"And, this is also when they would take back goods to your world to sell in their store. Nickalli knows very little about this world's deep truths and traditions."

"OK, fine," Ayden, again interrupted. "OK, fine, I will accept Nick had no clue about me and this whole prophecy thing. And, I can understand, somewhat, his parents need to keep him away from all this craziness in Eshra. But, what about Nick? Has anyone even considered what he wants? Have you Nadab? Or for that matter have his parents?" Ayden passionately asked.

"Ayden, this is the reason you have found Nickalli and I together today. He has come to me to ask a favor," Nadab stated.

Nadab turned to his nephew for permission to continue. Nick nodded his head in agreement. "Nickalli has asked me to speak to his father on his behalf. He wishes to stay in Eshra to be trained in our ways. And, he wants to start by going on an enlightenment journey."

"Nadab," Ayden began to talk fast with fear in her voice. "Nadab, Nick cannot come on our journey. It is too dangerous. I just found out downstairs there is something out there named Choran who I have to fight and nobody, I mean nobody has ever mentioned him, or it, to me the whole time I have lived here. And, to be honest I was pretty miffed at all of you for keeping this huge secret from me. Actually, I am still pretty upset about it. But, besides that, it is just too dangerous for Nick to be involved."

Nick stood up and looked at Ayden, and stated, "Wait just a second here, Ayden. I don't ever remember giving you permission to speak for me. I wish you no disrespect. But really! How different are you than my parents if you decide what I am allowed to do or not to do?"

Nadab once again stood in-between the two of them and calmly said, "OK, please both of you sit back down. Give me a chance to help you."

"First," Nadab began, "each of you has the perfect right to make your own decisions. Second, give yourselves a break from being angry or hurt because you feel others assume what is right for your life. Whenever you see someone try to protect you, it is not always a malicious selfish act. It can be a selfless act of love to protect you from real danger and harm," Nadab compassionately stated.

"It's just, when you love others and care about their wellbeing, you sometimes forget they have to be given the honor to grow and mature. It can be hard to let go and see those you love leave your caring arms and explore their world, their own way," Nadab's fatherly concern expressed.

"Third, Ayden, yes there is a terrible evil being out there who wants to destroy both of our worlds. All of us are concerned about your safety as well as those who go with you. But we have all had to look past our fear. We have got to stay strong in our belief you will succeed because of the truth of the prophecy," Nadab emphatically expressed.

"And, lastly, Ayden, you are right to feel hurt and lied to. We should have been more respectful to you and told you about Choran. But, for now, because the hour is getting late and the festival is soon to start, rest in trust I will make sure you learn as much as you can about Choran after the festival," Nadab pleaded.

Ayden could see Nick visibly relax, as she too felt the same as they listened to Nadab acknowledge their feelings. She turned to address Nick when Lydia walked through the door.

"Ayden, Lydia exclaimed. "What are you doing here? Oh! I see you have found Nickalli. I knew you two would become fast friends in Eshra. He is my sweet delight. You two will have plenty of time to talk later."

"But, right now, there is so much joy in the Great Tree tonight. And did I not send you to rest way earlier today? No, you must be alert for tonight and I am shooing you off to your room. Go, Girl!" Lydia said as she teasingly pushed Ayden on her way.

Ayden quickly turned around before she left the room, and said to Nick in a soft but firm voice, "Nick, we will talk real soon."

Ayden arrived back to the room with enough time to exhaustively fall on her pillow and sleep.

Journal Fifteen

I have been told before, "You can't judge a book by its' cover." That's a fairly accurate statement, most of the time. None of us know why another person's experiences will cause them to act in certain ways.

Or, even more importantly, cause them to hide for the world to not see. Heck, I was the master at hiding. I hid my bruises I got from my dad and mom. I hid my birthmark.

But I did not expect these words to 'not judge' to come back on me so strongly. I had judged Nick over in our world. I thought he was timid and shy because he was uncomfortable with himself.

In reality, he was uncomfortable with his knowledge of a world he wasn't allowed to talk about. What happened in his home to make him so timid? Was he chastised like I was over my birthmark?

No, I judged wrongly. I judged cruelly. There was a lot more to Nick, a.k.a. Nickalli, than I knew.

I had judged Nick like a book cover. So, yes, I discovered to not judge quickly. He was stronger than what I had thought.

Chapter Fifteen

The girls woke to music and laughter coming from the courtyard. Elora was the first to speak as she flitted around them in excitement stating, "Girls, girls, girls! Let's get movin'."

Ayden eyed Elora with suspicion while she stated, "Don't you guys feel like there is something up with Lydia? I mean she seems overly excited for just a celebration. Now, granted, none of us have seen an event like this before. But, it's like she is busting with a secret and can't wait to tell it."

"I felt the same thing, 'A'," Deborah piped in. "There is definitely something going on with Lydia that she isn't telling us."

"I know what it is," Elora chirped. "But I am not allowed to tell you guys. The ospreys flew in yesterday with the news. It's big for Lydia and Nadab. I mean really big!"

"Come on Elora," Ayden pouted, "You know it's not nice to say you know something and then tease others with the information."

Elora lifted her left wing and quickly put it back against her side. "It looked like she stomped her foot," Ayden thought while she hide her giggle.

"Come on Ayden!" Elora said. "Father told me just because I am little and can hide all of the time around others, I am not supposed to take tales from one person to another on what I overhear. It's not fair for you to ask me what I know!"

"Oh, Elora, I am so sorry," Ayden oozed with kindness. "Please forgive me for hurting your feelings. I know it is important for you to honor your father. I just thought, maybe, you needed to tell your very best friends because you knew we would always tell you if we knew something important about you. But, really, it's OK, Elora, you just keep quiet. Deborah and I will find out soon enough without your help."

"That's it!" Elora chirped. "You guys know I am your best friend, and I can tell you what I know and you guys will keep it secret."

"The ospreys were on a seeking mission with Tybin and Jerin. You know, checking out the best route for us to go when we leave here. Well, they are on their way back to the Great Tree and they sent the ospreys ahead to let Nadab and Lydia know they are almost home. Cuz Nadab and Lydia are their parents, and they knew they would be worried about them; with them having been gone for so long. So, they wanted them to know they are almost home and they will be here tonight to help celebrate. There! I told you," Elora exhaled.

"Wow!" Deborah expressed. "You really know how to deliver a punch of news, Elora. I don't think you took one single break to breathe."

"I guess I really never thought about Nadab and Lydia as parents, before," Ayden said. "Both of them are always so busy helping others. You just don't think about them having a family life."

Just like this," Ayden continued as she pointed to the table in their room. "Each of us has a special outfit made by Lydia for tonight. She is the greatest at showing us how she cares about us and how she knows each of our personalities. We know so little about her and Nadab. I feel kind of bad I have been so wrapped up in my life and haven't looked at how I could be there for someone else," Ayden stated with regret.

Deborah moved to the table and picked up her designated outfit and said, "I know, 'A', but we will be able to make it up to her. I promise we will find a way. OH! Look how absolutely beautiful this is! Come on guys, let's get ready," She finished.

Lydia had designed each of the girls a silky blouse woven with intricate patterns which represented their personal likes. Each had distinct uneven jagged cuts along the whole bottom where it draped down just below their knees.

Deborah's was a rich solid yellow with a beautiful tree of browns and greens that
flowed with movement while she walked. The leaves and limbs spiraled up along the front to her shoulders.

Ayden's was a deep night sky blue with a moon on the left side of her shoulder, and full of stars throughout which looked like they were crossing the sky when Ayden was in motion. To finish their look, Deborah had a pair of tights the color of dark green moss, while Ayden's tights were black berry purple.

The girls twirled around the room, each admiring the other's dress. Ayden turned to Elora and said, "I have something very special for you, Elora. I made them myself, long before we came to Eshra. And, I just kept forgetting about them. Maybe you weren't supposed to have them until now."

Ayden went to a drawer beside her bed and pulled out twelve little scarves which looked just like the ones she had brought with her in the backpack. As she laid them out on her bed, she kept talking to Elora, "I took a corner from each one of my scarves and cut it so it would look like mine, but your size."

Elora screamed with delight as she flew to the bed and hopped to look at each of the scarves. "Which one should I wear tonight?" She squealed.

"OH! Ayden, you do not know how happy you have just made me. She picked up a lilac one in her beak and tried to talk, "Rrrremmmm," she dropped the scarf, "remember when I asked you about the color purple? I am so-o-o-o excited; I have my very own scarves. Just like I wanted. Would you help me put it around my neck, Ayden?"

Deborah laughed so hard at Elora's joy; tears formed in her eyes. Watching Elora gave her such warmth over her happiness at receiving even the simplest little gestures of love. Ayden also joined in the laughter as she took the scarf and placed it around Elora's neck and tied a knot so each end fanned out perfectly.

Elora hopped over to the mirror and sashayed back and forth while looking at herself. "Do you see me, girls?" She declared. "Do you see me? I look so beautiful," she gushed as she hopped around the mirror.

Now, all three were ready for the big event. As they waited, anticipation was high as to what the night would bring. Ayden encouraged Elora to fly ahead to find Lydia to make sure it was OK for them to leave their room and arrive for the festival.

With Elora out of sight, Ayden turned to Deborah and said, "'D', I have got to tell you something real big. I didn't dare say anything with Elora around. You know how she can't keep a secret. But this is huge and you are gonna fall off the bed when you hear it!"

"OK, spill the news, 'A'. Get to the point, will ya." Deborah excitedly asked.

"OK," Ayden continued, But, seriously, this is big. While you guys were sleeping, I went on a little adventure down to the festival yard. I wanted to see what people were saying about us being here, and I didn't want them to know it was me."

"So, I dressed up like a man and just wandered around. It was pretty cool. I wasn't once questioned about who I was and did I hear a lot. Most people and animal, of course, are fine with us being chosen. But there are some who feel we are too "young," Ayden gestured with her two fingers, to be able to pull off this quest."

"Anyways," Ayden gained speed in her speech, "That is not the big news. There are two things that are big, though. One, there is this creepy thing, and I don't even know what it is; but it is evil, for sure. And we are supposed to battle it at some point, and its name is Choran."

"But, "'D'," the second thing is the biggest news ever." Ayden grabbed Deborah's hands in hers and said, "'D'," Nadab has a nephew, and we know him. It is Nick from our world!"

"W-W-What!" Deborah quizzically looked at Ayden. "Are you sure you are not hallucinating, 'A', Deborah asked. "Surely, he has to be someone who just really closely resembles Nick, 'A'," Deborah rationalized.

"No, 'D,' It is Nick, christened as Nickalli Lawliet, Ayden confidently said.

Before either one could process any more information, Lydia opened the door followed by Elora. "Come, my girls, it is time." Lydia happily said.

The courtyard had been transformed into a huge stage, with risers which held hundreds of chairs for everyone to get the perfect view of the performance. Everywhere were people and animal eating new types of festival foods the girls had not seen before. The room was full of laughter and happiness.

Eleea flew to Ayden's shoulder, while Elora stayed on Deborah's shoulder. All four looked around and soaked up the energy of the festivities. They walked around the bottom floor, and were instructed by Eleea to pick what they wanted to eat and drink while they sat and watched the performance.

Beautiful displays of silk portrayed full moons with eloquent cranes on them. Each one was designed differently, and all were absolutely phenomenal in their detail and artistic expression.

Ayden and Deborah were each given a basket to put their selected food and drink into. As she picked out her treats, Ayden would continuously stop and look around the whole area. Try as she could, she could not find Nick in the crowd.

Lydia regrouped with the girls, and said, "Here you are. "It's time for the show to start and I want you two to sit with Nadab and I, and with two other people I want you to meet."

Lydia directed the girls to the top back row of seats, directly in the center of the stage. Off to one side were two young men sitting with Nadab. When they saw Lydia and the girls, all three stood up.

Lydia, visibly glowed with pride. She turned to Ayden and Deborah and said, "Girls, I would like to introduce you to my sons." She pointed to one who had shoulder length curly brown locks of hair, and said, "This is Tybin." She then introduced the other son who had straight black hair tied back into a tight pony tail, stating, "And this is my other twin, Jerin." The boys bowed to the girls and smiled as they sat back down.

There was no time for the girls to talk to the young men as the performance had begun. They smiled and nodded as they tried to juggle their food to sit down.

It was a wonderful display of actors in costumes flowing with color. Song and acrobats were the mainstay of the show. Along with some humor from the choreographed interactions of man and animals.

All in all, it was a full night of beauty and relaxed fun. The grand finale came at midnight with a magical lowering of the lights. Slowly the walls and ceiling opened to the outdoors and transformed into a vibrant showcase of nighttime depicting thousands of stars and the most beautiful crane, proudly standing in the moon.

Fireworks went off in timed unison to music which brought all the spectators to their feet in applause. By the end of the night, the girls were exhausted and opted to go to bed shortly after the show ended.

The next day brought back their usual routine with Ayden sitting silent in the courtyard. She had her eyes closed, when suddenly, she felt the wind move towards her face. She instinctually lifted her hand to ward off what was coming at her. She opened her eyes to see Abner lower his hand away from her, as he smiled.

"Ah! my Ayden," he spoke with pride, "You are now ready to leave my tutelage. You have become a strong warrior. One I am proud to call my friend and my equal. And, may I humbly say to you what an honor it has been for me to have become part of your life. To have become part of your family," Abner stated as he lowered his stance and regally bowed to her.

Ayden stood, looked intently at Abner and said, "It is me who has had the privilege. To have been taught by one as great as you. And, to have been accepted by you where you consider me family is an honor, Abner."

As she spoke, she took Abner's forearm in her hand, and he took her forearm where their eyes held each other in deep respect as they sturdily grasped each other in the shake which would always define Ayden forevermore.

Deborah was already in the kitchen talking with Lydia, and surprisingly Nick also, when Ayden arrived for lunch. Deborah was deep in conversation with Nick when she looked up to see Ayden enter.

"Hey! 'A'," Deborah started, "You were right it is our Nick!"

Ayden felt perplexed. Deborah's free attitude about it being no big deal they were in Eshra, or no big deal how long it would take them to complete the quest. To now, no big deal Nick is here made her totally confused. No anger, no self-doubt. She just freely accepted everything.

Lydia sensed Ayden's uneasiness and said, "Ayden, my child, tell me what is wrong?"

Ayden could feel the pressure of everyone as they watched her, and she wasn't sure how to handle it.

Finally, she blurted, "I am really uncomfortable with how easy it has been for Deborah to just nonchalantly accept everything that is going on since we got here. From how long we will be here, to, 'Hey it's Nick' It just seems like nothing gets to her."

"I love you, Deborah, but aren't you even a bit confused and scared all of this is so not our normal way of life?"

Deborah moved closer to Ayden, took her hand and stared into her eyes saying, "Ayden, I love you more than any friend could. It's OK for you to feel overwhelmed," Deborah comfortingly said.

"No, it is not our normal life, like back in our world. Yes, it is full of confusion with all that is around us," Deborah quietly continued.

"But, from the moment we entered Eshra, when I totally lost it, to now I made the decision to accept and learn. Learn whatever I could, knowing there would be things which would drive me crazy. Because one, I couldn't control it and two, because it was completely unfamiliar to me."

"Ayden, if I had not chosen to accept and move forward, I would be a nut case right now," Deborah finished as she squeezed Ayden's hand and smiled at her.

"Fine," Ayden conceded, "It makes me feel a little better you understand what I am feeling and you, too, have some of those feelings. Actually, I do not know what I would have done if you were not here. Every day I realize more and more I need you with me on this journey."

Ayden turned to Nick and resolutely said, "So, just as Deborah has accepted you here, so too must I."

Nick looked at Ayden, and responded," Ayden, I am sorry you feel confused. I am truly sorry I could not tell you I knew about Eshra."

"Just because someone stays quiet about who they are or what they know, does not make them a bad person. A part of any journey is learning. Whether it be learning about the environment or learning about another person, or even learning, more importantly, about yourself...it is all enlightenment. But, in all fairness here, I too, did not know you knew about Eshra," Nick stated.

Ayden considered Nick's statement, as she realized she never really did know him. She assumed who he was, because he was awkward in their world. And here, in Eshra, he seemed more confident; still timid, but confident.

"OK, then," she finally said to Nick, "I agree to accept I don't know too much. I don't need to know everything all of the time. Or always be in control. And," she turned to include Deborah and Lydia, "it is my job to learn what I can to stop my confusion and to not freak out over it all of the time."

With the air somewhat cleared, the four of them began to enjoy their meal. Suddenly, they were interrupted by boisterous voices coming from the hallway.

Jerin entered the room laughing. He turned to Tybin who followed him and said, "Tybin, we both know I am the one with the brains in this family. You have always been the brawn."

Tybin slapped Jerin across the shoulder and stated, "Well Jerin, brains cannot help a person if they do not have common sense to match. At least my brawn compliments my awesome common sense."

"There is nothing wrong with my common sense," Jerin attacked back. "Let me remind you of what happened when you wanted to jump across the creek three days ago. What did I tell you about the slippery rocks on the side of the stream? Did I not tell you to think, first? And what happened! You took a running leap across the dead tree limb, landed on the slippery rock and down you went, straight into the water. Which was hilarious to watch, actually. Anyways, I have more than enough common sense to keep me dry," he triumphantly finished.

"Boys," Lydia broke into their competitive bantering, "Come join us at the table. I haven't had an afternoon meal with the two of you for months."

Both boys came over to their mother hugged her and kissed her on the forehead. They then, noticed Nick and reached under his arms and lifted him up out of his seat.

"Nickalli," Tybin began, "You have really gotten tall since the last time I saw you!" As he gave him a big bear hug.

Jerin gave him a hug too, and said, "It is so good to see you, Nickalli. I have missed you."

Ayden tried to not be rude by staring at them. She felt so full of love as she watched how they interacted with their mom and Nick; she wanted to soak in every single moment.

She stole a look at Deborah who was just as enthralled at watching the boys' actions. She turned to look at Ayden and they smiled at each other. Both knowing their silent look spoke volumes about how they felt right then.

Gethsemane flew into the room, which caused the boys to go into another fun rant.

"Gethsemane! Old Man. How have you been since we've been gone?" Tybin spouted as he went over to Gethsemane and gently rubbed his head.

Gethsemane tried to stand tall and composed under the head rub, but failed miserably. To see a human, rub a golden eagle's head in such a playful way was the most awkwardly funny thing to watch.

Gethsemane cleared his throat, and tried to act sophisticated and important saying, "Tybin, it is so good to see you and your brother have returned and you have not lost any of your childish ways."

"Ah, Gethse, don't be angry with me. You know I love and respect you. I'm just very happy to see you, that's all," Tybin cajoled him.

"Well, yes, it is so very good to see you are safe. I must admit, it has been fairly boring around here without you two and all of your antics. Although, I am thankful while you were gone, we have not had to do as many repairs in the courtyard," Gethsemane said in a fatherly tone.

He turned to Jerin, stating, "Well, my child, how was it taking care of your brother in the wilds of Eshra?"

Gethsemane took the tip of his wing and turned Jerin's head to see his sideburns. "Is this a bit of gray I see in your hair, Jerin?" he said with a mischievous glint in his eye.

"I'm only seventeen years old! I don't have gray!" Jerin yelled as he grabbed the mirror at the end of the table. "Mom! Do you see any gray in my hair?" He asked as he leaned into the mirror near his mother.

Gethsemane's laughter caused him to lose his balance as he tried to catch himself from falling by digging his claws into the wooden top of the chair. He then teetered back and forth to regain his stand. Which caused everyone to laugh with him.

"You will always bring me joy, Jerin," Gethsemane laughingly told him. "I can always count on you to over react when it comes to anything vanity based about you."

"My boys," Lydia chided all three of them. "We are being rude to our girls. They do not know all of you well enough to join in your games."

"That's OK, Mom. By the time we are done with this next journey, the girls will definitely be able to join in any game we come up with," Tybin said as he winked at Ayden.

Ayden could feel her cheeks warm as she tried to hide her face by putting her glass in front of her to take a drink. Regaining her composure, she said, "I don't know boys? Deborah and I have a few tricks we could teach you too. You may be surprised to find out our tactics are a little more challenging than yours."

Deborah joined the fun by saying, "Yeah, you guys do the man stuff, but once you're involved with women and their moves a whole new realm of circumstances may just put you off your game. And then you guys will be having to learn from us on how to win."

"Oh-h-h-h I see," Jerin teasingly said, "My brother and I respectfully accept you and Ayden's challenge. But I will remind you, it was your idea to make this a competition. So, I don't want to hear any complaining when it gets too tough for you two to keep up with us."

"So, now that we have settled that," Ayden stated as she turned to address Gethsemane, "When were you planning on telling Deborah and I about Tybin and Jerin traveling with us?"

"Ayden, I did not tell you because there was never the right moment to explain it. And, obviously, Jerin and Tybin have done a much better job than I telling you. Wouldn't you agree?" Gethsemane stated.

"Enough has been said," Gethsemane finished, "More will be revealed three nights from now when we will honor what you and Deborah have accomplished here. But, right now, I feel tired and need to nap. I will leave the six of you to your meal."

"No, Gethsemane, it is not enough for now," Ayden declared. There is still this huge matter of Choran. When were, you going to tell Deborah and I about him, or it, or whatever?" Ayden demanded.

"Choran is an extremely horrible being. He lives to make sure evil reigns in this world. There is no honor with him and wherever he is decay surrounds him. He resides in the Dead Trees. He sends out his minions to do his bidding from his throne. He is heartless and spineless," Tybin interjected.

"Our journey is to take away his death grip on our world and yours," Jerin followed up on what Tybin said. "He is an old decrypted being who uses twisted logic to fit his own sadistic and selfish means. Once he was a great owl, full of respect and honor and magnificent beauty. But his jealousy and pride relinquished him to a mere shell of his past glory," Jerin finished.

"Well said, boys," Gethsemane proudly said. "And, now I am tired." Gethsemane flew to a high perch in the kitchen to rest. He watched with admiration as the girls interacted with their new friends, old friend, and with Lydia. He thought back to the council meeting when he was unsure if Deborah should go with Ayden.

He silently observed Deborah for days. Watched how she took in everything she was taught. She was like a young bird with their mouth constantly open, wanting more food. He had felt uncertain about her going, but was leaning towards saying yes. Then he saw the girls greet each other with the handshake which cemented his decision.

For them to know the sacred shake, and to do it so naturally, just kept him in awe of them. They were meant to be together. They were meant to make this mission with each other.

"It was no accident Deborah fell through the entry with the others. There is a far greater magic here than any of us are aware of," Gethsemane reminded himself as he closed his eyes to sleep.

Journal Sixteen

In the two short months, I lived at the Great Tree, I had learned more about me than in all the years I have been alive. Maybe, it was because I was getting older and not because I was in Eshra.

All I really knew was I belonged in this world. It felt right and real. I wasn't afraid to voice my concerns or fears.

I guess, I had found my voice. Maybe this was why I felt I had grown and learned so much. I had freedom to be me. A person with thoughts and emotions that mattered. I had never known this type of freedom before.

My only concern with it, was I didn't want to abuse it. I didn't want to get cocky and treat anyone with disrespect.

In reality, I still had a lot to learn about how to handle this freedom. As I listened to Eleea, Nadab, Lydia, Gethsemane, Abner and all the rest from the Great Tree I knew I would be OK. The way they handled conflict and discomfort was so very respectful. They spoke everyday with dignity and respect.

I wanted their speech to be my destiny. I wanted to be able to speak with respect. Naturally speak with respect...where I didn't have to think about it...it just happened.

Chapter Sixteen

Lydia entered the workshop and saw Nadab sitting with a troubled look. She came in behind him and placed her hands on his shoulders and massaged them. "What, my love, has you so worried?" She asked.

"I am truly confused, Lydia," Nadab began. I have never known such confusion about what type of weapon or tool to design. Each time I think I have the right idea to make for Ayden, and I begin to forge it, I suddenly lose it."

"Everything seems to go well, while it is red hot and I am pounding its shape. Then I place it in the oil and as soon as I bring it out of the oil, it disintegrates to ash. I am just baffled. Now, I have less than three days to present her with her weapon, and I just don't know what to do."

"Come, sit with me in the courtyard for a while. Maybe, you need to leave the shop and look at this from a different perspective," Lydia said while she gently took his hand in hers.

Nadab followed his wife to the bench in the courtyard. The seat was covered in green vines which acted like a natural soft cushion when one sat on it. Quietly they looked at all of the beautiful colors of the flowers and greenery as they flowed in and out of each other. Stones all around the yard showed forth their brilliance in turquoise, lapis, agate, peridot, sapphire and many other colorful stones and designs.

"Isn't this just breathtaking, Nadab? The absolute natural beauty of everything in this yard speaks forth of how nature is so very important to all of us," Lydia expressed.

"How all of us are a part of it. We all fit together in this big picture of this world. It is no coincidence, you know, these two girls came into our lives. Just watching them can bring a person joy. They are so full of life and love, Nadab."

Nadab listened intently to Lydia. He loved spending time with her. She always knew how to bring him to a place of rest.

"Lydia," he began, "I am deeply aware of these girl's beauty and purpose here. And, I too, am very thankful to have them in our lives. But I feel as if I have let Ayden down by not being able to provide her with a weapon," he said with concerned sorrow.

"Did it ever occur to you, Nadab, maybe she doesn't need a weapon?" Lydia questioned him.

"You do not just make magnificently formed weapons, you know. Look at the turquoise, the lapis, the gold, and the silver running through the veins of these rocks. I still cherish the ornate jewelry you have created for me from these stones. Mixed with your unique design in metal, they are all purposefully made with intense beauty," Lydia said to him.

"And, what about when you and I create together? We have made some absolutely wonderful bags with cotton, leather, stone and metal work," she reminded him.

"You have put yourself into a vice and now you have squeezed the creativity out of yourself because of it. Think beyond weapon. Think beyond self. Think about what Ayden is all about, what she represents, and how beautiful she is. And what you are supposed to forge for her will come naturally to you," Lydia encouraged.

The two of them talked and laughed with each other for another hour, and then they went their separate ways. As Nadab walked back to his workshop, he felt strengthened by the time spent with his wife and her spot-on wisdom which always put him back to a proper perspective.

She inspired him, and this made him proud she had chosen him to be her husband.

At the entrance to his shop, Eleea, Gethsemane, and Nickalli met him. He nodded, and invited them in.

"To what do I owe this prestigious meeting," Nadab requested of the three, as he pulled up chairs for Gethsemane and Eleea to perch on the tall backs, and two individual benches for Nickalli and he.

Gethsemane started by saying, "Nadab, we come to you to discuss Nickalli's desire to make an enlightenment journey. Not any journey, but one which is highly unusual. He wishes to go with Ayden. Sincerely, I am very troubled by this request."

"I too have grave concern," Eleea quickly agreed. "Nickalli does not know this world like he knows the other. We do not know how much ability he has in difficult, let alone dangerous, situations."

"Gethsemane, Eleea, I have great respect for both of you and your deep concerns," Nadab began.

"I have known Nickalli longer than the two of you have, since he is my nephew. Yes, he would only spend his summers here in Eshra. But, during those days, I saw great strength in him. He is highly intelligent, quick to learn and skillful in working with woods, leathers and metals. The most impressive quality about this young man is his dignity. He holds value in our ways and he shows honorable respect to all he encounters. These attributes alone, are not common in either of our worlds. My boys view him as a little brother. And, I humbly ask the two of you to listen to Nickalli's reasoning as to why he has requested this journey," Nadab pleaded as he nodded to Nick to respond.

Nick stood and faced the three of them, stating, "I stand before the three of you with a heart full of tremendous honor because you have given me a chance to speak."

"All you have spoken is true. No one, including myself, know what I am truly capable of if allowed to join this utmost important mission. I know Ayden, and the depth of strength she possesses. She is a person who I highly value as a friend and the same goes for Deborah. Both of them are good people. All three of us live in a small town and we have interacted throughout the years; even if most of it was in a school setting. But I do not ask to go with them because I know them," Nick claimed.

"When I crossed over to Eshra this summer, I had no idea Ayden and Deborah were here. My decision to ask for an enlightenment journey was impressed on me when I crossed. I can only tell you I had a vision as I entered Eshra," Nick expressed.

"In this vision, I saw myself enter a forest I have never seen the likes of before. All around me was dead moss hanging from the trees. Almost as if it were spider webs.

I felt my body gain speed as I tried to rush through the moss to get to the other side of the forest. As I continued forward, I did not feel I was running on two legs, but I was running on four.

Large paws with long claws slapped the ground under me as I ran. Reaching the end of the moss forest, I abruptly stopped at the edge of a beautiful lake. When I looked at my reflection in the water, I saw a bear staring back at me," Nick explained.

"Then, as soon as my entry was complete and I was in Eshra, the vision vanished. My mind and heart were full of confusion as to what could this all mean," Nick expressed.

"The first chance I had; I spoke privately with my uncle about what I had experienced. I asked his advice and his help to convince all who were responsible for me to allow me the privilege to go on an enlightenment journey. I did not know until I got here, that this journey I was requesting was to be the one for the Messenger of Eshra," Nick stated.

"Deep within my soul, I know I am to be a part of this journey. I ask for your trust in my decision to ride with all who leave with Ayden," Nick intimately asked.

Gethsemane held Nickalli's eyes in his as he lifted his chin with his wing. Truly he was touched to the core of his heart to hear such wisdom and determination from such a young man as this.

He finally stated, "Child, you are more noble than you know. It is my honor to give you my blessing to go on this journey. A vision such as you have had is not to be taken lightly. It would seem, you were destined to be involved in this prophecy."

"I concur with Gethsemane," Eleea stated. "Any doubts I had have been removed by your words. And as far as your vision; the answer to its meaning will come when the time is right. It is with pride I ask you to join us," he finished.

"Nickalli," Nadab said as he slapped him on the back, "I know you will ride with skill and strength. I am very proud of you, my child. Now, stay and enjoy a meal with me. Eleea and Gethsemane need to leave to speak with Ayden and Deborah before the council meeting tonight."

Eleea and Gethsemane flew in to greet Ayden and Deborah, who were having dinner. The girls looked at the two of them, waiting to hear what they had to say.

Gethsemane addressed the girls, "Tonight you both will be received by the Council. Before all of us attend the feast, in two days, to honor all you have accomplished these last months, the Council wishes to see you first. This is a very high honor which is being bestowed on the two of you," Gethsemane impressed on them.

"We, Gethsemane and I, want both of you to be prepared," Eleea stated. "Do not speak unless you are first addressed. Show respect and listen to what is being said. Choose your words carefully when you answer someone," Eleea continued to instruct them.

The girls hurriedly finished their meal as they listened to what was to be expected of them. The sense they felt from Gethsemane and Eleea about this meeting made them both uneasy.

"Now, it is time for you to come with us," Gethsemane said.

The girls followed behind Gethsemane, Eleea, and Nadab who had joined them. Quietly they walked the corridors to the upper branches of the tree. They watched as Nadab took a vine from the banister and untangled it. As he lifted it upwards, they saw it disappear into the tree's trunk. Nadab used his index finger to trace a latch, which he used to open the secret door.

The room was magnificent in design. Colors used for each seat or perch, for each wall to floor design showed a brilliance the girls had not seen before in the Great Tree. Everywhere they looked was a human or animal sitting, with all eyes on them.

Ayden recognized Phum, the squirrel, who she had briefly met in her world, and who had taken the amulets from Nadab when they crossed over. Abner was also in attendance with Shamgar, Yabinith and Nekoh sitting beside them.

But, most of the council were foreign to her. The middle of the room held five high back ornately designed oak chairs facing a massive dark blue chair where Nadab went and sat.

Eleea flew to a perch on Nadab's chair; while Gethsemane flew to a stunning sapphire perch near Nadab. Three of the oak chairs held people who kept their heads forward. Nadab gestured to the girls to take the other two seats.

As Ayden reached the chairs, she realized it was Tybin and Jerin in two of them. She let out a small scared cry as she realized it was Nick in the third.

Nadab began the formal introductions, "Welcome Ayden, Deborah, Tybin, Jerin, and Nickalli to the Council. It is our honor and great privilege to speak with you tonight about your decision to undertake this great journey. To fulfill the prophecy of Eshra we will always be in your debt for your bravery and sacrifice."

'For it is your calling to take the hand of destiny and to ride its wings to victory.'

Before the feast, when all will honor you, we, here, wished to meet with you," Nadab continued. "Some of the Council have requested to address you. At this time, I pass the mantel to the Council to speak," Nadab finished.

Ayden watched as a badger dressed in short little pants and a vest made of leather with beaded tassels walk to the lapis chair and bow to them. He turned, nodded to Nadab, and then turned back to the five of them and stated, "Thank you for taking the time to speak with us. I just have one question for each of you to individually answer," he said as he intently looked at them.

"The question is this: *What was the one thing which gave you a true reason you needed to go on this journey?* I ask to start at this end," as he gestured to where Tybin was sitting.

Tybin stood to speak, "Pepion, my good sir. I have traveled far in our land. I have seen how the light has begun to dim. My father, Nadab, has taught me the deep truths of our world and has always inspired me to respect what we have been given. Whether it be skill or magic, honor what is true."

"My moment of clarity, to decide to take on this quest, came when I sat alone one day beside the riverbank. As I contemplated our world, my heart became heavy. What if we did not try to stop this darkness? What if we accepted the inevitable end to let it just happen? I could not let this be," Tybin reflectively stated.

"To do nothing, is still to do something. It is an active decision to walk away from what is right and good. I could not allow myself to do nothing. My heart is to take this task at hand and to protect all involved. To help all involved succeed." Tybin bowed and sat back down.

Jerin stood next, and said, "As you all know, Tybin and I have been given the freedom to travel throughout our land. He and I have seen this wondrous world in all its glory. The deep respect we have for it, is only because we have had people like our father and mother, and all of you instill in us qualities of how much dignity our world holds.

To stand by and do nothing, after all we have seen of this land, would be a true travesty. My soul, my heart would ache forever to see our world die. No, it is my calling and my heart to join in fulfilling the prophecy." Jerin bowed to Pepion and returned to his seat.

Nick rose and bowed to the badger, saying, "I have not had the same privileges as my two cousins, who sit next to me. I was not raised in this world. My parents choose a life for me on the other side. Yet, each summer I was allowed to spend time with my uncle Nadab, and my aunt Lydia. Through them I was taught how valuable Eshra was to my existence in the other world. The respect they taught me about our two worlds and what they showed me about myself has been carried deep in my soul for some time now.

I do not know my purpose in entering this decision to go on this quest. I only know from the moment I crossed over this time; I have had this burning desire in my heart which told me I must be a part of this journey. This is my time to stand. My time to cease this moment of history for both of our worlds." Nick bowed to all, and sat down.

Ayden stood, looked at all of the Council, and began, "I am only one person. Alone, I can accomplish very little."

"Together, with all who go with me, I am a mighty force. I have no idea what lies ahead of us. Or how we will overcome the obstacles set in place to try and stop us. Honestly, it is very scary to me. I do not see myself as anything great just because I have a mark on my back.

But your question is: 'what was the defining moment which led me to my decision.' My moment came when Lora died in my hands. She was my friend. My confidant. My teacher. Her and Eleea took me and comforted me in ways I cannot really explain. I only know because of them; I am ready to go forward and do what needs to be done for our worlds." Ayden bowed to the Council and sat down.

Deborah stood and bowed as she started, "I guess I am the only one who came into this plan unexpectedly. I wasn't supposed to be here. But because I love Ayden and felt this strong need to protect her, I crossed over with her.

I never gave it much care I was to have a defining moment to go on this journey. My thoughts were, I will go where Ayden needs me. And since she needs me, I need to learn all I can about this world through what I do best," Deborah informed the council.

"I have studied every plant and known terrain of your world. I have trained hard so I can help wherever I am needed. If someone is hurt, or sick, or needs to understand directions I am your girl to get the job done. This is an adventure. One where I have been given a gift to learn and help. This is why I am here. Thank you." And, Deborah sat back down.

The badger smiled and regally bowed to the five of them and returned to his seat.

Immediately, Phum stood up from his perch. He jumped down and took a stand on Nadab's arm of the chair.

Phum cleared his throat and said, "This request which has been given to each of you, is of grave importance to both of our worlds. It will not be easy. There will be danger. There will be uncertainty. There will be doubt. Each of you will be tested beyond anything you have ever experienced before when danger, uncertainty, and doubt arise" he authoritatively said.

"This is the time to ask yourself if you are determined to follow this path. Or, to accept you are not willing to put yourself in this serious situation," he queried them.

"No one on this Council," Phum gestured around him, "will regard you as weak or unworthy if you state right here and now you do not want to continue on this journey," he informed them.

"I ask each of you to take a moment of silence to reflect on your final decision. Then if you know deep in your soul this is the right destiny for you. Well, then stand," Phum stated.

The room became completely silent as Phum's words began to sink in to all who heard him. Phum nodded to Nadab and to the five sitting, and jumped back to his perch.

Ayden stood up, walked two steps forward and turned to face the four who sat with her. With great intensity, she looked at them.

She fixed her eyes on each of them and nodded to them, and then began, "This is my destiny; my purpose," she determinedly said. "The four of you who sit with me, know this: I will not feel any less of you if you choose to stay. Do not go with me out of pure emotion to protect me. If you must go; go with the truth in your heart it is what you need to do for yourself and for our worlds." Ayden smiled at them as she finished.

In one fluid movement, all four stood at the same time. Ayden stepped back to her chair and turned to stand with them. Proudly, each of them could feel their united strength as they stood together.

Silently and slowly, each person and each animal in the room stood in respect and support of the five.

Nadab raised his hand to all present and said, "Tonight has brought us all hope. It has shown us each one of these five was chosen by fate to fulfill their destiny. Our worlds thank you. And, know this, the five of you do not go alone. At the feast, you will meet the rest of your companions."

The council adjourned and everyone in the room expressed words of encouragement as they each shook the five adventurers' hands. Eleea, being the ever-present father figure finally led the girls out of the council room and made sure they crawled into their beds.

Journal Seventeen

One of my absolute favorite things in school was when we would learn about the psychology of people. Basically, psychology is the study of behavior watching.

Not that it is an exact science, though. Once again, you have to get beyond the surface of a person. The surface being, what they are willing to show others.

Only by observing and learning about the past and present of a person can you get a better understanding of who they were and are.

But still psychology tries to make sense out of people patterns and then label those consistent patterns into categories of types of psychology. For example, phobias, obsessive disorders, eating disorders, and sociopath disorders are all documented types of psychology.

And, from what everyone at the Great Tree believed, Choran was a sociopath. Full of himself. Angry. Felt he was entitled. Twisted sense of reality. All of it suggested a very troubled soul.

What I wanted to know; is how he got that way? I wanted to delve into his psyche and find out what made him so disoriented about life where he stayed angry and full of hate.

Bottom line, everybody wanted me to take him out of the picture. But if I was supposed to do that...shouldn't I know in my heart why I was doing it?

Chapter Seventeen

Very early the next morning, the girls ran down to the kitchen and asked Lydia if they could have breakfast in their room. They wanted to spend time with each other without interference from others. Lydia brought them a beautiful treat of fruit, cold cereal with milk, and jam with fresh baked bread and butter. They laid on their beds, as they ate, reminiscing about their time in Eshra, as well as their time in East Glacier.

"Doesn't it feel weird how we have grown so much here. And yet, I don't feel any older," Ayden said to Deborah.

"Yeah. It is hard to explain, huh? I know we've learned a lot in such a short time. And because of what we have been taught, it makes us feel so much older. But you are right, I still feel young and only fourteen," Deborah agreed.

"Are you scared, 'D'?" Ayden asked.

"Well, anytime someone goes into an unknown situation, there is some type of fear or trepidation," Deborah contemplated.

"But, 'Ayden', we have each other; we always have. Both of us are smart in our own way. We have determined personalities, we are not afraid to try new things, and we were sent here for a reason. It is not just us going off on some tangent to prove something. It is a weird divine intervention of some sort that has brought us to this place in our lives. Together we will triumph," Deborah continued. "Plus, we have Eleea, Elora, Jerin, Tybin, and Nick to help us." Deborah finally said.

Ayden nodded to Deborah's response to her question. Silence ensued as both girls lazily drifted off to sleep. Ayden suddenly woke in terror and muffled her scream to not wake Deborah. She sat up and put her face in her hands as she rocked back and forth quietly on her bed.

Tears slowly formed and drifted down her face. Memories of her past beatings by both her parents, taunts by children in her neighborhood and ridicule from her father engulfed her mind.

"When will these horrific memories stop?" She questioned herself. "When will I get rid of the fear," she silently muttered. "Why can't I just accept like Deborah does!" Ayden scolded herself. Slowly, she exited their room to spend her last full day with the domesticated animals at the back end of the Great Tree.

Ayden loved being with the animals. Whether it was grooming them or just sitting as they ate out of her hand, she felt at peace with them.

When she arrived, she filled her hand full of grain and sat on the clean straw floor. Immediately a dozen chickens, a goat, and several ducks surrounded her, all nudging her hand to be opened for them. She giggled at their impatience.

The chickens climbed all over her lap as the ducks stood in front of her and quacked for her attention. The goat gently head butted the back of her head. She positioned her back to lean against the barn door and methodically caressed each animal.

A young girl approached her with a bucket full of meal for the animals, she smiled and sat down next to Ayden. Ayden took several handfuls from the bucket and spread the contents out in front of her and on her right side.

She looked at the girl who looked nothing like the glacier clan people. Her dark olive skin and beautiful curly black hair was in stark contrast to her parent's appearance.

"Shora, tell me about yourself. How did you become one of the tree people?" Ayden quizzed her.

Shora aimlessly played with the grains of meal as she drew abstract designs with her finger. She intently looked at Ayden and began, "I am a child who was abducted by Choran's followers. What I have been told is, I was supposed to be a worker for Choran. Taken from my home when I was only four years old, I have very little recollection of my real family."

"What I do remember is the smell of burning wood surrounding this cottage as it went up in flames. Even the animals in their pens were destroyed by the fire. At times, I wake in horror as I hear their screams of terror as they were all burned alive."

Shora's eyes welled with tears as she caressed the goat who had laid down and placed his head in her lap. "When I first arrived here, I would not speak. They say it was the trauma I had experienced which caused me to be mute. I don't know?"

"Ever since I arrived here, I have been raised by two of the most beautiful people in this whole tree village. Not that all who live here are not beautiful. Because each soul is important to our very existence. I just feel very fortunate to live with Tarth and Verdith."

"Because I didn't speak, they had to name me. They say I came from very far away near the ocean shores. So, they named me Shora to always remind me of my roots. I love my name and one day, when I am old enough, I will take an enlightenment journey like you and travel to where I was born." Shora triumphantly announced.

Ayden put her arms around Shora and hugged her stating, "Shora I believe your enlightenment journey is going to be full of awe and excitement when it happens. Thank you for sharing your story with me. And, I, too, believe you have the greatest guardians anyone could ask for."

Ayden stood, brushed off the remnants of the grain and smiled saying, "Gotta, go. Will I see you tomorrow night for the banquet?" Shora smiled back and nodded her head up and down.

Deborah woke to see Ayden enter their room. "Let me guess," she teasingly said to Ayden. "You were down with the animals, again?"

"Yup!" Ayden stated as she smiled at Deborah.

Both girls lay on their beds, sensing the anticipation of what the next day and future days would bring.

Elora flew through the door and landed on Deborah's right foot which was dangling off of her crossed leg.

"Girls," Elora began. "I want both of you to know I will protect you from whatever comes our way. It is my duty to stand with you and be there for you."

Ayden and Deborah looked at each other and muffled their astonishment towards a small little bird who claimed she could protect them with valor.

"Thank you, Elora," Ayden finally was able to express.

"Good, now that we have this matter taken care of, I am here to tell you dinner is ready." Elora authoritatively said.

Eleea flew into the room exclaiming, "Elora! Elora, how many times do I have to tell you to wait for me? And, to be patient!"

"Oh, hello Father," Elora sweetly replied. "I was just telling the girls it was dinner time. That's all, Father. Patient, Father? It would seem you too have a problem with patience. Look how frazzled you are right now."

Eleea ruffled his feathers with a look of exasperation as he replied, "Elora, my child, do not twist my words to avoid your responsibility! I specifically asked you to wait for me to get the girls."

"Yes, you did Father." Elora concurred. "But sometimes a female's intuition is more accurate than a male's request. I strongly feel my mother would agree with me," Elora said as she flew to her father's side and tenderly nudged his head.

"Fine, fine, fine," Eleea succumbed. "But I am telling you, child, we are leaving and traveling into danger. You have to be more cautious and less impulsive in order to survive this journey."

"All of us," he stated as he lifted his wing to include the girls, "have to be aware of our surroundings and feelings and not react quickly to the unknown. We all need to assess before we act. It is late and dinner is served," he finally said.

Each traveling member was served their favorite dish for dinner. From fried chicken to pasta to spicy soup and roast, all were accommodated. The same fair went with the desserts and drink.

Ayden waited for a lull in the conversation at the table to ask, "So, I have a few questions for all of you." She looked around the room and began.

"Why is it Elora did not have to be brought in front of the Council last night? When will I be told more about Choran? And, does everyone in Eshra know about my world. Plus, if they do, can they all travel freely to my world and back whenever they want?"

"Elora did not need to go in front of the Council because it was always assumed, she would go wherever her father went," Nadab stated. "But you do have a point, Ayden." Nadab turned to Eleea and Elora saying, "What are your thoughts on this, you two?"

Eleea looked steadily at Ayden as he replied. "Elora is an extension of me in many ways, Ayden. I have great fear for her and this journey. It would devastate me if anything happened to her. But I could not even fathom the thought of leaving her behind. Yet, I never asked her if she wanted to go or not," he finished as he looked at Elora.

"Father, not once did it cross my heart to stay behind," Elora passionately stated. "Ayden," she continued as she looked at Ayden, "saved my life while I was still in the egg. Our souls belong together. Just as you and her, father, have forged a bond deep in your spirits; so too have I."

"As to your other question about Choran," Gethsemane started. "This enlightenment journey will bring you knowledge in many forms. As you travel, and as you converse with others and your companions, here, you will learn about Choran."

"What you will see and hear in the world of Eshra will give you more understanding to Choran than mere words spoken to you as you sit comfortably at a table. Trust Eshra to reveal to you who Choran truly is, Ayden." Gethsemane wisely finished.

"And, finally. The question of whether all in Eshra can enter your world, Ayden," Nadab stated. "A spiritual leader has to bestow the gift upon an individual to allow them the freedom to go freely between the worlds. Chaos would ensue if all of Eshra entered your world at their free will. Those who live here in our world and who do not completely comprehend the delicate balance between the two worlds could cause great distress in your world."

"Just as Deborah had great confusion when she first crossed over, so too would others in your world. And, yes all of Eshra does know about your world. Most do not give it any concern or have any desire to see it," Nadab said as he smiled at Ayden and Deborah.

"Hold up," Deborah proclaimed. "If a spiritual leader like Nadab has to bestow the gift for someone to cross over like you say. Then how did Ayden and I cross over without the spiritual gift?" She asked in a perplexed voice.

"Deborah, you crossed over because you held onto Ayden. Ayden crossed over because she is the Messenger," Nadab stated. "She did not need my gift. Because she has the crane on her back, we knew she would have the ability, probably through song, to make the leap. We believed her ability would override anything I could have given her," Nadab finished.

Ayden and Deborah nodded and smiled back as they contemplated all that was spoken. Everyone seemed to gladly say goodnight after the girls' questions were answered.

Lydia entered the girls' room early in the morning. "This morning has been set aside for pampering," she exclaimed. Behind her followed four women who were well known to the tree people.

Two women rubbed their bodies with lemon, arnica and lavender oils, working each of their muscles to relieve tension while the other women trimmed their hair. After the women left, Lydia turned to the girls and stated, "Rest, girls. Tonight, will be full of excitement and activity. So, now is your time to rest." She smiled at the girls and left the room.

Ayden walked over to Deborah and sat on her bed. She took her friends hand in hers, but could not formulate any words. Sitting there, she placed her hand over her other hand that was holding Deborah's.

Sighing, she finally stated, "Deborah, I want you to know how very relieved I am because you are going with me on this journey. I know it is dangerous, and I know it all seems crazy for two young girls to be put in this situation and I know, somehow, we will succeed. I do not think I could have handled any of this without you."

Deborah squeezed Ayden's hand and then let go as she put her arms around Ayden. "We, were always meant to be together, Ayden," Deborah softly stated.

"Our friendship has always been strong. Just as Elora said, I too will always be there to protect you, to protect us," Deborah fervently stated.

Ayden put her head into Deborah's chest and silently cried. Both girls slightly rocked back and forth as they both clung to each other and then laid down on Deborah's bed and fell asleep.

As early afternoon approached, Lydia knocked on the girls' door and entered with Elora and two others who carried their afternoon snack and a stack of clothes. Lydia explained they were to eat and then she would help them dress.

Lydia joined the girls in their meal, stating, "My girls, I want you to know how deeply I love you. Yes, you have only been here a few months; but time does not always determine an emotional energy. Just as in your case, a connection is made when souls first meet and immediately form a bond of deep respect. I have watched the three of you, daily, and this love I have for you has only grown deeper. You have brought great joy to my heart. And, I know our time together, forever more, will only bring more memories of joy and love."

"But, right now," Lydia smiled and said, "it is time to show you what I have made for you. I have designed a backpack with each of you in mind. First, Deborah, come see."

Deborah jumped up from her seat and went to sit next to her. Lydia produced a backpack which showed the colors of summer. Shades of yellows, greens and browns intertwined with zippers of pinks, purples and oranges.

Next, she gestured for Ayden to sit near her. Lydia pulled out her pack, which displayed the colors of a sunset. Mixtures of blues, whites, oranges, and purples with zippers that shined like a shimmery pearl, catching the color's reflections from the fabric of the pack.

"Now, my Miss Elora," Lydia expressed. "I did not forget you, my little chirp-per," she stated as she revealed a tiny pack like the girls' design. "See here, Elora," Lydia explained, "You have three small snaps; and, I choose purples and greens to compliment the girls' packs."

All three girls were thrilled with the colors and numerous pockets the packs had. Several times they would open and close each pocket area, and examine the whole pack inside and out.

Lydia explained, "I know you will have need to carry whatever items that are important for you for travel. Therefore, I made sure you could separate everything and keep track of where it is in the pack. Also, I wanted the pack to be very functional. So, not only can it be worn on the back, but it can also be used as a side pouch. There is magic sewn into it, girls. Whichever way you need it, it will transform. Elora, yours only goes around your neck and rests at your side, so it does not hinder you in flight." she concluded.

"This is not the only thing I have made for you," Lydia excitedly continued. "Here are your outfits for tonight," she said as she helped the girls dress.

Each girl had a pair of silk pants which looked like a loose pajama bottom, with a
smock to match in a darker color; also, made from silk. Deborah's was a beautiful purple lavender combo; while Ayden's was a deep fern green and chartreuse color. A belt made of dyed leather and rope was stained to match each girls' attire.

Both, Deborah and Ayden, had a long robe with a gradation of color matching their outfits, made out of dyed lace and cotton which magically shimmered. It highlighted the clothes underneath like glistening lights were constantly focused on them as they walked.

Even Elora had her own little robe colored purple and green to match the girl's dress. Lydia had designed Elora's to have large openings to allow her wings to slide through it and a belt held the robe under it so she could fly freely.

Ayden took Deborah's hand and they both stood in front of the oak mirror to admire their outfits.

Elora flew to Ayden's shoulder breathlessly saying, "We look so very beautiful, don't
we?"

Lydia proudly stood back and watched the girls as they giggled and talked. Not only was she pleased they liked their new clothing, she was also pleased with how well the clothes fit their bodies.

"I would like to help you pack your packs," Lydia stated. "But, before we start, I have one more item I want each of you to carry in them." Lydia ceremoniously handed each girl a set of scarves, crafted in designs acceptable to the culture of Eshra; and to their personalities.

"I know how much you love bandanas; and I could not let you leave me without these," she declared.

Each girl squealed with delight as they gave Lydia hugs. Then, they busily organized their pack to carry their belongings.

Deborah and Ayden slyly glanced at each other as Lydia helped Elora. With great care and stealth to avoid Lydia's eyes the girls each put several personal items in their packs from their world.

Taking a deep breath, Lydia sighed and said, "It's time for us to attend the ceremony girls."

Ayden didn't recognize the courtyard when they walked in. It had been transformed into stadium seating to hold the whole community of tree people.

Each row of seats had long tables in front of them, full of all sorts of food, drinks and decorations which represented the Great Crane. Several banners draped each table and walkway up the stairs.

Lit candles in intricately ornate pottery graced the whole yard. On the bottom level towards the back were more, round, tables decorated the same as the ones above.

 Everywhere Ayden looked, people and animal had filled a chair, and all eyes were on them. Two long tables faced each other towards the front of the center of the courtyard.

To the right, were five stallions in full dress. To the left was a table displaying several different items including tools, boxes and weapons.

Gethsemane flew in and perched on the chair directly in the middle of the front table. Nadab came in after him, followed by Lydia where both of them sat to the right of Gethsemane. Abner sat to the left of Gethsemane and Shamgar, Yabinith, and Nekoh sat to the right of Abner.

Another person Ayden only knew to be Beynor the master woodworker, sat to the left of Lydia. Phum, Pepion, and a few other council members sat to the left of Gethsemane.

Eleea flew to Ayden's shoulder while Elora took Deborah's. Eleea directed the girls to the long table facing those who sat with Gethsemane. Ayden and Deborah sat in the middle with Eleea on Ayden's left and Elora on Deborah's right. Next to Eleea sat Tybin and next to Elora sat Jerin. Each of the boys had an osprey perched on their respective chairs and Nick sat next to Jerin.

All in attendance enjoyed the food and celebration, being everything was delicious and full of laughter. Music played throughout the yard. Ayden could not see anyone playing the instruments or see who was singing which made her think some type of magic created all of the sounds.

Ayden turned to Tybin and asked, "What is the name of your osprey, Tybin?"

Tybin smiled at his bird and said, "This one is Lok, and Jerin's is Tari. Let me tell you the story about how we came to have these birds as our best friends."

"We had just returned from our enlightenment journey, three years ago, and there was a big celebration, kind of like the one we are having now. Gethsemane presented Jerin and I with two eggs."

"He told us it was our responsibility to make sure they stayed warm and incubated. When the birds began to hatch, Jerin and I were right there, helping them and the birds imprinted to us."

"The reason we have the birds and not their parents, is their parents were sent on a mission. It was just a short one, but they never returned; something happened to them. And, none of us know what it was. It still remains a mystery to this day. Speculation is the forces of darkness which are continuously gaining strength out in the unprotected world of Eshra took their lives," Tybin sadly said.

"What type of mission did they go on?" Ayden asked.

"When the council sends out a mission, it is not for the general population to know the purpose," Jerin interjected. "Gethsemane knows, but he keeps it to himself. I do feel though, he still feels the pain of losing them; the birds' parents, I mean. He was responsible for the eggs while they were gone. I sense he still regrets agreeing to Lok and Tari's parents requesting they both go when their eggs were so close to hatching," Jerin said with equal sadness.

"When he watches Lok and Tari, I see sorrow in his eyes. Giving Tybin and I the eggs to care for was an extremely high honor of respect from Gethsemane. He trusted us to do the right thing," Jerin confessed.

"OK, then I am a little confused? If the missions are not known by the general population, how come everyone is here celebrating with us, and knows we are going on a mission?" Ayden asked.

"It was pretty hard to keep this mission secret when you two entered the Great Tree," Tybin began.

"Everyone knows the prophecy, and everyone knows about your birthmark. Plus, you two definitely did not grow up around here or anywhere in Eshra. You were too different and lacked knowledge of our ways. It worked to Gethsemane's advantage to be honest with everyone about who you were and why you were here."

"This way all who trained you and helped you would feel like they had a part in saving Eshra. It created a strong bond of hope and promise," Tybin respectfully stated.

Deborah waited patiently for Jerin and Tybin to explain the birds and the different types of missions and then asked. "Do the birds talk to you guys? I mean, I know some animals are domesticated and some animals talk. Which has always confused me as to how come some do and some don't," Deborah said with frustration.

"Yes, the birds talk to us," Jerin acknowledged. "But they do not feel the need to talk to others very often. It is their choice and we respect their decision," he explained.

"As to your question of why some animals can and others can't. Well, it has to do with lineage of the species and the magic of Eshra.

The domesticated animals and the feral animals in the wilds of Eshra have always existed here. Just as they have always existed in your world. All magic is a gift, Deborah. The gift of speech and reasoning given to an animal is deeply respected.

We know we are fortunate to live in a world where animals are more than simple companions. They are our teachers, friends and equals." Jerin reverently explained.

Ayden and Deborah nodded their heads in understanding as they deeply thought about everything Tybin and Jerin told them.

Gethsemane moved to a perch above where he was seated and begin to speak, "To all here, I want to express my deepest gratitude for your help in making this day possible. Without you we would not have been able to move forward so quickly. Each of you are a part of this history which belongs to Eshra. *'The promise of Eshra lives in each of you.'*

Gethsemane turned to Ayden and those who sat with her and passionately stated, "Ayden, you and your companions will leave us this evening to begin a most treacherous mission. All of us, here," he gestured with his wings, "are proud to have been a part of your journey."

"This moment in time is your destiny. Each who go with you, tonight, have been divinely chosen to stand with you. *'May the Great Crane guide you, protect you, and return all of you home safely into our fold.'*

"Before all of you leave," Gethsemane continued, "there are friends here who would like to present you with gifts to help you on your journey." Gethsemane turned and nodded as he acknowledged Beynor.

Beynor stood and went to the table where the gifts were. He gestured to his intern to follow him with his presents. He handed each person their own specially designed wooden bowl, inlayed with metal around the rim, stating, "These bowls have been molded with a specific magic. When you are in the wilderness and cannot make a fire, fill the bowl and run your finger around the metal rim and it will cook the contents."

He then handed each of them new wooden utensils with the marks of the glacier clan engraved on them. "Use these in good health and in peace wherever you sit and eat. *'May the wings of the Great Crane guide you safely,'* Beynor concluded and bowed to them.

Abner stood next and presented each of them with the stallions waiting patiently on the side of the courtyard.

Speaking to Ayden, he said, "You have been a worthy student and I could not be prouder than I am this day. I look at you as one who came to me as a child, and now leaves me as a young woman with character beyond anything I have ever seen before." He too, bowed and asked the Great Crane to protect their journey.

Shamgar, Yabinith, and Nekoh presented together which didn't surprise Deborah since she had always seen them work as one mind.

Shamgar began, "It has been one of the most rewarding experiences of our lives to have been the instructors for Deborah. Deborah, your beautiful mind continually brought light to our hearts. The three of us sat for hours trying to decide what would be the greatest gift we could give to bring all of you the most significant need for your journey," he stated.

"And, with much deliberation, it always came back to the first idea we had. I present to you Nekoh. The three of us agree he should be beside Deborah and the rest of you on this mission," Shamgar humbly said as he and Yabinith bowed.

Deborah's eyes immediately filled with tears as she heard Shamgar's words. She loved Nekoh and felt so honored to have him with her.

Nekoh came down from the stage, jumped onto the table next to Deborah and waited for her to scratch his head. He looked at her and said, "You didn't really think I was going to lose out on being pampered by you all of the time, did you?"

Phum stood next, stating, "This mission of prophecy will take you deep into unknown land. What trials will lie ahead for you, no one knows. But I have great faith each of you stand in this moment where you are supposed to stand," he paused for a moment as he looked at the five.

"With this being said, I too believe I am where I am supposed to be...and this is to stand with you on this journey. '*May the winds of Eshra carry us to victory,*' Phum ended, as he bowed to his companions.

Lydia gave individual clothes to each one in the group, and explained the uniqueness of each item to them. She specifically revealed the hidden pocket where they were to keep their utensils. A strong reminder from her they were to always use them while they journeyed so as to not bring unwanted attention to themselves and put their journey in jeopardy. Lydia smiled at each of them, bowed and sat back down.

Nadab stepped forward and reverently said, "Now, I would like each of you to come forward and stand with me. It is common knowledge my gifts hold special meaning and purpose. Whatever I forge is specifically designed for one person, one animal. Although others can use it in its normal capacity, each tool is meant to bond with its true owner," Nadab informed them.

"Each gift will not burden you as you travel. Each gift holds deep magic and will only show forth when it is needed by you. No one, not even I know what magic it will perform, but each gift will never harm its owner," he humbly told the group.

"But, in order for this bond to take hold, a ceremonial act will need to be performed on each of you. As I hand you your gift, I want you to stay silent and continue to stand in front of me," Nadab instructed them as he handed each of them their gift.

Tybin received a wooden staff embedded with intricate geometrical designs of various silver, gold and bronze metal. This staff matched his enlightenment gift from three years ago of a hunting knife.

Jerin received a bow and arrows, with each arrow tip a different colored honed stone of red agate, emerald, opal and lapis. This, also matched his hunting knife from three years ago.

Nick received an enlightenment hunting knife with leatherwork embedded in it depicting a bear. He also received wrist bands made of dark stained leather with brass inlaid to resemble bear paws.

Phum received a belt of leather, dyed a rich black to accent his fur. A highly polished oval silver buckle connected the belt around his waist. Fine chain attached to opposite sides of the buckle were able to retract into the structure. On each end of the links were small daggers with a hook just below the tip of the blade. Both blade handles were intricately wrapped in a crisscrossed leather. The knives fit into their sheath sideways along the belt, and were partially hidden by the silver buckle.

Elora received armor to fit around her chest and head and metal to spread the length of her wings with each feathered section designed to form a blade. The whole metal piece was forged in an ancient method where it was like a light sheath of feathers which could move in motion with her and had no weight to hinder her.

Eleea received armor that fit across his chest with a leather strap attached to metal to fit around his forehead. When he lowered the metal, it covered his beak. He also had metal which formed over his feet and had blades at the tip of his claws. Just like Elora, he was not burdened by the armor.

Nekoh received a cotton bag filled with numerous pouches made of leather which held several empty and filled vials.

Deborah received a hand carved box containing a foraging blade etched with a majestic oak tree on one side and the words *'Within each seed a soul emerges to live...protect these souls,'* etched on the other side; a mortar vessel was also included. She received a small hunting knife, to honor her enlightenment journey. It mimicked the same design as the larger foraging knife, and was made to strap around her ankle in a sheath.

Ayden received a small hunting knife which fit around her ankle in a sheath, also. It had an intricately carved handle portraying several scenes of a journey ending at a rising full moon. Next, she was handed a small sterling silver etched box with the words, *'May the winds of Eshra carry you'* written on it. Inside lay a necklace of the same silver as the box. The chain was created with seven woven strands, and at the end of the necklace rested an intricately etched sterling silver crane feather.

Ayden wanted to scream and cry, but was afraid to let anyone know her shock at seeing what was in the box. Even though her mind was raging with emotional confusion over Nadab designing her a feather like her mother had given her, she was too overwhelmed with the ceremony and its importance to everyone to bring attention to herself.

Nadab formally bowed to each of the recipients, as a low, but powerfully emotional, melodic sound began to echo around the room.

He began, *"These gifts carry deep magic within their framework. As they are, they can be used in any normal fashion, necessary. Each gift will show forth its secrets when you most need it to help you. But, to release the full potential of their magic a sacred ritual must be performed over them,"* he stated.

Lifting his hand, Nadab gestured to have the two pottery basins on each side of him be lit. An aroma of incense and smoke seemed to dance out of the pots in rhythmic unison with the music.

"I ask each of you to hold out your gifts in front of you. When I clap my hands, I want you to breathe over them, like you are blowing on a fire ember to make it ignite," Nadab instructed.

He nodded his head and drums began to slowly pound. Raising his hands straight above his head with palms facing them he began to chant. The sound of his comforting voice echoed throughout the courtyard as all eyes watched him.

In one swift motion, Nadab dropped his arms in a circular arch, as he forcefully brought his hands together in a powerful clap in front of him.

Immediately, each of the sojourners engulfed their gifts with their breath. As they blew, the air came forth and mixed with the smoke of the incense.

The mixture began to intertwine in an upward motion towards the ceiling. Each individual swirl formed a funnel cloud straight above their extended hands.

Suddenly, a flash of lightening pierced directly through each funnel and struck the gifts. Followed by the loud crack of thunder.

Nadab lowered his hands, and emotionally looked at each of them as he spoke, *"Forever more these gifts will be bound to your souls. If you should find yourself in danger or in need, they will come to your aid to help you and guide you. And, since they are linked to the inner depths of your core, if by chance they should fall into enemy hands, they cannot harm you."* Somber silence of respect lingered as the drum beats slowly lessened and stopped while Nadab walked back to his seat.

Gethsemane moved in and said, "The time has come for you to depart."

Lydia took the girls behind a curtain and helped them get into their riding gear. It was difficult for her to keep from crying while she helped dress them. Ayden and Deborah took turns to give her a warm hug, and then went to stand beside their horses. Ayden noticed while they were gone someone had readied their horses with their personal belongings, including the backpacks from their room.

Lydia then went to the boys to make sure they were properly prepared and cried again. Nadab came beside her and put his arm around her waist as they watched the five travelers mount their horses.

Eleea flew to Jerin's shoulder, while Elora flew to Ayden's. Phum took his place with Nick, jumping to the crown of Nick's horse's head. And Nekoh stood beside Deborah.

Gethsemane gave one final warning before they left, stating, "Remember, all of you, be careful with whom you speak to about what you are truly doing. Keep your conversation with each other guarded in case unseen forces hear you. Deep magic goes with you, but you must be on guard at all times for there is evil magic in Eshra too," he warned.

"Jerin and Tybin know the direction to get to the Dead Trees. Trust their guidance and listen to their decisions for they know this land and its ways," Gethsemane reminded them.

'The Great Crane is a lamp to your soul. Follow with your heart and he will light your path. He rides with you,' Gethsemane humbly finished.

Gethsemane flew to a limb by the waterfall on the far end of the hall. He raised his right wing to the top of it and as he lowered it, he sliced the water in half. The water magically separated and Tybin, with Lok riding on his horse's head, led the small caravan through the opening, while Jerin, Eleea, and Tari brought up the rear to begin their journey to take the messenger to meet her prophecy.

Journal Eighteen

Confusion and fear shrouded me as we left the Great Tree that night. It made absolutely no sense to me my locket from my mom was the same as my gift from Nadab.

How did she receive it? Did it hold powers for her? Why didn't she tell me? Had she been to Eshra before? And, did Nick know Nadab had made the one he found in the rubble of the fire?

Of course, Nadab had made the first one. But, how could it be?

Would I ever find the answers to all my questions? My mind was a whirlwind of confusion.

And, I dared not tell anyone what I knew. I had to find the answers, first, before I could explain it to others. I even questioned if I should privately speak to Nick about it. But I knew when I found a private moment with him, I would not hold my tongue.

Well, there's an interesting statement.... 'hold my tongue.' Both Eleea and Lora had drilled into me all spring this very issue, kinda.

I would mouth off about someone I felt offended me and justified to myself and them I had a right to speak what I thought.

Their constant statement to me was, "Ayden, you can always think what you want when you are mad and hurt. But do not let it cross your lips immediately.

Think about what you wish to say, so you do not regret what you have just spoken. Be careful to not harm.

Yes, it may be true what you feel. But, will what you say harm you further? Will it get you in bigger trouble? Will it make you be viewed wrongly? Will you cause harm to another by what you speak?

Think before you speak. Always remember, you can think anything...just don't let it cross your lips."

Fine, maybe I would talk to Nick and maybe I wouldn't. I had to think long and serious before I made my decision.

Chapter Eighteen

Tybin made sure all were outside the entrance to the Great Tree and then stopped. Jerin pulled up next to him, and stated, "We leave at night to ensure our exit remains secret. We will travel through the day, until early next evening. The trail we take is an easy one to traverse and should not be difficult for all of you to keep up."

Tybin took over the instructions saying, "Once we get past the known path, the terrain will become harder. We will need the light of day to find our way. The plan is to make up as much time as possible during the first leg of the journey, before we have to slow down."

Jerin followed Tybin's statement with, "Tybin and I have been through the area past the first mountain range twice. The rest of the journey is unknown land."

"To find our way we will be dependent on our senses, people we meet who have knowledge of the area and the spirit of the Great Crane himself." Jerin turned his horse and positioned himself at the end of the caravan. While Tybin turned, and set the pace for the travelers.

Even though it was a clear night with the moon almost full, the darkness of the forest fit the somber mood of the inexperienced expedition. Ayden noticed she was very comfortable on her horse. The saddle surrounded her in fluffy natural wool with wispy mixtures of midnight blues for her down feather mini blanket.

Elora was settled in front of Ayden on the lower neck of the horse, cradled in her own little leather nest covered in wool which was attached to the saddle. Eleea had the same setup as Elora on Jerin's horse. Deborah had the same set-up as Ayden except for her blanket being a beautiful mixture of greens.

The boys' ospreys were sometimes on their shoulders, or flew ahead, or circled around everyone, or perched on the horse's heads of their respective partner. They were like little sentinels, always on guard and watch.

Nick positioned himself second to last in the caravan. Phum had a makeshift leather bowl, almost like the chickadee's nest, but bigger, on Nick's horse to rest in when he wasn't on watch.

At times, Phum would leap into the trees, jumping from limb to limb as he went ahead to check the perimeters for danger.

Nekoh walked with the horses, but when he felt tired, he would jump up to Deborah and lay, the best he could, in her semi-lap as she rubbed his coat. It was a funny sight to see his legs sprawled on the sides of the horse while being rubbed down.

Ayden felt secure in the hands of Tybin and Jerin, and enjoyed the peacefulness of the horse's stride as they traveled. All of them stayed fairly quiet while they rode.

To keep their spirits up, Tybin periodically handed everyone little snacks Lydia had specially prepared for them. Each traveler had their own water bladder hanging from their saddle to quench their thirst. They moved through the night into the next day.

As evening approached Tybin gestured for them to stop to set up camp. The three boys worked quickly cutting down evergreen boughs to cushion each of their beds, making a fire ring for cooking and warmth, taking the gear off the horses and rubbing them down before feeding and watering them. And then, finally placing a magical ring around the camp to keep out any unwanted visitors.

Ayden loved the smell of the mountains. It was the clean pine tree scent which permeated throughout. Coupled with the crisp night air, it caused her to think about East Glacier and how much she missed being there.

Sitting by the fire while they ate their meal, her mind wandered as she watched the mesmerizing flicker of the flames. Deborah sat next to her and seemed to be in the same mindset, as she was just as quiet.

Shortly after dinner, Tybin showed up with five twigs he had sharpened to a point at one end. Jerin opened his pack and took out a neatly tied cloth pouch.

As Jerin started untying the bag he said, "Mom warned us you two may become sad, especially your first night rest in the wilderness. So, she packed a special treat for all of us to help you two with your homesickness. She sent father to, 'you know where' to gather special things for you two."

Jerin handed marshmallows to Nick, who placed them on the end of the sticks. He handed Ayden the graham crackers and to Deborah he gave the chocolate bars. Each of them took their own stick and placed it in the fire to melt the marshmallow.

By the time they had finished their first s'mores, the girls were talkative and laughing. Ayden looked at the boys and said, "Thank you."

Their first night and day of travel had brought them high into the familiar mountains of Eshra. Tybin explained to them the next day would have them cross over the mountains and start to descend into the valley where the meadow people lived.

It would take them two days past the meadow to get to the village and they would spend the evening in the inn there. After the village, they would begin to travel into the unknown land.

The second day of travel was fairly uneventful. It was getting close to the time for all of them to retire for the evening when Ayden sensed a presence outside the camp's ring.

She didn't feel scared, just curious as to what it could be. Little eyes seemed to glisten in the light of the dying fire, but she could not be sure her eyes were tricking her in the night light. She laid down on her bed with her head facing outward in case she could catch the eyes and was able to follow their path. Before too long, she was sound asleep.

Deborah was helping Jerin with the fire when Ayden woke the next morning. She decided to go help Tybin get the horses ready for the day. With everything packed, they all sat down to enjoy their breakfast. Ayden still couldn't shake the feeling they were being watched by someone, and kept looking around to see who it was.

Finally, Ayden said, "Have you guys felt uncomfortable lately, like we are being watched?"

Deborah responded with her head cocked to the right, "Well, it is not abnormal for there to be many different species of animals in the woods. Most people do not even realize they are being watched by nature because they are so focused on what they are doing."

"And, the animals are only trying to stay out of harm's way when they are watching us. They don't want us to hurt them. So, to answer your question, yes, we are being watched and no, I do not feel uncomfortable about it."

Ayden didn't feel any better after Deborah's lecture on the species in the wild. "Naturally, all of us know there are animals in the wild and they watch us," she disgustedly said to herself. "That is not what I meant," she mumbled as she mounted her horse.

Riding through the forest reminded Ayden of being at home. The same flora and fauna graced the landscape. From meadowlarks singing in the grass to the little ground flower known as the bitterroot, she felt like she belonged in this land.

Tybin pulled up beside Ayden as they started the descent into the valley. "I agree with you, there is something following and watching us," he said.

"I am not sure, but I think it might be chipmunks or something of the sort because they are running through the trees. I can hear them as they pass over us. I am curious to see if when we will leave them behind in the forest, when we reach the valley, if they will still continue to track us," he told Ayden.

"I don't think we need to be too alarmed by them, as I do not sense danger, nor do the ospreys or Phum feel threatened. So, we'll just keep a close watch on the situation," Tybin stated.

Ayden nodded her head in agreement; thankful someone understood her concern.

Soon, they left the mountains behind and started their trek into the valley. The girls found the floppy hats Lydia had secretly packed for them were the perfect accessory for traveling through the open meadows. Even though it was overcast, the sun was still hot, and the hats helped them stay cool and comfortable.

Tybin found a secluded area beside the riverbank for their third night camp. "The meadow people live farther inland," he stated. "Most of them are good folk, but our first encounter with them left Jerin and I somewhat uneasy. We avoided them on our return trip and felt we should do the same this time."

The river was deep and wide, and, yet, it peacefully flowed in a natural course. Ayden stepped to the water's edge and was amazed at its clearness.

Large colored pebbles of red, orange, green, brown, black and yellow covered the riverbed as if they had been laid there by an artist in a mosaic pattern. The water, itself, was a dark bluish green, and Ayden could see tiny minnows swimming everywhere.

Deborah came up behind Ayden and scared the baby fish when she put her bare feet in the water. "Come on, 'A', join me. It feels so-o-o-o good!" Deborah exclaimed.

Ayden hurriedly took off her shoes, unzipped her magic pants at the calf, and stepped into the pure water. She walked around and let the rocks massage her feet. She watched as Nick and Phum walked out of sight and headed downstream to fish for their dinner.

"Well," Ayden whispered to Deborah, "if it weren't for talking animals, it would seem like we were still in East Glacier. All of this feels like Lake McDonald in the park. Except the colors are more intense and this is a river, not a lake."

"Yeah," Deborah whispered back, "Even the mountains are just like home. Of course, the plant species from the snakeweed to the whitebark pine grow in the same pattern and size but, the colors are exceedingly more vibrant here," she finished.

Eleea and Elora joined the girls as they flitted around the bushes to look for bugs to eat. Nekoh just lazily stayed far enough away to stay dry and sunned himself. Tybin and Jerin started to prepare the camp as they had every night.

Phum and Nick returned with freshly cleaned rainbow trout, except for two of the largest ones still intact for the ospreys. Lok and Tari circled above Nick as he carried the dinner.

Nick chuckled and said, "I see the two of you. I just don't know? I am really, really hungry tonight. What do you think Jerin, do we share, or do we make them go find their own fish?"

Jerin smiled with tender eyes, and retorted, "Nickalli, I hear your pangs of hunger all the way over here. But I love my birds more than I care about your stomach. We share. They deserve it. They have traveled many miles back and forth making sure our path is danger-free."

Nick nodded his head and smiled in agreement as he took the two-intact trout outside of the camp for the birds. Lok and Tari hopped and squawked in delight at their feast.

Tybin helped Nick fry the dinner on the open flame while Jerin prepared the side dishes from their food pack. The girls sat back and reaped the benefits of it all.

Phum, also enjoyed the benefits of others preparing food for him. Sitting on his haunches, his belly protruded out as he patted it with satisfaction.

"You know, once, I crossed over for," he paused to think, "oh let's just say for a vacation, to the other world. I watched humans do some really strange things. They are a curious lot, you know," he stated as he scratched his ear with his back paw.

"They transport to other worlds through the strangest ways. I have seen them use these doors with lighted numbers on the top where they enter and the door shuts where they either go up or down in number. And *jazing* they are in another world."

"It's a *jazing* world over there. Where you thought, they were, is *jazinged* right into another world. And it happens so very fast. Kind of makes your mind go fuzzy trying to figure out how they did it, or even where they are at in their new world," Phum finished with awe in his voice.

Deborah looked at him with disbelief, stating, "Another world, Phum? Seriously, is that what you believe? Because a mechanized contraption uses a series of pulleys and wenches or pneumatic pressure, you think it transports people to other worlds? Phum, this is not what is taking place," Deborah tried to explain.

Phum stood up and put his paws on his hips and said, "I know what I saw. There are hundreds of other worlds over there. And it only takes a door opening and closing to get to it. Are you saying I am lying?" he asked with indignation.

Nick jumped up and got between the two, stating, "Whoa, whoa, whoa, guys. Phum, let me help you see, OK," he said with tenderness.

"You know how the Great Tree has the large basket at the back of it. The one where the gatherers bring food from the forest for the kitchen? Remember how it travels several floors up the tree to get to the kitchen? Well, this is how elevators, that's what they are called in the other world, get people from one floor to another. It is the same world, but, just a different floor," he said with compassion.

Phum sat back down and said, "Well, yes, that makes more sense, I suppose. But I did not lie about what I saw," he emphatically stated.

Deborah looked at Ayden who was determinedly staring at her with a firm face while slightly shaking her head no. She decided she better take Nick's lead, and stated, "I can totally get it Phum, If I had seen it for the first time, I too would have thought it was a *"jazing"* moment. You were right in how you witnessed it."

Eleea watched in anticipation as the whole scenario unraveled. Thankful Nickalli took great care in protecting Phum's dignity, he realized there was much more to him than he had previously thought when they were at the Great Tree.

"Yes," Eleea thought, "it was a wise decision to include him in their quest. He would prove to be a valuable asset," he was sure.

Phum cordially acknowledged Deborah with a nod and took out his left knife from its sheath. He acted like he no longer needed to be involved in the conversation and started to pick at his teeth with his knife.

Nick sat back down with relief on his face. Eleea caught his eye and gave him a gesture of approval for how he handled what could have been a very difficult situation.

Tybin directed the group to help clean up the camp before they retired. Everyone settled in for the night as a peaceful sleep came over them while the night air filled their dreams.

At breakfast, Jerin informed the group of his expectations for when they would enter civilization later in the day.

"I want you girls to rest, about thirty minutes, before we reach the village. Walk around, stretch, get a snack, and relax a little. What I don't want you guys to be is nervous when we enter. Act like you own this journey and you belong here."

"Both of you were chosen to take this enlightenment journey because it was felt you two would bring back to your community great knowledge and experience. The spiritual leader, who sent you two on this mission, wants you to learn what you can from those you meet and from the land you travel."

"Ask questions and listen to the answers. And, most importantly, do not get into debates over another's perception. Remember, it is this world you come from not another where how should I say it," Jerin stopped to think. "Where the world is full of jazing moments," he cleverly finished. The girls smiled at Jerin in agreement.

Travel through the open fields was easy on the horses with the level landscape, in comparison to a mountainous terrain. Ayden's mind wandered as the horses kept their steady progress.

She thought back to Eleea's description of the land of Eshra. He had told her there were natural paths made by the flowers, etc. But, now, ever since they began the journey, she could see no natural walkways. All of the foliage had grown together, and they had to blaze their own trail. To see with her own eyes how Eshra had changed, caused her to feel Eleea's pain for his homeland.

Granted, the mountain terrain was vastly different than the meadow tundra, but all of it still had lost its ability to show its uniqueness with natural pathways. It caused her to be sad by the loss.

Deep in her thoughts, it took her awhile to notice the little birds darting in and out throughout the meadow, especially as they got closer to the village. It was hard to see them as they were so fast when they flew by.

Deborah started to name the different plants along their route. "That's cardinal flower, butterfly bush, trumpet vine, bee balm, salvia, and lilac. I know what these plants are for! The birds flying around us are black chinned hummingbirds! Aren't they beautiful, Ayden?"

"The flowers or the birds?" Ayden asked, a little confused.

"Both, of course," Deborah said excitedly. "Hummingbirds are fascinating. They take about two hundred and fifty breaths every minute. Their eggs are the size of a jelly bean, and they have to drink almost twice their weight in nectar each day."

"They drink with their little tongues. The beating of their wings at 50 times per second makes them look like a blur and is the reason it is hard to see what they look like. All of these flowers and plants are their feeding grounds, they love these plants. It's their nectar," Deborah scholarly informed everyone.

"If they have to fly so fast to live, I'll bet it's hard to talk to them, then," Ayden decided.

"Actually," Eleea stated, "It is kind of hard to understand them. You have to be patient when you talk with them. They are very excitable and full of energy. But they are intelligent and can be fun to be around. Look at it like talking to Elora times ten, and you will get the idea about how fast they talk."

"This community we will be entering soon, has taken on the responsibility to nurture and protect the hummingbirds of this region," Jerin explained. "People travel from great distances to watch the birds in their natural habitat. They believe there is some magical power the birds possess."

Deborah and Elora chatted back and forth about how wonderful the flowers smelled, and how cute the hummingbirds looked. The closer they got to civilization; Ayden felt surrounded by the birds.

They constantly dived in and around her, as if they knew her and were trying to talk to her. It was beginning to annoy her. Like a mosquito trying to land on her to suck the blood out of her, she had to continually, gently, bat them away. When they stopped to rest outside the village, she finally felt some relief as the birds flew off towards the town.

The sun was just beginning to set and the sky looked as beautiful as Eleea used to describe it to her. Brilliant pinks, yellows and purples playfully mixed with the bluish white clouds as they covered the horizon in vivid color.

She wanted to continue her daydreaming into the painted hues of the sky, but she noticed Tybin wanted their attention. Causing her to come back to the present.

Tybin quietly gestured to the group to mount their horses. Before Jerin took his place at the rear, he cautiously reminded them, "Act within the boundaries of Eshra culture, everyone."

Journal Nineteen

The greatest difference between Eshra and my world was technology. Eshra was old school. No electricity. No cars. No automatic anything.

I didn't really miss the convenience of my world, though. Maybe it was because I knew I would be back there, one day, and get to, once again, enjoy the niceties of technology.

It did make me curious, though. Did everyone in Eshra who got to travel to my world do it often?

How did the spiritual leader determine who got to come to my world? And, did they all enter the worlds the same way I did?

There were a lot of questions I wanted answered. But, like everything else I had learned while I was in Eshra; it's all about timing.

Watch and observe, first. You will eventually find out your answer. Just be patient.

Chapter Nineteen

Ayden noticed as they got closer and closer to the village the natural pathways Eleea had talked about while in East Glacier started to emerge. Flowers and grass swayed in unison, as if they glided out of their way when the horse's hooves touched the ground. A distinctive dirt path lay under the foliage and guided them in the direction to the village.

Turning to Eleea, Ayden asked, "How come, Eleea, the path is forming in front of us, when we haven't seen it do this in other parts of Eshra?"

"The hummingbirds, Ayden," Eleea began. "They have this deep mutual respect for all life here in Eshra. Maybe it is because they are so little. Or because, as many believe, they hold magical properties. All around this area, known as Sunbird Village, is directly linked to these birds."

"Legend holds the hummingbirds are the caretakers of the sun. So, it makes sense the sun is at its brightest and normal state closest to their home. And, it makes sense we would see the natural paths because of them and the sun," he concluded.

Ayden pondered Eleea's answer as they continued on course towards the village. "All these legends and lore" she confusingly thought.

"Prophecies and legends. Every damn one of them are vague and no one really knows an exact meaning about any of them! And! And! They want me to blindly follow them and fulfill something they have no idea about! This is absolutely crazy! Now! Now! I am stuck on this stupid path to stupidity! Crap! We are all doomed," she forlornly thought.

"Well," Ayden continued to think as she looked ahead, "there's not a lot I can do about it, now. There's the town. And, I don't want to be seen as a whiny moody brat for everyone else to feel bad about it, too. So, I'll just deal with it later. Besides, I've got plenty of time before the 'Eshra Plan' anyways," she convinced herself.

Entering the town, they saw several two-story homes, with quaint picket fences lining the main street of the entrance to the village. Signs, some hanging and others painted on the house fronts, were everywhere on the homes with art of hummingbirds and flowers.

All sorts of nectar feeders and flora covered the yards and porches. People and animal were walking the streets and working in their yards. No one seemed too concerned Ayden and her friends passed by them. Yet, they were all friendly when eye contact was made and they all acknowledged them in a nice manner.

Farther into the town, was what looked like the business district. Stores with wooden signs hanging from chain represented a bakery, an apothecary, linen and leather goods, a grocer, a blacksmith shop and a stable for the horses.

Finally, all the way at the end of the village was the Sunbird Inn, where they were to stay. Ayden, like all with her, were thankful they were able to stop and rest in comfort for almost two full days.

The stable hand took the travelers' horses as he said, "Good to see you boys again. Dinner at the inn tonight is one of your favorites," he smiled as he rubbed his stomach. The boys smiled back as they helped with the horses.

The keeper of the inn stood behind the bar and smiled as they entered the building and said, "Welcome, my name is Nora. Have a seat and I will bring you tonight's dinner. You can put everyone's belongings over by the stairs, Jerin and Tybin. It is so good to see you two again," she stated. The boys acknowledged her statement and took the bags to the stairs.

The inn was a rustic cabin design with a big open room for several wooden tables and chairs. A long single piece of a gigantic tree was cut in half to make up the bar counter, and measured over three fourths the length of the room with stools all along it.

The middle of the bar had waist height swinging doors to allow a person to come out from behind the counter.

Directly behind the counter opening was an entrance which led to another room. "Possibly the kitchen," Ayden thought as she could see steam coming from the area. Towards the far-right end of the room were two sets of winding stairs leading to the left and to the right.

Nora brought a big pot of chicken stew to the table with individual bowls. Everyone produced their designated utensils and properly blessed the meal.

The most delicious aroma of freshly baked bread Ayden had ever smelled accompanied the stew. Their drink was some type of sweet tasting, syrupy delight mixed with cool spring water. Fresh fruit with a dipping sauce of goat cheese, pomegranate and sweetened whipped cream finished off the meal.

After dinner, Tybin, Nick and Jerin went to grab the bags to carry up to their room when Nora said, "Before all of you retire for bed tonight, please join us back in the main room for some entertainment and snacks."

Everyone was to sleep in one large room, much like they did when they were in the wilderness; except for the nice fluffy individual beds to lie down on. The girls jumped onto their beds and tried to relax. But they were too full of excitement and wanted to go explore the town.

Jerin put a damper on their plans, stating, "It would be best to explore the village when it is daylight and not as dangerous." So, everyone opted to go downstairs for the night's entertainment.

The room was already full of people and animals when they arrived which caused them to have to break up and sit apart. Deborah went with Jerin, Phum, Elora and Nekoh while Ayden, Eleea, Nick and Tybin sat together.

Ayden sat next to Nora, who looked at her and said, "I would like you to meet my dear friend, Callie. She has lived here for over ninety years."

Ayden reached her hand out to shake Callie's. As she did, Callie would not give her hand back. Holding it in her two hands, Callie said "You, my child, who are you?"

"I am Ayden from the glacier clan and this is my brother Tybin and my cousin Nick and my sister Deborah and Jerin, my other brother, are over there," Ayden said before she could even think about what she was saying. She sensed this fear to protect and blurted out the information.

"I do not get the sense you are from this clan," Callie insisted.

Tybin looked at Ayden, smiled, and then looked at Callie, and stated, "Our family comes from a distant glacier clan which has almost disappeared. This is what you are probably sensing."

"Maybe you are right," Callie said unconvincingly as she let go of Ayden's hand.

Ayden sighed with relief as several men and women came in with their instruments and broke up the interrogation.

Before the music started, Ayden quickly went over to Deborah and whispered in her ear, "If anyone asks, you are my sister, Nick is our cousin, and the boys are our brothers, tell Jerin and the others," she said and grabbed Deborah's forearm to secretly shake, as they looked at each other.

Ayden sat back down with her group, but could not even hear the music. She was in such a whirlwind of emotions, full of fear they may have compromised the mission, already. All she wanted to do was go upstairs and forget about having to interact with anyone but those close to her.

Tybin took her hand in his and patted it, silently telling her everything was going to be OK. But she still felt like all eyes were on her, yelling at her saying she was a phony.

After the music, Ayden slowly worked her way up the stairs, trying to stay under the radar of those around her. She almost made it too.

Until a mountain lion sitting at the top of the stairs said, "Ayden sit with me for a few minutes, will you."

"How do you know my name," Ayden asked, startled.

"I am Joshua, and I am a prophet," he said. "I saw you coming in my dreams last week, Ayden."

"Please, do not tell anyone you know me," Ayden pleaded.

"Do not be afraid, Young One," Joshua soothingly told her. "It is a great honor for me to meet you. And, to spend time with you. Your secret is safe with me."

"What is my secret, really?" Ayden asked. "I mean I know what we are going to do, kinda, but do you have a deeper understanding of what I am all about?"

"Young One, because of you, we live," Joshua spoke with authority. He then intently looked off, as if he was reading something written in the air and said,

'Surrounded by dead limbs and bones, deep from the bowels will rise the crane.

Sing, child. Sing with joy, sing with fear, sing to hear the stars respond,' Joshua finished.

"Joshua, what does that mean? I am totally confused," Ayden frustratingly expressed.

"It means when the time is right you will completely understand the words spoken tonight. And, you will take action when needed and you will succeed," Joshua said as he took Ayden's chin in his paw and smiled at her with his eyes. "Just know I am very proud of you, and I have the greatest respect for you, Young One," "We will meet again, Ayden," Joshua said as he stood up, stretched, and walked away.

The rest of Ayden's group headed up the stairs, laughing and talking; totally unaware Ayden had spoken to Joshua. Deborah grabbed Ayden's hand, pulled her up to walk with her and said, "Wasn't it fun, 'A'? All of the music and food and the people and animals all talking and enjoying everything? It was a great night!" Deborah cried with glee.

Ayden smiled back at her and followed her into their room. Everyone busied themselves with their nightly rituals.

Ayden deliberately let all of them go before her. Once the room started to settle in their perspective sleeping areas, Ayden took her backpack and slipped into the bathroom down the hall. She locked the door and sat on the floor.

Her breath began to become heavy as she pulled the chain with the sterling silver locket on it out from under her blouse and, then, looked at her backpack. Quietly, she slowly unsnapped the pocket to reveal the locket from her mom.

She put the necklace locket next to it. This was the first time she had seen the two pieces together. There was no mistake, the artist who made them was one in the same. "How," she thought, "how could it be true? And, more importantly, what did it mean?"

Tears pooled in her eyes, refusing to drop down. She sat and tried to stare through the tears at the two lockets as she rubbed their beautifully etched skin.

Finally, the pressure of more tears caused the buildup to flow down her face. She took her right arm sleeve and swiped it across her eyes and face to clean herself. Ayden loosened the locket from her backpack and placed it on the chain with the other one.

She moved to the mirror and stood and stared again. This time in shock. The lockets were opposite of each other, not the same shape one would have thought them to be. They formed a perfect set of wings. Lightly she ran her fingers across their profiles, while she felt the splendor of their presence on her neck.

Jolted back to reality by Deborah knocking on the door, she rapidly hid the chain and lockets under her blouse and responded. "I'm almost done, 'D'." Ayden stepped out and looped Deborah's arm in hers and said, "Let's get to bed so we can wake early and explore this town."

They nestled into the wonderful down blankets and pillows and drifted off to sleep with the windows open. The night air lazily breezed in and brought all of the smells of lilac and pine, mixed with all of the other flowers the hummingbirds enjoyed.

Everyone woke rested after sleeping in a bed rather than a forest floor. Tybin set the pace for all to refresh with a bath before allowed to head out on their adventures for the day.

Ayden and Deborah voted to go shopping right away. Their first stop was to be the apothecary store. But they were shot down by Jerin and Tybin.

"Before all of us go, there is a small thing called breakfast downstairs," Tybin stated. "I am not going to shop and explore without food. Plus, did you two forget you need coin to shop?"

"Well, maybe we could barter," Deborah started to dig through her bags. "What can we use, Ayden? What do you have in your bag?"

"You don't need to barter," Jerin said. "Gethsemane gave us silver and gold coins for both of you. He knew you were girls, first, and your hearts were meant to shop. He prepared Tybin and I," He slyly smiled.

"OH! That is so not cool," Deborah argued. "Just because we are girls doesn't mean we only need to shop. And, I bet you two like new things too! It's not just a girl thing."

Jerin and Tybin laughed at them as Jerin reached into his bag and produced the coins.

"You're right, Deborah," Tybin consoled her, "We like to shop too. We were just having fun with you. But we eat first."

"Wait! Before we go downstairs, I have a question," Ayden stated. "How come we have not had to buy anything until now? I mean, I thought everything was on barter and exchange here in Eshra?"

"Yes and no," Nekoh began to explain. "Yes, in the fact most everything is an exchange of goods through equal work or wares. No, in the reality of towns which are tourist attractions like this one. Here the exchange of goods and work do not help as the people do not stay long enough to be able to exchange."

"Although, some do bring in items for trade from their homelands. If a person wished to have coin instead of trade, they are free to ask for it. All who live in Eshra have coin, but do not value it like those who are from your world, Ayden," Nekoh concluded.

The smells of breakfast wafted up to their room as Ayden smiled at Nekoh when he finished answering her question. The girls concurred with the boys' breakfast was definitely the first order of business on their day's agenda.

It was a wonderful morning as they sat around the big tables and enjoyed all of the food Nora had prepared for them. Eggs, bacon, homemade jams and biscuits, fresh fruit and squeezed orange juice, and even honey butter.

Ayden glanced around the room, while eating, and realized it was just the most peaceful little town. It was obvious people and animal everywhere showed delight in their meal by the constant laughter and excited talk throughout the inn.

Jerin stood and stated, "Let's get movin' crew; time's a wastin', with a whole town waiting to be conquered with things to buy."

The girls ran upstairs to get their money and to make sure they looked nice for everyone on the streets to see them. Eleea and Nekoh choose to stay back at the inn while the others explored.

Deborah was beyond excited as they walked down the street to the apothecary. Entering the store was like going back in time. Rows and rows of old-fashioned jars and boxes with herbs, dried plants, and candy in them. Mortar and pestles of all sizes and design were everywhere, along with books, plants and other gifts.

As Deborah spoke to the store clerk, Ayden noticed a small box containing several empty small glass bottles. Attached to it was a ball of twine, and other needed supplies to gather herbs, mix them, and even small pots with a stand to put the pots on the fire to heat ingredients when needed. She decided to buy it for Deborah as a gift for her birthday, which was just around the corner.

Deborah asked the clerk about a box with a plant she had not seen before. "This houses a plant called buffalo ear," the worker said as she opened the drawer of the box. "It helps heal broken bones when mixed with gopher weed and silver grass," she explained.

"And," she continued, "ancient people once said a plant known as snail fern, which does not exist anymore, could be mixed with all of these ingredients to make an elixir which could cause anything to grow exponentially larger than normal size," she finished.

Deborah bought several different types of dried plants and herbs, a couple of books, and a tethered bound field manual showing hundreds of different kinds of plants. She walked out of the store joyfully happy with her purchases. "Where next?" she asked with glee.

"I want to go to the grocer's," Ayden quickly said before anyone else had an idea. "I want to get some apples and pomegranates to take with us when we leave here."

The grocer was a bubbly older woman with cats and kittens all around her. She had baskets full of vegetables and fruit displayed throughout the store; plus, dried vegetables, fruits, and nuts to snack on.

There were potted plants for the hummingbirds. And several other types of gifts like crane and hummingbird banners, hummingbird nectar containers, pottery dishes and mugs. As well as, beautifully made small stuffed animals of foxes, cranes, bears, wolves and hummingbirds.

Deborah and Jerin spent most of their time talking with the grocer who was full of laughter and chatter. Ayden, Elora, Nick and Tybin sat with the kittens while the others talked. One tiny kitten, the runt of the litter, kept climbing into Ayden's lap and using her little finger like a pacifier.

Every time Ayden tried to get her to go back to her mother, she would meow incessantly until she found her way back to Ayden. Finally, Ayden picked the kitten up and walked around with her while she picked out items to buy. Tybin held the basket for Ayden, so she could put the items into it.

After Ayden made her purchases the grocer looked at her and said, "You know, animals have a sixth sense about people. They know when to have fear or when to feel safe. This kitten has made a very unique connection with you, she feels safe in your presence. I would like to give her to you, as a gift from me."

Ayden looked at Tybin and Jerin to see their reaction to this news. Jerin answered by saying, "A gift is a gift and it should not be taken lightly. For whatever reason, the only honorable thing to do, is to accept the gift."

Ayden turned back to the owner, asking, "Isn't she too little to leave her mother, though?"

"No, she is beyond her mother's milk. She seems needy because of her size. The others usually pick on her because she is tiny and can't defend herself. It would be a better life for her if she was taken care of by you and your friends," the store owner said.

"Well then," Ayden decided, "It is our privilege to take this little one with us, and I thank you for your kindness. What is her name? And, are you sure we can't pay you for her?"

"Animals are generally not bought, here. An animal who is young can be given by a parent or guardian or when old enough make their own decision about where they choose to live," the owner said in a troubled voice. "And, she has no name yet as we did not feel she would live long," the woman concluded as she eyed Ayden with suspicion.

Jerin quickly stepped in and said, "The only reason we asked about payment is you said she was a gift. All of us know animals make their own choice. We just thought because she is looked at as a gift then maybe the mother owed a debt to you and therefore was here until she payed you back. And, this way we could help to loosen the burden of this debt by paying you."

"Oh, yes," the owner said, "That makes perfect sense why you thought you should pay for her. And, no there is no debt. Her mother and I felt since she had so quickly become attached to this young girl, the only right thing would be to let the kitten go where she wanted and give her as a companion to her and the rest of you."

Ayden knew she had just messed up big time. She had almost given this person a reason to question who she and Deborah were; as well as the boys, too.

If Jerin had not jumped in and rescued her, she would have caused all of them to be in danger. All she wanted to do now was get out of the store and go back to the inn before she jeopardized them anymore.

Journal Twenty

We, Deborah and I, were thrust into this crazy world of animals who could talk to people. As a young child, how many times did I fantasize about being able to talk to animals? Now, it was real. Their personalities were no different than ours, really. They cried, got angry, laughed and had fear. It was fun being around them.

Nekoh and Phum were the most animated of the group. Well, I guess you could put Elora in this mix. But Elora was innocent; she didn't hide her feelings. She just told it like it was.

Nekoh and Phum tried to pull off they were 'adult-like' and had no need for childlike behavior.

Jazing was not an adult word, though. It proved to me Phum had a lot he was trying to hide. He had childish awe over learning new things. Behind his important demeanor was a little kid excited to see everything new.

Nekoh, just by his cat nature, was full of curiosity. Most of the time he tried to hide it. He always was playing with something. He'd bat it with his paw and watch as it moved out of range and then he'd pounce on it and do it all over again.

His tufted ears and black tipped tail exuded cuteness. Then you had his whitish hair under his chin which looked like a beard and made him look wise. His markings were a gorgeous golden brown and white.

Actually, his fur looked a lot like Deborah's hair. No wonder those two have bonded, they were like twins.

Anyways, all of the animals we got to meet, talk to and watch throughout Eshra gave Deborah and I insight into animal behavior.

Something we could have never experienced in our world. It was only one of the many blessings we received while we traveled this land called Eshra.

Chapter Twenty

On the way, back from the grocer, it was decided all of them would rest for the afternoon. And then, they would join everyone downstairs for dinner as evening approached.

Ayden was still troubled over her misstep at the grocer's, and was quiet while the rest of them talked aimlessly. She took two of the cloth bags from her purchases at the grocer and started to make a sling out of them to carry the little kitten in front of her.

Deborah asked, "What are you going to name her Ayden?"

"I don't know, 'D'," Ayden stated. "Maybe we should watch her personality for a while and see if she comes up with her own name through her actions? She just seems so tiny to be away from her mom, doesn't she?"

"Yeah, she is very small," Deborah agreed. "But look at her beauty. She looks like a tortoiseshell brooch with swirls of orange, brown, black, and yellow. Yet, she has very distinct black markings from the bridge of her nose to her eyes that almost look like feathers or whiskers all along her whole face," Deborah concluded.

Ayden finished her sling and tested it for comfort by fitting it on both her and the kitten. Laying down, she stroked the kitten until they both drifted off to sleep.

Jerin and Tybin left them to rest while Eleea followed the boys out of the room. Soon, the rest of them were asleep as the morning's excitement overcame them.

Nick was the first to wake and sound the call they needed to prepare for dinner. "By my calculation the sun should set in about twenty minutes and we will be considered rudely late for dinner if we don't hurry," he stated.

Nekoh decided to stay in the room with the kitten while everyone met the others to eat. He liked the kitten, but he had an uneasy feeling about her and didn't want to leave her alone.

"Maybe, it is because she is so little and needy," he thought to himself, "maybe this is why I am annoyed with her."

The kitten fell asleep lying next to Nekoh, and he was happy he too could lazily sleep the evening away. All this traveling had made him a little grumpy. He was a cat and cats love to sleep.

Nekoh felt like he hadn't even hardly slept when he heard noise coming from the end of Deborah's bed. Groggily he opened one eye to see what the noise was all about.

And, there she was, his little annoyance, rummaging through Deborah's bag from the apothecary. She was rolling around and acting kind of goofy, he thought as he watched her.

"Hey! Little one, what are you doing," he questioned her.

She popped her head out of the bag and her muzzle was full of dried leaves. Her eyes crossed as she tried to eat the leaves off her chin. She looked at Nekoh and kept falling over each time she tried to use her paw to clean her face.

"OK," Nekoh said as he walked towards her, "What have you gotten yourself into." He started to lick her face to clean it for her. The more he cleaned her, the more excited he got.

"This is catnip," he declared. He took his paw and dragged the catnip bag out and started eating it and rolling in it.

The whole contents ended up emptied on Deborah's bed with both of them sliding along the covers like they were doing swimming strokes in a pool.

Deborah and Ayden walked in to find Nekoh dangling over the bed and the kitten sitting on his hind legs. Both of them looked drunk and seemed to be smiling with their eyes barely open slits.

Deborah noticed immediately the catnip bag had been discovered, and stated, "'A', they found the catnip." Both girls burst into laughter as they looked at the cats sprawled out in pleasure.

Jerin, Nick, and Tybin, Eleea and Elora entered the room, and looked confused when they saw the animals. Deborah explained the problem, and they too began to laugh at the sight.

Nekoh tried to regain his composure as he quickly sat up, stating, "OK, OK I, I was just trying to clean up the kitten who found the catnip. It's not my, my, my fault all of it is strewn all over Deborah's bed."

Deborah assuredly said, "Nekoh it is no problem. I bought the nip especially for you to enjoy. How you decided to use it, is totally up to you."

Through their laughter, Ayden said, "That's her name, 'D', it is Nip. Because she got into the catnip."

Nekoh, in his drunken catnip stupor continued to try and plead his case, stating, "This little annoyance. She is a total annoyance, Deborah. She is the one who wasted every bit of my catnip in one swoop. I tried to stop her, really, you have got to believe meeeee," he meowed long and loud.

Deborah tried desperately to comfort Nekoh and help him regain his dignity as she cleaned up her bed from the residual catnip.

"It's OK, Nekoh," she soothingly calmed him as she scratched his head. "You just go back to sleep for a while, my precious Nekoh. We're gonna go down and enjoy the music and snacks. And, you just need to sleep and rest for a while," she comfortingly said.

As Deborah talked to Nekoh, everybody quietly started to leave the room to avoid him feeling anymore embarrassed.

"Here, Nekoh," Deborah stated. "I also bought fresh catnip for you. How about I place it in your apothecary bag you received for our journey? That way you can keep it fresh and away from Nip," Deborah concluded.

Ayden grabbed Nip and put her in the sling so Nekoh could have some peace. She insisted they wait for Deborah outside, so they could all sit together this time for the entertainment. She wanted no more chances for close calls of exposure of being found out.

When they got downstairs, she placed herself in the middle of the group. She kept Nip quiet in her sling by using her pinky as a pacifier. Since they were early, they had time to visit with each other.

Soon, Joshua came up beside Ayden and nodded. "My name is Joshua he told the group. I have brought my friend Callie to talk with you. I believe the two of you have already met?" He stated as he looked at Ayden. "I want her to tell you about the hummingbirds and how important they are to our world."

Deborah stood up and repositioned herself next to Ayden and intently prepared herself to listen to Joshua. "I knew there was something important about them, and why they are protected in this village," she stated.

"Yes," Joshua responded. "These little birds have a history, and a special place in the hearts of those who live in this town. But, let me stop and give Callie the chance to explain what I am talking about."

Callie looked at the girls, sat down in a chair in front of them and began.

"There was a time when this world was young. The moon was home to the Great Crane who watched over the night. And the sun was bright with the Great Red Fox residing in it.

The land was formed in its brilliance because they stood guard over the world. Each was needed to keep the sun and moon in the sky for every living thing to survive.

Majesty and glory reigned in their presence." She stopped to allow her words to take hold in the girls' hearts.

"There needed to be a connection between the night and the day," Callie continued. *"A thread which tied the two together.*

The Great Crane and the Great Red Fox pondered many days on what they needed to do to keep their world united, as one. Many animals offered their suggestions on what it should be."

The wolf said, "I am fast and strong. My image would fit beautifully in the shadow of the moon. Go hummingbirds and tell the crane and fox, I accept their decision to choose me."

The antelope said, "I am faster than the wolf. My whole realm is the great plains where the sun rests beautifully on my sleek body. Go hummingbirds and tell the crane and fox, I accept their decision to choose me."

The great horned owl said, "I have more intelligence and power than either the wolf or the antelope. I rule the night air and own the day air. Go hummingbirds and tell the crane and fox, I accept their decision to choose me."

"Nothing suggested held the power or the source the Great Crane and the Great Red Fox knew they needed."

"Finally, the Great Crane turned to the Great Red Fox and said, "Truly, we have been wrong in where we have looked, Dear Fox. What friends have been the most faithful and humble in this whole search?"

"The Great Red Fox replied, "You are so right my good Crane. There is only one true choice. They have traveled great distances to speak to each of us. And, never once lost their energy to accomplish what was asked of them."

"Then it is settled." the Great Crane said. He turned to the hummingbirds to say, "It is clear to Fox and I; you alone can handle this great responsibility for the day and night."

"You will be our binding thread and become the stars."

"In the day, you will rest in the sky with the Great Red Fox and the sun. And, at night you will shine brightly with me and the moon."

Callie explained, "The hummingbirds, in their humble desire to help and not call attention to themselves became the stars in the sky. Always beating their wings to show forth their light. Always looking down on those who live in this world."

Deborah and Ayden sat in awe at what they had just heard. "No wonder," Ayden thought, "this town took such pride in nurturing the hummingbirds. They were the missing connection between the night and day. They kept the world in balance."

"What a wonderful lore," Deborah said to break the silence, while she rubbed Nekoh's neck, who had sauntered up to join them before Callie had started the story.

Ayden nodded her head in agreement as she readjusted the kitten in the sling.

Callie watched as the kitten snuggled to get comfortable. "May I see your new little one?" she asked.

Ayden handed the kitten to Callie, who examined the kitten's whole body with a concerned look on her face. "Will you and Deborah come with me," Callie urgently asked the girls.

Callie led the girls to the kitchen of the inn, as Joshua, Eleea, Elora and Nekoh followed behind. With precision, Callie pulled together several ingredients from different drawers and glass bottles. Placing all of the contents in a large pot of water she brought them to a boil.

Callie turned to Eleea and said, Go, find Errol and tell him we need the powder. Callie then turned to the girls and asked them to tell her the whole story of how they received the kitten. She, then, asked the girls if they noticed anything peculiar about the kitten.

"Well, she is overly needy and quiet; she hasn't talked to us. She only meows," Ayden said as she looked at Deborah worriedly.

Both girls sensed Callie was upset, maybe even angry, and they did not know how to react to her.

The mixture in the pot steeped together into a thick mush, where Callie then put all of it into the sink filled with cool water. She took the kitten from Ayden and put her in the sink.

She rubbed her down with the mixture, making sure every part of her body was covered. Gently she started to rinse her off and soothed her with cooing words.

Once she was completely cleaned from all of the cooked substance Callie turned to the girls. Saying, "Now, she will be able to live a happy life with you. There was dark magic on her. A film, if you will, which caused her to be muted and it arrested her development. It was literally killing her. This type of magic is used to secretly gain information."

She took a dry towel and rubbed the kitten as she spoke. "From the film, they are able to hear and see everything this kitten can hear and see. Once they acquired the information which they needed from her, she would have been left to die. Because she was so young, she did not know what was happening to her when they covered her in the magic," Callie said as she tenderly dried the kitten.

Both girls welled up with tears while they petted Nip. Ayden turned to Joshua and Nekoh saying, "We were in real danger, weren't we?"

"Yes," Nekoh began, "I am sorry I did not catch why I was troubled with her, earlier. I should have researched my feelings for why I was feeling annoyed with her."

"Not many can see this magic, Nekoh," Joshua consoled him. "I knew something was wrong with the kitten when Ayden brought her into the inn. Even I did not know what we were dealing with."

"This is why I had Callie talk to the girls. I had already consulted with her and our alchemist, Errol, about what I suspected. I needed her to be close to the kitten to discern what magic surrounded her," Joshua stated.

Eleea returned with Errol, where Callie then asked, "Eleea would you go tell Jerin, Tybin and Nickalli what has happened. And, would you also have them gather the items bought at the grocers. Thank you, Eleea."

Soon, Jerin, Nick and Tybin came into the kitchen with Ayden's last bag she had purchased from the grocery store. Callie opened the bag and took out the apples, pomegranates, nuts and the little stuffed animals Ayden had bought and put them in the sink. She took the bags made into a sling for Nip and the bag which contained the food and gifts and put them in the sink.

Callie looked at Ayden and said, "All of these things have been strategically planted on you in the hopes one of them would kill you. If at any time one of these items would have gotten wet from your spittle while you ate it or used it, it would have poisoned you," she commandingly said. "Anyone around you would have been totally puzzled by what caused you to die as it would have disappeared immediately after you got it wet."

"And, if another would have mistakenly eaten or used it, they too could have died," she gravely continued as she opened the inside of the bag. "See this bluish tint shimmering in the light?" She explained to them. "It is the poison placed inside the bags and it covered everything you bought," Callie stated.

Errol stepped to the sink, pulled out a small bag of powder, he took a pinch in his fingers, and sprinkled it on everything in the sink and then spit in the sink. Within seconds of the powder touching all of the objects began to burn and magically disappear.

Ayden slumped into a chair at the kitchen table. "What about the things I bought at the apothecary, are they full of poison too?" She asked.

"No. Only the grocer and her friends are involved in this endeavor. This is Errol, he owns the apothecary and he would never fall prey to an evil scheme like this one. He is a good man," Callie concluded.

"Matter of fact, he is the one who mixed the powder for us. The powder neutralized the poison so when it went up in flames none of us would breath it in and die," she finished.

"How come the kitten or I didn't die when she was in the sling? I mean, she used my finger as a pacifier, and it was full of spit," Ayden asked in a perplexed voice.

"This magic required human saliva and not animal. They sent the kitten as a ruse to gain information, and knew they could not hinder receiving the information by an animal's accidental spit. This was planned with great detail and care for success," Callie perceptively stated.

"What about my clothes and my hands. Or even the bedspread where Nip was sleeping?" Ayden asked. "Won't they also have poisonous residue on them, too?"

"Errol has determined there was not enough poison on those items to give you harm," Callie stated. "Plus, this poison cannot be exposed to open air and light. The darkness of the bags was needed to set its properties in action."

"Generally, the nonfood items would not have caused you any problem, but we decided to destroy it all just in case. The food items in the bag would have absorbed the poison and set their plan into motion. Yet, for all to be safe, Nora has already sent workers to clean your room and linen," Callie concluded.

"Now, what will happen to them since they have been found out?" Deborah asked.

Joshua spoke up, saying, "Sentries have already been sent to the store and are all around the perimeter of the building, standing guard. They will not be able to do any more harm to anyone."

"The Council has sent men to take care of this problem and it will no longer compromise anyone in this community. The moment you brought the kitten to the inn, Eleea and I have been working on making sure all of us are safe," Joshua concluded.

Eleea looked at Ayden and said, "Child, the eyes are the window to the soul. When I saw the kitten's eyes at the grocer's, I knew she was deeply troubled within her soul, as her eyes were distant and confused."

"She sensed the good in you and in her own way was crying out for help. She just didn't know what was going on or why she needed you. Even though they meant her for evil, she had no concept of their plan," Eleea continued.

"It was their work to use her to get close to you for surveillance. But it was totally her innocence to cling to you. She was oppressed and her soul showed it. She was desperately trying to survive her circumstances, and saw her chance with you. I am sure she was probably abused daily, and was just trying to live. You were her freedom, her hope," he sadly stated.

"Not only did I sense her struggle, I also sensed the presence of evil in the store. My heart told me the whole curious question about the gift was the woman trying to trip you up so she could cause discord amongst this community and us." Eleea revealed.

"She would have gossiped about you and tried to have those around her doubt your sincerity of being on an enlightenment journey. Plus, the whole curious thing of the kitten not having a name and they suspected she would die and not need one was confirmation, for me, she was being used for evil." Eleea finished.

"But I thought you were staying back with Nekoh this morning, Eleea?" Deborah questioned.

"Yes, this was my original plan, Deborah. My heart was heavy with concern. I could not shake this feeling of evil around us," Eleea expressed.

"To better understand it, I decided to privately speak with Phum so he and I could observe the people and town more closely. As soon as we knew about the grocer, Phum was sent to meet with the Council. Riding on the wings of the red-tailed hawk, one of our fastest allies, he has already returned to us from his mission," Eleea stated.

"All of what has happened today has the signature of Choran on it," Joshua proclaimed.

"Wait, we have to go and fight this Choran at the Dead Trees. It would seem this little adventure of ours has taken a turn for the deadly," Deborah expressed in a fearful voice.

"I'm with Deborah on this," Ayden stated, as Elora flew to her shoulder and hid her head in Ayden's hair. "We are going straight into the lion's lair. And this lair is full of evil. This is definitely scarier than either Deborah or I imagined it would be."

"You are not going into this alone, remember," Tybin reminded the girls. "Fear is a natural reaction to any unknown situation; especially something like this. But, both of you have been trained, as well as Jerin's and my training. And, I include Eleea, Nekoh, Phum, Nickalli and Elora who have also been trained," Tybin continued.

"Do not look at the negatives or at what could have happened today. We were given protection when it was needed. Go into this with the attitude there are greater forces out there which will protect all of us. Use your skills and trust your heart to take you through this," Jerin reassured them.

"Ayden and Deborah," Joshua said as he started to address their concerns, "Yes, there is evil all around. Yes, it is scary. And, yes, there is great unknown about what will happen as you continue your journey."

"But, to choose to go through life in fear, is to live no life at all. Stunted by doubt and fear will only make you bitter. Bitter you never tried, or trusted or believed in yourself to take a leap of faith. Bitter will eat at you and destroy you from the inside out. Each day you live, is a day of unknown. For, do we really know what will truly happen in any minute we have not yet lived?" Joshua asked them.

"I ask you, Deborah and Ayden, which path do your hearts tell you to follow?" Joshua beseeched them. "The one which stops you in fear...or the one which embraces you as you rise to the call of the Great Crane?" Joshua humbly finished.

Ayden firmly looked at Joshua and then panned to the rest of them as their eyes fixed on her, and said, "I have no great words of wisdom to speak, here. All I know, is I am scared. I don't like all of this evil at every turn wanting to kill me or my friends."

"Even though I have great, I mean great fear, I do not want to stop in it and wallow in self-pity. My heart tells me I will continue with the strength of everyone who goes with me," Ayden sighed deeply as she turned to look at Deborah.

Deborah immediately nodded in agreement as their eyes locked on each other. Simultaneously they both grasped each other's arms in their familiar handshake.

Ayden turned to look at Eleea, saying, "I do have a request, though. A request for all of you," she said as she looked at Deborah and Nick.

"It is exhausting to me, emotionally I mean, because there is always someone who has to keep secrets from me. Or secrets from Deborah, Elora and Nick. The four of us deserve your respect and the truth," Ayden declared.

"None of us knew about the grocer. It could have been very real with death happening. You, all of you," Ayden expressed as she swept the room with her hand, "felt fear about the grocer but left us in the dark. This time it turned out to our advantage. But, what about the next time? It could be life or death with death prevailing. Seriously, it is time to stop keeping secrets," Ayden finished with determination.

Eleea, Nekoh, Phum, Jerin, Tybin and Joshua nodded their heads in agreement to Ayden's request.

"Everything is well, right now," Callie encouraged them. "Let's not dwell on fear and let it consume us. Everything will work towards good, girls. We need to stay focused on the present and not the what ifs of fear."

"And, yes, it is time for all of you to be completely upfront and honest with each other. Now, let's rest our minds and our hearts by joining everyone for tonight's entertainment and snacks," Callie finished.

The resolved group shook their heads in agreement and filed out of the kitchen and joined the inn's guests for the night's activities.

Journal Twenty-One

Our little group of mix and match personalities was finally becoming a cohesive unit. We watched out for each other. We learned about each other through how we reacted to things.

We enjoyed each other's company.

I no longer felt I was looked at with reverence. I felt like I belonged as a part of a team; with the same goal.

The freedom to not be looked at as special was exhilarating. Yes, there were still statements made about me as 'the one,' but, it was different than before. I didn't feel the burden of having to carry it by myself.

Everyone with me, helped me carry it. The burden had become bearable.

I knew I had a lot, still, to learn and experience through this journey; but I no longer felt alone. Everyone with me was also learning and experiencing the same things I was. We had finally become a team of friends.

And, more importantly, like Deborah had told me about the poet Maya Angelou: We had become a family.

Chapter Twenty-One

Ayden lazily looked around early the next morning. Jerin and Nick had left to get the horses, Tybin was off with Eleea to settle their inn bill, and the girls were left to themselves in the room.

Nekoh was curled up tight next to Deborah's legs, asleep. Nip was sleeping at the top of Ayden's pillow. She seemed to be less needy, but still stayed very close to Ayden.

"Their journey to destiny had become a lot more intense now," she thought as she gently woke Deborah and the rest to tell them it was time to pack.

Tybin walked into the room saying, "We are ready girls. It's time to go."

Lok and Tari followed him into the room, apparently excited to be traveling again.

"Where have Lok and Tari been?" Ayden asked. "I have not seen them since yesterday afternoon?"

"Once we realized the danger of the store, it was decided to send them ahead to listen for news in the woods. To see if any danger was nearby. We, now, begin to trek into the unknown. Extra caution has got to be taken for all of us to succeed." Tybin warily stated.

Nekoh decided to check on his fresh catnip before he left the room. "Just to make sure Nip didn't get into it," he said to himself.

When he opened the bag, and saw it, he was slightly surprised. Turning to Deborah, he stated, "Look, Deborah. This pocket you put my catnip in has immediately dried it!" He exclaimed.

Deborah came over to Nekoh's bag and looked at its contents. "Well, isn't this a cool trick of the bag, Nekoh?" She said with excitement. "I love Eshra magic," she expressed with glee as she rubbed the top of Nekoh's head.

Everyone went downstairs to eat breakfast before they continued their journey. Their table was full with Joshua, Callie, Errol, and Nora joining them. Mostly, it was light conversation during the meal, interspersed with some elderly advice for all of them to stay careful and guarded.

Callie nudged Ayden with her elbow, causing Ayden to look at her. With a twinkle in her eye, she said, "One day, Ayden, these three," she gestured to Tybin Jerin and Nick, "will mean more to you than just brothers and a cousin."

"I'm sorry, Callie, for lying to you," Ayden said.

"No, no, no," Callie began, "Do not apologize for protecting yourself and your friends. You did not know me, and it is always more important to protect yourself from strangers."

"People who you do not know may not have your best interests in mind. Never divulge a lot of information about yourself or anyone you love to a stranger, ever. The next time you are presented with a conflict like this, tell the person you are not comfortable talking about personal information, then you can avoid lying," Callie instructed her.

Eleea flew to Ayden's shoulder saying, "It's time to go, Ayden."

Callie hugged Ayden and then pulled a bunched-up piece of tie-dyed tan, brown, off white, and turquoise cloth from her bag which was sitting next to her.

"For Nip," she stated, "I'm sure she will appreciate resting next to your body while traveling."

Ayden took the cloth and examined it. She smiled at Callie saying, "A new sling, and it is way more beautiful than the one I tried to make. Thank you so much Callie."

Ayden hugged her again, and then placed the sling over her neck and arranged it to fit comfortably before placing Nip inside it.

Errol walked out with Deborah, and handed her a small cloth pouch with drawstrings. "This is the same powder we used yesterday," he stated. "Use it sparingly, and only when absolutely necessary. It is designed to neutralize any poisonous substance, making it harmless. But whatever you use it on, it will cause everything it touches to disappear." Deborah nodded her head in understanding as she placed the pouch in her pants pocket.

With the last good-byes spoken and everyone mounted, ready to ride, Nora left the inn porch and handed two small baskets to Jerin. "A small meal for all of you, and good apples, nuts, and pomegranates for a treat," she said as she smiled at Ayden.

Leaving was a bit difficult for the girls. They truly enjoyed spending time in this comfortable little town and they knew by leaving it they were going towards many more uncomfortable situations.

Their journey would take them over the last mountain ranges and into the valley where the Dead Trees stood. It would take two days to cross the mountains before they could begin the trek down into the valley. And then, another day and a half before they would, only, be near the Dead Trees.

Errol and another man had spoken extensively with the boys, Phum, and Eleea the night before, after the entertainment. Their knowledge of the area past their town was instrumental for the caravan to be able to travel in, somewhat, safety.

Once again, their movement was methodic and quiet as the air became noticeably thinner each step they climbed. Ayden reflected on all that had taken place since they entered Eshra while they silently rode.

Her child-like mind had no understanding of what she would experience before Eshra. And, now it seemed to her she had lived twenty years in three months with the knowledge and the daily life happenings which had taken place.

From being just a young child when she entered Eshra, she was now a grown young woman, and a warrior. She was a wanted person by those who worked evil, a friend to several new people and animals, and she no longer saw her life as a child looking to gain selfish pleasure. She could never go back to childhood, she had crossed over, at fourteen, into adulthood.

"I really thought I had become an adult when my mom died," she thought. "Brother, I had no idea what it was to be an adult. Even now, I question myself if I am aware of what it is to be a true adult. I'm just a child, even if I don't feel like one," she frantically said to herself.

While she was thinking, she watched Tybin. "Curious," she pondered, "he's standing up on his horse. What is he trying to do? Be a trick rider," she questioned.

Suddenly, he grabbed an overhanging tree limb on the side of the trail and lifted himself up and swung around it with lightning-like speed. From the momentum of the swing, he propelled to the next tree.

Standing on the limb, he darted to a higher outer limb and grabbed something. With ease, he jumped from limb to limb until he had reached the ground; all with the use of only one hand.

In his other hand, he held a furry small animal. He had a tight hold of him by the back of his neck, and the animal was fighting with all his might to try and free himself from the grip.

"If it wasn't so scary to watch, it would have been hilarious to see the raccoon try to get away," Ayden thought.

"What the heck, Tybin! Why did you ambush this poor little thing," Ayden asked?

Everybody else stopped frozen by the event, except Jerin. He jumped off his horse, and with blade in hand went to Tybin's aid.

"Let me go, you fool, and get that knife away from my throat. You are both madmen and you don't know who you are messing with," the little guy said as he tried to get loose with his legs dangling and paws clawing the air.

"Reveal who you are," Jerin yelled as he held the knife to the animal's throat.

Phum jumped to Jerin's free shoulder with both his knives unsheathed, ready to help where needed.

"Oh-h-h-h big boy, you think you know me? You think you have me where you want me? Watch this, you silly boys!" The raccoon impatiently yelled as he began a low-pitched whistle, followed by a high-pitched whistle. All around them the trees rustled with activity, and little noises of "hut, hut, hut."

Jerin and Tybin were surrounded by seven raccoons. Each stood poised with a weapon, ready to take action to help their comrade.

Everyone was baffled by how quickly everything had escalated to a serious and potentially harmful situation. Eleea and Nekoh stepped in and began to negotiate with the raccoons.

"Whoa, whoa, whoa," Nekoh started.

"Now let's all stay calm and sort this out," Eleea chimed in.

"How about we let this little guy down, Tybin?" Nekoh continued.

Tybin looked at Nekoh saying, "I am not willing to release him and give him the chance to run with his friends. We need answers, and if we let him go, we will have no chance of knowing why they have been following us since we left the Great Tree."

"Why don't you ask Gethsemane, little man. I am sure he could give you the answers you seek," the raccoon taunted Tybin.

"What are you talking about," Jerin questioned him as he lifted the animal's chin with the blade of his knife. "Be careful how you talk about Gethsemane," Jerin warned.

This act caused the other raccoons to close in ranks around the boys.

"Enough!" Eleea said with authority. "What is your name," he asked the captured raccoon.

"I am Trevin, leader extraordinaire, information broker, and barter king," he said.

"Who are you working for and do not talk in riddles." Eleea continued.

"Fair enough, but I request respect, and respect does not come in the form of being held by the back of my neck, with a knife to my throat" Trevin demanded.

Tybin slowly put him down on the ground. But he and Jerin stayed ready to leap if need be to capture him again.

"Gethsemane bartered with me and my men to follow you and provide extra
protection as needed. As my foe who captured me has noted, we have been with you since you left the Great Tree. There is more I can tell you, but it will cost you," Trevin bartered.

"Cost us!" Tybin yelled. "What kind of game are you playing? You and your buddies! I could have killed you, and you want to charge us a price for more information!"

"Everything comes with a price," Trevin said nonchalantly. "How do you think I be barter king? It didn't just happen because I said poof, I am barter king. We are raccoons, and raccoons live for pretties. We live for the next great shiny."

"Now, the way I see it," Trevin continued, "since I am the broker of information; I have what you need to get past the Dead Trees to complete your mission. You see, there is great magic surrounding the area. You cannot walk into the trees; you have to walk through the trees."

"What the Crane is that supposed to mean!" Jerin asked. "Can't walk into, but have to walk through!"

"You will understand once we arrive at your destination, little man," Trevin stated. But, now, we must continue on and not talk in open about our plans," Trevin finished.

"Yes, we must continue," Eleea agreed. "Dusk is upon us," he revealed, "It is time to make camp for the evening. Trevin, do I have your word you will stay with us and join our night meal? I do believe, there are pretties to be given by the end of the meal," he slyly said.

Trevin placed his fists on his hips, cocked his head and took a long look at Eleea. "My team could use a nice hot meal, I guess. I mean we have had to smell your cooked food for days without even a nice, 'Would you and your men like to join us, Trevin.'

"So, yes I will join you. Trevin Two, Trevin Three, Trevin Four, Trevin Five, Trevin Six, Trevin Seven, and Trevin Eight," he yelled. "Stand guard around the camp, men. Keep out of sight, and be alert," he barked.

Everyone stood silent, unable to move. Not sure their ears had heard what they had heard. Ayden turned to Nick and gently put her fingers under his chin and lifted them up to close his mouth.

Nick looked at Ayden, smiled, regained his composure and went to aid Tybin and Jerin with camp preparation. While the rest of the group tried to keep close watch over the Trevins.

Deborah inched near the closest Trevin who was supposed to be on guard outside of the camp. He was busy with his little dagger, cleaning his paws.

Casually, she asked, "So, your name is Trevin, huh?"

"No ma'am, my name is Finch. Our leader has named us after him. I am Two, if you need to call me to help you," he stated politely.

"OK, let me get this straight," Deborah pressed on. "All of you have a real name. But you choose to follow a leader who only wants to call you by a number? And, all of you," Deborah lifted her hand and gestured around the trees, "are perfectly happy to be addressed in this way?"

"Ma'am," Two stated as he tried to explain, "Once you get to know Trevin, I
promise you will totally understand it is easier to just go with the flow and accept his way of reasoning. Trust me," he finished, as he put his knife away, nodded to her and jumped away into the trees.

Deborah walked back to Ayden, gave her a raised eyebrow and shook her head.

The girls and Elora sat on a log and warmed themselves by the fire as they waited for the work to be done to set up the rest of the camp.

Trevin sat on his hind legs by the girls, and watched every move Ayden and Deborah made. Deborah reached into her bag and pulled out her gray bandana from her world to wipe her face.

Trevin jumped to attention when he saw the bandana. "Madame," Trevin began, "What an interesting piece of material you have there. It sparkles in the light. How much would it cost to relieve you of this rag?"

"Whoa, back it up!" Tybin halted Trevin, while he took the scarf from Deborah and dangled in front of him. "If this is a rag, then you do not want it, now do you? But, if it is, as I suspect, a pretty, then it must have value. Great value I would assume since it caught your eye so quickly."

"Hey!" Deborah broke in. "Don't I have a say in this transaction, since it is my bandana? Who says I want to sell it? Maybe I want to keep it since Ayden gave it to me as a gift."

"It's OK with me, if it's OK with you, 'D', to sell it," Ayden interjected.

"Well, I just don't know, 'A'. It's a pretty big deal for me ya know? Because it is so special. If I sold it," Deborah stopped and coyly looked at Trevin, "if I sold it, I would have to get a very big price for it. Because it real-l-l-ly means a lot to me," she finished.

Tybin followed Deborah's lead by saying, "It is a beautiful scarf, Deborah. I would feel bad for you, if you did not get a decent price for it."

"Alright, alright," Trevin succumbed, "I will tell you all I know about how to get past the magic once we get to the Dead Trees for the bandana."

"Deal!" Deborah quickly agreed. "The scarf is yours. Now, would you like me to cut it into perfect sizes for you and your friends? For a price, of course, though?"

"What's your price?" Trevin asked.

"How about we decide on a truce? Instead of each of us trying to work to get one over on the other, we work to help each other during this journey," Deborah suggested.

"That's not how we raccoons work. You can't ask us to involve emotions in our decision making. It makes everything discombobulated, and then we get confused and then we cry because we are so discombobulated. No, we cannot get emotions involved. Nope, you will have to come up with some other price," Trevin concluded.

"How about I just cut the bandanas and you agree to stay with us as we travel and not try to hide from us?" Deborah compromised.

"Fine, we will not hide for you," Trevin decided.

Deborah looked at Trevin saying, "You mean from us not for you, right?"

"No, I mean for you," Trevin claimed. "This is a gift for you, get it?" He questioned her.

Deborah smiled at Trevin and nodded her head in agreement as she eyed Ayden with a look of disbelief.

She was excited she was finally able to use her new knife. She took it out of the sheath where it was attached to her belt, and began to prepare the scarf by folding it into a pyramid. As she began to slice it, it cut like soft butter. Almost like it knew what she wanted it to do.

She lifted the knife to look at it, curious by its ability to follow her lead. Taking the two pieces, she again folded them into pyramids and sliced each of them with the same ease as the first cut.

Ayden took each scarf and rolled it to make one long band to be tied around each raccoon's head. Trevin stepped up first as Ayden adjusted the scarf to look its best around his head. Trevin than picked Trevin Two, Trevin Five, and Trevin Eight to wear the same look.

Deborah picked up her knife and said, "Here, look at the blade, it is a mirror for you to see yourself."

While Trevin was admiring his new look in the knife's reflection, Ayden asked, "How did you know 'D', it would be a mirror?"

"I don't know, 'A'. I just felt if I wanted it to do it, it would do it. This knife is very
awesome!" Deborah excitedly stated.

The girls, including Elora and the boys, watched with humor as Trevin strutted around the camp with his new look. He would take a stance and display his sword as if preparing to attack. Walk some more and do the same act. Then he would try and see himself in the mirror while he was strutting around. Immediately his crew of misfits mimicked his actions.

Jerin set a magic perimeter around the camp to allow them to talk somewhat more freely without fear of others listening in. Tybin secured all of the sleeping quarters in a circle near the campfire while Eleea directed the girls on how to prepare the night meal.

The raccoons joined in the dinner and seemed to really enjoy being involved with everyone, rather than hiding in the trees. They were chatty with Nekoh and Elora, especially.

Trevin Two took a spot on the log near Deborah as he ate his meal. Deborah liked that he felt comfortable enough to join her and the others.

Respectful of his pride, she cautiously included him in their conversation. "I like your name, Finch. It has a regal sound to it."

"Thank you, ma'am, he replied, as he continued to eat.

Deborah reached into her backpack and pulled out a small silver metal charm with the words 'My Friend, My Hero' etched on it. She looked at Finch and said, "I want you to have this," as she opened the lobster claw clasp and clipped it onto his belt.

Trevin Two stood up, grabbed the charm, and examined it with intense care. He looked at Deborah and said, "This is a great honor to receive a shiny of such value, ma'am."

Before he could finish his statement all of the Trevins had surrounded him to see his new pretty. His chest puffed out as he stood tall for them to see it dangle perfectly off his belt.

Phum remained distant, staying close to Jerin and Tybin, who were as wary about the raccoons as Phum.

Trevin pulled out a little five-tiered flute from his pouch and handed it to one of the other raccoons after everyone had finished their dinner and were done admiring Two's new accessory. Trevin announced he and his comrades would be honored to entertain everyone.

The raccoon began with a slow melodic flute sound which truly sounded like echoes of an Irish folk song. The other raccoons started to dance to the sound of the flute; all in perfect harmony. As the music increased in intensity, they moved faster in dance.

Their movement reminded Ayden of the old river dance gig she used to watch with her parents when she was little.

Even Jerin and Tybin seemed to watch with enjoyment, as they laid back and relaxed. Nip walked behind the raccoons as if she were trying to dance with them, but just didn't understand their steps.

Phum, still leery of the whole scene, watched with his knife in his hand. He tried to look casual like he was using it to pick at the log he sat on, but it was obvious he was ready to jump into action if needed. The dance finished, and all sat around the fire, as Nick filled everyone's cup with hot tea.

Trevin gazed at Phum and said, "Dear sir, over there on the log. I know I did not catch your name. Therefore, to make it easy on all of us, I will call you Nine."

Phum stood up, his paws in tight fists, and said indignantly, "I, sir, am no Nine!"

"Hey! Nine! I mean no disrespect," Trevin responded. "We are on the same side here, Nine. It's no wonder you look so discombobulated, my good sir," Trevin informed him.

"Your emotions have over taken you. Here, come sit next to me and enjoy some drink. Let's talk about tree strategy and the best way to climb out of sight. I am sure you have great skills that could help my men." Trevin matter-of-factly finished.

Phum, stood stunned listening to Trevin. Not only did he continue to call him Nine, it didn't even phase him he was being disrespectful to Phum.

Nick moved over to Phum and said, "Let it go Phum, pick your battles, friend. This is not one you will win, nor is it one worth fighting."

Phum looked at Nick, shook his head in disbelief and finally, nodded his head in agreement. Nick handed him a cup of tea, and he sat down to drink it as he kept his wary eyes on the newest members of his group.

Deborah listened to the whole 'Nine' debacles as she sat in the dirt with her knife. She mindlessly dug up the dirt to avoid eye contact with any of the actors involved in the confrontation.

Once the heightened emotions settled, she turned to Ayden and said, "Ya know, A, I really wish I could find some of the old plant snail fern which used to grow here. It was used with the buffalo ear, silver grass, and the gopher weed to make things large, remember?"

She stuck her knife in the ground, as she freed her hands. And pulled out her notebook of plants she had gotten at the apothecary to show Ayden the dried plants she had purchased.

Ayden and Deborah were intently looking at the chart when Nekoh let out a cry. Both girls slightly jumped off their seats and looked at him. "What is this," Nekoh asked with astonishment.

Deborah looked at what Nekoh was staring at and saw the knife was covered in a plant. "OH, Wow! I don't believe it!" She expressed excitedly. "This is snail fern, look," she stated while she pointed to the chart.

Ayden saw a plant growing where Deborah's knife had broken the ground. But it didn't mean anything to her as it was Deborah's world of plants.

"Look!" Deborah exuberantly exclaimed. "'A', look!" She said again as she started to dig with great care around the plant with her knife.

"This is the extinct plant of this world, Deborah cried out. "This is snail fern! Oh! Wow! This is the find of the century. I need to cultivate it and record it. Plus, I need to take some right now and dry it so I can use it when needed. This is snail fern! I just can't believe it," Deborah kept talking in disbelief. "I can make an elixir with this to help us, somehow. I don't know how, but I know it will help us."

Ayden reached into her bag and pulled out her gifts she had gotten at the apothecary for Deborah. Saying, "I bought this as a birthday gift for you, but I think it would serve us better if you had it now, 'D'."

"Wow! It is a whole pharm- I mean apothecary set to help me make anything I want. It is the best gift I have ever received. 'A', Thank you!" Deborah stated. Deborah immediately started harvesting the snail fern so she could prepare it for drying.

Eleea flew to Deborah's shoulder and stated, "Well, Deborah, it would seem this knife of yours possesses some pretty amazing gifts. May I make one suggestion, because it seems to read your words and mind, giving you what you need. Be careful what you think and say when it is in use, so it does not turn into something treacherous." Deborah looked at Eleea and nodded in agreement.

"May I also suggest," Eleea continued, "It is time for all of us to turn in for the night."

The summer air brought all of the outdoor smells into the camp and engulfed them as they blissfully slept the night away. Nekoh slept at the foot of Deborah's bed, Nip slept at the top of Ayden's head, and Eleea and Elora nestled together in one basket from the saddle.

Jerin and Tybin were on each side of the girls protecting them with Lok and Tari close by. Nick and Phum were at each end of the girls' feet and heads to make sure they were safe. The raccoons strategically surrounded all of them as if they thought they were the only protectors of the group.

Journal Twenty-Two

What was it about food in the wilderness? Everything tasted so much better than if you were sitting in your home.

Each meal, I felt like I was famished. I devoured everything in my bowl. Deborah and I hadn't had soda or real candy for months. Maybe this was why we ate with such joy?

Our taste buds could finally taste and weren't tricked anymore by preservatives. Oops, we had one candy with the s'mores, but none other since that night.

Tricked. There's another interesting word which has changed meaning for me since I crossed over. Or, should I say 'shape shifter'?

I was raised with the adage 'sly like a fox' but, never shape shifter. Although, some cultures believed the fox could change shapes on my side of the world. Like Japan for instance.

The image of the fox on the amulet created a sly trick to take our bodies shape so we would not be missed. Nor, would we, when we went back, lose out on knowing what the amulet did in our place. It would tell us everything.

Most of us, including me, saw sly like a fox as deceptive and like a trickster. Now, I saw it differently.

Sly didn't always have to be negative. Deborah and I slyly were able to save the world of Eshra and our own world without being missed by her parents or anyone else in East Glacier.

Brilliant is what it was. We got the best of both worlds. Which gave us the freedom to not worry about anyone missing us in our world.

Chapter Twenty-Two

Eleea woke the girls earlier than usual, saying, "Today, I want to take you to a special area of the forest. It is not a place many know about. All who have lived in Eshra have heard about it one time or another. Most believe it to be only lore and not real."

"When we were at the village, I asked Joshua to give me directions to reach it. I want you to experience the beauty of this place. We will walk for a couple of miles to get to it, but it will truly be worth it. Our destination is an area called Eclipse Lake, which is hidden deep in this area."

Everyone ate breakfast and prepared for the hike. The girls took their water bladders, and each tied their hair back with a bandana around their head and put their sun hat on top of the bandana.

Eleea and Elora rode their shoulders, Nip was tucked in her sling, and all the rest either walked, climbed or flew with them into the depths of the woods.

The first part of the hike had them gradually climbing higher. To reach the top of the summit they had to take the trail at an angle on the mountain side as it curved around to make the ascent easier to traverse.

Each step they took raised the elevation, and the terrain became increasingly more difficult to predict. The trees and forest floor became dense and, at times, difficult to maneuver.

The closer they got to the top, the harsher it was to see due to the thick shroud of clouds which floated around the mountain. After they reached the peak, they began to wind down around the other side of it. Halfway down, Eleea stopped the caravan and told them they had to go straight down.

The boys and the girls slowly walked sideways, digging the side of their shoes into the dirt to help them slow their descent. At times, a cry would ring out from one of the hikers as they lost their footing and begin to slide too fast down its surface.

As the clouds began to disappear, a trail appeared allowing them to gain a better footing where they could walk normally to the bottom of the mountain. Once they reached the base, the raccoons used their swords to break down the heavy leaves.

The sun began to shine through and revealed a mystical looking lake surrounded on three sides by a mountainous fortress. The closer they got to it, a sandy beach with downed trees and an expansive blanket of moss led up to the lake.

Flowers emerged and littered the whole area with every color imaginable. Large beautiful ferns swayed in the light breeze and seemed to beckon the onlooker to lie in them and rest. The lake water was perfectly clear as It illuminated colors of emerald green, blue, and turquoise in its depths.

The girls and Nick took off their shoes, walked onto the moss which led to the sand and to the edge of the lake. Before they could step a foot in the water, the raccoons beat them.

They jumped around, splashing everywhere trying to catch the 'shineys' at the bottom of it. Not realizing it was the sun's reflection on the water.

Tybin and Jerin chose to swim out into the deep, where there was a ledge on the side of the mountain. Each tried to out skill one another with different aerial tricks into the water.

When they tired of their competitive antics, they decided to sneak back to the shallow water, where they would attack Nick and the girls with sprays of water, which caused a major water fight.

Everyone did what they could to participate and win the battle. Some of the raccoons took Nick and the girls' side by trying to climb on top of each other to look taller. But it totally failed with them trying to fight off the boys.

They would fall and then clamber back onto each other's shoulders. It was hilarious to watch them try to maintain their composure and desire to be strong and warrior-like.

Lok, Tari, and Nekoh took the boys' side and did much better in the battle. With the batting of the wings from the birds and Nekoh coyly tripping the raccoons, the girls' team didn't have a chance.

Elora tried to warn them, but her voice was drowned out by Lok and Tari.

Eleea just stood back, riding on Nip's head, and watched with laughter. Phum, being Phum, watched from a tall tree limb like a typical guard on lookout.

Trevin slyly left the group as he went over to Ayden's backpack and produced a can of spray. With the help of Eight, their little palms held the nozzle down as they tried to spray it at Jerin and Tybin.

The force of the pressurized can caused the two raccoons to lose control of its aim and everyone around the boys got sprayed. The whole group began to cough uncontrollably as their eyes watered and their sight was lost.

Trevin screamed as he let go of the can while he and Eight ran high up into a tree.

"Trevin are you mad!" Tybin yelled through his sputtering cough.

Not moving from his limb, Trevin stated as he looked down on the group, "My good sir, this is not my fault. A shiny from the other world is not supposed to act with such disgust coming out of its mouth. Eight and I were only trying to help the girls win in an unfair battle."

Deborah, on her hands and knees coughing, yelled, "get, your whole body in the water. This is the only way to neutralize the spray with tons of water!" She exclaimed. Everyone followed her instructions.

Soon, each of them felt they could leave the water as they all tried to focus as they exited the lake. Their red eyes and runny noses looked and sounded like all of them had a terrible cold.

Ayden turned to Trevin who still refused to leave his limb of safety. "Trevin, seriously, what do you have to say for yourself? You know better than to take from someone else without permission?" She questioned him.

"Madame, you were in peril," he proclaimed. "I was only thinking of your care. And, it would seem this is your fault, anyways! How could you not let us know you had a can from your world that could cause such puke-y sprays," he claimed as he put his paws on his hips.

Nick chuckled at Trevin's determination to not be responsible for the pepper spray mishap. He turned to Ayden with a glint in his eyes and stated, "Yeah, Ayden! How could you not let them know about your puke-y spray?"

Ayden looked at Nick with horror. "So, this is my fault," she declared.

"Well, yes. In a sense, it is your fault, Ayden," Nekoh stated. "Technically, you girls were told to leave your world belongings at the Great Tree."

"But, Trevin." Nekoh continued as he looked up at the safe limb where Trevin refused to leave. "You do know better than to rummage through another's belongings without permission."

"Fine," Trevin stated. "I say we all just forget about this little misstep of misfortune and eat."

Deborah looked at Ayden and smiled while Ayden shook her head and smiled back. Deborah handed her the can and Ayden looked at Trevin with determination as she put the bear spray back in her pack.

After all of the chaos, everyone lay on the beach to let the sun warm them. Tybin and Jerin prepared lunch and all devoured the food as if they hadn't eaten for weeks.

Everyone refilled their bladder with lake water more than once. The taste of the pure liquid seemed to do more than quench their thirst. It rejuvenated their souls.

Ayden looked out beyond the lake where the gorgeous scenery surrounded the whole area. The mystical setting of trees which lined the lake and climbed up the mountains with green moss riding up their trunks looked like a painted picture from an artist's mind. It just didn't seem to be a real place because it was so perfectly still and beautiful.

Eleea flew to Ayden's knee and said, "Ayden, I would like you and Elora to come with me. There is a special place I want you two to see."

Ayden rose, with Elora on her shoulder, and began to walk the path directed by Eleea. He guided them up a small trail farther down the side of the lake by the base of the mountain.

Deep in the foliage of extremely tall ferns, they walked through to the side of the fortress. She saw water streaming down the rock face like a peaceful waterfall.

"This is called the 'Wall of Tears,' girls," Eleea stated. "I want you to sit here and listen and watch while I go to the wall."

Ayden obediently did as Eleea asked. But she felt strange and scared by his request.

Eleea flew to a tree limb directly in front of the wall and began to sing in a soft voice. The wall of water began to move in a circular motion, and then it spread open to expose the rock behind it. Lora appeared in the center of the circle.

Ayden had to catch her breath to not scream out. Tears silently fell down her face as she watched Eleea speak to Lora in soft tones. Elora nudged her chin, trying to stop the tears. Ayden looked at her and petted her head trying to comfort her, knowing Elora did not know Eleea was talking to her mom.

After some time, Eleea turned to the girls and said, "Come closer and talk with us girls."

Ayden went to Eleea and said, "It is so good to see you again Lora. I have missed you. And I love you, Lora."

Elora lost her balance and caught herself by flying to the perch Eleea was on.

"*Momma!*" Elora spoke softly.

"*Yes, my preciousl daughter,*" Lora said.

"*OH! Momma, you are so beautiful!*" Elora continued.

"*And you, yourself are just as beautiful,*" Lora responded. "*Eleea has told me so much about you, Elora. I am so very proud of you. Remember, my spirit lives on in you. Wherever you go, I go with. I have loved you from the first time I saw you in your egg. I will always love you as you live your wonderful life.*"

Lora began to fade as she spoke, "*I love you too, Ayden.*"

"*Elora, my beautiful child, live your destiny.*"

"*Eleea, my love, it is time for you to move on from the past.*"

Elora began to cry out to her. "Momma! Don't leave me just yet," she cried.

Eleea drew closer to Elora and whispered, "Elora, she has to go. She was able to tell you how much you mean to her, but her place is there and yours is here."

"It is not for us to dwell on the past and the what ifs of this world. It is for us to accept what happens, and to make our time here a better place by what we choose to do with our life. Rest assured, she will always love you. And as she said, her spirit lives on in you," Eleea comforted her.

Elora laid her head on her father's chest and cried.

Ayden slowly walked closer to Eleea and Elora, feeling their pain, she silently gave them her support.

Once again, the wall began to move and an image slowly appeared. Ayden, startled, blurted out, "Mom!"

"Ayden, please forgive me," her mom started.

"You don't need to apologize, Mom," Ayden began.

"NO, do not justify what I did to you, Ayden! I was wrong, your stepfather was wrong. There is something I need to tell you. I need you to listen carefully."

Ayden fell to her knees in tears.

Eleea flew to her shoulder and comfortingly said, "Ayden listen."

"I was a young girl when I conceived you, Ayden. I was in love and felt like the world would always be full of love.

Then tragedy happened. The man I loved disappeared, never to be heard from again. I felt abandoned and cheated.

It turned me into a desperate woman and one who was very angry. I lost all hope of ever being happy again.

I cheated you, Ayden. You were a beautiful gift, and I did not even know it until it was too late.

My world was still full of love with you in it, and I missed it because of my selfish sorrow."

Ayden lifted her eyes to her mother, trying to comprehend all she was hearing.

"Ayden," Her mother continued.

"Listen to me. Do not ever let one experience in your life turn you into a person who loses hope. Look at each obstacle you face as an opportunity to turn it into good.

I love you, and I am sorry for not turning my obstacles into good for you."

Slowly the image began to swirl. Ayden jumped to her feet, knowing she was beginning to disappear. "NO! Don't go yet! I have too many questions, and you haven't answered them!" Ayden screamed.

"I'm sorry Ayden, please forgive me," her mom's voice said as she faded away.

Ayden turned to Eleea who had flown back to where Elora was perched and said, "Eleea! No! I need to know who my true father was! I need to know!"

"Ayden, time will give you the answer you seek. I am sure what you heard from your mother was meant to be heard, and the answer will come," Eleea soothingly told her.

"Eleea, please bring her back. You can bring her back; you know how to do it!" Ayden begged.

"It is not in my power, Ayden," Eleea whispered. "The Wall of Tears brings forth what it wishes, when it wishes. When I came to the Wall today, I hoped I would see Lora, but I had no idea if she would show. And, I was completely taken off guard when your mom showed. I did not expect for you to see her. Truly, it is confusing to me, too, that she came to you. I always had thought this Wall was for those of this world, not yours."

"Eleea, what does it all mean? I am so confused," Ayden moaned.

"All I can tell you, Ayden, is to take what you have been told and use it for positive. *Your character is forged by how you face your obstacles,"* Eleea stated.

The three quietly made their way back to the rest of the group at the lake. When they reached them, Ayden grabbed Deborah's arm and sat down to tell her and the others all that happened. "I don't know how to take in all of this." Ayden stated.

Deborah put her arms around Ayden and said, "What you have just experienced is not something you can resolve in one minute or even one day, 'A'. This information is a journey of self-reflection and growth. One day it will all make sense, I promise you."

"D', I am just so tired of all of this wait and see for answers stuff. I just found out my dad is not my dad. Who knows who my dad really is! I just want to get back to camp." Ayden impatiently stated.

The Trevins huddled around Ayden. Each of them gently patted her with their little paws. The tenderness of their actions warmed her heart.

I love Deborah. She is a friend for life. Her wisdom and insight always cause me to see her as one of the smartest people I have ever known.

When she said to me, "This information is a journey of self-reflection and growth." It just really hit me.

Because, this whole quest is a journey and it is all reflection and growth. I am finding out about myself, about others and about what it takes to be a family.

I love the sound of those words....to be a family. I have a family! A family who loves me like I love them.

Chapter Twenty-Three

By the time they reached the camp, it was late afternoon. Jerin, Tybin, and Nick worked quickly to feed the horses and settle them for the night. The girls busied themselves with meal preparation.

A heavy mood had followed them from the lake, and it still lingered. The Trevins stayed as close to Ayden as they could while they watched the perimeters. All the others slept or watched the girls.

Deborah decided since the meal was on the fire it would also be a good time to cook her plants for her elixir. Gathering all of the ingredients together, she was thankful they had discovered one of Nekoh's pouches quickly dried the fresh plant she had cultivated earlier and she didn't have to wait days for drying to occur.

Ayden stared aimlessly as she watched between Deborah and the raccoons who were playing and reenacting their fighting moves. Off in the distance a bird's caw could vaguely be heard.

Ayden shook her head from her daydream, and turned to Eleea. She tried to closely listen to hear the cry again as it got closer.

She jumped to her feet, ran towards Eleea and said, "Eleea, listen! Listen to the caw. I know that cry."

Eleea tipped his head to hear the bird's sound. He flew to Ayden's shoulder excitedly saying, "It's him Ayden!"

"Jerin!! Tybin! Come quickly," Ayden yelled. "Listen! Do you hear the hawk?" She asked. The boys came to her side and nodded.

"This, I know it in my heart, is the hawk that killed Lora. I need you to hide outside the camp and look for a hawk with only one eye. When you see him, grab him and bring him here," she informed them. Lok and Tari followed closely behind their friends.

Trevin called his crew and looked at Ayden and said, "We are here to serve, we will assist the boys in your request." The raccoons scurried up the trees and were quickly out of sight.

Eleea started to fly with them when Ayden yelled, "Stop Eleea! This is not, yet, your battle. Let them bring him to us, please." Eleea turned to look at Ayden, and finally nodded in agreement.

Those who stayed at the camp huddled close to each other, yet far enough away to not look obvious as they waited for the search party to return. Deborah slowly pulled her knife and set it next to her hip as she sat down near the fire. Nekoh laid next to Deborah's other side, with his back legs ready to spring.

Elora tried to hide in Ayden's hair while on her shoulder. Eleea tensely perched on one of the logs by the fire.

Phum stood in pounce stance, blades unsheathed near them. Nick, also unsheathed, stood by the closest tree to the fire, warily watchful.

Nip hid in the sling around Ayden's neck. And, Ayden sat with her legs crossed and eyes closed. Listening as she was taught back at the Great Tree.

Ayden knew in her heart she needed to keep still and concentrate. No matter how scary it sounded, she needed to stay focused. All around her she could sense the tension of everyone who waited with her.

At first, there was only the sound of the forest breeze amongst the trees and distant sounds of the hawk's caw.

Suddenly, the hawk's cry sounded distressed. It was far enough away where Ayden could only hear muffled voices yelling back and forth. Nick moved closer to Ayden and Deborah as the sounds became more intense.

The crack of limbs breaking mixed with loud voices calling out "I got you. That was close. Watch out there's another fireball coming right at you!" And, "He's right behind you," rang throughout the chase.

The resounding chaos of their words and the obvious fight taking place by those in pursuit of the hawk caused the whole camp, who couldn't see anything, to stay alert with fear.

Another round of excited cries, closer to the camp, rang out with, "Trevin, you almost had him, good work man." "Jerin, get the Trevins to flank you." "Tybin, grab him, now!" And, "Wrap his mouth tight, when you have him."

Ayden could sense Deborah fidgeting more as the party got louder. She felt concern over Deborah's movement, but felt the strong determination to stay in the position she had chosen with eyes closed.

She heard Jerin call out, "Bring him over to the campfire," as he jumped into the circle by the fire.

Jerin's voice startled Deborah which caused her to stand, grab for her knife and throw it. Ayden felt the wind of the knife fly by her and instinctually leaped and reached for it. The knife stopped within an inch of Jerin's throat.

Deborah screamed, falling to her knees as she trembled and cried, saying, "Jerin, I am so sorry. I could have killed you!"

Jerin lifted Deborah to her feet and put his hands on her shoulders as he stated, "Deborah, I am still alive, OK. Let this be a lesson for you. Do not react with dangerous weapons until you are sure how your reaction will turn out. Remember to keep emotions out of the equation."

Deborah nodded her head, while sniffling, and sat back down. Ayden walked behind her, handed her the knife and then put her arms around her shoulders and hugged her; reassuring Deborah she would be fine.

Tybin jumped down from the trees holding a hawk by its wings, with its mouth tied together. The raccoons hurriedly filed in close behind the boys and surrounded Tybin while he placed the bird on the ground. Each had their knife in hand ready to help if the hawk tried to escape.

"Reveal who you are and who sent you," Jerin demanded as he slightly loosed the rope around the hawk's beak.

He readjusted the rope to quickly cinch it closed in case he had to tighten it to avoid any flame the hawk could spew. Around one foot, he secured another rope so the hawk could only hop a short distance. Jerin held on to the ropes to make sure he couldn't fly away as Tybin slowly took his hands off the hawk's wings.

"I am Garis," the hawk said as he pushed out his chest. "My allegiance is to Choran. The true ruler of this land," he stated with pride.

Garis noticed a faint familiar smell as he spoke and looked around the fire pit. He kept his eyes on Jerin while he continued to talk. "Only Choran is the true ruler of the night and day of this land," Garis smugly told them.

"What is the reason behind you stalking us!" Jerin demanded.

"My purpose is to foil any plan you have, at any cost. Whether it be sacrifice of life or to just stall your progress," Garis retorted with a smirky cackle as he inched closer to the pot which held the aroma, he knew to be magical.

"Of course, when I say, sacrifice of life," he cackled in an evil tone, "I do not mean my life."

"You had no need to kill Lora, she did nothing to you!" Eleea cried out.

"Why do you think I wear this patch?" Garis vehemently spewed back at Eleea, while he skillfully kept his momentum towards the pot.

"It is you who caused me to lose sight in my eye, Eleea," Garis hissed. "I lose an eye; you lose a wife. Seems fair enough don't you think?" Garis sarcastically stated.

Eleea flew towards Garis, but was stopped in mid-flight by Nekoh who caught him in his paw. "Eleea, you know he is deliberately provoking you," Nekoh soothed him.

Eleea, resolutely let his wings rest at his sides and looked at Nekoh, and stated, "I know Nekoh, I know," as he flew to the top of Nekoh's head to watch and listen.

Garis continued his rant, saying, "I was sent to watch you and to stop that girl," Garis motioned towards Ayden. "She is trouble! Every tactical move I have made against her has been thwarted. I found great joy in watching her parents beat her, and even that didn't kill her."

Deborah swiftly turned to look at Ayden, confused and concerned by what he was saying about Ayden's parents. Ayden caught her eyes, slightly nodded to let her know it did really happen and then grabbed her arm to let her know she was fine and to not worry about her.

"Long before you, Eleea, our great Choran knew who she was. I have been watching her for years. But, Choran never felt she was any major threat until you got involved," Garis snarled at Eleea, while he continued his steps to get closer to the pot.

"Of course, we toyed with getting rid of her, and did try. I told Choran sending that stupid blind snake was a wrong move. If she wouldn't have handed the backpack to her friend, she would have been dead. But no, he could only smell her and not see her, which caused her to save her and her friend from his bite." Garis disgustingly said.

Garis slowly moved within inches of the pot Deborah had mixed earlier in the day as he slyly continued to talk about how he and his comrades were much more knowledgeable about Ayden compared to her friends.

"Strange magic surrounds her," Garis frustratingly stated. "No one knows what it is. There are periods of time where none of us can find her or get near her. We have tried, and we end up either in our realm, or far away from her in her world."

"We have to struggle to regain our senses and our surroundings to get back to her. Then there are other times where we think we are on the right course to finish her off and she isn't where we expected her to be. Just like the night we set fire to her house." Garis informed them.

Ayden's heart swirled with emotions as she listened to Garis. He was directly responsible for killing her parents. He killed Lora. He knew about Deborah's brush with death by the rattlesnake. He'd been watching her for years. He wanted to kill her.

All of these thoughts stirred up anger in her. She began fidgeting while she sat next to Deborah. Elora flew to her shoulder to try and comfort her. Deborah took her hand in hers and held onto it tightly.

"What I don't get, is what makes her so special to this world?" Garis haughtily asked. "Maybe you could tell me Eleea? She is not of our world! She has no right to be here!"

"Garis, I doubt you have the capacity to understand, let alone recognize emotions of love, or to even think on your own. You have been groomed to be a pawn and a machine of destruction. Delusion surrounds you, causing you to think you will be rewarded for your loyalty to evil," Eleea stated.

"One thing you have forgotten, Garis, concerning your allegiance. Evil has no allegiance. When it is done with you, you are disposable and no longer needed," Eleea finished.

"It still does not explain her being here, Eleea!" Garis fought back. "Your eloquent speech for your friends about evil, has no bearing on me. I will live far beyond your short time in this world."

"I will have power far greater than what she seems to possess. And I will conquer all of you!" Garis declared as he determined he could aimlessly talk and inch his way closer to the fire with each speech he gave. The smell from the pot which filled his nostrils was the same elixir Choran continuously drank to keep his body enormously huge and powerful.

"Choran will stop her from fulfilling her prophecy. She will never get to the Dead Trees to fight him. He will rule this world," Garis cackled in glee as he shoved the pot with his body, which caused it to tip on its side.

Rapidly he drank its contents. Immediately his body began to grow in size as he horrifically coughed and coughed like he was choking.

The ties around his legs became taunt and burst as his legs grew to the size of a horse's leg. His feet looked like huge gnarled roots of a tree sticking out of the ground.

Rather than having wings, his body appeared to represent layers of shingles on a roof. With every beat of his heart his chest protruded out like a balloon which was about to explode.

The eye patch burst away from his head leaving his left eye socket exposed looking like a hollow crater of an abyss. The straps for his beak broke away as if they were wispy strings of cotton candy.

He glared with his one good eye at Ayden and her friends with such intensity it looked like he would attack them right there. Instead, he flew straight up into the sky, above the camp. He peered down at all of them, laughing and cawing at their stupor.

The sound of his voice roared throughout the camp as he started to flap his wings above them. The air surrounding the flapping began to create a funnel directly above the camp. It filled their ears with the sound of rolling thunder ready to build into a major explosive storm.

Garis heaved his chest full of air and blew. He repeated the same act three more times until a fiery ball came out of his mouth and filled the center of the funnel.

The ball twisted and turned, and gained in strength from the wind of Garis' wings as it started to descend. Reaching closer and closer to the camp, he fueled the speed of the ball's trajectory by blowing it towards them.

Ayden watched in horror as the hawk gained in stature and strength, while he seemed to visibly enjoy his power over them. As he hovered above the camp, his eerie laughter gripped her heart with a cold chill she felt down in the pit of her stomach. She watched as his ball of fire grew and began its descent to the ground.

She vaulted to her feet and ran to the outside of the camp where everyone stood
as they watched the hawk. She leaned, instinctively, with her body towards the middle of the camp, outstretched her arms, and lowered her head into her chest. She could feel the heat and the wind of the fireball soar closer to her back as she kept her position.

Then, suddenly out of her back emerged an enormous set of wings of pure sterling silver which immediately covered everyone around her. The roaring ball of flame hit her wings and burst apart, leaving everyone underneath her stunned. Not only by her action, but because she had wings come out of her back.

Ayden lifted her head, looked at her sides to see the wings. She looked around at all of them and realized no one was harmed by the fireball. She stood up straight, lowered her wings which then began to disappear and looked at Eleea.

"Eleea, what does this mean," she began.

She was stopped from asking anymore by Eleea frantically calling at Elora who had flown to the remaining elixir and had put her beak in it.

Eleea screamed, "No Elora! don't do it!" But it was too late. Elora drank the rest of it and started to grow.

Her body became the size of a miniature pony. Elora's wing tips locked into place, each of them glistening from the blades of armor Nadab had made for her.

A mask came down over her face, covering her beak with a sharp pointed blade and finally a helmet on her head. She repeatedly coughed, trying to catch her breath as she grew. Elora looked at her body, looked at Eleea and Ayden, then looked up into the sky and took off into it.

Eleea yelled, "NO! Elora do not do it!"

Ayden raced to Eleea's side to try and comfort him. Both looked towards the sky at the hawk, who was reeling backwards with his wings flapping.

He looked confused his ball of fire had not destroyed all of them. Everyone looked to the sky as they watched Elora.

Within seconds there came screams from Garis. The only thing seen were instant flashes of light, trailed by blood which looked like it was suspended in the air.

They could see dozens of slashes of light moving back and forth across the sky. Then, there was a formidable silence, followed by hundreds of pieces of Garis' body falling to the ground.

Finally, a loud thunderous thud sounded as Elora landed near the campsite. Elora took her wings, fanned them outward, shook them and released all of the blood which was left on them. Her armor disappeared as she put her wings back against her body and looked at everyone.

Eleea was first to speak, saying, "Elora it is not right to kill someone in an emotional rage of vengeance. It is not our place to take justice into our own hands."

Elora intently looked at Eleea and said, "Father, I remember back to when you spoke to Deborah about her weapon and how it was not to be used with emotions involved, just as Jerin also told her."

"I had no emotion of revenge when I took to the sky to save my friends and you. He wanted us dead and I reacted to this danger. In my heart, with the purest motive, I attacked to protect all of us. Now, since we are all safe from him, I cannot lie. I feel no sorrow he is dead. I assure you I did not do this act out of vengeance, Father," Elora expressed.

Eleea nodded acceptance to his daughter's response.

Nekoh turned to Eleea and stated, "We cannot go any further in our journey until we are sure about what will happen to Elora as the elixir leaves her body. And, with her this size, she will cause too much attention to our party and alert Choran and his dominions about our location and purpose."

"What will be the consequences of this elixir leaving Elora's body?" Eleea asked Nekoh.

"I have never seen this before, Eleea. Deborah and I know a lot about plants and their properties, but this is new to both of us. We only can keep a strong vigilance over her and help her, as we can, when symptoms show forth," Nekoh concluded.

"So be it," Eleea decided. "We will stay here at camp until Elora is back to being normal. And then we will move forward," he finished.

Journal Twenty-Four

The first of our weapons Nadab had made for us came forth through Elora and I.
Yes, Deborah's weapon had already been used; but not in battle.

To see Elora in her full armor, and at the size she had become was, well it was mind blowing awesome. She didn't freak out or lose her focus. She just attacked. She saw a very real danger and took charge to take it out. Very impressive!

Garis, what an evil being. He killed for joy and false honor. He was just a hawk. And look at the damage he created.

And, for how many years had he caused me and others harm? He only told us about some of things he did to me and those I loved. And! Since he was only a small hawk, what would we face the closer we got to the Dead Trees? Animals and people can be really dangerous when they want to kill.

Then, there was the big matter of my weapon. Wings! Not just any ordinary wings like Eleea's or Elora's...but wings of sterling silver.

Granted, they were beautiful as they flickered in the shadows of light. Each feather was detailed and moved with the wind like a real bird's feather would do when a breeze caught it and slightly lifted it up, like hair blowing in the wind.

Plus, in battle, they became as hard as steel. But I didn't have time to freak out over my weapon because Elora's dilemma was just a tad bit more important. I am sure I would have, if I had been given the chance.

Yet, this was my world in Eshra. Make sure everyone else was taken care of first. And, I would have to deal with me later.

Chapter Twenty-Four

Jerin and Tybin came over to Elora, both of them slapped her on the back. Evidently proud of her actions, they continued to slap her as they spoke to her.

"That was one of the most epic battles I have ever seen, Elora," Jerin started.

"Yeah!" Tybin jumped in, "I can't believe this little body of yours grew into such a
great warrior with those wing-tipped blades. Absolutely awesome Elora!"

Elora had never known respect like she felt from the boys, and all she could do was inwardly smile at their compliments. She did not like being so big, now that she had time to think about what she had done.

She looked at Deborah and said, "How long do you think I will be like this?"

"I honestly don't know, Elora," Deborah responded. "I doubt it will last. You didn't take very much, because there wasn't very much left to take since Garis got to it first."

Elora turned to Eleea and said, "Father, I do feel sad, now. It is not a good feeling to take someone's life. It is really scary to be so strong where one dies because of what I did."

"Elora," Eleea began, "It is important to not fight with anger; especially when emotions run high. The choice you made today, is one which had to be made. It took courage for you to think so quickly to protect all of us. I trust what you have already said, you reacted for our safety. Not for vengeance." He comfortingly said.

Nekoh came along side Eleea and said, "Elora, all of us feel the pain of the loss of your mother. She was taken by pure evil for the sake of evil, alone. I do not believe you reacted to this knowledge of evil, and what it has done to you and your father. You reacted to a need for the far greater good of all of us. And, most importantly, you saved Ayden from harm," he finished.

Nekoh then turned to the group and stated, "Today brings a somber reality to our mission. Each step we take from this point forward needs to be done with extreme caution. Choran's whole purpose is to stop us."

"It is evident from what Garis said, Choran is scared we will succeed. There is no other reason he would dispatch his followers to try and stop Ayden. His fear will fuel him to send more to harm us the closer we get to the Dead Trees. All of us need to stay alert and be ready to fight. Just as Elora took action today, we too need to be willing to do the same," he said with a formidable wisdom.

Everyone respectfully listened to Nekoh as they began to process the seriousness of their mission.

Trevin turned to the other Trevins and directed them to follow him. Ayden watched the raccoons begin to gather all of what was left of Garis and pile his body parts on a pile of wood far away from the camp in an open area.

Ayden decided she should go and help them in their endeavor. It was a solemn task to pick up what was left of his body as it reminded her of all she had lost so early in her young life.

Without provocation, everyone seemed to sense the moment and began to help the raccoons. Trevin strategically placed dried grass all around the bottom of the pyre and stepped back to look at everyone's handiwork.

He turned to Eleea and said, "we should say a few kind words, Eleea. Would you do the honors?"

Eleea flew to Ayden's shoulder as the rest of the party stood around them like a congregation would at a church funeral ceremony. Eleea began:

"Each life enters the world to bring forth its soul to live with purpose.

Purpose propels their destiny and determines their path.

Some choose to accept their circumstances by taking the easy path.

While others choose to conquer their circumstances by taking the path of adversity and turning it into a path of life.

Regardless of their destiny, each life is meant to be cherished, honored, and forgiven.

Because true purpose for each of us who lives is to move beyond the circumstances and the obstacles.

To become a soul to help others and ourselves to achieve a true and honorable life."

Eleea looked at Trevin and nodded to indicate he was done speaking. Trevin held a lit stick with oil soaked on it from the campfire and kept it upright, like a beacon, throughout Eleea's speech. After he nodded back at Eleea, he lit the dried grass.

Everyone quietly watched as Garis' body returned to ash and dust. One by one they walked away, with the raccoons being the last to leave.

Deborah took Nekoh aside after the evening meal to ask him his opinion on what to expect about Elora's condition? "Nekoh, could this be dangerous for Elora when the elixir wears off?" she asked.

"Deborah, I just don't know what we are up against. You and I will have to watch her throughout the night. And, it would not be a bad idea to make some salve to help heal her wounds. Use your knife to ask for milkweed, lemonwood, aloe Vera cactus, arnica, and salt weed. Plus, we need some strong tea to help us stay awake throughout the night. Get us some elderberry root," Nekoh directed her.

Deborah started her makeshift laboratory off to the side of the campfire. She set down a blanket to use as a tabletop. She then drew a line in the dirt with the blade, and as the blade passed the dirt, sprouts emerged and matured instantaneously.

She organized all of the plants she had cultivated with the knife. She placed them in the order to how she needed to make the different salves and drink. Quickly she took the plants that needed to be dried and placed them in Nekoh's bag.

Ayden did what she could to help her. While Nekoh watched, and supervised.

Eleea was acutely aware of Elora's demeanor even before she grew exponentially larger than he had ever seen her. He could sense she wasn't feeling well and questioned her.

"Elora, tell me how your body is feeling?"

"Father, I am uncomfortable in my skin," Elora started. "I don't know how to react with what I am feeling. I don't know how to stand, how to sit or even how to perch with this body. I don't want to eat. And the biggest thing is I am so large I can't hide from those around me and watch everything quietly. I am miserable, Father," Elora confided.

"It will be fine, Elora," Eleea soothed her. "You will be back to normal soon. Deborah and Nekoh are working right now on herbs to help you transition through this, and they will not leave your side."

Nekoh directed the boys to bring water for Elora to drink, and for Ayden to take a soaked cloth and gently wash her face and neck to help her feel somewhat more comfortable. Deborah brewed a special mixture of the ingredients she had received from Sunbird Village for Elora to drink. The concoction would help her rid her body of poison.

As Ayden was wiping Elora's brow, she sensed Elora becoming extremely nervous. She looked into Elora's eyes, questioning what was wrong. Elora stood up and began to heave. Her whole-body wretched forward as a large black mass ejected out of her mouth. Elora looked at Ayden with fear permeating deep in her eyes.

Ayden reached for Elora's head and cradled it in her hand, telling her, "It's OK Elora, you need to get the poison out. Your body is just trying to release it for you. Just go with it and don't try to fight it, we are here for you, Elora."

Deborah jumped to attention when she saw Elora throw up. Ayden was amazed by how proficient Deborah became once she saw Elora having difficulty.

She was a skilled nurse who worked around her sick patient trying to ease her fear and pain. About every ten or fifteen minutes, Elora would heave and throw up more mass. This went on for hours, and Deborah stayed by her, unwilling to leave her side.

With each expulsion of gunk, Elora's body was slowly diminishing in size. But, with the smaller size, one could see areas between her skin and feathers which looked sore with blood oozing out.

Plus, it sounded like her bones were cracking and twisting as they shrank. Deborah went and got the salves she had prepared earlier in the evening and began rubbing down Elora's skin. Gently massaging each area.

Trevin sat and watched everything that was happening with Elora. When he saw Deborah struggle to try to keep her body massaged with the salve while still helping her when she was throwing up, he stepped in to help.

He directed his team to help with the salve; one raccoon would administer the salve and the other would massage. Their little hands were able to reach deep into the areas of Elora's skin where it needed the most treatment.

Phum had positioned himself high in a tree above them from the moment everyone started to attend to Elora. He kept watch over his comrades and listened for danger while the rest stay focused on her care.

Nick and Tybin worked through the night preparing food and drink for all of them. Every once in a while, Nick would coax Phum down to eat or drink. Phum would quickly consume what was offered and then scramble back up to his perch.

Finally, in the early morning hours Trevin said to Deborah, "Madame it is time for you to take a break and sit. Go drink some tea and eat. My men and I have watched you long enough to know how to help without you right here. Allow us the privilege to help both of you."

Ayden handed Deborah a cup of hot tea with honey mixed in, which Nick continuously kept on the fire throughout the night. She went behind Deborah and started to massage her shoulders, knowing Deborah had been going non-stop helping Elora and needed to be taken care of too.

She looked at Eleea who had stayed near Nekoh since the beginning with a constant worried look on his face. "Eleea, she will be fine, I promise you it is almost over. Look she is triple the size of Nip, now," Ayden said trying to calm his nerves.

"We have been going through this for over ten hours," Eleea worriedly responded to Ayden. "All of us are exhausted, can you imagine how Elora must be feeling. How much more can she take? It is obvious she is in tremendous pain. And, she has not cried out once, but has borne her dilemma with silent grace and dignity," he finished.

"I know, Eleea," Ayden agreed as she watched Deborah cut an apple and peel the outer skin. She then took out the meat of the apple by shaving it and putting it into a bowl. "What are you doing, Deborah," Ayden asked.

"There's an old remedy for an upset stomach. You shave the inside of an apple, let it sit until it turns brown and then eat it. It is supposed to stop nausea and I believe Elora is in need of some type of food since she has only had small sips of water for the last ten plus hours. By her eating this, she should be able to get some sustenance out of it."

"Plus, she has gone from throwing up every fifteen minutes to throwing up every hour or so. I think we are about done with her heaving, and now she can eat and rest. Hopefully we all will be able to sleep soon," Deborah explained.

Deborah went back to her patient and made her eat the apple. Soon Elora was done vomiting and resting against Deborah's chest where both of them fell asleep.

Jerin made a makeshift wall with a couple of large pieces of firewood and sat up against it. He put Deborah's body next to his to help her sleep more peacefully with Elora.

The Trevins lined themselves all around Jerin and fell asleep almost immediately. Nekoh sprawled out next to Deborah's and Jerin's side and became dead weight as he fell into a deep sleep.

Nick and Tybin positioned themselves up against the tree where Phum had staked out his guard post. And soon they too were asleep.

Eleea flew to Ayden who was preparing a bed for herself. Exhausted, but feeling slightly relieved Elora was sleeping, he began, "Ayden I know there is opportunity behind every negative situation to turn the negative to a positive. But when it involves someone you love so deeply; you begin to question if it is worth it. The elixir saved our lives, sort of, I mean if it hadn't of been for the elixir, we wouldn't have needed to be saved. In reality, Ayden, you saved us first."

"Eleea, I have been too afraid to talk with you about it. I was, actually, relieved we had the crisis with Elora to take my mind off it," Ayden expressed.

"We will deal with this new information and your new-found wings after all of us have rested, Ayden. I just wanted you to know how very much I appreciate you saving all of us. Do not worry and, once again, out of evil came good. Rest for now, my dear child and friend," Eleea finished as they both laid down to sleep.

Journal Twenty-Five

The Trevins were the best gift we had received on the trail to our destiny. When I think about how Trevin One tried to act so bad and important. I still chuckle and smile.

Calling Jerin and Tybin, "Little man" was hilarious. Tybin had him by the neck and he was still acting bad.

Saying they do not 'do' emotions because they would get all confused if they did. Jokes, really. They were nothing but emotions. Constantly trying to make sure Deborah, Elora, and I were OK if we got emotional.

When you really had a chance to watch Trevin One, you would see he was the most tender-hearted animal anyone could have the privilege to know. And the other Trevins were all the spittin' image of him.

They added humor and warmth to our mission and I loved all of them for those moments of pure love, concern and fun.

Chapter Twenty-Five

Ayden woke to little chirps from Elora as Deborah administered small drops of water to her. "Luckily, she was back to her original size and seemed to be no worse for her ordeal," she thought.

"See, girls," Elora stated. "I told you guys I would protect you," Elora expressed with pride.

Deborah and Ayden smiled at Elora as they both said in unison, "Yes, you did, Elora."

Ayden watched as Jerin worked on breakfast and Tybin approached with his arms full of wood for the fire.

Tybin stacked the wood, stood up and said, "After breakfast, we all need to talk about our next move as we begin to travel tomorrow. I feel we need to stay here one more day for Elora. We have to be confident she will be fine for travel. Or, if we need to send her riding the ospreys to Sunbird Village for their help in mending her."

Elora's voice was full of anxiety as she stated, "I feel fine, Tybin. I don't need to ride the ospreys, really! Please don't make me go away. Please!"

Tybin moved closer to her and Deborah, saying in a tender voice, "Elora, honey, I am not trying to be mean, here. You are valuable to all of us, and we can't afford to lose you for our selfish desires to keep you with us if you need greater care than we can give you at our camp," he concluded.

"I agree, Tybin," Eleea joined in the conversation. "We must be sure Elora is healthy enough to continue with us. And, to stay at camp another full day should give us a good read on whether she can handle further travel into the unknown," Eleea stated in a fatherly tone.

Phum interjected, "Not only is it good for us to stay here until tomorrow; but it is of utmost importance to deal with the gnawing questions we all have from the events of yesterday," he said as he turned to look at Ayden.

"We know Nadab gave you, Ayden, one feather locket as your weapon," Phum began his inquiry. "What I would like to know, is how one feather locket turned into two wings rather than just one?"

Ayden stood and moved to the center of the group to address them. *"When Nadab gave me my gift at the Great Tree, I was very confused wondering if he knew I already had a feather locket from my past. I had told no one, not even Deborah.*

The only person, here, who knew of this other locket was Nick. He had found it in the rubble of the fire at my home. My mother had given it to me when I was twelve. And, Nick returned it to me at the funeral of my parents." Ayden, pulled the chain from around her neck out from under her shirt to show them both lockets.

A stunned gasp echoed from the onlookers when she revealed both halves of the same perfect design. Ayden opened the first locket to show them the picture of her mother and her as a baby.

"I honestly do not understand how Nadab could have known I already had a locket. Or, maybe he didn't know and just made one like it...except it is the opposite from the first, being it is the other side of the wing," she said with confusion.

"The only thing I really do know about Nadab's decision to make it," Ayden continued, looking for insight to the question. "Is he told me he was having difficulty trying to figure out what weapon to make for me."

"I can attest to that," Eleea stepped in and said. "He had never known such confusion in designing a weapon, is what he told me, too. It was Lydia who broke his confusion when she told him to loosen his vice grip, and look beyond a normal weapon. She reminded him of all the beautiful jewelry he had made over the years for her and others," Eleea finished with awe in his voice.

"Nickalli," Nekoh began to question him, "Tell us what you know of this locket. Surely, you must have some deep knowledge of its origin?"

Nick stood up and went to stand by Ayden, stating *"When I saw the locket in the debris of the fire, I recognized my uncle's mark on it. It made no sense to me this piece of jewelry could belong to Ayden, until I opened it and recognized her mother. I figured the baby beside her had to be Ayden.*

My heart told me I had to return it to her. I did not know the importance or the meaning behind it belonging to her. I just knew she needed it.

I choose not to ask my uncle about it while at the Great Tree. As one, it never came up in conversation, and two, at no time while we were there, did my heart weigh with heaviness to address it.

I choose to believe the Great Crane guided my uncle to forge it, and it was not my place to be confused and confrontational about it. And, from what happened yesterday, with Ayden saving all of us, the Great Crane has obviously spoken here," he wisely finished.

"You, Nickalli, are a rare find," Nekoh admiringly stated. "Your depth of insight and patience is something all of us could learn from. I am with you. It is not our place to question; only to accept. And, if it had not been for Ayden, all of us would have perished yesterday," he respectfully stated.

Trevin stepped forward and stated, "Madame, may I be so bold to ask you a question?" Ayden nodded to him with approval. "My question is this, have you looked inside the second pretty to see if there is an image in it?"

Ayden held the locket higher so she could see it closer, as she stated, "No, Trevin, I have not. There has been no time or privacy for me to examine it closely. I guess this is as good of a time as any. Let's all look inside it," she said with a tinge of excitement.

Ayden glanced at everyone, then steadied her hand on the charm to open it. She turned it around in a complete circle and then looked at its back.

She raised her eyes to the group and stated with confusion, "I don't get it. There is no clasp to open it like the other one."

Jerin stepped forward and took it from her. He examined it with intensity. "No," he stated, "There is no way to force it to open. It is one solid piece, or so it seems anyway."

"Well, Phum said as he continued, "it would appear there must be other magic surrounding it. I propose when the time is right, an answer will show itself as to whether it will contain anything or not."

Trevin and Trevin Two jumped onto Ayden's shoulders for a better view and started to examine the locket. With the locket still attached to the long chain around her neck, Trevin pulled her head to the left as he was hunched on her left shoulder. He looked at it from all angles. Lifted it straight up, as her head jerked with it, to let the sun shine on it.

Trevin stated, "Look Two," as he lifted the locket on its side. "There is a line right here where it should easily come apart."

Two took it from Trevin and pulled Ayden's neck to the right, as he was sitting on her right shoulder. He did the same thing, jerking her neck up to see it better in the light, and said, "Yes, yes, I see what you are seeing," Two agreed.

"The shiny has a fine line when you hold it just right in the sunlight. It, it really should pull apart right here," he said with fascination.

Ayden grabbed the necklace out of Two's hand and said, "Guys! Guys! This is my neck you are jerking around here. Stop!"

Both raccoons looked at Ayden and simultaneously said, "Sorry, Ayden." They jumped down, bowed, and stood at attention.

"It's OK, guys. I'm not mad at you. It was kind of painful, But, it's OK, and I thank both of for trying to help me," she tenderly told them. They bowed again, and scurried off to a higher advantage point to watch the rest of the group.

Eleea took control of the situation by saying, "I think it is best to just let it go for now. And, since we are spending the day here, and all of us are existing off of a very high emotional drain from the last twenty-four plus hours. We all should just enjoy some free time and relax."

Everyone nodded in relief and started to go their separate ways.

Elora looked at Ayden and Deborah as she burrowed into her saddle bed. "I am going to sleep now, girls. But before I do. I am so proud I told you guys I would protect both of you?" She sleepily said as she closed her eyes.

The girls smiled at each other as Deborah grabbed her water bladder and apothecary pack. "Finch, come explore with me while I gather some plants," she stated as she started to walk into the woods.

Trevin Two excitedly ran to her side. Standing proud, he said, "It would be a great honor for me to go with you, Deborah, and assist you in your quest."

Jerin watched in subtle amusement at Deborah choosing a raccoon to be her partner in foraging. Curious by their bond, he decided he would quietly follow out of sight. Convincing himself they needed stronger protection in case any danger lurked behind a tree.

The two of them, and the silent one, Jerin, walked approximately a quarter of a mile away from the camp. Deborah sat down on a slightly raised flat rock and took a drink of water.

She turned to Finch, and offered him a drink as she said, "Tell me Finch, about your life before the Trevin regime existed."

Two took a drink and said, "Well, where do I start," he reflected. "I guess the easiest place would be where we are at right now. All of the Trevins grew up in this area. We know this forest front and back. It is our playground. This is why Gethsemane contracted with us to get you through it and beyond it, through the Dead Trees."

Two stood up and looked around at the landscape and continued, "All of the Trevins are orphaned, Deborah. The true Trevin took us in when Choran sent his bobcat, Dariat, to kill off our families. He individually, methodically stalked each of our homes and killed all but us Trevins," he sadly stated. He sat back down next to Deborah. She could see sadness in his eyes as he continued.

"If it were not for Trevin, we would have died too. He attacked Dariat with brutal force, he rode his back and would not let go. He dug his teeth into Dariat's neck and caught an artery, spewing blood rapidly. The force he showed in battle was that of a true leader. We were all wounded, and could not help him. Nor, were we old enough to even succeed in coming to his aid," he said with strong respect.

"After the battle, he took to our wounds and nursed each of us back to health. All the while, he held vigilance to make sure Dariat did not return to find us. He is a warrior of great beauty and love," Two stated as he looked past Deborah, remembering how Trevin saved them.

"We owe him, Deborah. Not out of obligation, but out of love for what he did for us." Two stated with humble regard for Trevin.

Deborah felt tears stream down her face as she grabbed Two in her arms. "I am so sorry for your loss, Finch," She cried. "No wonder you show Trevin such great respect. And, what a wonderful raccoon for what he did for all of you. I love him even more, now!" She exclaimed as she set Two back down.

Two was taken aback with Deborah's show of emotion and tried to regain his composure and hide his embarrassment. He stood again and said, "Deborah, would you mind staying here by yourself for a few minutes. I will be right back." He jumped high into the limbs of the tree they were sitting by and took off out of sight.

Deborah wasted time by looking through her plant book and tried to identify the plants around her. She felt a little uncomfortable by herself and worried she may be too exposed. She kept her mind occupied with her book, and hoped he would return shortly and not leave her alone for long.

Fifteen minutes later, he returned the same way he left. He stood directly in front of Deborah like a soldier would stand.

Two bowed to her and said, "Deborah as you know, we raccoons live for pretties. Actually, we have pretties stashed everywhere. It's just our way. I told you earlier this is our homeland. And, I have a private stash none of the other Trevins know about. This is where I went when I asked you if you were fine with me leaving you alone," he continued to say.

"Deborah, I would like to give you my most precious pretty I have ever found. A
gift for you. Because I believe it needs to be in your collection of pretties," he stated with pride.

Two opened his pack on the side of his hip and pulled out a tiny rectangle, intricately embossed bottle with different shades of sapphire and emerald stones inlaid in copper all around its one side. Gradually, the stones wove around to the other side of it. The stopper top was made of pure copper forged to resemble a tiny peacock head and neck, with its body of colorful wings played out in the stones on the bottle.

Deborah started to cry again as she took the gift from Finch. Her hands caressed the bottle as she said through her tears, "Finch it is the most beautiful bottle I have ever seen. It must have belonged to royalty it is so absolutely beautiful."

Again, she grabbed Finch and hugged him so tight his legs awkwardly dangled below him. She set him down and said, "Finch, I will treasure this for the rest of my life. I love you, Finch!"

Once again Two tried to regain his composure. Finally, he said, "Deborah, I am proud you like my gift. But I feel we have been gone too long and need to return to camp."

Deborah nodded in accordance with his request and the two of them began their walk back.

Jerin sat high above them in a tree and watched the whole scene unfold. Amazed at the degree of warmth Two had shown to a human being with giving her a shiny.

As well as the depth of respect he had for his savior, Trevin. He watched them walk far enough away before he jumped down to cautiously follow behind them.

"I will forever be changed by his story and his generosity," Jerin thought as he walked back to camp.

Journal Twenty-Six

Jerin and Tybin didn't look like twins in their appearance. Yet, their actions sometimes proved they were.

If one was in trouble, the other, almost instinctually, knew how to help. What one was thinking, the other would voice.

Their bond stirred from the womb, and carried on to their lives. Seriously, when you thought of one, the other was also in those thoughts. You just automatically looked for the other if you only saw one of them.

Nick was like a mini Jerin/Tybin. He looked a little like Jerin, with the same hair color. But his actions were a combination of the two of them.

Where Tybin was more athletic than Jerin, Jerin was more analytical in nature. Nick had both of these attributes. Nick's exposure to Nadab and his family had obviously given him a great gift to learn from some of the best.

The three of them were strong in so many different ways.

The gift each of them gave me...was the honor to learn from them.

Chapter Twenty-Six

By the time Deborah and Finch arrived back at camp, the evening meal was
simmering in the pot on the fire. Elora excitedly flew over to them and said, "I have been waiting and waiting and waiting for the two of you for a long time. Where were you guys? We have company!"

Deborah looked at Elora, and then turned her focus to the guest Elora spoke about. Tybin turned around to face Deborah and when he moved, the view of the woman standing with him was unobstructed.

She had long deep, dark brown hair, parted in the center as it flowed down her back to her waist. She kept it out of her face by placing it behind her ears.

Earrings of brass and silver with turquoise and blue lapis insets dangled three inches below her lobes. A fine silk and cotton mixture of multicolored blue, green, red, and turquoise full skirt swayed with her movement as it stopped just above her ankles. Above her left foot were several bracelets designed like her earrings.

A silk blouse of dark blue with sleeves reaching just above her wrists accented her rings of lapis, turquoise, coral, and sterling silver on six of her fingers. Bangle bracelets of copper, brass, and silver inlaid with the same stones rode up her right wrist and finished her look.

Tybin walked over to Two, Deborah and Jerin and said, "I would like to introduce Zetia. She is traveling to her homeland beyond the Dead Trees and ran into us on her return journey," he explained as he gave Jerin and Deborah a look of be careful what you say.

Deborah cordially shook her hand and searched at the same time for Ayden. She found her sitting with Nick and Nekoh against a tree outside of the campfire.

Ayden caught Deborah's eye, where she slightly shook her head to let Deborah know she was not sure of this woman. Deborah nonchalantly walked over to Ayden and Nick and sat down with them.

Jerin approached Zetia, bowed and said, "It is a pleasure to meet you, and it would be an honor for us to have you join us for an evening meal. Our young wards here, are on an enlightenment journey and would greatly benefit from your knowledge," he slyly concluded.

Zetia bowed back to Jerin and said, "I would very much appreciate the company this evening, and the hot meal. Then you could explain to me what this enlightenment journey is and why your wards have embarked on it."

Tybin drew closer to Zetia and said, "Let me help you break down the gear off your horses and ready them for the night." Zetia acknowledged Tybin's offer and the two of them retreated to tend to the horses.

Deborah turned to Ayden and whispered, "Whoa, this is a script right out of
Gethsemane's playbook, huh, 'A'? Thank the Crane, he had us play out dozens of scenarios at the Great Tree."

Ayden responded with, "Yeah, it makes it all very real, doesn't it? I just do not know how to read her? Friend or foe? But you and I are prepared, no matter what, to handle this very peculiar situation. I am just thankful Elora is back to normal and we have no need to let her know about your special skills or knowledge with your weapon's gifts," Ayden stated with relief in her voice.

The other Trevins returned from their recognizance search to find the best path to continue the journey. They excitedly jumped down in front of Ayden and the others.

Trevin leaned in to speak, "What is this? A new woman in camp! And, did you see the pretties all over her, Ayden?"

Trevin Five chimed in, "Not only on her body, sir, but on her horses, too. Look, at Tybin unload her bags. They are full of shineys. Even her horses wear the pretties," he stated with pure glee.

"Yes, yes, Five, I see," Trevin confirmed as he continued to address the group, "Is she to be with us on the rest of the journey, or is this just for tonight?"

"No one knows at this point, Trevin," Nekoh answered. "But we are all of one accord we say nothing to her about our true mission. She is a stranger, and we know not of her allegiance in Eshra," Nekoh cautioned them.

Trevin nodded to Nekoh and stated, "I am sure we will be able to spy out some truth tonight when she is not looking. We will dig through her belongings to see what we can find," Trevin said assuredly.

Nekoh lifted his paw in a gesture to stop and said, "Trevin, I respect you and your position but, we do not need to make an enemy here. Look, but do not take, my good sir. Agreed?"

Trevin put his paws on his hips and peered at Nekoh. "Fine," he sighed, "We just look. But, if I were to engage her in barter, I am free to get what I want," he stated triumphantly as he and the Trevins scampered off to get a closer look of the woman and her horses from high in the branches above.

Deborah turned to Nekoh and said, "Give him a break, Nekoh, it is his nature to find treasures. He is honorable, even if, sometimes, he goes about it in unconventional ways."

Deborah proceeded to tell the group, including Phum, Eleea and Elora who had joined them, about her outing with Finch and all he had told her about Trevin. She also explained the reason Gethsemane had chosen the Trevins to help them on their journey. Finally, she produced the bottle Finch had given her.

As Ayden admired its craftsmanship, Zetia approached them.

With intrigued interest, she said, "What a lovely artifact you have there." She reached out her hand, and said, "May I take a closer look?" Ayden looked at Deborah for approval.

Deborah reluctantly said, "Yes, you can hold it."

Zetia examined the bottle with great care as she turned it all around and intently followed the design with her fingers. She turned to Deborah and asked, "Where did you get this magnificent piece?"

Deborah's eyes became fixed as she piercingly tried to not glare at her. She reached for the bottle and took it out of Zetia's hand, and held it tight in her hand while she said, "It was a gift from a dear friend."

Zetia respectfully smiled at Deborah, sat down in front of the group, and said, "Let me give you some history about this piece. The copper you see around it was mined from a very ancient mining site."

"The history of the site is well known. What is not known anymore, is where the exact site is located. The type of copper and the method used to forge it and polish it have all been lost to modern Eshra."

"When you look at it, you will notice it still shines as if brand new. It has not turned green and does not show any patina which would normally be seen with its age." Zetia stopped to see if Deborah was intrigued enough to want to hear more.

Deborah's need to learn got the best of her, as she said, "So, what you are saying is, there is an old, lost, method to a) mining, b) forging, and c) polishing which no one knows anything about, now? Or is it the majority of people don't know of it? But you may just have some secret knowledge you keep to yourself because you are old Eshra?"

Zetia chuckled at Deborah and said, "You, Deborah, are an astute listener. I know partial methods, but not all. It truly is a lost art form. This piece you possess is exquisite in design. I would estimate it at, hmmm, five hundred years old."

"Five hundred," Ayden exclaimed. "Holy crap, that is ancient. How valuable is it?"

"Its value is a hard one to say," Zetia pondered thoughtfully. "My first reaction would be to say it is priceless. But, as we all know, there is always someone willing to pay for what they desire."

Phum watched the whole, what he considered a sideshow, of Zetia's playing with the girls' emotions. He finally said, "Enough. One, it is not for sale and two, and more pressing for me is, who are you and want do you want with us?"

Deborah followed Phum's comment with, "Yeah, I agree, Phum, what are you really doing here?"

Tybin stepped between all of them, saying, "OK, OK, it is all good. How about we all sit down to eat and have a friendly conversation where all questions, both sides, can be respectfully answered."

Nick and Jerin hurriedly finished the preparations for the whole meal. Which included fresh Marion and Huckleberries the Trevins had retrieved earlier while out on their mission.

Everyone sat around the fire to enjoy their meal. Deborah and Ayden made sure they pulled out their utensils from their outfits and placed them in front of them. Ayden was thankful Lydia had the forethought to design each garment they owned with an inside pocket to carry the utensils for easy access. She and Deborah gave thanks for the food, and all began to eat the meal.

Zetia visibly enjoyed everything set before her. She cautiously observed the whole group while she ate. A squirrel, a lynx, two chickadees, eight raccoons, a small kitten, two ospreys, and five humans she knew was far too big for an enlightenment party.

Yes, she knew through her travels what some in Eshra did at fourteen; but, never one this large. "They stand out like wearing a raincoat when the sun is brightly shining," she thought.

"Surely, they must realize how peculiar they look. And, what those who wish them evil would realize at the size of this group," she silently questioned, as she watched them.

"Tell me, Zetia, what is the purpose for all the art and jewelry you carry on your spare horses," Tybin asked.

"I am a curator of fine art," Zetia began. "I travel all across Eshra and between the worlds, throughout the northwest to sell and buy art. It is my livelihood to know what quality art looks like and what it is worth. I make a very decent living doing what I love. And, that is the true appreciation of past and present art of all forms," she concluded.

"Where do your roots originate from, Zetia," Nekoh endearingly asked with underlying subtle suspicion.

"Actually, I am on my home," Zetia revealed. "My home is beyond the Dead Trees, in a land known as Oshyama. My home is one of gorgeous mountains with trees far different than the ones you see here."

"Our trees are more bamboo-like, intermixed with white barked trees which hang heavy with a fruit unknown to any part of Eshra or the other world. This fruit is encased in a shell which when you break it open reveals a delicious soft orange outside core with a semi sour and sweet lemon nectar inside of it."

"Then there are the waters surrounding our land. The mountains gradually taper off into a beach full of beautiful grass and flowers which sway with pure art as they lead to the sand and the clearest ocean waters you have ever seen," Zetia dreamily finished.

"So, you are taking all of this art and trinkets to your land to sell," Deborah questioned Zetia. "And, all of this valuable merchandise, you carry, does not cause you any concern for harm by traveling alone," she continued to probe.

"I will sell or barter with most of it, Deborah," Zetia answered. "A few very unique pieces I have purchased for my private collection. And, as far as fear traveling alone, it is of no consequence. I may look fragile, but I promise you, I can hold my own against anyone or thing who tries to harm me or my horses," she said with authority.

"But the hour is late," Zetia stated as she turned to Tybin and Jerin. "I would like to ask permission to spend a few days with you as we seem to be traveling the same direction. And, even though I can take care of myself, I am not very good company when I only have myself to talk with. I would so enjoy having companions to converse with on the trail."

Jerin cautiously looked around the group, and then stated, "It would be our pleasure to have you join us for a few days, Zetia. The girls and Nickalli have already learned a tremendous amount about unknown lands in Eshra. Whatever knowledge you can impart to them is an added bonus for their enlightenment journey. And, I agree, it is late and we all need to retire for the evening."

Zetia left the group to check on her horses and to ready her bed for the night. Instead of joining the others around the campfire, Zetia laid out her sleeping gear in between her horses.

"Curious," Deborah whispered to Ayden as they lay in their beds. "She stays with her horses. She claims to be a force to be reckoned with in battles. She knows more than she is saying about this lost mine. And, now, she wants to ride with us, when it is very obvious, she is used to being alone...and likes it as a loner since she sleeps with her horses," she worriedly finished.

"Plus, 'A', I have a very uneasy feeling about my bottle from Finch. She liked it way too much. I saw the glint of greed in her eyes. We have got to do something, now, to protect it from her," Deborah said with determination.

"I know!" Deborah continued on her rant. "I'll lick the bottle and I bet my knife will protect it for me if I tell it to!" She yelled in a whispered tone as she started to dig for her knife and the bottle.

"'D'," Ayden expressed with frustration. "'D', your spit is not going to protect your bottle. Your knife is not going to protect your bottle. A bottle stolen is not a life or death situation where it would cause your knife to come to your aid. You are being irrational right now."

"Fine, but I am still going to lick it to make it my property. And, to be doubly sure she can't get it I am going to put it in Nekoh's apothecary bag. She'll never think to look for it there," Deborah smugly decided as she tried to stealthily inch towards Nekoh's bag as she licked the bottle.

"Nekoh, Nekoh," Deborah whispered right into his ear. Nekoh jumped, ready to pounce, until he realized it was Deborah.

"Good Crane, Deborah! What is wrong with you," he stated as he rubbed his ear with his paw.

"Nekoh I need your help, now!" She screamed in a soft tone. "Give me your apothecary bag. I have to hide my bottle in it," she claimed.

"Your bottle! Really, Deborah? You have to hide a bottle!" Nekoh asked in disbelief. "You wake me from my sweet dream, in a very rude manner I might add, to hide a bottle?"

"Yesssss, Nekoh, yes," Deborah urgently said. "Yes, I need your help. I need your apothecary bag, you know, the one given to you as a gift from Nadab and Lydia. I did not feel right getting your bag myself without your permission. Are you going to help me!" she quietly demanded.

"Fine, fine, fine, Deborah," he said as he turned over on his side. "Take it and do with it as you wish," he sleepily said as he laid back down on his other side.

Deborah found the bag, unlatched it and placed her precious bottle inside one of the empty leather pouches. "There, this bag will keep it hidden until I need it." She said as she closed the bag and breathed a sigh of relief.

'A', I feel much better, now." Deborah said as she slipped into position to sleep. "But maybe I better check it to make sure I strapped it in there tight. I do not want to lose this treasure so soon upon receiving it. As you know, Finch gave it to me and raccoons do not part with their pretties so quickly. It is so very special to me. It means a lot I was honored by him to have it." She sat back up and inched towards the bag.

Ayden rolled her eyes and said, "'D'," get done with it already. Whatever it takes for you to finally get some sleep do it. Because it appears, the only way I am going to get some sleep is for you to shut up and finish your obsession," Ayden impatiently stated.

"OK, 'A'," Deborah agreed. "I'll be quick," she said as she, again, unlatched the bag. Deborah let out a small muffled scream, and said, "AYDEN, it's gone! The bottle is gone!"

Deborah quickly turned the bag and its contents out beside the light of the fire. She dug through its contents, as she squinted in the dim light to see. Quickly, she grabbed her backpack and produced a tiny flashlight to help her see more clearly.

Trevin lit out of his perch above the campfire, and landed directly in front of Deborah. "OH! Deborah," he whispered. "You have a new kind of pretty!"

Deborah shushed him by saying, "You can have it when I am done, Trevin, but leave me be right now." Deborah desperately looked for the bottle as she started to hyperventilate.

Trevin Two jumped down from his tree perch and began to pat her hand, as he said, "It will be fine, Deborah. I will help you look for it." Deborah rubbed his head, between his ears to acknowledge him.

Ayden quickly came to her side and whispered, "We will find it Deborah, stay calm. And, stay quiet, OK. Let's take it back to when you first put it in the bag."

Ayden grabbed the empty bag and reenacted the scene by pretending she was putting the bottle in the bag. "What did you say when you got the bottle in the bag, Deborah," she encouraged her.

"I, I said, there, this bag will keep it hidden until I need it. And then I closed the bag." Deborah played along with Ayden's idea and closed the bag.

"OK, 'D', I know this is going to sound crazy, but I want you to pick up the bag. Then I want you to say, "I need the bottle I got from Finch and open the bag." Ayden quietly instructed her.

Deborah followed Ayden's instructions and said, "I need the bottle I got from Finch." And, then she opened the bag. She looked at the leather strap where she had first placed the bottle. "Ayden!" She screamed softly. "There it is. It's safe where I put it!"

Deborah moved over to Nekoh and whispered in his ear, "Nekoh, Nekoh!"

Once again, Nekoh jumped in the same fashion as he had the first time. "Deborah! Have you lost your mind, tonight," he cried in a meowing sort of way as he raised his body to sit on his haunches?

"Nekoh," Deborah said in a low voice. "You have got to see this." Deborah played out the previous events of the bag to show Nekoh how it hid things in plain sight when asked.

"Interesting," Nekoh claimed. "What a nice new discovery this is. I suggest, Deborah, we put your snail fern in this bag and do the same act over it to hide it from wrongful hands."

"Good idea, Nekoh," Deborah said with excitement as she dug through her belongings to get the plant parts. To make sure she had every bit of it, she used the flashlight to see better.

Nekoh jumped up and put his paw over her hand and said, "Deborah you cannot bring that out in the open. It is not of Eshra," he cried with fear in his whispered voice.

Deborah quickly flipped the switch off to draw no more attention to it. "Oh! Nekoh, I am so sorry I forgot we have company over there; and we have no idea who is watching us. It is, just, I was so scared I had lost the bottle. And, it felt so right to use it to help me find all of the snail fern. I am sorry," she said with remorse.

Trevin stepped in saying, "Nekoh, I will take it from Deborah and keep it hidden until it can be used safely. No one would think twice if a raccoon owned it. Especially since we are well known for gathering pretties and shineys from both worlds. Plus, Deborah has already told me I can have it." He masterfully finished.

Nekoh nodded his head in agreement to Trevin's solution. Trevin gleefully grabbed the flashlight and placed it in his bag. He and Two scampered back into the trees, utterly pleased with their barter skills.

Nekoh turned back to Deborah and said, "Child, we have to be extra careful, now. We are close to the Dead Trees and our mission will only get more and more dangerous."

"With this being said, do not let this misstep cause you to lose sleep; danger has been averted. And, with your new-found identification of the apothecary pouch and its hidden use, I believe tonight has been a very successful event," he finished as he nudged Deborah with affection.

Eleea, Elora, Phum and the three boys watched the night's activities with quiet trepidation. Thankful all went well with no major incident; they all laid their heads down and fell asleep.

Journal Twenty-Seven

Deborah and I grew up together. Granted, we only started when we were ten, but we were at the age where we could be on our own to explore our world.

No adults had to watch over us in East Glacier, because they trusted Deborah and I would keep close to each other.

A small town is different than a city. There is more freedom to roam the streets and alleys and the amenities like stores or the movie house.

The only time we ever had to be held more accountable of our whereabouts was when the height of the tourist season was in full bloom or when there were fires. Then, the whole town was on high alert. No one trusted the foreigners who entered our town, nor the unpredictable fire and where it would ignite next.

The freedom we had, gave us precious memories and insight into each other. What I never expected to see, was Deborah lose control.

I mean emotional control like she did over her bottle from Finch. She was always the calm, methodical, one who rationalized everything.

It would seem the Trevins, 'who were not emotional at all', had a strong effect on all of us. Their presence in our lives caused us to emotionally feel deeper than we ever had before.

Chapter Twenty-Seven

The sound of birds singing for the morning sun, gently woke the late sleepers from their slumber. Zetia already had her horses packed for the day as she walked over to the fire, and poked at it with a stick. She added tinder to help it ignite as she gradually placed larger sticks on it for the breakfast preparation.

She smiled at everyone, and said, "Good morning, fellow journeyers. What a beautiful day for travel. The sun is rising, the birds are singing, and soon we will have a wonderful breakfast to fuel us for our day. Does it get any better than this," she exclaimed with delight?

Tybin and Jerin returned on their horses, with Lok and Tari just ahead of them. The Trevins and Phum ran through the trees right behind the horses.

"It looks like we will continue to head due south once we reach the bottom of the tree line," Tybin stated.

"This day's ride will keep us in the trees, and tomorrow should bring us closer to the valley," Jerin added.

"Time to prepare for our journey, and get your horses packed," Jerin continued. "Tybin and I will get breakfast ready for all of you while you take care of your chores," he stated.

After breakfast, the boys worked with precision to quench the fire and safe guard it from any embers being left behind.

Ayden felt uneasy with Zetia around them. The whole morning meal was her talking aimlessly about her art and the 'exposition of its composition.'

Ayden considered it to be the most boring and uncomfortable time since she had entered Eshra. Throughout the meal, her and Deborah would give each other the look of, "Really, is this what you feel is important? Do you only talk about yourself and your greatness?"

The group filed into their normal riding sequence with one exception, Zetia rode behind Tybin. Ayden felt no ill will with the choice to have her ride there. She actually liked to be able to keep an eye on her, rather than wonder throughout the day if she was planning a sneak attack on her or her friends.

It was evident their mood was subdued by their silence as they rode and when they took short breaks to stretch their legs. The eerie lack of conversation, except for Zetia's incessant rambling of her superficial exploits, caused Ayden to grow in discomfort. She wasn't sure if it was really Zetia, or if it was the unknown dangers which may be ahead of them.

In one hand, Ayden was impatiently waiting for the sun to set so they could make camp for the night. But, on the other hand, she dreaded the thought of having to listen to Zetia spout her personal accolades for any length of time until they could all go to sleep.

Tybin must have sensed everyone's dreary thoughts about Zetia. Because way before it was time to stop, he yelled, "Jerin, this looks like a good spot to set up for the night."

Jerin called back with, "Thinking the same, Tybin." The boys set camp after they took care of the horses, while the girls prepared the meal.

Trevin yelled, "Nine, come join us on patrol. Let's see what fun we can stir up before dinner."

Phum looked at Nick perplexed, and said, "I really do not like I am called Nine, Nickalli. But, after Deborah's story about how he saved the other Trevins, I do have a heart for the weird little guy. And, I guess, I should feel privileged he considers me an equal, somewhat, to him. I mean, me being a squirrel and him twice my size, he sees me as an important part of his world," he said as he jumped into the trees to meet up with the Trevins.

Nick smiled as he watched Phum jump higher in the branches and soon disappear from his sight. "Yes," he thought, "Phum could argue all he wanted he didn't like the Trevins. But, since he accepted they were friend and not foe, Phum had been way easier going to be around. He laughed and he played more readily than when he was at the Great Tree. Yes, the Trevins had proven to be good for Phum," Nick happily decided.

Soon, the camp was busy with activity as everyone tended to their personal needs and wants. Ayden watched as Nip played with Elora. They would hop after each other, as if they were playing tag.

Slowly, each day, Nip was gaining strength in speech. It was like watching a baby speak her first words. You want to help, but it had to be their decision to do it. With you always encouraging them to push forward and try. Nip could say Ayd and Debd for Deborah, and Eyor for Elora. Full sentences were a little too advanced for her yet, but the girls took it as a personal challenge to work with her daily.

Eleea flew to Ayden's shoulder and said, "Does your heart good, huh, Ayden? To see a young soul, begin to learn. I remember the pride I felt when Elora took her first flight. It is exhilarating to see them grow. Cherish these moments, Ayden, for they are precious," he affectionately said.

Ayden turned to smile at Eleea as she realized he was right about seeing young life learn. It gave her great peace to see Nip free from oppression and able to grow in a loving environment with all of them.

The trees came alive with the return of the Trevins and Phum. They were full of laughter and more excitable than usual.

Trevin dropped down and said, "We chased a feral raccoon through the forest. They are not the brightest of the animal species, ya know, Deborah," he laughingly disclosed.

"You should have seen him chitter at us as he tried to scold us and run at the same time," Trevin stated as he fell over in laughter.

"Sometimes, he would get so discombobulated with us he could only run along the branches, and he would forget how to jump. It was hilarious," Trevin chuckled as he patted the other Trevins on the back.

"Nine," Trevin yelled. "You sir, are a true comrade. When I saw, you dangle below the branch and rise up ahead of him, and scare his heart into paralysis, I thought I would fall to the ground I was crying so hard from laughter."

"Hey! That is not cool, you guys," Ayden chastised them. "To scare a little guy like that is just plain cruel."

"I am very disappointed in all of you," Deborah declared. "This is not how any of us were taught at the Great Tree. What happened to showing respect to all," she declared?

"Deborah, ma'am," Two said as he bowed, "We did not leave him scared. We made him an ally before we left him. Each of us gave him a pretty from our own personal stash so he would feel he belonged and was a part of our troop. Truly, Deborah, we left him with food too. Lots of food for him to enjoy. He was sitting surrounded with his treasures, completely happy when we left him."

"Fine," Deborah stated. "But I still want all of you to seriously think about your actions and how scared the little raccoon felt. Because, boys, he did not know in the beginning you guys were just playing. He had real fear. You guys just sit here in time out and think about it," she finished as she stomped her foot.

Eight raccoons and one squirrel, all with their tails limp, filed into obedience with
Deborah's scolding. They just sat there, sitting, staring at the fire.

Ayden had to turn her head to mute her laughter and so they could not see her face. She walked behind Nick and beckoned him to stand with her behind the first tree she could find. The two of them watched from their advantage point as Deborah walked up and down the line gently chiding them for their inconsiderate behaviors.

True to how Deborah was trained by her parents, she stopped the scolding and began the healing process by telling each of them something she appreciated about them. She would hand them a special bowl of food, prepared by her hands, only.

And, as she handed them their bowl, she would tell them a specific trait she liked about them. Then she would gently rub their fur in a nurturing way to let them know she loved them.

Slowly, the line of tails began to perk up as she talked to them. And, all was well, once again, in the Trevins and Phum world.

Jerin and Tybin sat in stunned amusement, eating their dinner, as they watched Deborah demand her crew of shamed children repent for their actions.

Eleea flew strategically to Jerin's shoulder which was closest to Tybin's ear and said to the two of them, "Well, my boys, it would seem there is much much more to Deborah than any of us realized." The boys nodded in agreement as they smiled at Deborah and her misbehaved children.

Ayden and Nick joined the rest of them to eat their meal. Zetia, too, came from where she stood on the outside of camp and sat to eat. With their feelings mended, Phum and the Trevins, except for Two, climbed into the trees to take watch over their friends and to make sure there would be no surprises from unwanted foes in the woods.

Two timidly approached Deborah and said, "When we were out in the forest, I found this pretty for you Deborah." He took his paw out of his bag and handed her a stone.

Deborah gazed at the olive-green gem which looked like it had just been mined out of the ground. Dirt mixed with rock was on one side, while the brilliant colored stone itself jutted out of the dirty rock it was encased in.

She looked at Finch, grabbed him in her arms and hugged him, and then put him back down as she said, "Finch, this is an uncommon find. Look at its luster and clarity even in its natural state. It is absolutely one of the most breathtaking pieces of stone I have ever seen."

Two smiled with pride as he watched Deborah admire her rare gift. He bowed to her and jumped into the trees to join the others.

Zetia said, "Deborah, do you know what kind of stone it is?"

"No, I actually am not sure if it is yellow jade, emerald or maybe yellow sapphire?" Deborah stated.

"It is peridot, Deborah." Zetia stated, as she continued, "It can look like emerald, but it is its own stone. This piece Finch has found is exquisite. In the other world, it is the birthstone for August." Zetia smiled at Deborah and said, "What a friend Finch has become to you."

Deborah nodded as she looked at her new 'shiny'.

Ayden's heart was full of love for Two and Deborah as she watched their exchange of emotions.

"D'," Ayden said, "Finch has really bonded with you. Ever since the Trevins have joined us, life out here has gotten a lot more meaningful, wouldn't you agree?"

Deborah looked at Ayden with tears in her eyes, and said, "'A', I love that little guy. He is so tenderhearted. I just want to take him and protect him all of the time," she finished.

It was still early afternoon as they put away the supplies and cleaned up after the meal. Each looked to relax in their own way, when Ayden noticed Nip was agitated.

She intently looked at her, and said, "What's wrong Nip?" Deborah moved closer to Ayden to try and help.

Nip looked into Ayden's eyes and tried to speak, "Ayd, sme, sme," she said with a concerned look on her face.

"OK," Deborah said. "We know she has certain difficulty with some letters when she speaks. We know Ayd is Ayden. So, all we have left is 'sme.' "Smen, maybe? No, I don't think so. OK, smet, no. Smesh it could be smesh, like smash. No, none of it makes sense. Nip became more excited and fearful with each try Deborah made.

Ayden said, "No, 'D', none of those sounds like sme. What's another letter she can't pronounce? She says Debd for you and Eyor for Elora. 'L' it's got to be 'L'". Ayden turned to Nip and said, "Is it smell, Nip?" Nip jumped into Ayden's arms and rapidly repeated, "sme, sme, sme." Ayden noticed she was trembling with fear as she spoke.

"It's smell, Nip, what do you smell?" Nip jumped out of her arms and took a firm stance and bared her teeth, like she was angry and mean.

Jerin, Nick and Tybin began to take notice of what the girls were trying to do with Nip and joined in to help. All of them could feel each other's frustration when Zetia stepped in.

"I think she is trying to tell us she smells something dangerous. A smell she knows from her past and it is scaring her," Zetia determined.

Nip immediately climbed into Zetia's arms and started to lick her face.

Zetia gently placed Nip on the ground, and stood up. "Jerin, Tybin, and the rest of you," Zetia stated with urgency,

"I believe it is time to gather your weapons and prepare for battle. Nip's senses are highly sensitive to smells and she knows we are about to be attacked."

Wrapping her skirt tightly around her hips and tucking the ends of it into her waist, Zetia revealed several sheathed blades attached to her leggings.

She called out again, "Ospreys, call the Trevins and warn them. Each of you take a hidden position outside of camp on my backside, as I sit here with Nip and lure them in closer. Know the Great Crane fights with us today," she said as everyone scrambled to their posts.

Journal Twenty-Eight

The Great Crane. Everyone in Eshra held him in high regard. For me, he was just a bird who was well liked by the people I was traveling with.

I had no reference other than what he looked like. And, the cool story Callie told us which was lore of Eshra with a lot of symbolism.

It showed the crane full of wisdom. He was the decision maker of everyone. He recognized good and evil. And meted out his decisions by what he saw.

He valued humble behavior like what the hummingbirds possessed.

He wasn't afraid to make others angry with his decisions. He had deep love for everything Eshra.

And, I had his mark on my back. Why? Why did I have to bear his body on me was beyond anything I could figure out. One day, I hoped I would be able to ask him why.

Chapter Twenty-Eight

Zetia sat and soothingly spoke to Nip, while she stroked her fur. "Little one, you will be safe. When the fight starts, see here," Zetia pointed to a hole she had dug under the log behind her legs, "I want you to hide in this hole. And, I want you to stay there until I tell you it is safe to come out," she finished.

She then, strategically placed the tip of a thin, long, log into the fire, and made sure she could maneuver it with her foot. She poured herself a steaming cup of tea and sat with Nip on her lap. Zetia positioned herself to look like she was just relaxing and enjoying her afternoon with her kitten.

Tybin and Jerin grabbed the horses and put them far on the left side of the camp behind Zetia. They then, respectively flanked the girls.

"Ayden," Tybin whispered, "I want you to go directly back another two hundred feet. You stay out of sight and do not engage in battle. If need be, you jump on your horse and you ride back as fast as you can to Sunbird Village. The horses know the way if you get confused."

"Deborah!" Jerin began, "The same goes for you. Go straight back from where I will stand over there," he gestured. And, keep hidden like Ayden. And, if she goes for her horse, you go with her. Understand?"

Ayden began to object, but Tybin cut her off. "No, Ayden! We need to protect you and not lose you this day. Your time will come soon enough. Stay out of sight," he tenderly demanded.

Jerin motioned to Deborah to follow him and he positioned them across from Tybin, approximately 500 feet, and hid from site.

Making sure they could see the campfire, the boys turned to the girls and motioned for them to move farther back and hide. The girls nodded at the boys and did as they were told.

Once they reached their new positions, they looked at each other from across the distance which separated them. Their eyes locked with noticeable fear.

Ayden nodded and smiled at Deborah to reassure her they would be fine. Even though, she didn't feel fine, she wanted to help Deborah manage her fears and not react to them.

She then lowered herself to her knees and sat back on her legs as she hid, slightly behind a large tree; making sure she could freely jump up or see if need be. She questioned if she should close her eyes or watch. She sensed she needed to stay focused by observing all that was going on around her, rather than hear in sequestered darkness.

Deborah crouched down behind a boulder that had fallen onto a tree and had split the trunk. She was able to lean comfortably inside the trunk, and still stay mostly hidden. And, as a bonus, she could see all around their camp. She noticed Eleea had taken to a limb close to Ayden, while Elora landed on a branch in-between her and Ayden.

Farther past the campfire, Deborah saw several of the Trevins high in the trees look down at Zetia. She heard whispers between her and them, and then the Trevins took off into the trees.

Phum had both his knives in his paws as he perched to the right of the trees by the girls. As she looked up, she saw the ospreys; each were perched high above their best friends. Try as she could, she could not find Nick or Nekoh.

Ayden flashed back to the Great Tree as she sat, straining to listen and see around her. All Abner had taught her, she thought, at the time, was foolish and a waste of time. Now, was proof he knew what she would need to survive in battle.

Her ability to stay focused with fear surrounding her, gave her a stronger advantage to react with the needed skill she must have to fight at the right moment. Abner had continuously drilled these skills into her and she was very thankful for him as she waited to see what would happen.

Sounds in the distance, past the campfire, suggested people and animals would soon be approaching. Ayden could hear at least two horses. She knew each had someone on its back by the weight of the rider causing their feet to hit the ground a little harder.

Simultaneously, Ayden heard above her right and her left a sound of metal moving across itself. Like when a person is using a sharpening stone for knives.

She knew it was the chickadees armor appearing on their bodies. Remembering Elora's weapons, she visualized in her mind how it formed over her wings, becoming a solid mass of feathered steel as she heard each section snap into place.

Ayden sensed everyone around her become tense as the intruders drew close to the campfire.

A woman's voice said, "Zetia, this is not your battle. We have no quarrel with you. Leave now, and we will spare your life."

"Nahrita, I too, wish you no harm. It would seem you have been sorely mistaken by your scouts as there is no one here to battle," Zetia stated.

Zetia sized up Nahrita's war party and said, "Twelve hawks, a pack of wolves, three badgers, five boars, your friend on his horse, and you and Dariat, Nahrita. Do you really believe I should be concerned about my life because of who is with you?"

"It would seem you and your friend Dariat have chosen to throw good sense to the wind and follow Choran's misguided herbology," Zetia slyly taunted Nahrita.

"How much snail fern does it take to become the size of an amazon woman and a bobcat to become the size of a horse, Nahrita?" Zetia asked.

"What is it to you, Zetia!" Nahrita spewed in retaliation. "You could have given us a much better way to accomplish our goals. But your righteous desire to stay neutral, or so you told Choran, caused us to take other methods into our own hands. Whatever it takes, we will have our victory!" Nahrita yelled at her.

"Yes, victory, Nahrita," Zetia stated, calmly, as she continued to speak. "At what cost to your body are you willing to achieve this victory? If you continue to take the elixir, you will end up as Choran. A shell without a soul, and no hope to return to your natural glory."

"Do not take me for a fool, Zetia," Nahrita vehemently stated. "Your words mean nothing to me, except for the fact this conversation allows her and those with her to escape from our grasp. You know the messenger is on the move in Eshra. And, you out of all of us, know the prophecy more intimately. I can guarantee you spoke to Joshua at Sunbird, and were warned by him to be on the watch for these fools who travel to the Dead Trees. Where is she, Zetia? This camp you sit at is not your style. Give us the direction she is running to hide from us."

"Yes, I spoke to my dear friend Joshua three days back," Zetia stated. "And, yes he did tell me the prophecy from old would soon come to pass here in Eshra. Which brings me to a question for you, Nahrita?" Zetia said as she placed Nip down by her legs. "What makes you so sure she is running?"

Zetia flipped the log out of the fire causing the flames and hot embers to land on Nahrita and her companions. She quickly stood and reached down her legs and pulled a knife to each hand.

Zetia propelled her body upwards, swirled around and kicked Nahrita off the back of Dariat. She calculated her kick to allow herself to land on Dariat's back and plant her feet as she launched herself into another swirl. In midair, she raised her blades and jabbed them into the neck of the other horseman.

Nahrita's hawks dived at Zetia as she hit the ground running deep into the forest while the hawks chased her.

Deborah sat stunned as she listened and watched the whole Nahrita/Zetia interaction unfold. "She's a good guy," Deborah thought to herself. "Crazy, Zetia is a good guy and on our side. There are a lot of questions I have for her when this is over. I knew she had more knowledge than she let on to when we first talked," she disgustedly concluded.

Deborah's thoughts jolted back to reality as she watched Zetia fly into action as she unseated Nahrita and killed the other rider.

The minute she began to run, the ospreys bolted towards her and Deborah could
hear stressed cries from the hawks, as she knew Lok and Tari had connected with their targets.

Nahrita scrambled to her feet, jumped onto Dariat's back and took off in the same direction as Zetia. Followed closely by the badgers running after Nahrita.

Tybin and Jerin seemed to fly into the trees above them as they easily traversed the limbs to reach the wolves. Tybin's staff flipped the first wolf as he twisted his staff with lightning-speed to stab the animal dead with its tip in the wolf's head.

Another wolf jumped onto Tybin's back causing him to fall. The wolf lunged at Tybin's throat just as an arrow pierced the wolf's neck. The arrow exploded in a blue haze of smoke and flashed light when it made contact causing all who were close to blink excessively to regain focus around them.

Jerin, took advantage of the wolves disorientated vision, and rapidly shot three arrows into three different wolves who were the closet to Tybin. Each arrow exploded with a different color of haze. White froze the wolf like brittle ice where the wolf shattered into pieces as the arrow hit him. Another ignited into flames when the arrow passed through its side. A third one puffed with green smoke upon impact and paralyzed the wolf in mid-flight.

Tybin jumped up and out of the way of the dying wolves. As he turned, another wolf latched on to his right ankle with such force it brought him to his knees. The wolf and Tybin began to roll on the ground as the animal loosened his grip and put his full body weight on top of Tybin and bared his teeth. Tybin grabbed the wolf's neck fur as he tried to get the wolf off his body.

Again, Tybin and the wolf started to roll as they each tried to gain the upper hand on one another. The wolf quickly sunk his teeth into Tybin's right wrist to disable his hand. Letting go of the wrist, he moved with precision towards Tybin's neck. Taking the dagger from his left side sheath, Tybin brought it up and sunk it into the wolf's chest. He twisted the blade until the wolf's body went limp.

Another wolf made a wide circle around the fight and caught Jerin from behind. The weight of his body and the force of his attack knocked Jerin to the ground. Jerin's head hit a rock and busted his right eyebrow open. The wolf promptly moved to Jerin's throat as he looked for an opening to dig in with his teeth.

Phum, who was watching from above, left his perch and pounced directly down onto Jerin's wolf with his two blades in his paws. He scrambled up the wolf's back to his head, Phum forcefully jabbed his blades into both of the wolf's eyes; disabling the wolf's attack on Jerin.

Tybin came in and finished the wolf with his staff. The last two wolves ran into the woods, leaving the three warriors to regain their strength and bearings. Tybin took Jerin's hand and pulled him up to a standing position.

The boars, who were waiting to join the fight, ran away when the other wolves retreated. But, instead of continuing to go the same direction, they suddenly veered to the left as they came directly towards Deborah.

In a full run, with their noses to the ground, they called out to each other, "I smell her! She is at the downed tree. Quick before they see us, get her!"

Deborah pulled her knife out and readied it by her side. Fear began to rise in her throat as she tried to figure out which one to attack first. The huge tusks protruding out of their jaws caused her to question her sanity and her ability to conquer them.

The closer they came, the more she felt the fear. She began to lift her body from its resting position as she prepared for their attack. She readied herself to stand, when she felt a flash of wind pass by her from Nick, Two, and Nekoh who ran towards the boars.

As Nick ran, his wrist bands began to grow. The leather grew like lava flowing while it covered his elbows to his wrists and hands. Each hand formed into a huge paw, while his five fingers became formidable sharp claws.

Nick reached the first boar and slashed him with his claws. The force of his actions was so intense the boar went flying through the air and landed on the ground.

Two and Nekoh jumped onto the downed wild pig. Nekoh sunk his teeth into its neck, while Two went for his eyes with his knife. The boar raised his head and thrashed it to break Nekoh's hold. As he did, Two went flying into the bark of a tree.

Nekoh lost his grip and fell back. The boar took his left tusk and slashed Nekoh's right hip. Tybin swiftly charged with his dagger and impaled the boar, leaving its guts spilling out.

Nick attacked the next boar with his claws as Elora swooped in with her feathered blades. While Nick held the boar in his claws, she methodically flapped her wings to take out his eyes. Tybin twirled around from his first kill and finished off Nick and Elora's victim.

Nekoh ran from behind to jump on the back of the next boar as it barreled down on to Nick who was watching Tybin. He made contact with the wild pig's neck and large streams of blood spurted everywhere as his teeth found the carotid artery.

Jerin, running to help, reached in his quiver and held two arrows in his left hand as he lined them up on the left side of his bow. With rapid succession, he let loose of the two arrows into the fourth and fifth boar, where one exploded into slivers of ice and the other one burst into flames.

Within seconds of the boar fight, what was left of the hawks, circled around Ayden.
Eleea and Elora took flight, as Phum and Two scrambled to reach the highest branches just above the hawks.

Eleea set his steel claws into the back of a hawk who ferociously flapped his wings to get Eleea off of him. The two of them began a free fall as the wings action caused them to spiral out of control.

Phum grabbed his left knife and threw it, where it landed in the hawk's chest. He yanked on the chain as it began to retract into his belt buckle. With all of his body strength he tried to stop their dangerous descent.

Two came up behind him and held him in a tight body hug as they both struggled to hold their bearings. Within inches from the ground, the hawk's body went limp as it slowed its momentum and dangled from the chain. Eleea flew off the hawk and looked for the next one to attack.

Elora flew high above the trees to get away from the two hawks who flanked her. Instinctually, she changed her flight pattern by diving back down into the trees. She darted in and out of the limbs with the hawks close behind her.

She caught Nekoh out of the corner of her eye as she navigated the branches and flew directly at him. Nekoh leaped up at her and caught one of the hawks in his claws. The bird fell to the ground, where Nekoh pounced on him and broke his neck with the weight of his body. Elora swiftly turned away from Nekoh's claws and began to climb high into the sky with the other hawk in quick pursuit.

Eleea followed behind the hawk and gained speed as he reached the back of the hawk's wings. Elora flew into position on the other side of Eleea. Both of them used their feathered steel wings to slash at the hawk's body. The hawk tried to defend himself by darting back to the ground.

Immediately Eleea flew under the hawk to stop his downward trajectory. Elora flapped her winged blades into the hawk's body as she flew beside it. As the hawk's dead body fell to the ground, blood dripped from every cut made by Elora's blades.

With danger averted away from the girls, Tybin turned to his comrades and stated, "Nekoh, Eleea, and Nickalli, the three of you stay with the girls. The rest of us go to assist Zetia and the Trevins."

Jerin had retrieved the horses while Tybin gave his instructions. Phum and Two jumped onto Tybin's horse, while Elora flew to Jerin's as they hurriedly took off in the direction of Zetia.

Ayden sat in total awe by what she had just witnessed. Seven of the nine wolves were gone. Five boars with really big tusks, dead. Three hawks annihilated. Blood was everywhere; and, not one of her friends were mortally wounded. The reality of the battle began to sink into her heart, as she slumped back in her sitting position.

She closed her eyes in deep thought. "I could have never survived this type of battle," she whispered to herself. "I don't even have a real weapon from Nadab like the others nor do I have the agility to wield a weapon like they did."

Her mind began to wander as she thought about the past, present and future. The past and life with her parents seemed so long ago; almost like a bad dream.

The present was way too present and real right now. Life and death happened. And, obviously, any decision made, had consequences. All of these dead animals made a choice to live for Choran and now their choice got them killed.

And, then there was the future. What will it hold? "Will her friends die like these animals who lay here," she questioned, as she tried to hold back tears.

"*I am really scared,*" she softly breathed.

A gentle breeze played with her hair as she spoke those words. A voice she thought she heard in her mind said,

"*Ayden, my child, fear is not defeat. Fear is awareness.*
Have courage, child.
For courage….is not the absence of fear.
But, the determination against all odds
To hold your head high, and
To persevere with dignity and respect."

Ayden, flashed her eyes open to see who was talking to her, knowing it wasn't her mind giving her this type of wisdom. Off to her left she could see an outline of an image.

At first it appeared to be a blurry blob. As she focused her eyes intently on its form, she gasped.

Standing by her was a magnificent regal bird. It looked just like the picture etched on her journal. The journal Lydia had slipped into her backpack before they left the Great Tree.

"Help me," she said to the crane. "I am so afraid. I am just a child playing a very serious game of real consequences. What can I do, I have no weapon to help my friends," she said through her tears?

"*Ayden, you are the weapon, child. Those wings you see when you need them, are real and powerful. Take flight with them, and you will begin to see,*" the crane said.

"Take flight! Take flight," Ayden softly screamed. "I am a human! How do I learn how to fly? I am a human!"

"To know how to fly does not come from the act of doing it," the crane explained. *"To learn how to fly comes from the soul. Allow your soul to give your wings flight,"* he concluded, as he slowly disappeared.

Ayden watched his image vanish, knowing it was no use to call him back. Just like the Wall of Tears, she knew the magic of Eshra only gave a certain amount of time to deliver its message. Even if those messages created more confusion than answers, this was all she would get.

As she pondered this new concept she was supposed to freely embrace and own. She determined to keep the meeting with the crane to herself.

"There's no use to get the others confused like she was," she thought. "It's better to stay in the present and help everyone when they come back from the Zetia battle," she silently determined.

Journal Twenty-Nine

Is anything what it seems when we first encounter it? I mean, really, can we trust our first impression on anything?

When we see, or hear something, we can only evaluate it from our past experiences. What we already know is how we determine to handle any new information.

That which is familiar to us is our reference points to future understanding.

How someone deceived us with subtle words of trickery could cause us to feel less sure about another who speaks to us with the same type of wording.

Or, here is where our gut reaction comes into play. Once we have been deceived...a little voice deep in our hearts says, "Be careful of this person. This person may be the same type as before."

Bottom line, we all have to take what we hear and see and wait. Wait and watch for further information, to form a solid opinion of whether the person or event is real, good or bad.

Wait to decide if our first impression is valid or needs to be changed.

Zetia was a perfect example of how I needed to wait and watch.

We all had those gut reactions to our first encounter with her. But there was a lot more to her than any one of us realized.

Chapter Twenty-Nine

Zetia swiftly ran through the dense forest to lure Nahrita and the badgers away from Ayden. Confident the rest of Ayden's friends could handle the other combatants, she knew, from past encounters, Nahrita would stop at nothing to prove to Choran she was loyal. Her desire to please him made her extremely unpredictable and dangerous.

The only chance everyone at the camp had was to get Nahrita and the other aggressors far away from Ayden. Her chosen path led her pursuers with her for about a quarter mile where the Trevins were high in the trees.

As soon as Nahrita and Dariat passed them, the Trevins dropped to the ground. Four on one side, and three on the other. They quickly drew a rope taunt, like a tug-of-war line.

The badgers, in full chase, tumbled over each other as the rope caught the leader under his neck. Trevin dropped the rope and leapt onto the stomach of the first badger.

Teeth bared, he latched onto its throat as they rolled on the ground with Trevin on top thrusting his dagger into its stomach repetitively. The badger gnashed his teeth as his clawed front foot swiped across Trevins face on the left side and cut him.

Trevin held on tighter, blood oozing and dripping onto the badger. Trevin situated his head, and let his blood drip into the badger's eyes which caused the animal to blink and lose his focus.

Trevin Four quickly moved in and slashed the badger's throat. Trevin stepped off the animal and then wiped his head on the badger's fur to get rid of the blood from off of his face.

Trevin Three, Five and Eight jumped on the second badger, who viciously rolled over to regain his footing. Three ended up underneath the animal while Eight took his knife and thrust it straight up into the badger's bottom jaw. The badger reeled straight up where Five immediately took his knife and dug it deep into the animal's chest. Three, who was able to scurry out from under the badger when Eight used his knife in the animal's jaw, came around to his other side and swiped his knife across the badger's throat.

Trevin Six and Seven tackled the last badger who stood straight up on his hind legs. He grabbed Six and Seven in each of his sharp claw paws and smashed their heads together. The Trevins fell to the ground, dazed.

The badger turned on Seven and bit down on his chest. Six crawled on top of him and put his paws on his forehead as he stuck his fingers into his eyes and pulled his head back to get him to release his grip on Seven.

The badger fiercely shook his head and threw Six onto the ground. Three, Four and Eight jumped on the badger and wrestled his front arms down to stop him from wounding them. Trevin sprung up to reach his neck and made a deep clean cut to kill him.

Trevin surveyed the battle scene to make sure the badgers were dead. Then he ran over to Seven. He lifted Seven's head in his paw and said, "Seven, talk to me."

Seven slowly opened his eyes and focused on Trevin, and quietly said, "I'm fine, sir. I promise I won't die." He closed his eyes as his chest heaved.

Trevin put his ear to his chest to listen to make sure he was still breathing and no gurgling sound came from his chest cavity. Trevin lifted his ear off of Seven and turned to the rest and said, "Six and Eight, stay with him until he can walk, then get him back to camp for Deborah to take care of him."

He turned back to Seven and said, "Seven, you will make it, son, I promise."

Trevin jumped up and said, "Three, Four, and Five, the fight continues. We go to help Zetia, men!" The four of them took to the trees and rapidly disappeared from sight.

Zetia reached the end of the thick trees where her horse stood waiting. Running at full speed, she jumped onto his bare back and held onto his mane as the horse raced through the trees. She put her hand into her waist pocket and produced a drawstring pouch. With her teeth, she opened it and placed it and her hand behind her back. The contents of the bag spilled out like a poof of flour as they rode.

Nahrita and Dariat were fast approaching Zetia when the powdery substance hit them. Both began to cough and choke as it reached their lungs. Nahrita pushed her heels into Dariat, demanding he keep running as they both gasped to get clean air in their lungs.

Dariat continued another three hundred feet before he collapsed from lack of oxygen. Nahrita jumped off of him and opened her bladder to give him water and then took some herself.

Angrily, Nahrita said, "Dariat," but she could not continue as she and he began to heave up black masses from their stomachs. Both lay on the forest floor, in agony, as their bones began to creak and twist as if they were breaking.

Zetia watched from a distance to make sure Nahrita and Dariat were disabled. She trotted her horse back to where they lay and said, "Go back to Choran, Nahrita."

Nahrita looked up at her and scowled, saying through coughing and spitting, "I will never give up, Zetia."

Nahrita tried to catch her breath as she continued to speak, "You have made your choice! Now, I no longer have to honor Choran's request to leave you alone. I will see you die by my hand, Zetia!"

"You fight a battle you can never win, Nahrita. My heart aches for you. Not because of what you have become, but for what you saw as a child. The horrors you have seen should have never been a child's life. You were terribly wronged and abused. But, as an adult, you are responsible for your choice to follow evil rather than good. Go home, Nahrita," Zetia sadly said.

Zetia gently heeled her horse as they began to pick up speed to get back to the others. The Trevins were the first to see her, as she stopped to assess them.

They quickly told her of their exploits as she helped them climb up on her horse. By the time they reached Seven, he was sitting up, taking small sips of water given to him by Six.

In order to get him on Zetia's horse, Eight got on Five's shoulders and stood up. Four and Three picked up Seven like they were handling a baby and handed him off to Eight. Trevin jumped back on Zetia's horse and reached down to stabilize Seven's move to lay him in front of her. Just as they finished getting Seven secure, the others reached them.

Zetia listened to Tybin and Jerin as they told her all that happened back at camp. She looked at all of them and said, "This battle is finished, but more will follow. Two have escaped and will go to the aid of Nahrita and Dariat. The wolves will stay with them to make sure they recover from my potion to expel the snail fern in their bodies. The wolves will not leave them and will protect them from predators. For now, this battle is over."

"Why did you not kill them when you had a chance, Zetia?" Jerin questioned.

"Jerin, I know it is hard for all of you to see my reasoning. Yes, I could have ended their lives, easily. But, what would that make me? Any better than them? They could not fight. They were not attacking me where I had to defend myself. In my training, it is wrong to take a life when they are unable to fight back," Zetia humbly explained.

Jerin nodded to her in acceptance, and said, "The hour is late and we need to secure the camp for tonight.

Deborah could hear the Trevins' happy voices before she could see all of them return. She looked at Ayden and yelled, "'A', it's OK, you can relax they're home." Ayden turned to Deborah and smiled, acknowledging she could relax.

Ayden had watched with overwhelming fear and pride as each battle unfolded. The biggest moment of sheer terror for her was when she felt the need to run to Deborah as the boars started to come at her. Thankful she could relax, she audibly let out a large sigh.

Eleea flew in the direction of the returning party, as Nick stood in-between the girls and watched. Deborah ran for her apothecary bag and began to organize her supplies to help the wounded.

Her first priority was Nekoh, as she examined his gash. She turned to Ayden and Nick, saying, I need lots of hot water and any rags you can find. Nick and Ayden jumped to action to fulfill her requests.

Deborah drove her knife into the ground, where plants began to grow around it. Peppers, horsefly weed, aloe Vera, Wooly Lamb's Ear, monkshood, common daisy, and marigold all came forth to help her.

With everyone back at camp, Deborah continued to direct them to help her. She sent the Trevins to gather large green leaves from trees for dressing. She asked Elora and Eleea to find honey bees and when they found them, to return and get Jerin and Tybin to retrieve the honey for a salve.

Zetia handed Seven off to Nick and jumped off her horse as she called to Nip, saying, "It's OK, now little one, you can come out, it's safe." Nip slowly came out and ran to Ayden, where Ayden opened her sling and Nip jumped in to hide again.

Nick rolled up a blanket and set Seven on top of it, making sure he was comfortable. Deborah evaluated his wounds and quickly administered some of her concoctions.

Zetia watched Deborah with admiration, as she realized she had impressive herbalism skills.

"Deborah, while you work, let me talk with you," Zetia asked. "It appears you have great knowledge of our land and its resources. I too, know some of these skills. I was able to disarm Nahrita and Dariat from their ingestion of snail fern with a powder mixture through the use of plant properties. I would like to teach you how to make it and administer it after everything is settled. Maybe tomorrow, we could spend some time together," she stated.

Deborah, with her eyes focused on her patient, nodded her head and said, "I would be thrilled to learn what you know, Zetia."

Deborah silently continued her meticulous triage, not wanting to be bothered with conversation. After the serious wounds of each friend were given the appropriate ointments and dressed, Deborah turned to the others.

She intimately examined every single one who was in a battle. Methodically, she cared for each, even if they claimed they had no wounds. Their bodies were not theirs when she reached them and made them show almost everything.

Deborah stood up and looked at her handiwork. She mentally counted off each patient she had seen and cared for. She twisted her head around to look for Jerin. He had avoided her and she knew he was hurt when he battled the wolves and boars.

Tybin caught her eye and nodded his head to the left where the horses were kept for the night. Deborah grabbed her bag of aids and walked down to the horses. She found Jerin leaning up against a tree, acting like he was busy with his dagger and sheath.

"Do you really think you can avoid me when above your right eye has a good-sized gash," she asked him.

"I do not need any special medicine or care, Deborah. I am fine," Jerin tried to say with authority.

"Jerin," Deborah compassionately said, "you and all of the others saved not only my life, but Ayden's. I watched how brave you were when you were fighting. Sit right here. Now!" She told him firmly.

Jerin reluctantly sat while Deborah examined his wound. Two had followed her and she enlisted his help while she worked. He held her salve and leaves as she cleaned and dressed the cut. Deborah took one of her bandanas, a dark blue, and tied it around Jerin's head to hold the leaf and salve in place.

"There." Deborah said as she finished and packed her belongings back into her bag. "Now, I want you to join us at the fire to eat and to drink my special tea all of you are required to consume to help your injuries heal faster," she informed Jerin.

Deborah looped her arm through Jerin's as they walked back to the fire, and said, "Again, Jerin I want to thank you for keeping us safe. I was really really scared when those boars came at me."

Jerin patted her hand, saying, "Deborah it took all of us and our special skills today to survive and to be able to talk about it. The Great Crane, as Zetia said, was with us."

Food was served by Nick and Ayden and everyone ate in deep reflection over the day's events. Ayden looked around as she noted most had some type of a scar they would carry for the rest of their lives. Whether it would be on their body or in their heart, all of them were scarred this day.

Tybin looked at Zetia and said, "Who are you, really?"

Zetia set her bowl down and took a long sip of her tea before she spoke. "I am a person who loves Eshra, Tybin. My travels have given me great freedom to learn about people and places. My business allows me the privileged insight to all different kinds of people and customs."

"Good or evil. I learned at a young age how to defend myself and how to take advantage of each circumstance I encounter. I strive to look for the good in people and in life. I am very capable of discerning motives from others, which has kept me safe for many years," Zetia finished, while she took another sip of her tea.

"That is all fine and good," Tybin continued. "And, I am very thankful you were on our side in this battle today. But, all of those attributes you claim do not tell me who you really are," he stated with authoritative confusion in his voice.

"Tybin, I ask you, all of you, to take me at my word. I wish none of you any harm. It has been a great honor for me to help you today as we fought off evil and protected Ayden and her quest. Yes, I knew from the beginning who all of you were."

"Then, why did you act so, so shallow with your nonstop talk about frivolous topics and act like you knew nothing about us," Deborah blurted out in frustration.

"Do you know the term 'ruse' Deborah?" Zetia asked.

"Ruse: To trick; a strategy to trick." Deborah instructed.

"Yes, you are right, Deborah," Zetia stated. "I used a ruse of frivolous, as you call it, talk to ward off evil around us. We do not know who is watching your every move; especially the closer you get to the Dead Trees. With me talking nonsense, people and animal get bored of listening to it. Just as all of you did. They try to distance themselves from it, as it is annoying."

"My purpose was to keep Choran's scouts confused and annoyed so we would not be attacked unexpectedly. Their guard would be down and they would leave the area to get away from the stupid conversation."

"Thus, they would go back and give poor information to those who wanted to harm you. They would have seen you as nonthreatening," Zetia concluded.

"And, by today's actions, it would seem my ruse worked as we were not attacked by an army or ambushed out in the open, exposed. Nahrita was a scouting party. Not an army. The hawks gave her weak information. When she came up on your camp, I could tell by her facial expressions she was taken off guard. She quickly put two and two together, as she noted, this is not my style of a camp. She knew it belonged to the Messenger and her friends," Zetia wisely stated.

"OK, fine," Ayden stated. "But, back to the original question," she insisted. "Who are you? You are more than a traveler of Eshra. Because you called Joshua a dear friend which tells me you have very special knowledge and skills uncommon to most in Eshra," Ayden inquired with confrontation in her voice.

"I will tell you this, Ayden," Zetia said as she tenderly continued, "I have belonged to Eshra for many many years. I have known Joshua since he was very young. He has been an integral part of my life. I know Gethsemane, and Nadab, also. Those who are full of sage wisdom have come to me for help at one time or another. I walk this land, and yours unhindered and I show up where I am needed most. The Great Crane guides my decisions and I follow his guidance. Again, I tell you, my heart is full of pride I was guided here to help you and your friends this day," Zetia stated.

"Well, that just keeps me confused," Deborah responded. "Thanks for your help and wisdom, I guess. But, what about tomorrow? Nahrita is still out there with Dariat and the wolves. Actually, very close to us, out there."

"Plus, you mentioned an army, and they could be gearing up to come after us right now. How do you propose we stay safe from them and still be able to continue on this quest? I, for one, do not feel very safe or confident after I have spent all evening tending to the wounds of my friends," Deborah stated with a tinge of nervousness.

"Deborah," Zetia began, "You have the greatest weapon you will ever need sitting right next to you. Today Ayden did not have to help, but when she senses the need to take flight, she will be there for all of you. But, as far as tonight and tomorrow, Nahrita and Dariat will not be able to move for another ten to twelve hours and the wolves will not leave them. And, since those are the only four who survived today, no one will be able to reach Choran for at least four days to let him know what has happened."

"Nahrita is filled with anger and vengeance, but even she will not attack with only the four of them left," Zetia reassured them.

"Even if all you say is true, Zetia," Jerin began, "I still feel it would be wise for us to have the ospreys travel ahead and bring back news of whether it is safe, or not, to continue the way we are heading. And, the Trevins need to strategically place themselves in the trees to alert us quickly if we need to join in a fight," he determined.

"Jerin," Zetia stated, "If it would make you feel safer, I can call out for others to ride with you."

Zetia lifted her right arm away from her body and whistled in a long low pitch. As she finished the last note, an enormous black raven landed on her arm.

Zetia lovingly caressed his head and back, while she said, "This is my friend Uri. Uri, I would like you to meet the Messenger and her friends. They are in need of your services. Go to your friends and call them to arms. From every part of Eshra have them ride, for the Great Crane is in need of their protection. Have them stay hidden, but close, until the time is set for them to rise and answer the call," she finished.

Uri turned to look at Ayden, bowed to her and cawed. He lifted his wings slightly off his body as if he was preparing to take flight and disappeared in a puff of smoke.

Everyone looked at Zetia's arm where the raven had been and watched as one lone black feather lightly swayed back and forth as it landed next to Zetia's foot.

Zetia picked the feather up and presented it to Ayden, saying, "Let this feather be a promise for you to remember. A promise of hope. A promise of a tomorrow. A promise you are the Messenger of Eshra."

Journal Thirty

The first big battle, of what I knew would be more, had left me emotionally drained. To watch animals so viciously attack for no natural reason was unsettling.

Humans always did things for personal gain...even if it was misguided and selfish. But, animals?

Eshra, this land of beauty and of a culture where animals had human emotions, was not always beautiful. It was scary and unpredictable.

At every move, we would have to watch closely to make sure we didn't walk into danger unexpectedly.

The quest, our journey, had taken on a whole new perspective. It no longer was an adventure, like a camping trip. It was a mission to protect everything.

Everything we held dear and valued was at stake. There were forces out there who wanted evil to win.

And it was our job, our prophecy, to stop the rising tide of evil.

Chapter Thirty

The hour was late when everyone finally was able to sleep. The much-needed rest was not very peaceful. Evidenced by a lot of tossing and turning which could be heard throughout the whole camp.

Jerin, Tybin, Nick, and the Trevins woke earlier than usual in the morning to clean up the carnage from the day before. The twins downed six long tree poles to make travois' while Nick cut boughs from pine trees.

The Trevins stripped long pieces of bark off of the downed lodge pole pines. Each pair of poles was crisscrossed at one end and wrapped in the bark strips to make them sturdy. A large 'V' shape was made after the crossed sections were complete.

All of them worked together to weave the bark through the structure to give it a bed frame. They then placed the tree boughs on top of the frame and secured them with more of the bark. As a team, they lifted each of the apparatus' and placed them on the rump of a horse.

Using rope, they tied the travois to a horse's body to secure it for transportation. Jerin, Nick, and half of the Trevins took off to where the badger fight occurred and lifted the dead bodies onto the structure. Upon their return, they searched for any hawks who fell in the area.

Tybin, Ayden, and the other Trevins took care of the man, wolves, boars, and hawks. The job of retrieving all of the bodies was a long and somber process. Deborah and Zetia kept the fire stoked with food and drink on it to help the laborers in their task.

Ayden noticed, while they worked, Zetia and Deborah were deep in the tethered notebook of plants, as they talked excitedly about their mutual interest. Soon, little pots joined the food pots and several brews of herbs were simmering. Deborah had laid out a blanket, and plants grew all around them from where she dug her knife into the ground. She strategically organized them on her makeshift table.

Tybin approached the girls at the campfire and told them it was time. Jerin, Tybin, and Nick led the procession on the horses, who bore the burden of their load. All the rest of the group followed behind as they traveled beyond a part of the forest where a grassy meadow covered the area. The boys took the poles apart after they emptied them of the dead and cut the logs into firewood. They then built a pyramid shaped structure which would allow the embers to breath from their heavy load of bodies.

The Trevins worked tirelessly gathering dead pine needles and other dried grasses to place all around the pyre. Even Eleea, Elora, and the ospreys would fly back and forth with pieces of wild cotton or other material they found which could ignite easily. Phum ran around the whole structure making sure each spot had tinder to help the burn go smoothly.

Nekoh and Seven, who were hurt the worst in the battle, lay by Deborah, sleeping in the sun. With the fallen bodies placed, the workers took a moment to rest.

Zetia turned to them and said, "Allow me the privilege to say the eulogy for these fallen comrades of Choran." The group nodded with approval.

Zetia began, *"Each moment we breath, is precious. We may not have shared the same goals as these who have fallen, but we all shared the same air.*

Our purpose to live may have been in direct opposition to their purpose, but the same maker made all of us. He cries for each soul who falls. And, because He cries, we, too, cry.

We cry for their loss to do good and for their choice to follow evil. They did not know what it was to find their true purpose.

To not live life full of joy and love is the deepest death we feel for them today. May their souls unite in the beyond and may they find the peace they were searching for here on Eshra," Zetia said as she bowed her head.

Everyone bowed with her, as Trevin started the tinder burning. Ayden and Deborah held hands and cried as they watched the flames consume the bodies. The Trevins surrounded the girls, trying to console them. The girls picked up two Trevins, one in each arm as they watched. Deborah had Two and Eight, while Ayden had Three and Four. The others helped the boys contain the blaze so it did not get out of control.

Zetia moved forward and took a pouch from her right hip pocket. She opened it and poured its contents as she walked the perimeter of the pyre, laying a thin line of powder all around it.

Zetia stood back and directed all of the others to stand behind her. She snapped her fingers and the whole pyre imploded and disappeared in smoke. Zetia turned to the group and said, "There, now we don't have to stay here for hours tending to a fire. Let's get back to camp and eat."

Ayden walked back in silence with the others as she replayed the past moments in her mind. "Zetia was a strange duck," she thought.

"First, she acts ditzy, then she acts warrior, from there it is teacher of plants etc. To finally magician, where poof it's all gone. Yes, she has a kind heart, cuz she was wonderful with Nip. But who the hell is she? Her sly answers helped her to avoid stating the truth about herself. Not that she lied, she just avoided the whole truth. Yep, she is a strange duck," Ayden concluded.

Reaching camp, Tybin said, "The hour is getting late, we will stay here tonight. And, tomorrow morning we start the journey to the Dead Trees." He then turned to Zetia and said, "Will you be traveling with us?"

Zetia smiled and said, "We go the same direction until the Dead Trees. After that, I travel on to Oshyama. So, to answer your question, yes, I travel with you tomorrow."

Everything seemed to be back to a normal pace as they sat around the fire and ate. The sounds and smells of the night were calm and full of the beautiful scents of pine.

Ayden felt anything than normal. Her encounter with the Great Crane and Zetia's speech at the funeral made her more determined than ever to speak to her.

Ayden watched as Zetia said her niceties to everyone before she retired to sleep with her horses. She turned to Deborah and said, "I'll be fine, but I have got to talk to Zetia privately."

Eleea overheard Ayden's conversation with Deborah and sensed he needed to be near her as she confronted Zetia. He watched high above the tree limbs as Ayden approached Zetia.

Ayden looked down at Zetia and said, "I need to know who you are. And, I need to know if you can help me."

Zetia sat up and crossed her legs. She gestured for Ayden to sit down on her blanket, and said, "Ayden, I will help you anyway I can. What do you need help with?"

It didn't surprise Ayden she chose to avoid the first question and address the second. It was true to her form to avoid. But her need for help overruled her desire to confront her avoidance.

"I need to know how to fly. Because you and the Great Crane, both, have said I am the greatest weapon we all have. And, I know you know I have wings I can call when I need them. I don't know how to use them as weapons and it is very real right now with all that happened yesterday and I need to know how to use them to protect my friends. I know you can help me to understand," Ayden desperately finished.

"Ayden, First, let me address the Great Crane," Zetia stated. "It would seem He came to you, recently?"

"Yes, I talked to him yesterday during the battles. He said the same thing you said, I am the greatest weapon for all of us. He said courage is not the absence of fear and a whole bunch of other things. He told me I had to fly. And, to fly came from the soul," Ayden stated.

"Walk with me Ayden," Zetia said as she stood up and reached her hand down to pull Ayden to her feet.

"It is a very very rare occurrence for the Great Crane to show himself to someone," Zetia said with wonder. "Even more rare for him to speak."

"And, it would seem he needed you to hear from your heart and not from your head," Zetia said as she contemplated what Ayden told her.

"So, Ayden," Zetia stated as they walked. "By Him saying, 'You have to fly from your soul,' He is telling you to get out of your head. For example, baby birds are programmed from birth to instinctually fly. It is a part of their natural order of existence."

"And, because you have knowledge of this through your educational training, you can only see it from this view. In your mind, it is not natural for you to be able to fly," Zetia explained.

"Here, sit with me, on these rocks, Ayden," Zetia said. "Look at the view! The moon is shining more brightly tonight than I have ever seen it shine in Eshra. The stars are even more vivid than usual; they are twinkling everywhere. You can see the valley down below. This is a very special night, Ayden," Zetia said with awe.

"How so," Ayden asked.

"The moon and stars are calling you, Ayden," Zetia said. "They are talking to you tonight. Listen with your heart, Ayden," she encouraged her.

Ayden looked out into the valley and then up into the night sky. "Yes," she thought everything did seem much brighter than she had ever seen it before." She looked at Zetia and said, "Help me."

Zetia stood up and put her hands-on Ayden's arms as she helped her to stand. With her right arm around Ayden's shoulders, she started to hum. A slow soothing sound emitted from her throat, as she began to sway to the tune.

Ayden felt her body move with the song as she too began to hum the same melody. She felt Zetia take her arm off her shoulders as they stood together and began to softly sing together.

Slowly, Ayden felt the wings on her back emerge. She turned to look at Zetia and was stunned by what she saw.

On Zetia's back were two beautiful shimmery white wings, each with a distinct midnight blue outline all around them. And the same blue lightly splattered each individual feather. Their shape and size looked just like Ayden's sterling silver ones. Each individual feather of the wings slightly moved in the night breeze.

Zetia smiled at Ayden, turned, and lifted her body up off of the rock, and began to fly. Without even thinking, Ayden followed her lead and let her feet leave the ground. The two of them soared as their wings continuously caught the light of the celestial bodies of the sky.

Instantaneously, a cascading shower of shooting stars began to flash across the sky. Almost as if they were welcoming Ayden to their world with brilliant white fireworks.

Ayden turned to her right and saw Eleea flying with them. She lost her concentration for a second, and thought she was going to fall.

Eleea saw her fear and said, "Listen to your soul, Ayden. You will never forget how to fly. It will always be a part of you."

Ayden smiled and regained her composure while she climbed the winds with Zetia and Eleea.

"Ayden," Zetia said. "To land without breaking your nose, takes a little understanding. Keep your head up as you come into the landing. Pull your chest back towards your wings, and let your wings slow you down as you plant your feet on the ground."

"Watch Eleea land first, and then I will land. Both of us will guide you if you feel scared and can't do it, OK?"

Ayden nodded and watched Eleea land with perfect ease. Eleea looked up at Ayden as Zetia flew in next to him. Ayden flew around them three times before she felt she could follow Zetia's instructions.

Making sure her feet would be flat for the landing; she pulled her chest back as her wings slowed her descent. She touched the ground as she kept her head high while her wings automatically folded into her sides.

She let out a sigh of glee, and turned to her teachers. "I did it!" She exclaimed with delight.

Zetia and Eleea laughed like two proud parents as they watched Ayden's joy over her new-found independence.

"How? How did you know all of this, Zetia? How could you have known? We have never met before and yet you know so much about me?" Ayden questioned her with a perplexed voice.

"Sit, Ayden," Zetia tenderly said. Zetia pulled her water bladder from her side and gave it to Ayden. "Drink, child, I have lots to explain," she stated.

"It was not by coincidence Eleea was sent to be the seeker. The prophecy told us you would have the mark of the crane on your back. We did not know how, but we knew you would, one day, fly the winds of Eshra."

"The birds of this world cross over between the two worlds through humming and song. Eleea had to teach you how to use your vocal cords to produce music; through humming and singing. Because, not only do they cross over in this way, but all birds hum and sing to give first flight to their wings. We had to prepare you," Zetia stated.

Ayden listened intently and then said, "But how come? You have wings like me. Why don't you save Eshra, instead of me?" she questioned.

"Ayden," Eleea began, "The prophecy is not about wings. It is about you and your mark. No, we do not completely understand what the prophecy states. What we do know is your mark is our answer."

"Still, what does it mean by messenger? And why is everyone so, so reverent about it?" Ayden questioned them.

"There will come a day, Ayden," Zetia stated, "when you will have to speak, sing, or whatever. You will bring a message to the darkness which will ignite the end of Choran."

"Only you can deliver this message, no one else. The prophecy has made it very clear you, the Messenger, are the one, who's voice will be heard throughout Eshra. It is your destiny." Zetia triumphantly said.

"Well, I understand everything a little more than when I entered Eshra." Ayden agreed. "But I still don't get it. You have wings like me? Ayden stated with confusion.

"My wings, Ayden, come from my ancestry." Zetia said. "My people belong to the Great Crane. Not that He owned us; but that we belong together as a family. In a sense, we were His messengers."

"We traveled the land and helped the people of Eshra in whatever way was needed. Our purpose was to bring peace and enlightenment to their world. To gently remind them of the importance of the moon and the sun. As well as the importance of their responsibility to follow their hearts for good and not evil," Zetia stated.

"So, how many are there of you," Ayden asked.

"In the beginning there were many of us who belonged. Now, I am the last one I know of." Zetia said sadly.

"When Choran started to become more and more powerful, my people went into hiding out of fear they would end up in the clutches of Choran. I had a brother, Ayden. A brother named Zayden."

"He stayed strong with me and did not hide. One day he was there, and the next day no one could find him. Of course, the assumption is Choran took him, but none of us know for sure." Zetia stated with sorrow.

"Ayden, I am going to tell you a truth I believe," Zetia said as she fixed her eyes on Ayden. "Your name is also no coincidence. I believe you are my brother's child. And this is why you have wings."

Ayden reached for her lockets and pulled them out from under her shirt and held them tight in her hand. She stared at Zetia, dumbfounded.

Zetia gently took the locket of her mother and her, opened it and smiled. Next, she took the one which could not be opened. As she caressed it with her thumb, a latch appeared on it. She met Ayden's eyes and smiled, saying, "Allow me the privilege to introduce you to your father, Ayden."

Zetia kissed the locket, and as her lips touched it, the latch opened. With tears running down her face, she gazed on the picture of a man, a woman and a baby. Zetia turned the charm for Ayden to see, and they cried together.

Eleea flew to the middle of them and began to softly sing, as if he was soothing their tears. Across the sky a show of brilliant lighted stars bounced in and out of brightness as they seemed to dance with joy at their reunion.

Journal Thirty-One

Zetia was my aunt! This was not what I expected when I went to talk to her to help me. And, she had wings like me.

Confusion just seemed to be my best friend this whole Eshra trip!

Did I need the lockets to have wings? Or, since she said she and my dad had wings, did I always have wings and just didn't know it?

Did they have birthmarks, too? And, how did my mom meet someone from Eshra?

Plus, would I ever get all my questions answered? Being confused was so very tiring.

Rather than dwelling on the "I don't know," it was much easier to just accept and move on.

Move on to what I knew needed to be done...help my friends survive.

Chapter Thirty-One

Ayden, Zetia and Eleea started back to camp to tell the others about all of their new discoveries. The whole group was sitting around the fire in obvious anticipation of their arrival.

"It would appear the moon and stars are happy with the three of you," Tybin stated happily as they approached.

Deborah handed Zetia and Ayden a cup of hot tea saying, "I want to know every single detail and I mean every detail."

Ayden smiled at everyone and sat down to begin to tell them what happened. After an hour of replaying the night's events, with Zetia and Eleea filling in some of the content, Ayden stopped. She looked at everyone and started to cry.

Deborah moved close to her and took her hand as she said, "It's OK, 'A', everything is going to be OK."

"I know, 'D', it's just our worlds, yours and mine, have been turned upside down in a matter of three months. We will never be the same, again. We can't go back to just being carefree kids, and it's just so scary," Ayden stated.

"I know I don't want to go back, but I am very overwhelmed right now. Plus, I am so confused about how Nadab had a picture of my mom and I, and my real dad. Where did he get it?" Ayden said with bewilderment.

"I can answer this question for you, Ayden," Nick stated with a bit of anxiety as he looked around the camp fire at everyone. He sighed as he stood to deliver his message.

"When I found your locket with the picture of you and your mom, I knew I wasn't finished. I kept searching, not knowing what I was looking for. I was just driven to find something you had to have. It took me hours of lifting debris with no success."

"I almost gave up, thinking I was too obsessed because I felt so bad for you and your loss. I started to walk away and kicked a piece of wood in frustration. The burnt board flew through the air and landed on another piece of wood causing it to jut out of its resting place."

"Peeking under the second piece of wood was a small metal box. I opened it and found the picture of you and your mom and dad in it. I had already looked in the locket I had found earlier, and realized it was the same picture, but, your real dad had been cut out of the photo.

I figured your mom had kept this picture hidden from you and who you thought was your father. I didn't want to scare you with it. So, I waited until I crossed over and spoke to my uncle about it.

I asked him to make a gift for a friend of mine on the other side, and put the photo in it. I thought one day I could give it to you, when the time was right. I actually forgot I had given it to Nadab."

Nick looked at Ayden and finished with, "I never wanted to deceive you, Ayden. But to tell you when I found it, would have devastated you."

Ayden listened to Nick and her heart burst with pride for this friend she had no idea cared so deeply for her. His compassion made her feel, strangely, secure as he spoke.

"Nick, you are one of the most beautiful souls I have ever known," Ayden exclaimed as she went over and hugged him.

"Thank you, for never giving up. And, you are right, I would have freaked out bad if I had seen the picture before tonight," she concluded.

"It has been a night full of twists and turns for fate," Zetia stated. But we have to be on the move early, so let's all of us get some sleep." Everyone nodded in agreement and prepared their beds for the night.

The next morning the Trevins took off right after breakfast to scout ahead. While the rest of the party packed up and cleared the campsite. With the horses ready for the ride, they fell into their designated order for travel.

The sounds of early morning rang throughout the land as they soaked in the beauty of the landscape. Their travel took them past the pyre of the day before, and all of them silently paid their respects in their own way as they passed it.

This was their last mountain range before they got to the Dead Trees. But, before they reached their true destination, they had three days' travel of grassland and small rolling hills.

The journeyers stayed fairly quiet as they traveled, knowing they were probably not hidden from eyes and ears of Choran's devotees. The ospreys darted ahead and back as they scoured the land high in the sky for unwelcome life.

Suddenly, yelling and sounds of some type of ruckus could be heard off in the distance. Tybin stopped the group and had them make a circle with the horses. He put Ayden, Deborah, and Nekoh inside the circle, while he, Jerin, Nick and Zetia stood on the outside with weapons ready.

Phum, Eleea and Elora stood on the back of one of the horses, also ready with their weapons, to fight. Ayden and Deborah leaned into the horses' sides closest to the warriors who were protecting them, trying to see past them.

The hootin' and hollerin' rapidly came closer as the girls strained to see. Nip peeked out of her sling, slightly nervous since she could feel Ayden's heart beating somewhat faster.

Jerin started to laugh, causing Tybin, Nick, and Zetia to join him. Nick gently slapped one of the horses' behind to move him out of the way of Deborah's and Ayden's obstructed view.

A horse galloped towards them with his bridle in the hands of Trevin. Trevin stood on the horse's neck yelling, "We ride the winds of Eshra men! Go? Go, I will name you Ten. Go, Ten, and take us to our family!" he cried.

Down the full back of the horse stood seven other Trevins holding on as tight as they could with their leader commanding the horse to do his bidding. Their tails, completely out of sync with each other, flopped up and down as the speed of the horse bounced their bodies.

As they got within hearing distance, Jerin yelled, "Where, by the Crane, did you find this horse, Trevin?"

Trevin pulled up close to Jerin saying, "Whoa, Ten, you can stop now. Stop, Ten, stop!" he yelled frantically. The horse broke his run and the Trevin's all jolted forward with their back feet flying in the air as they tried to hold on to not fall off of the horse.

Trevin quickly hid his fear and stood tall with chest puffed out as he said, "This horse was mindlessly eating grass in the meadow. From his gear, he wears we determined it was the horse belonging to the rider Zetia eliminated back at camp two days ago. He no longer has an owner," Trevin stated with guarded glee.

"Therefore, according to the Barter King code of ownership, this horse belongs to us," Trevin triumphantly declared as he patted the horse's neck.

Zetia looked at Trevin with a sly glint in her eyes and said, "technically, Trevin, wouldn't the Barter King code say it was my horse?"

"Finders, keepers," Trevin blurted out, nervously. "You forfeited your chance when you did not go after him the day he became free property."

"We rescued Ten from a life of wandering in his gear, with no one to help him get it off. Ten has become our ward. We are responsible for him now," Trevin stated with authority.

Zetia chuckled as she said, "I totally agree with you Trevin. He is your responsibility. And, I believe he is in the best hands possible. He is one lucky horse to have such caring hands, sixteen of them to be exact, watching over him."

"Actually, Trevin," Zetia declared. "I believe fate has handed us the golden key. What better way to get deep into the bowels of the Dead Trees undetected? A smell of a horse they already know to be theirs would not set off alarms. And, if it is timed correctly, Nahrita and the others will not be in the vicinity to notice."

Yes," Zetia said with joy, "This is a great shiny you and the Trevins have found today. And, this is a good time, I think, for a rest. You are right Trevin, Ten needs to have a break from his gear, after two days of it on his back," Zetia concluded.

The Trevins hurriedly untangled their horse from the gear they could handle. The boys helped them with the saddle and blankets which would have been too heavy for their little bodies to hold. Sixteen small hands began to rub the body of the horse with great care and skill. Several of the areas were scarred with dry blood or had briars in the hair.

Trevin got salve from Deborah to use on the horse's sores. He directed his men to take a specific section to rub. "This part is your responsibility from now on," he instructed them.

"Ten, Ten, you need to learn your name. We will help you," Trevin exclaimed.

Ayden watched as they led the horse around calling his name at every turn. They would stop him, call his name and then call his name again and pull him in another direction.

Jerin and Tybin decided it would be wise to gather everyone's bowls and make a cooked meal with Abner's magic to create a delectable afternoon treat rather than start a fire.

Deborah and Ayden moved closer to Zetia who picked up the last rider's pouches and had begun to look through them. Clothes, dried food, leather rope belts, and weapons were the mainstay of the items found.

Zetia turned to Tybin, saying, "These clothes would make for a good cover to enter Choran's chambers. Put this hooded jacket and pants in your bag, please."

She then turned to Deborah and said, "Take this food and put it over there, where no one is sitting. I am not going to take a chance it is free from any kind of magic; we need to destroy it. We have to rid it from harming anyone."

Deborah stated, "I have a potion from Errol which takes care of poisonous substances." Deborah explained to Zetia how she had received her gift from Errol. Both girls told her the whole story of how they got Nip and how Callie and Errol had saved her.

Zetia acknowledged the girls' information as she led them to the food. She closely monitored Deborah spreading the potion over all of it.

Telling her, "The trick is to not waste it. A small amount goes a long way." After they had covered all of the food, Zetia said to Deborah, "Take your water bladder, put some in this bowl, and spit in the cup." Deborah did as she was told.

"Now, empty the bowl's contents into the middle of the pile," Zetia stated. Again, Deborah followed the directions. As the water hit the food, it ignited and permeated to the edges in a puff of smoke and disappeared.

"There, done." Zetia stated as she continued, "Now, to move onto the pressing matter of making Ten able to carry his riders with ease."

Zetia called Nick over to her. "Nickalli, I need to take this leather, blanket, and saddle and turn it into eight pieces of riding gear. Would you help design it," she asked.

Nick looked at the pieces she had and started to turn them in his hands as he thought.

Deborah stepped forward and said, "Remember, Nick, my knife will cut anything I want, like butter."

Nick took the saddle and told Deborah, "I want eight horns, approximately four inches in diameter, cut from the thick part of this saddle. The Trevins will need to hold onto the horn in their small hands while they are riding."

He directed Deborah on each cut, as she took her knife and breezed through the leather. Next, he took the leather rope and measured around the belly of the horse and cut eight strips to fit each piece around each part of the horse's belly.

He added a loop on one end so it could work through the other end to allow each section to be tightened as needed.

Nick looked at Zetia and said, "I need the horns to fit securely on this rope, do you have any ideas?" Zetia picked up one of the horns and one of the belts to examine how to attach them.

Jerin and Tybin came over to see if they could help. All the while, the Trevins sat in a group near them, watching intently as their new gear was being made.

"How about," Jerin started, "We take the leather belts and run them through a cut in each of the horns, like a belt loop."

"And, then, we take each belt and attach it to the rope Nickalli has already cut," Tybin stated.

Jerin pulled out his enlightenment knife and seared the leather ends together. He looked at the girls, saying, "this is my knife's gift. Whatever I need to bind together, it does it for me," he smiled at them as he continued to work.

Everyone worked diligently to make the new Trevin gear work. They even rubbed the leather into a soft consistency with some of Deborah's salve so it wouldn't hurt the Trevins or Ten with its freshly cut sharp edges.

"Call Ten over," Jerin said to Trevin. The raccoons ran and got Ten, as a team. Eight little bodies proudly presented their horse to be fitted with his new attire. The boys worked the rope around the horse's body, constantly readjusting the horns to fit right.

Ayden stepped into their work area and said, "Maybe, we need a long piece of leather running the length of Ten's body. From the back of his bridle, by his ears to the last horn. This way, when they are riding fast, the horns won't end up under Ten's body."

"Nice," Jerin said as he retrieved another piece of leather. "Very smart idea, Ayden," he said with admiration. Again, the boys worked out the kinks of the leather which would keep the Trevins upright and not fall under the belly of Ten.

Tybin turned to Trevin and said, "Get your men, Trevin. Let's see how well this works."

The raccoons took their place on Ten. Jerin, Tybin and Nick walked around with them to see if they needed to make any more adjustments.

Every now and then, one of the boys would stop them and add another piece of material to make it more secure, or more comfortable for their friends. Finally, everyone seemed to agree the Trevins would be safe riding Ten.

Zetia looked at the group, and said, "We can go about another two hours before we need to camp for the night. I know of a safe place away from dangerous eyes and ears. There is a lake on the other side of these trees. Just before we start traveling into the meadows and small hills. It is at the edge of the forest and valley. A beautiful spot for a night's rest," Zetia assured them.

The group agreed and climbed back on their horses. They traveled in silence, again, as everyone seemed to enjoy the last of the forest.

Soon, there came a sense of sorrow over leaving the mountains, knowing it would be a long time before they would smell the pine, or see the beauty of the land with trees all around them.

Journal Thirty-Two

So many new things were happening around me that I felt bad I didn't have very much time for Elora. She is such a beautiful soul, and she just patiently waited to be noticed.

I hadn't been fair to her. She, too, didn't have a mom and needed to know how important she was to all of us.

Sometimes, I felt so selfish even though I wasn't trying to be. I have got to determine to be there for all of my friends.

To look past myself and be a true friend. Ask them how they are doing. Listen to them when they need me to be their ear.

I just need to stop getting wrapped up in the drama of Eshra. My friends needed me just as much as I needed them.

Chapter Thirty-Two

The group was led for over two hours as they wound their way down to the edge of the forest. Looking past, the trees, as far as the eye could see, was a vast meadow mixed with rolling hills.

Zetia stopped, jumped down from her horse and stood beside a very crooked, tall sage brush tree. She lifted her arms out to her sides and her wings appeared as if they were ready for flight.

When her wings came into full view, the sage brush creaked and straightened as it revealed an entrance. She turned to the group and gestured for them to enter. They single file entered through the door into a place which looked like it belonged in a fairytale.

Very old oak, pine, cottonwood, and aspen trees stood hundreds of feet tall with the most beautiful roots protruding out of them. They looked like chairs waiting for a person to rest in their root-arms.

Their full dress of leaves above the trunks hung in lush greenery as it draped over the tree's body. The brilliant colors of different shades of green and brown filled the whole forest.

Their pathway was full of all kinds of flowers in bloom; except where they were to walk. There it was soft dirt leading to a rock and wooden mansion with moss and vines growing up its walls, intermixed with purple, yellow, and white flowers.

Zetia watched as the doorway closed after them and then said, "This is one of my homes. It is surrounded by magic and we are free from danger and people or animals who wish to harm us." She smiled and continued to lead them to the front doors of the mansion.

"Zetia! You are here!" A voice cried out as they came down the path.

Zetia smiled and went to the woman and hugged her. "Tarhana, it is so good to be here with you! Come meet my friends," Zetia said.

"I heard the sage creak and I knew it was you," Tarhana said. She looked at her guests and smiled, saying, "Come, come, Uri told us you would be arriving shortly. We have rooms for everyone, just the way you each will like them. Uri's friends have watched you for some time, and they sent messengers to me. They told me what I needed to know."

"Oh! Tarhana, you are such a perfect heart. Always making sure everyone is comfortable around you," Zetia said with affection.

Ayden watched Zetia and Tarhana as they continued on the path where more friendly animals and people came out to meet them.

Tarhana turned to the group and said, "This is Sahl, he is our wonderful groundskeeper for this whole area. Sahl bowed to the travelers and gestured to two men, who came forward and bowed also. They took the reins of the horses as the group dismounted their rides.

"Your animals, will be in good hands while you rest here," Sahl smiled at them.

The group were in awe at the friendliness of its occupants, as well as the splendor of beauty they saw all around them.

Zetia stopped talking to Tarhana, and turned to the group saying, "You are all safe here. No evil can enter. My wish is for you to stay at least two days. Then I will show you a shortcut to the Dead Trees. When you leave here, I will not be going with you. I want all of you to be rested and prepared for what lies ahead."

Ayden and the rest walked through the doors into a main room full of activity. A large table held the place settings for its guests. A fireplace as big as her bed at the Great Tree was in its full glory, with the sound of pine crackling as the embers surrounded it in flame.

Full grown pine and aspen trees lined the walls in their natural majesty, while smaller plants covered almost every empty space in between the trees. One side of the room was dedicated to a ten-foot waterfall with inlaid rock and thin lines of copper, gold, silver and semi-precious stones which created a mountain scene with the sun peeking over the bottom of the horizon. It gently played its water song as it flowed into a waist deep pool of about fifteen feet long and five feet wide.

Beautiful mosaic pottery graced several areas of the room. Most of them held potted plants with flowers in full bloom. Others housed ferns of all types, as well as other green plants.

Ayden let out a small gasp as her eyes caught a glimpse of a figure by the other side of the fireplace. Laying peacefully, waiting for all of them to enter the room was Joshua. He stood and stretched like a cat from its slumber and began to walk over to meet the sojourners.

"Did I not tell you I would meet you again, Ayden." Joshua mischievously stated.

"Joshua, it is so good to see you. I have come to a point in my Eshra journey to no longer be surprised by what I see or hear. And with you standing right there, it would seem I am right to not be shocked by anything." Ayden said matter-of-factly. "With this being said, I am very happy I get to visit with you again," she finished.

"Callie!" Deborah screamed. "I never would have expected to see you. This is a great day when we get to see our friends from Sunbird," she said with joy.

Zetia excused herself and said, "I will be back within the hour, but I have something I must do before we eat. Why don't each of you look at your rooms and freshen up." Zetia gestured to her staff, and each took the belongings of the travelers as they directed them to their designated sleeping areas.

Deborah, Ayden, and Elora were assigned a room together, with two huge beds and Elora a sweet little, but huge, nest in between the girls' beds. Again, just like at the Great Tree their bedding was down feathers. But instead of silk, they had cotton linen. Rich beautiful designs of flowers, plants and trees were dyed into the fabric.

The bed frame was an oak tree trunk with its highly glossed roots protruding out to form the whole bed. It even had a sitting bench at the foot of it, made from its roots. When they laid on their beds, they noticed the sky could be seen through a strange window design which let the light enter the room. It looked like glass, but it was so clear, it didn't seem to be really there. Windows across the room had the same type of glass.

The floor was inlaid with different colors of wood and copper which formed a huge sun pattern. At different sections of the design, intricate little copper hummingbirds could be seen as they led to each bed and out the door to other areas of the mansion. They looked like markers on a treasure map, directing where you should go.

The girls, each took a luxurious bath; both visibly excited they had a private bathroom in the room. They then changed into one of Lydia's party outfits before they set out to find the others. The boys met them as they exited their room. By the look on their faces, the girls could tell their rooms were just as nice.

Tarhana called the group to attention by saying, "It is time for all of us to sit and eat. Come, join us and our spirits shall commune with each other over a good meal."

Their seating order was Nick, Ayden, Deborah, Jerin, and Tybin all together in the middle of the table. Callie sat close to the front and the rest were directed by Tarhana on where to sit or perch.

Ayden looked around at her friends. She felt deep respect for how each of them had special accommodations where they sat.

Eleea and Elora had little perches adjusted to fit perfectly at the edge of the table. Phum had a bigger perch which allowed him to sit back with ease or stand on his hind legs, if he wished. Nekoh and Joshua had a sort of bed setup which gave them freedom to relax or sit on their haunches and eat.

Nip had her own little area like the big cats. Even the Trevins and the ospreys had their own special platform where it was easy for them to sit and enjoy the meal.

Zetia entered from the back of the room and sat at the head of the table. Servers began to present the food to each person and animal so no one had to reach across the table or over one another to get what they wanted. As the meal progressed, if you wanted a second serving, you could go to a secondary table, much like a buffet, and take another helping.

"I don't think the Trevins have ever been treated so special," Ayden whispered to Deborah. "Look at how proud they are to be with us at the table."

Deborah leaned into Ayden's ear and said, "Isn't it just so beautiful to watch their little souls being honored like this?"

"So, tell me, Eleea, how have your wards faired on this journey?" Joshua asked.

"Well, as you can see, my original count of ward duty has turned from four, Elora, Nickalli, Deborah, and Ayden, to thirteen with the Trevins and Nip being added." Eleea chuckled. "But I will have to say, it has been a very enlightening experience for me as well."

"How so, my good friend," Joshua queried.

"What they have taught me, is a person, an animal, may seem young or small but, when the test of conflict rises, each of them have proven to be most valuable. I doubt we would have survived if not for each of them showing their courage when needed," Eleea concluded.

"I concur, Eleea," Phum joined in. "Each of them has proven they are tough and tried as true warriors. And I include Jerin and Tybin in this statement. Yet, their hearts are full of love and respect. It has been my greatest privilege to be counted as friend to all of them," he finished.

"This is great news," Joshua said as he acknowledged Eleea's and Phum's statements. He turned to Nekoh and said, "my dear, dear comrade I see you have a limp. How is the wound healing?"

"Joshua, no battle is won with just eyes and desire. It takes physical and mental strength to conquer. A small wound is not defeat. Only, a reminder of who we are fighting and why." Nekoh emphatically stated.

"Yes, true, true," Joshua said while in deep thought. "Yet, I believe we are in need of some more weaponry to thwart this type of wound from occurring again."

"May I introduce someone who has been waiting to see all of you and who can help with this weaponry," Joshua said with a twinkle in his eye.

The group looked in the direction Joshua's eyes were leading them as a man and a woman came through the kitchen doors with a very large bird.

Ayden and Deborah simultaneously stood up as they saw Lydia, Nadab, and Gethsemane come into view. The girls ran over to Lydia and hugged her, as Nadab went to the three boys and patted each one on the back. Gethsemane took his perch at the opposite end of the table from Zetia, while Nadab and Lydia sat across from the boys and girls.

"How can this be?" Deborah began to say, as her rational mind tried to wrap around all she saw. "If they can time travel here so quickly where it has taken us several days. Why didn't we just travel like them?" she confusingly questioned.

"There are different ways to travel quickly throughout Eshra, but it is not really time travel per se," Joshua addressed the group. "This type of travel which brought Nadab, Lydia, and Gethsemane comes at a cost. The bearer who brings people or animal across the skies of Eshra does so with great risk of exposure to Choran. They are vulnerable to his attacks if they were to be seen. And, large groups, like yourselves, cannot be easily transported in this manner." Joshua stated with grave respect and concern.

"Zetia has risked her life to bring us here," Gethsemane stated. "We flew on her back from the Great Tree. She is capable of carrying heavy loads and traveling across the sky at speeds where what would take days and weeks to arrive at some place, only takes less than an hour on her back. If, Choran saw her in the sky, traveling this rapidly, he could take flight and kill her," Gethsemane stated.

"This is why my people have chosen to hide," Zetia explained. "Throughout the land, Choran killed whoever he could when we were in flight. He had spies everywhere who could see us in the sky and would send word to him and he would quickly take us out."

"He knew we were the first he had to destroy if he wanted to succeed in ruling Eshra. I knew I had a window of opportunity, because he would not have expected me to fly."

"I have a pact with him where I will not travel the winds of Eshra. And, because of this pact, he would let me travel and sell and buy my wares without fear of harm from him. The agreement included I would stay out of his business and he would stay out of mine," Zetia interpreted for them.

"Nahrita would not have reached him, yet, to tell him our pact was broken. He would not have expected me to be in the air. Therefore, he would have his guard down and not have spies out looking for me. And, I could quickly go to the Great Tree and back without him being on alert," she finished.

"And my, Child," Gethsemane stated. "If we had you travel as we did today, no lessons would have been learned. No forging of bonds with whom you traveled would have been made.

No life experiences would have been discovered. And, most importantly, the world of Eshra would have no hope. For, you see," Gethsemane continued, "All of Eshra now knows the Messenger is on the move. Word has spread throughout the land, and hope has risen in the hearts of all Eshra."

To add to Gethsemane's wisdom," Joshua continued, "Nothing of value comes easy. Life has to test you to make you realize what you truly value. Then, and only then are you able to discern what you are capable of. And, what you are needed to do to make your life one of worth to self and others."

"Hold up," Deborah started again, "How can all of Eshra know about us when we had to train to be discreet? Our enlightenment journey and our whole cloak and dagger personification we have played is for naught? And, how did you and Callie get here so fast?"

"Not totally, Deborah," Callie tenderly began. "Yes, Eshra knows the Messenger is on the move. Yes, you are to continue to stay discreet and use your cover story."

"Just because the people of this world know, does not mean they know who you are. And this includes Ayden and who she is. It is to your advantage to stay hidden from those you meet. In this way, all of you are protected from serious danger which may happen upon you."

"Then the matter of how Joshua and I arrived here before you. There are certain windows of entrance that can be used to travel to other realms of the land. Special magic, if you will, can be used when needed to travel quickly. Only a select few know the magic and can use it; the whole of Eshra are not aware of this ability," Callie explained.

"How, though, do they know I am on the move?" Ayden questioned them.

"Nothing of this magnitude stays secret, Ayden," Eleea soothingly said to her. "Our large group drew attention. We knew it would raise questions. The incident at Sunbird Village confirmed our worst fears of Choran sending out spies everywhere to harm anybody who seemed out of place," he stated.

"But, the biggest sign no one expected came through you," Eleea proudly explained. "When you took flight, the moon and stars reacted to your presence in their world. Well, the whole world of Eshra saw the glory of what the stars performed for your maiden flight. It was absolutely beautiful. And, hope rang throughout the land." Eleea stated as he stood and bowed to Ayden.

Ayden was emotionally taken aback; she had never seen Eleea bow to her before. And, then because he bowed, everyone stood up around the table and bowed to her. Her level of uneasiness started to rise as she felt her face begin to flush.

Zetia walked over to her, put her arms around her and said, "Ayden, it is OK. Own who you are. You already have the greatest gift that comes with your position: humility. You are going to be fine. Your friends will hold you up and keep you safe in all areas of your life."

"Now, let's all enjoy our stay here." Zetia said as she took her arms off of Ayden. "The waterfall over there is a natural hot spring and is one of the best ways I know to rid one of travel fatigue."

"Tomorrow all of you can explore the grounds. There are wonders all around. Plus, the lake is breathtaking in the morning as the sun rises on it and the birds sing to the glory of a new day," Zetia informed them.

"Throughout this sanctuary you will come across many people and animals who will provide you with knowledge and entertainment. And, remember, you have at least two days here. Maybe more depending on Nadab's need to keep you while he makes new weapons," Zetia ended as she walked over to Tarhana.

Tarhana handed her two swimming suits for Ayden and Deborah. Zetia smiled and said girls follow me.

"Zetia, I don't wear swimsuits," Ayden said with fear.

"Child, it is time for you to not only own your position, but to own your body." Zetia warmly said to her.

"You cannot change how you were born. Nor what you were born with on your back. No scrubbing, no hiding will take it away. Stand proud and enjoy the freedom of accepting all of you." she finished.

Journal Thirty-Three

I was overwhelmed with everyone bowing to me. They did not need to put me on a pedestal. They were my friends, my equals. I doubt I would ever accept people bowing to me. It just seemed wrong.

Accepting my back. Well, I had to come to terms with it. Zetia was right. I could not rub it off with soap and water. And, I had tried several times when I was younger.

Letting others see it, would be a process of allowing myself to uncover it. I knew it would not just happen. Gradually I would get more comfortable with it being exposed. I just felt so vulnerable.

Exposing the mark was exposing me to emotional pain which I was so good at protecting myself from.

Maybe, when I got back to our world, I would just have a huge tattoo of the crane incorporated with color and design to make it prominently stand out.

Chapter Thirty-Three

"Girls, girls, girls," woke Ayden and Deborah from their peaceful rest. They immediately knew Elora had been out exploring their new surroundings.

"You have got to come see everything. It is enormously beautiful and free from danger. I have been everywhere," Elora excitedly told them.

"No Father saying," Elora lowered her voice like a male's saying, 'Elora, stay close to me. There is evil all around us.' Nope! I do not have to ask anyone if I can go. I just go and come back and go again and come back."

"Girls, girls, girls! Hurry up and get dressed. We have lots to do today." Elora impatiently said.

Ayden rose out of bed and tied a bandana around her head as she looked for her clothes to wear. All she could find was a pair of cotton pants and a smock. "Where have all of our clothes gone to," she asked as she looked at Deborah.

Deborah dug through her bag, looked at Ayden and said, "They must have taken everything to wash it. We have been on the road for over two weeks and all we own is pretty nasty, 'A'." Deborah took her pants and smock and put them on as she spoke.

"You know what, Ayden," Elora said, "When you named me you Put an 'E' in front of my mother's name Lora. Have you thought about your name? Your mom and dad must have decided to take the 'Z' off of your dad's name for you to be named Ayden. Get it Zayden, Ayden." Elora triumphantly finished her deduction.

"Yeah, Elora, I kind of figured that is what happened. It just still blows my mind to think my mom knew someone from Eshra. Or did my dad keep it a secret from her?" Ayden contemplated.

"And, the sad thing is, you can't ask her." Deborah expounded. "And, even sadder is all of her things were destroyed in the fire, so you can't look for old pictures or letters or anything else to help you form a solid hypothesis of how they met." Deborah finished.

"Yup, just another mystery of Eshra," Ayden said perplexed. "But I am not going to dwell on the what ifs of everything. The time is for the here and now. And it is Elora's day, or at least morning, to show us what she has learned. So, let's go."

Elora flew to Ayden's shoulder, visibly proud she got to be their guide through Zetia's home.

"Let's start down this hallway to the right," Elora instructed. "Behind us is the boys' room and it is bor-r-ring, let me tell you. We do not want to go that way. Here you have several more bedrooms for guests and residents of Zetia's home. Which I will refer to from now on as the Home, OK?"

Elora continued as guide. "This big room with all the windows is a sunroom, a lot of guests use it for relaxation and meditation. It looks out into the outdoor courtyard. Down these back steps lead to the inside courtyard. Isn't it beautiful?" Elora stated.

The girls walked down a set of steps into a yard full of bustling noise. It almost looked like a mini mall full of stores with several sections corded off for each activity.

There was the potter making his wares. The weaver making macramé art of all sorts for both display and functional use. The basket weaver, whose baskets were gorgeous with color and native or scenic design.

The apothecary mix master with pots on the fire all around him; not to mention dried plants hanging above him everywhere. The metal bender who worked all kinds of metals into art for jewelry, display and use.

Beautiful skirts and blouses like the outfit Zetia wore when the girls first saw her. The leather master who made too many things to even count. The wood worker who crafted the most outlandish mixed woods into bowls utensils, furniture and art.

The canvas painter who used the natural pigments of the earth to mix her colors. And, the gemologist who used everyone's art form in the courtyard to make his jewelry and other treasures.

"Holy!" Deborah stated. "Zetia would not have to go anywhere else to get her stuff for sale. It's all here, and every bit of it is absolutely gorgeous."

"Come girls, there is more." Elora took them under the stairs, where they walked into a kitchen full of laughter and smells.

"Wow! I forgot how hungry I am," Ayden stated as she smelled the baked bread on the counter.

"Oh! girls," Tarhana stated and continued, "I see our little Elora has been your tour guide this early morning. How about sitting at the bench and enjoying a cup of tea, or," Tarhana leaned into the girls and whispered, "I have coffee from Zetia's travels if you wish," she said with delight.

Both Ayden and Deborah blurted, "We'll take the coffee, please."

Tarhana begin to brew the crushed beans while she cut huge slices of fresh bread and put the pieces on two plates.

Taking a smaller plate, she crumbled up a corner of the bread for Elora. She brought butter, honey butter, and jams of all sorts for the girls.

As the girls enjoyed the fresh goodness, she filled two glasses each. One with ice cold milk and the other with freshly squeezed orange juice.

The girls sat in their glory with food overwhelmingly delicious, it melted in their mouths. Both of them smelled the aroma of the coffee for several minutes before they took their first sip.

"I never want to leave this place," Deborah expressed as she drank her coffee.

"You are welcome here anytime you like," Zetia said as she entered the room.

"But how, Zetia?" Deborah questioned. "It takes special magic to enter your home."

"Simple, my dear, Deborah." Zetia claimed. "Before you finish your stay here, we will put a," Zetia took Deborah's hand and traced it as she talked, "little hummingbird on each of your palms. No one will see them as it is a special mark. When you are near one of my homes, it will show itself and guide you through the opening," she finished.

"I love Eshra," Deborah shouted. "Do you have homes in our world too? Please say you do, Zetia." Deborah begged.

Zetia laughed and said, "Yes, my little, 'D' I have homes everywhere they are needed. These sanctuaries are not just because I love beauty of art and nature and those who create magnificent art."

"They are homes to help those who are wounded physically and emotionally to heal. They are hidden in secret to allow the residents freedom to explore their pain and to grow out of it. When they are comfortable, they can return from where they came. Or, if they choose, they can stay on and be a part of the staff who keep this place at its best. Whatever they decide is up to them, and we honor their choice," Zetia told the girls.

"Have you ever been deceived by someone entering a sanctuary?" Ayden asked.

"As a human or a talking animal, all of us have to be wary of deception from others," Zetia began.

"There are those who practice deceit like you and I enjoy this fresh bread with butter. They take a twisted pride fooling others into thinking their sad story of woes is true. They work at your common decency and emotions to weave a web of deception.

Then, they try to reel you in deeper and deeper by telling you when you question the truth of something they said or did that you just saw it wrong. You really did not see their actions as inappropriate. They make you to start to question yourself and what you know you perceived. It can make you feel crazy, at times. They are extremely quick to read you and thwart you from believing yourself."

Zetia continued, "But, I digress. To answer if we have been deceived by anyone wrongly entering a sanctuary was your question. We have a built-in warning system at each entrance. The eyes are the gateway to the soul."

And, the entry will not allow the soul in, if it is dark. For you see, dark souls cannot be saved by human means. It takes an awakening for them to see their wrongs and repent. Nothing we try to do will mend their ways for them. They have to reach this point through their own trials and experiences. And, unfortunately, some never see their wrongs and die in their pain and misery." Zetia sadly concluded.

"But enough on this subject," Zetia stated. "It is time for you two girls to be pampered. Massages, haircuts, and other fun as well as relaxing in the hot spring are all in order now." Zetia led the girls out of the kitchen to their next adventure.

The Trevins and Phum had wildly explored the whole outdoors around the Home all morning. They jumped from limb to limb, full of excitement at each new thing they discovered.

From beautiful shiny metals, which hung from the trees as ornaments and wind chimes to the lake where clams were just waiting to be devoured; the nine of them were full and happy. By the time the afternoon was upon them, they were lazily resting in the tree branches above the outside courtyard.

Below, Nekoh was making his way to explore the outdoors and all of the noises he heard in the courtyard. He walked slowly, smelling new scents and chewing on the grass which grew naturally all around.

He found a bench, warmed by the sun, and jumped up to lay his full body on its surface. Nip, who was always close by Nekoh, laid underneath the bench.

With his paw, Nekoh played with the tall grass. Repositioning himself, he leaned his head back to the edge of the seat and watched a beautiful color palate of feathers with distinct eyes all around them.

As the feathers moved in the light afternoon breeze, Nekoh felt himself become mesmerized by their movement. His head started to sway with the eyes and he felt kind of dizzy. He reached out with his paw to stop the movement.

Suddenly he was batted in the face by three tiny little claws jolting him off the bench.

A voice screamed, "No! Bad Touch! Bad Touch!" very loudly as it kept batting Nekoh across his face.

Nekoh's head bounced back and forth as he tried to scramble away from the foot. He hissed with fear and indignation as he tried to regain his balance and dignity.

Nip stood with all four paws wide apart. She stiffly jumped at the thing and hissed in fear with each jump.

The Trevins and Phum, who had seen the whole display of 'Bad Touch' were holding onto each other as their laughter nearly made them fall out of the trees.

Zetia came rushing in and said in a tender voice, "Kit, Kit, it is OK. He doesn't want to hurt you. He is a friend. He's not bad touch, OK?"

Deborah and Ayden who were sitting in the sunroom saw the whole debacle go down. Deborah jumped to her feet and ran to Nekoh with Ayden close behind. They arrived in the yard, hearing Zetia trying to calm the peacock.

Deborah ran over to Nekoh to assess his new wounds around his head. She looked at Zetia and said, "What is wrong with that thing!" Ayden quickly picked up Nip, holding on to her tightly.

Zetia stated as she calmly caressed the peacocks head, "This is Kit and he has been traumatized by people and animals. He is emotionally geared to see any unfamiliar movement as bad touch, and he reacts negatively.

"So, what do you call his actions, then," Deborah demanded, "Good Touch because it's OK for him to beat the crap out of someone?" Deborah, emotionally, held Nekoh in her arms as she protected him from Kit.

Zetia turned to Kit and said, "Kit we have talked about you being safe here, right? There is no need to bat someone crazy because you feel fear. Remember you can run and hide to your safe place if you feel threatened."

The Trevins and Phum jumped down from the trees, and cautiously made a very wide turn to reach the injured party. Not taking their eyes off of Kit, they stood behind the bench where Nekoh was being protected by Deborah.

"Hey Nekoh, you want me to pluck one of his feathers for you as a souvenir. Or maybe just a reminder. A reminder of how a bird took you down with one claw," Trevin said as he began rolling on the ground in laughter at his 'funny' he made about Nekoh.

Nekoh turned to him and stated, "I'd like to see you get a feather, Trevin. Make sure I am here when you try. And, you better make sure Deborah is close so she can tend to your wounds when that animal tears you a new one."

Kit turned to Nekoh and said, "I am sorry big cat for hurting you." He looked at Zetia who nodded her approval and Kit ran off to hide.

Zetia stated, "Well, that went better than I anticipated. Let's go eat dinner."

The dinner started with the retelling of the Nekoh fight and everyone laughing at the scene of Nekoh being taken down by a peacock.

Nekoh was a good sport and laughed with everyone over the 'Bad Touch' story. Which led into the story of how the Trevins acquired Ten and how the raccoons could hardly stay on or stop the horse. Which made Nekoh feel less embarrassed by his encounter.

Just like Tarhana said, "good conversation and the communing of their spirits" was the beauty of the night's meal. After they atel, everyone sat around the fire and continued to talk.

"Ayden," Joshua began, "Tell me how you feel about your conversation with the Great Crane? Ever since you arrived, I have sensed an aura around you. This aura only comes from being in the presence of the Great One," Joshua revealed.

Ayden choked on her drink as Joshua exposed her secret. Everyone in the room turned to see what she would say. Some with mouths dropped, and others with admiration waited patiently for her to respond.

"It was a little unsettling at first, because the battle with the wolves and boars had just ended," Ayden began.

"I was scared because I realized I was out of my league with my weapons in this type of battle. I could never had done what all the rest of you had done to save each of us. Jerin, Tybin, Nick, Elora, Phum, Two, and Eleea were all so amazing to watch. Even the first act where Zetia strategically lured them in with a calmness was just jaw dropping amazing." Ayden stopped to think about what to say next.

"Everyone except Deborah and I, and Eleea, Nick, and Phum who were closer to the campfire listened in anticipation to make sure they were not needed as the rest went ahead to help the Trevins and Zetia. All of these thoughts were swirling in my mind about how serious everything had just become. That this battle was real and to the death." Ayden again stopped and looked at everyone.

"How was I supposed to justify putting my friends in danger? I quietly said out loud, 'I am scared.' And, an image began to form on my side. The clearer I saw the Great Crane, all sound around ceased to exist. It was just he and I in this vacuum," she stated.

"He told me to not be afraid. Because fear is not defeat, it is awareness. He said, 'courage is not the absence of fear, but the determination against all odds to persevere with dignity and respect.' He said I was the greatest weapon we all had and I needed to hear my soul with my heart not my head in order to fly."

Ayden sighed and continued. "I told him I couldn't fly. And he said I could when I let my soul give my wings flight. Then he disappeared." Ayden finished and fixed her eyes on Joshua.

"Ayden," Joshua started, "I have heard of many instances where the Crane has shown himself and silently guided someone to safety. Or stood off in the distance as encouragement. Even fewer have told of him giving them words of encouragement. Yet, he not only showed himself to you, he encouraged you and, he had a conversation with you. Very impressive." Joshua stated.

"Do you know the rule of three, Ayden," Joshua asked.

"No, I don't, Joshua," Ayden stated.

"The rule of three is a symbolic affirmation which can be used to help you determine difficult decisions," Joshua explained.

"Some believe it comes from three because you have the Great Crane, the Great Fox, and the hummingbirds. Three entities of high value represent good decisions. So, let's say you are perplexed in which way you should go with a decision. And, you keep this concern to yourself and do not audibly express your feelings."

"Then, three different statements at randomly three different times are made to you on the exact subject which was concerning you. And it is a confirmation for you, usually, on which right path to follow with your gut decision," Joshua stated.

"You have received three different experiences from the Great Crane in one meeting," Joshua said with awe. "He gave you full view of himself, he gave you wisdom to hear, and he answered your questions. Extremely rare, Ayden. He obviously holds you in high esteem," Joshua concluded.

"But, Joshua," Ayden began, "Just like everything I have seen in Eshra, I didn't get all my questions answered. It just feels so frustrating to have half answers which leave you with a lot more questions. For example, my mom at the Wall of Tears loved Zayden, my father, but she didn't tell me. Zetia told me. So, how," Ayden turned to stare at Nadab, "could you not tell me about the second locket at the Great Tree, Nadab?"

Nadab looked at Ayden with eyes of compassion and said, "Ayden, when Nickalli came to me with the picture, I had this gut reaction and didn't know why. I believe this is why I could not make a weapon for you. My confusion had gotten in the way of my abilities. Something kept nagging at me, and I could not put my finger on it."

"Yes, Zayden asked me to make the first locket. He never showed me a picture or told me who it was for. Yes, I recognized Zayden in the picture Nickalli had given me. But to tell Nickalli what I knew would confuse him. And, it was not a fair thing to do to him," Nadab explained.

Nadab turned to Lydia and took her hand, "It was Lydia who helped me to see what I needed to do. Together, she and I, figured it out. Your name came from Zayden. It all made sense. The 'Z' was removed to create you, Ayden. But, again to tell you what we knew, or suspected, would have caused you great confusion. We had no answers for you and could only burden you with more questions. So, we decided to stay quiet until the time came when we could give you answers."

"When I started to forge the second locket, it just happened naturally. I didn't plan on it, my hands and mind just wanted to do it." Nadab stated.

"Joshua spoke of the rule of three," Nadab continued. "Well, this is how the picture ended up in the locket. The first was a dream I had. I saw you looking across the mountains while you held the locket in your hands. You were crying. The next affirmation came when I saw you at the festival in your beautiful outfit Lydia had made for you. The night scene flowed across your body, and walking next to you was Zayden. I almost cried right there, at seeing his image with you."

"And, the third came when I had completed the locket. As I stared at its detail, the picture of you, your mom and Zayden caught wind from off my bench shelf where I had it tucked away, and it gently landed on my work bench. I knew then the picture needed to go in the locket. As soon as I got it placed the way I wanted it, the locket closed and I could no longer open it." Nadab finished, as he looked at Ayden with love, and grabbed her hand.

Ayden rose from her seat and went over and hugged Nadab and Lydia, she turned to Nick and hugged him. She saw Zetia with tears running down her face. Ayden walked over to Zetia and took her arms to have her stand, and she hugged Zetia as they cried together.

Deborah came over to Ayden, and Ayden grabbed her and pulled her into the hug, where all three of them cried, holding on to each other. The effect of the moment caused everyone to stand and start hugging each other. The whole group went from one to the other giving hugs. All either crying or with tears in their eyes.

The Trevins were a mess. Big tears rolled down their faces as they hugged legs all around the group. Phum hugged the Trevins, the Trevins hugged Phum. Nekoh and Nip meandered through the legs of everybody, and Eleea and Elora softly sang for the whole group. Gethsemane perched above them and watched with pride.

Ayden turned and looked at the whole assembly of friends she had become so very fond of. She raised her hand to get their attention and said, "I truly believe it is best we stay here with Zetia for at least three more days. This time of rest will be our last until we defeat Choran."

She looked at the group with intense emotional power in her eyes and said, "The love I hold for each of you, has never been known by me before. I wish to have time with each of you before we leave. My heart tells me I need to spend time with all of you, alone."

Ayden looked at Gethsemane and Zetia, who was standing by him, and nodded. In turn, they both nodded to her with approval.

Journal Thirty-Four

"Fear is Awareness" the Crane told me. Well, I was aware there was a real possibility all of us would not survive this battle with Choran.

I was aware Jerin and Deborah were developing strong feelings for each other, even if she couldn't see it.

I was aware I had some really awesome people and animals going with me into battle.

I was aware I wanted answers to my most pressing questions. Like how my mom knew my dad, and where was my dad, and what did I have to do to stop Choran.

I was aware we were all going into a very dangerous part of our journey and it would test all of us beyond anything we had ever known before.

I was aware of the need to let everyone know what they meant to me.

And, deep in my heart, I was aware something was going to happen that would deeply

> *change me forever.*

Chapter Thirty-Four

Nahrita and Dariat arrived at the entrance to the Dead Trees with the wolves close behind them. She looked up at the sky as she breathed heavily from their long walk back.

It had taken three difficult days to reach the trees. Her and Dariat were back to normal size and had lost any chance of riding the horse belonging to Jaeh. The stupid horse didn't follow the wolves and got lost in the woods.

Nahrita dreaded her entrance into the Trees. Knowing, all too well, the anger of Choran when he found out she had failed, again. She sighed, and looked at the tree which held the secret mark of Choran.

A lone tree amongst twenty other larger trees around it. It stood inconspicuous as its' withered branches hung high in the sky like gnarled fingers on an arthritic woman. The dried-out trunk, weathered, from years of the wind circling it and very little water had turned to almost cement with deep crevasses where the roots protruded out.

She walked to the tree and felt the mark on the bark with her fingers. Three long lines, curved at each tip, and connected at the base, depicting Choran's footprint were hidden by the natural design of the tree's surface.

Nahrita placed her palm directly on the mark as she lowered her head in anticipation of where she was going. She took her hand away and walked around the tree. Three times to the left, then four times to the right, and one more half round to the left.

The tree's roots crawled up in the air and grabbed the trunk, pulling it apart to reveal a dark staircase leading into the underground. Nahrita, Dariat and the wolves began their walk down the winding platform which looked like twisted vines of the tree.

Their walk wound deeper and deeper into the darkness of the cavern beneath the tree. Upon reaching the bottom, Nahrita took a five-foot walking stick wrapped at the top with cloth from a basin at the side of the walkway. She dipped the tip in another smaller basin which held a liquid. When the cloth touched the wet substance, and was removed from the liquid, it ignited into flame. Nahrita used the flame as light to continue down one of the rooted corridors of the massive underground fortress.

They traveled in silence for twenty minutes before they reached a set of huge doors etched in the depiction of Choran's claws. Nahrita pulled the lever on the right side, and the doors loudly creaked open to allow their way through. She turned to her left and placed the tip of the walking stick in a gooey substance, which extinguished the flame, and then put the stick in a basin.

Nahrita was welcomed by workers who were behind the doors, and who continued at their tasks after they acknowledged her. She walked past several blacksmiths, leatherworkers, weavers, seamstresses, potters and bakers for another ten minutes before she stopped at a little cottage. She opened the door and entered with Dariat. The wolves laid down outside the cottage like sentries on each side of the door.

A woman looked up from the fire she was tending and said, "Nahrita, take heart. No war is won with the first battle. Stay here tonight and meet with Choran tomorrow. You need your rest to be able to speak to him intelligently and not emotionally."

"Iza, we lost your brother, Jaeh, in this battle we did not win," Nahrita stated with sorrow as she sat down. "My emotions will not leave easily. Zetia has broken the pact and killed him," she said with anger.

Iza came to Nahrita's side and hesitantly put her hand on her chair. "Jaeh made his choice long ago, and knew it could mean death, Nahrita," she said. "I have sorrow for my loss, and for you at his loss, but we have to accept as the time draws near, more will die before the end."

"I need a hot meal, clean clothes and a horse, Iza," Nahrita coldly stated. "There is no time to rest, I have news for Choran."

Iza handed her a bowl of stew with bread, turned to Dariat and placed a bowl on the floor for him and then exited the cottage with two bowls for the wolves. She returned five minutes later and handed Nahrita new clothing.

"Your horse is tethered outside. I beg you to rest until morning," Iza pleaded.

"No, Iza, my news cannot wait until morning," Nahrita impatiently stated as she stood to change her clothes. Nahrita somberly nodded at Iza and left the cottage to mount her horse.

Dariat followed on foot as they began their journey deeper into the recesses of the cavern. The wolves followed behind the horse with lowered heads, as if they feared what was to come.

It would take her throughout the night to reach Choran. The homes of the people of the Dark Cell, who resided throughout the cavern, would dimly light her path.

Early morning brought Nahrita to the Land of Bones, where Choran kept his army of regurgitated pellets he released from his kills. Each pellet could be called by him when he desired. They laid in wait to break out of their deathly cocoon to do Choran's bidding. Layers of pellets lined the path to his chambers.

Nahrita had personally witnessed the release of the pellets on several occasions.

Whenever Choran became angry with one of his disciples or wanted to eliminate a captured soul, he would call for the pellets to rise and tear the body apart to make it easier for Choran to devour it. At other times, Choran would have the pellets destroy the victim for fun and not food.

There was no real surefire way to not anger Choran. The longer he had to wait for his revenge on the Great Crane, the more unpredictable he had become. He sat in the dark on his high perch, wallowing in hate, waiting for his followers to come back to him with the news he desired. News the Messenger was no longer a threat.

When he felt hunger, he would release his pellets, known as Bones, to bring him food from the world above. The Bones were hindered by the light. They would break and fall to the ground if direct sunlight or moonlight hit their bodies. Therefore, the Bones had to be helped by specifically trained Dark Cell dwellers.

The Cellers, as they were known, had a special formulated powder Choran was
continuously perfecting. They would use it to throw over the Bones so the light would not affect them. The powder, still, was unstable which sent Choran into a tirade of accusations when it failed. Generally, he would devour the potion makers, who he felt failed him and start fresh with a new group.

The closer she got to the Chamber; she could see the workers who were dedicated to making the elixir. There were the cultivators of the snail fern who used artificial light to nurture the plants to maturation. They also grew the buffalo ear, gopher weed, and silver grass plants which were needed to create the potion to make a body grow to an enormous size.

Choran drank the elixir throughout the day and night, and would become outraged if the workers fell behind in their task of running out of his drug infused euphoric drink. Many cultivators were in the bone pile, which motivated those still alive with fear of meeting the same fate.

Next to the cultivators dwelled the dryers and herbalists. The first, took the plants, dried and crushed them in the proper manner and readied them for the herbalists. The herbalists cooked the plants in the required combinations to create the drink. There were three shifts of laborers who kept the bowls full of the elixir. All, feared the wrath of Choran and worked tirelessly to keep his eyes off of them.

Nahrita reached the entry to the Chamber and stopped. She exhaled a very heavy sigh, lifted her head high and walked into Choran's presence.

High on a ledge of jagged rock with a monstrous cave behind him perched Choran. Huge trees jutted out and around his entrance. The limbs, gnarled, barren and hardened, eerily climbed up the sides of the rock to its highest point as if seeking water and light to survive.

All around his chamber, and beyond, vast roots from thousands of trees covered the landscape. The Forest of Roots, as it was called, led far into the Dark Cell kingdom and reached up into the world of Eshra.

One, lone, heavily knobbed branch extended out and away from his cave and provided Choran a throne to look down on those who entered his domain. Darkness surrounded his world and gave him superiority over all who dared speak to him.

Being an owl, he was able to see clearly in the dark, and he liked this advantage over all he spoke to. But he did allow, at times, a solitary walking stick to burn when he wished to show his immense size, or speak to his subjects with more than auditory dominance.

Nahrita picked up a walking stick and lit it as she came into view of Choran. He was sitting at the entrance to his cave, and seemed larger than usual.

He was a great horned owl by birth. Yet, after years and years of snail fern potion, he had lost any resemblance to the great bird.

His feet and legs looked like the gnarled roots of the trees around him, as they spread into his black claws which resembled cast iron curved hooks.

His massive wings no longer held the natural flow of a bird's wing. Each feather jutted out and away from his body, looking like a child had tried to glue feathers on an oblong ball, but couldn't get the feathers positioned in a uniformed manner. Rather than looking like feathers should, where each layer created the beauty of the color of the wings of a great horned owl, his took on the appearance of sinew barely holding on to the bones.

Choran's head looked out of place on his body as it seemed to perch weakly on his shoulders. Just as the feathers on his lower body were mangled, so too were the ones around his neck and head. The horned feathers which gave his breed its name stood out like misplaced sticks on top of his head.

His enormous gold and black eyes bulged out of his skull with a menacing stare that could make your skin crawl in disgust or fear. Despite his decrepit appearance, his stature emanated power and might. When his eyes focused on you, it felt like your inner core would be crushed by his malice.

"Nahrita," Choran stated as he slowly climbed onto his limb. "What good news do you bring me," he asked.

"Choran, my leader," Nahrita said as she bowed to him. "I come with no good news. Jaeh has been killed and we lost all the boars, hawks, and badgers. Only the two wolves you see with me and Dariat survived the onslaught of Zetia's attack."

Choran roared as he stood up off his perch and his wings left his side, showing their enormous wing span. "YOU NAHRITA! You were on a scouting mission, not a battle mission," he yelled. "I never gave you permission to attack, you fool!" He screamed.

"Choran, my leader, it was not my choice to do battle," Nahrita pleaded as she bowed lower. "Zetia broke the pact and attacked first. We had no choice but to defend ourselves," she declared as the wolves' ears fell back in a submissive stance and their bodies tried to lay as flat as their tails.

"The Messenger and her followers finished off all our comrades, Choran," Nahrita continued to explain. "They ambushed us. If we had not run, we too would be dead." Nahrita tried to convince him.

Choran lowered his wings and glared at Nahrita, and asked, "Did you see her? This thing? This messenger?"

"No, my leader, Zetia kept her hidden from our view," Nahrita explained.

"ZETIA!" Choran roared. "She knows the cost of crossing me," he stated with venom in his voice.

"Zetia has made her choice. She will pay for her stupidity. How close is this thing Eshra has put their hope in," Choran demanded from Nahrita?

"Two maybe three days' ride. I am not sure if they chose to stay at their camp or have rode with speed to the Dead Trees. Zetia's magic is at play here," Nahrita said as she avoided telling Choran she was tricked by Zetia and lost her size from the potion.

"Gather," Choran started to say as he began to heave and catch his breath. He turned to his left and raised his wing to have a worker fill his dish with elixir. He flew down to the floor of his chamber and took a long slow drink from the bowl, and then spread his wings to regain air in his lungs.

He coughed again and said, "Gather the Bones and send them to the Front at the Dead Trees. Keep them underground and prepare them for the attack."

Continuous coughing stopped him throughout his orders as he finally stated, "But, you, Nahrita, wait for my order to begin the siege."

"Send the Cellers to the surface with twenty Bones and have them scout the area. Task the potion makers to triple their supply and pick those who you know can handle the elixir. But do not drink until I give the signal." Choran ordered.

He flew back to the entrance of his cave still coughing and said, "I am very disappointed in you, Nahrita. You are lucky I need you to be my eyes and ears right now, or you would reside with the Bones."

"I have half a mind to rid my view of Dariat and those two wolves who could not even take down a small group of inexperienced warriors," he warned as he walked into the darkness of his cave where is coughing was magnified by the vibration of the walls.

Nahrita quietly backed out of his view. She turned around to leave the area, when she was stopped by Choran.

"Nahrita," Choran's voice echoed from deep in his cave. "I know you have not told me the whole story about your meeting with Zetia. Remember what happens to those who lie to me one too many times."

Silence surrounded the Chamber as Nahrita, Dariat and the wolves quickly exited the room.

"Find me a strong hawk, Dariat. One with speed and good speaking skills," Nahrita ordered. "He needs to be able to go swiftly back and forth and take accurate messages from Choran and I. Look for one like Garis, who is not afraid to be in Choran's presence," she finished.

"You two wolves stay here with the potion makers," Nahrita commanded. "Make sure they triple their output and they store it properly. Pick a bird who can bring messages to me at the Front on your progress," she instructed.

"Dariat, after you find the hawk, get the Cellers to move the Bones to the Front. I will speak to Nargaut on the way out on getting Bone scouts above ground," Nahrita stated.

Nahrita left the three of them and began her trek back to the front of the Dead Trees. She stopped at the main home of the Cellers and walked through the doors.

Nargaut stood as she entered, and said, "Nahrita, it is good to see you."

"There is no time for niceties, Nargaut," Nahrita stated. "You and I know we have no like of each other, so save your words. Choran wants twenty Bones above ground scouting for the Messenger and her followers. Whatever you find, you tell me first before you go to Choran," she said as she stared at him with a long look of determination.

"And, I am serious, Nargaut! Me first, no mistake." She ended as she walked back out and slammed the door.

Nahrita traveled late into the evening before she arrived back at the cottage. She opened the door and slid into the chair at the table. She put her arms on the table and her head on her arms and fell asleep.

Iza walked over to Nahrita and placed a blanket around her shoulders. She sat down in the chair across from her and sadly looked at the woman who was so full of anger.

Iza brushed Nahrita's hair out of her face and Nahrita stirred and lifted her head.

"Iza," Nahrita said, "Jaeh is gone. Gone."

Iza took her hand and silently sat with her.

"I will kill Zetia, Iza." Nahrita confessed.

"She killed the one thing I loved. I will have my revenge." Nahrita said as she fell back to sleep.

Journal Thirty-Five

I knew I had to make special memories with each of my friends. Not only for their emotional wellbeing, but for mine too.

I wanted memories I could relive. And, I wanted them to know how much I valued them.

We were always together as a group and I wanted the freedom, without other ears, to tell them how I felt.

Zetia's home was the perfect backdrop for my planned execution of letting each of them know how strong and beautiful they were.

I was excited to get to tell them what made them special to me.

It was going to be a great couple of days at Zetia's sanctuary.

Chapter Thirty-Five

Ayden woke very early in the morning to hearing Elora singing, but she wasn't in their room. She quickly got dressed and went outside their door to look over the balcony which graced the whole upstairs rooms.

And, there was Elora in the main area of the Home by the waterfall. Singing to herself. It was obvious by her movements she was enjoying her sounds, mixed with the falling water.

Ayden began to walk down the stairs and yelled to Elora, "Hey, Elora let me get something to eat and join you, OK?"

"OK, Ayden, I will stay here and wait for you," Elora yelled back.

Ayden quickly went to the kitchen and got a plate of cheeses, fruits, and bread with jam. She then got a small plate for Elora, and coffee for herself.

She juggled her plates as she tried to hurry back to Elora. She sat down next to her and asked, "What were you singing?"

"I was singing a song of joy because this is such a very peaceful spot to be. The sound of the water falling down the pretty rock scene is so very nice to be near. It kind of reminds me of the Wall of Tears and the lake," Elora dreamily said.

"You know, you are right," Ayden said. "This does look like the whole Wall of Tears area. What was a crazy day, huh? I never got to ask you how you felt about meeting your mom, Elora," Ayden asked.

"Well, I was happy and sad at the same time," Elora said thoughtfully. "My mom, she is beautiful. I got to hear her voice, and it was something I never thought I would get to do. I will always have the memory, now. But, to see her leave so fast. Well, this is also a memory and I don't like it," Elora said with sadness.

"Do you remember what she told you, Elora?" Ayden questioned her.

"I remember her telling me she loved me from the egg. And I was a beautiful child, and she was proud of me. And to live my destiny," Elora stated as she tried to recall all her mom said.

"Yes, she told you all of those wonderful things, Elora. And they are all true," Ayden said. "One of the most beautiful things she told you, that I remember, is this Elora," Ayden put her finger under Elora's little beak and lightly lifted it to meet her eyes, and began: *"My spirit lives on in you, Elora. Wherever you go, I go with you."*

Elora burst into tears as she listened to Ayden repeat her mother's words.

"This is what I know about your mother, Elora," Ayden revealed as she clasped her hands in her lap.

"She was a heart who knew how to give extraordinary love. Her advice she gave to me, was to always look for the good in any situation. To be careful how I speak and to never stop loving those I held dear. I was to always let them know how special they were to me. Her ability to see deep into my soul, healed my heart," Ayden told her.

"What I saw in her, I see in you. She was determined and strong just like you. Her spirit does live on in you, Elora. You are the most beautiful friend and you are my family. And, Lora is right, wherever you go, she is with you," Ayden soothingly said to Elora.

Elora looked at Ayden for over a minute before she spoke, "Ayden, I love you. I will never forget my mom lives in me and goes with me. Thank you, for reminding me she is here in my heart...every flight I take, she flies with me. And, Ayden, I carry you with me too." Elora said as she flew to Ayden's shoulder and rubbed her head against Ayden's neck.

Ayden and Elora stayed by the waterfall for another thirty minutes. As they sat, they began humming together in perfect harmony.

Deborah came down the stairs and said, "Hey there you guys are. I wondered what happened to you two. It's still early in the morning! And, you guys had breakfast and coffee without me!" Deborah teasingly exclaimed.

Ayden laughed and said, "Come on we'll go to the kitchen with you while you eat. I could use another cup of coffee, anyways."

After Deborah finished her breakfast and second cup of coffee, she turned to Ayden and said, "Today, I plan on spending time in the courtyard with the herbalists. I think I saw some unfamiliar plants. So, I want to learn about what they are doing with them. What are you going to do today, 'A'?"

"Oh, I'm going to find others to talk to and just let my day lead me where I need to be, I guess," Ayden said.

"OK, then, I am off. See you guys later," Deborah said as she left the kitchen.

Ayden watched as Elora flew in the direction of Deborah. She stood up from the kitchen table to leave when Tybin came in and sat across from her. Ayden looked at him and thoughtfully decided, "Why not," and sat back down.

"How ya doin', Tybin," Ayden asked.

Tybin grabbed a huge piece of bread slapped a large portion of butter on it. He then got a tall glass of milk and said, "Lovin' it here, that's for sure," as he devoured the bread and went for another slice.

"Tybin, I want to thank you for saving Deborah and I at the battle," Ayden began. "I have learned a lot from you. You are very calm in a crisis. And I wouldn't mind learning some of those acrobatic moves you do so well in the trees," she stated.

"Hey! No problem. Zetia has a very cool sparring hut down by the lake. I'd be glad to meet you down there later this morning and give you some pointers," Tybin said.

"Great, I'll meet you later then," Ayden decided.

"Sounds good," Tybin said as he grabbed another piece of bread and walked out of the kitchen.

"Well," Ayden thought, "That didn't go as planned. He is not one to talk emotions and he definitely doesn't like to stick around for small talk. Maybe, physical activity will open him up," she decided.

"On to my next victim," Ayden thought as she left the kitchen.

She walked outside where she heard the Trevins animated wild behavior down by the lake. She hadn't seen the lake and decided it was a perfect opportunity to see the grandeur of its place on Zetia's property.

She walked through the pine trees for about three hundred yards where it opened onto a grass filled beach before the water. A large building was off to the left, which Ayden assumed was the sparring hut Tybin spoke about.

To the right was a long boat dock made from the most beautiful hard wood, weathered like an old barn house, yet it had a dull shine on it to keep it from breaking down from the elements. It reached at least fifty feet out into the water, and chairs and benches of wood were dotted all along its path.

Between the hut and the dock was a pebbly beach, and this is where the Trevins were. Eating clams and gabbing endlessly while their little fingers slammed the clam shells on the rocks to open and reveal their treasures.

Ayden took her shoes off and walked down to the edge of the water where they were, and said, "May I join you guys?"

"Ayden!" Trevin said. "I did not know you liked raw clams. Here, let me break open some for you."

"No, no, no, Trevin," Ayden quickly said. "I didn't mean join in your feast. I meant join in your conversation."

"Oh, sure," Trevin said with understanding. "Come sit and we will be proud to talk with you, Ayden."

Seven little bodies lined up on the beach and sat on their haunches; all staring at Ayden. It was hard for her figure out which one was which, as they all had matted wet fur.

"Hey!" Ayden said, "One of you is missing. Let me guess, it is Two." The seven of them nodded at her in agreement.

"Well, I will talk to him later, then," she said. "I guess, I have called you all together, even though you are always together, to tell you how much I appreciate each of you," Ayden began.

"Gethsemane was very wise to ask you guys to help us. When I first met you, I thought you guys were a chaotic group of misfits." Ayden said as she let her feet enter the water. And, I mean that with respect. You guys crashed into our camp in a very crazy and emotional way. Especially with all of you named Trevin."

"But," Ayden continued, "the Trevins works for you. You guys are not misfits; you guys are a family. And for you to say the rest of us are your family too...well, it means so much to me. Because I see each of you as my family, and I love you guys."

"You have taught me a very valuable lesson, actually more than one. The biggest one is to respect those who die and give them a proper burial," Ayden stated. "My life would not be as full of love if you guys were not in it." Ayden told them as she looked at them affectionately.

Seven little bodies climbed up into her lap, all vying for the center position. In unison, they said, "Ayden, we love you too."

Trevin jumped down beside her and took her hand in his paws, he looked into her eyes, and said, "You are the best thing to happen to us, Ayden. If we had not agreed to watch over you, we would have never found our true family. We will go wherever you go. We will fight wherever you fight." Trevin said as he climbed up to hug her neck.

Ayden started to cry, which caused the Trevins to hug her and cry too. She took each one by the face with her hands, looked them in the eyes and kissed their cheeks on both sides.

Tybin was just walking into the hut when Ayden had kissed the last of the Trevins. She got up and said, "Gotta go boys, I'll talk to you later," as she walked towards the hut.

Ayden entered the building to a massive view of an inside forest along three of the walls. The center was open like a gymnasium floor, and the far side had mats and other accessories for combat and workout practice.

The ceiling was arched with windows and huge beams. Off of the beams hung leather straps for trapeze type exercises. Tybin looked up as Ayden entered the room.

Ayden caught his eyes and said, "This is a pretty impressive training room."

Tybin came over to her, and smiled, saying, "Yep, it is a perfect place to teach you how to reach for the stars, Ayden."

He grabbed two of the leather straps and lifted Ayden up for her to grab them. "I want you to start gaining momentum while you are gently swinging. Don't try to do it fast. Just get the feel for the movement. Let your arms and hands get used to the pull as they gain strength in this position. Once you feel strong, move your body back and forth with more force," Tybin instructed her.

Ayden followed Tybin's instructions and as she began to gain speed, he would hold onto her hips and stop her. He made her let go of the straps and stand on the floor with her arms down. Instructing her to shake her arms and hands. He would then tell her to repeat the whole process over and over again.

"Are you teaching me how to go through the trees like you and the others, Tybin?" Ayden asked.

"Anything worth learning takes practice, Ayden. And, yes to answer your question, this will help you to go through the trees," Tybin stated.

"What you want is to get to a point where it is second nature to you. You don't think, you just do. You see a limb or a rope hanging, and you just grab and start the movement to propel you to another area. But, to get to where you propel, you first have to know how to hang and start the movement," he finished. He gestured to her to continue the same pattern.

Ayden became used to the drill, and said while swinging, "Tybin, we need to talk. Promise me you will protect Deborah. I mean if something should happen to me, and she tries to come after me. I want you to stop her from danger, OK?"

Tybin grabbed her hips and stopped her, looked into her eyes and said, "What do you know, Ayden? What are you not telling me?"

Ayden dropped the straps and landed on the floor. She returned his gaze and said, "Tybin when we were at Sunbird, Joshua gave me a prophecy. He said, *"Surrounded by dead limbs and bones, deep from the bowels will rise the crane. Sing, child. Sing with joy, sing with fear, sing to hear the stars respond."*

"I do not know what it really means, but I do believe it will happen. And, Deborah has no real skill to survive in a place like Joshua described. She is not a fighter, nor an athlete. You and Jerin have got to protect her for me. Promise?" Ayden pleaded with Tybin.

Tybin looked long into Ayden's eyes and then said, "I promise you we will keep Deborah safe. Just as we will keep you safe, Ayden. But, yes, I will let Jerin know of your decision."

"Tybin, you are a beautiful soul," Ayden began. "You have your mother's beauty and your father's strength. When I look at you, I see a majestic tree with the sun shining down on its branches and trunk. The leaves glisten like brilliant emeralds as you talk, and the whole tree is you, sturdy and strong."

"Thank you for being my friend, Tybin. Thank you, for being my family," Ayden finished as she took his forearm and he grabbed hers in the same manner. They stood there for a lengthy time as their eyes fixed on each other.

Tybin smiled, and said, "Let's finish your training, Ayden." He had her do the same steps again. And then told her, "When you get the force of the momentum going fast enough you can grab for another branch or whatever is closest to propel you forth." He came up next to her and took two straps and showed her how to do it. For the next two hours, Ayden practiced what she had been taught.

Zetia walked in with a tray of cheeses, fruit and drink saying, "Ah! I see valuable time is being used wisely," as she smiled at Ayden and Tybin. She walked over to a chair, and said, "Let me see what Tybin has taught you, Ayden?"

Ayden showed her how she could now propel to other limbs around the room by using the trees. She used the full three walls to demonstrate her new ability, and came back to stand in front of Zetia and Tybin.

Tybin stated, "I do believe my expert training methods have made Ayden an honorary raccoon," he smiled with mischievousness. "Now, that my time is done with you, Ayden, I have a kitchen to raid," he said as he used the trees to trapeze out of the hut.

Zetia looked at Ayden, and said, "It is my turn to help you train, but first we eat for strength." After they enjoyed their light snack, Zetia stood and raised her skirt. She wrapped it tight, and stuck the end in her waist.

"Come, Ayden," Zetia said, "It is time for you to learn how to use your wings in all areas of your life."

Ayden ran through drills throughout the late afternoon. Zetia instructed her to stand still, lift her wings half way so she could feel the wings strength. From there she would have her feel the wings on how they could help her jump high to get where she needed to be.

Zetia taught Ayden how to land with her feet secure, much like when a person stands to deliver a punch and not lose their balance.

Next, she had Ayden let her wings go into full display beside her body, and taught her how to gauge the distance between her wings and objects close to her. And how to avoid her wings getting trapped between a structure and her body.

Finally, Zetia said, "The hour is late. Tomorrow we start before sunrise, as there is much more you need to know. But, now, let's go and enjoy dinner with our friends.

Ayden walked out with Zetia, and as they walked the path back to the big house, she said, "I was wondering, Zetia, I might like to start dressing differently. I love your look with the skirts and leggings, but I want to make it my own. Maybe a little more modified for my benefit, but I think I need a change."

"Absolutely, Ayden," Zetia said. "We will sit with Lydia after dinner and come up with a design you will be happy with. It will be a fun project for Lydia. She loves to design outfits and it will make her feel so special you have asked for her help," Zetia finished as they walked into the room full of the aroma of dinner.

Everyone was around the table already, talking and eating with joyful contentment. After the meal, Zetia asked if everyone would stay at the table until she returned.

Zetia came back with Tarhana and another woman, who were both straight behind her. She moved out of the way for the two women to stand next to each other. In their hands were two beautifully decorated birthday cakes. Deborah and Ayden gasped at the cakes, lit with fifteen little candles.

Zetia started singing: 'Happy are our hearts for this is the day you were born. Happy are our lives for you came to us and brought us joy. Happy Birthday to both of you.' The group joined in and repeated the song as the women placed a cake in front of each of the girls.

The girls waited for the song to end and then blew out the candles. The women took the cakes and cut them and served both to all at the table. One piece was a three-layered white with lemon filling and the other was the same white layered with raspberry filing.

Zetia turned to the girls, and said, "Since your birthdays are a day apart, September 7th and 9th, we thought it would be OK with you two if we celebrated them together the day before the first birthday. This way neither one of you would have known and would both be surprised," she said as she smiled at Ayden and Deborah.

"Thank you, Zetia," Ayden began, "I had really, forgotten about my birthday. And, thankfully I gave Deborah her birthday present early or I wouldn't have had anything prepared for her."

"I am so sorry, Ayden, I have been so wrapped up in everything, I didn't even do anything for you, yet," Deborah forlornly said.

"Girls," Zetia called them to attention, "There is no time here for sorrow. It is all good. Give yourselves a break, your lives have been anything but normal for the last three plus months. Let us enjoy your day with each of you and celebrate," she finished as she raised a glass to toast the girls.

Zetia's glass came back down and the room filled with magical bubbles which started at the floor and floated up. As they reached the ceiling, they burst into an array of color lighting the whole room with fireworks.

Nadab stood and faced the girls, "I am in the process of making a ring for each of you. Today, I asked Nickalli what stone I should use, and he told me of a peridot stone you are in possession of, Deborah. Would you consider letting me use it for a ring for both of you," Nadab humbly asked.

"What is a great idea, Nadab," Deborah exclaimed. "Then, Ayden and I will have something from each other. Something unique and special. I can't wait to see what you come up with. Can Ayden and I have a say on how it looks, so we are part of the surprise," Deborah asked.

"Here, Nadab, it is in my pocket. I was going to show it to the gemologist in the courtyard, but got too involved with the herbalists today." Deborah said as she pulled it out and gave it to Nadab.

"Of course," Nadab said. "That is a wonderful plan. I will meet with both of you, privately, tonight and discuss the details." He said as he took the stone and hurriedly left for the workshop.

Everyone finished their dessert and went their separate ways for the night. Ayden wound her way to Nadab's to design Deborah's ring.

"Ah! My, Ayden," Nadab stated as she entered, "I have truly missed being able to spend time alone with you," he said as he got the clamp around the stone to see how he was to break it apart from the dirt and gray stone.

"This is an exquisite rock and so very big, Ayden. I have never seen such clarity in a peridot like this one," he said with admiration.

"Nadab, I too, am thankful we get to spend time together," Ayden said. "I wanted to thank you for all you," Ayden turned to see Lydia standing in the doorway, "and Lydia have done for Deborah and I," she continued.

"I have a special request for the two of you," Ayden explained to them as Nadab stopped working and looked at Ayden.

"I know Deborah and I are only fifteen this week, but we have become so much more than fifteen these last few months. We have both matured into young women," Ayden said as she sat in front of Nadab and Lydia. "This world of Eshra, and both of you, as well as all who live here, will always be a part of our new lives. We will come and go several times over the years ahead," Ayden continued towards her request.

"I have seen the way Jerin looks at and tries to protect Deborah. And, I have seen Deborah try to steal looks at Jerin when she thinks no one sees her. There is something very special happening between the two of them. Even if they do not totally see it." Ayden explained.

"If something," Ayden paused, and started again, "If something should happen to me at the Dead Trees. I want Deborah to have a very special gift from me for her wedding day. I know it won't happen for several years, but I know it is going to happen with Jerin. I feel it deep in my soul. So, what I ask is for you to help me design something for her from me for that day and keep it to give to her, OK," Ayden asked both of them.

"Child," Lydia expressed. "Do not talk doom and gloom, you will have victory at the Dead Trees." She said as she grabbed Ayden's hand.

"Lydia, I believe we will have victory, but I do not think it is going to happen easily. There will be great loss before we succeed, I know it. I just don't know what we will lose?" Ayden stated with foreboding exasperation.

"Ayden, we will honor your request," Nadab stepped in to say. "And, as I talk with you about Deborah's birthday ring, we will figure out what to make for her wedding day," he said as he reassured his wife by rubbing her shoulder.

"Thank you, both of you," Ayden said as she sighed. "Now, could you two tell me about my dad?" She asked.

"Zayden was a man," Nadab started as he went back to working the stone. "A man, who knew what he needed to do to help others. He always watched and listened to everyone." Nadab stopped speaking and looked at Ayden. "Kind of like you, Ayden. He always put others first," he concluded.

"His hair was like the color of Nickalli's," Lydia interjected. "It flowed down his back, like Zetia wears her hair; yet he generally had it in a ponytail. He was tall and slender like Zetia. And walked with the same grace and confidence Zetia has," Lydia explained.

"We did not see him very often," Nadab said with his brow furrowed as he tried to bring up memories. "He did love to come to the Great Tree on the New Year, though. He loved celebrations and conversations. Not, that he made everyone, but, when he did make it, he would show up unexpectedly before the festival and partook of the joy with great enthusiasm."

"I remember he had this thirst to know how things were made. It didn't matter what the craft was, he wanted to have his hands in the process," Nadab stated.

"His dress was usually the same," Lydia said as she too pulled memories from her mind. "He liked to wear a semi heavy dark tan cotton pant which fit fairly tightly around his legs. Yet, he loved color. His shirt would be off white or tan, with pockets everywhere. And, it hung loosely around his frame. The pocket buttons were always colored; whether it be blue turquoise with midnight blue, or emerald green with purple amethyst, he loved color. And, Oh! He always had a bandana wrapped around his wrist to match his buttons," Lydia finished with delight.

Zetia walked into the room as Lydia was explaining Zayden's dress. She laughed with tenderness as she said, "Yes, my brother loved color. But, not too flashy to affect his manliness," she said with a smile.

"Have you told Lydia of your desire to change your dress, Ayden," Zetia asked.

"Well, after how you explained my dad's dress, I was wondering about something like the same look," Ayden stated.

"I like Zetia's skirts and leggings but, maybe not as full of color and design. Something a little subtler, like my dad."

"I am concerned about movement, though," Ayden said as she tried to explain what she wanted. "I don't want to be hindered by the skirt, so I am not sure I want a skirt or a loose pant. But, then again, I love the look of the skirt and its freedom to hide things under it. So, I guess I am kind of confused to what I really want," Ayden said with doubt in her voice.

"How about Lydia and I take off to the sewing room and work on your ideas, while you finish with Nadab," Zetia decided. "I will see you tomorrow, Ayden. I will come for you before the sun rises," she said as she smiled and left with Lydia.

"Nadab," Ayden said as she rubbed the stone with her fingers, "I would like to see a ring for Deborah with vines and leaves. This is such a beautiful olive-green color," she said as she gazed at it.

"I would like to see a fairly big, slightly oblong stone, polished without cuts on it. Set in a ring where the sterling silver or even the copper we see around here, either one, is vines and leaves which hold the stone in place, but do not hide the stone. And, if you could, on one side have a secret compartment door open to underneath the stone for her to put some type of concoction there that she always makes," Ayden finished with satisfaction as she looked at Nadab for approval.

"That is a very beautiful design, Ayden," Nadab admiringly said. "I believe you have given me a perfect idea to fit Deborah with the exact personality of her in it," he determined.

Deborah walked in and said, "Hey! I do believe it is my turn, you two."

"Yes, it is, and I am going to bed because Zetia says she is getting me up before the sun rises," Ayden said as she started to leave.

"'A', would you mind if I wrote in your journal tonight?" Deborah asked.

"Sure," Ayden said hesitantly. "But, why, 'D'?"

"Oh, I just feel like word exploding onto a page of paper," Deborah stated as she continued. "And, I wanted to have it in a place where I wouldn't lose it."

Ayden nodded as she left the two of them and wound her way up to her bed. She fell asleep immediately, as her body told her the workout with Tybin and Zetia had worn her out.

Journal Thirty-Six

I turn fifteen today, and I thought it would be a good start to write my thoughts down. It is early in the morning, like midnight, so I am just a fresh fifteen-year-old.

My life has been good. I grew up with two beautiful people who made sure I was well taken care of, with all my needs met. I didn't have to worry about being beaten, or being yelled at, or told I was worthless, or being embarrassed because of what was on my body.

My life was almost picture perfect for a child. I am very thankful for this being my beginning destiny.

Ayden coming into my life was the most important moment in my growing years, besides my parents. She caused me to see beyond a happy childhood. She caused me to learn deep compassion for another.

I watched her struggle from the first time I met her. She was afraid to take me to her house and meet her parents. She was even more afraid for my parents to meet her parents.

Great at avoidance was her motto.

Fear was her driving force.

One, she did not want to expose her family's dark secret of drinking, anger, and beatings.

Two, she did not want to look like she was vulnerable.

Ayden was proud, and determined to not let her childhood define her as a victim.

Protecting her became second nature to me.

The hurt I would see in her eyes, always cut to my heart.

If she wouldn't protect herself...well, then, I would do it for her... when I could.

I made sure the kids at school left her alone. I choreographed whatever I could to keep her out of danger or from being hurt.

I knew from the beginning she would do very great and important things in her life. What I didn't really think about, until Eshra, was that I would be so deeply involved in her making her mark.

*I am so very proud to be her friend. To call her my family.
And, I would not have it any other way, but to be by her side as we
move forward for her to fulfill her greatest moment, yet, in her road
to destiny.*
I love her.

Chapter Thirty-Six

Zetia woke Ayden very early the next morning. Ayden literally crawled out of bed, trying to not wake Deborah and Elora. She put a bandana over her head and crawled on her knees out the door.

Zetia, smiled down on Ayden, said, "Let's go my girl, it is time to see the beauty of the morning in flight." Zetia led Ayden down the path to the lake.

Ayden thought to herself, "How can she see where to go? It is pitch black out here," as she took a tight grip onto the back of Zetia's skirt for guidance.

Zetia guided Ayden out to the edge of the dock and began to hum. Ayden stood next to her, and matched Zetia's pitch. As their humming increased in intensity, the sun began to slowly peak over the horizon. Zetia looked at Ayden and nodded, as her wings emerged out of her back.

Ayden, again followed Zetia's lead and allowed her wings to show forth in full glory. Zetia lifted off and Ayden kept right beside her. The sun's light rose with them as they soared over the lake.

They followed the shore line all the way to the end of the lake and then turned to the right. They flew past the lake into the forest. Ayden saw an old-fashioned mine entrance and workers standing around it.

Past the mine was a meadow where beautiful flowers of all sorts, glistened from the morning dew. Farther out were gorgeous mountains with purple flowers all along their backs. Ayden smiled as the mountains looked like dragons with their dainty petals following the spine of their formation.

Coming back towards the main house were several pathways leading to personal cottages for the residents who lived there. Zetia continued to fly to the hut and landed.

Ayden easily followed and stood beside her. "Boy, do I have a lot of questions," Ayden stated as she intently looked at Zetia.

"Where would you like to start," Zetia asked Ayden as she opened the door to the hut.

"Where would I like to start in training or questions," Ayden asked.

"Both," Zetia said matter-of-factly as she prepared the room for their first lesson.

"OK," Ayden started, "I want to know about the mine. I want to know why our wings disappear into our body like we don't even have them. I want to know why you are not going with us to the Dead Trees. And, I want to know more about my dad," Ayden finished just as matter-of-factly as Zetia.

"Well, since you assume, I am going to teach you about your wings and how to use them effectively," Zetia began. "Let's start with a simple lesson and I will answer your questions while you are practicing."

Zetia directed Ayden to stand in the middle of the room with a wooden horse rolled out approximately eight feet away from her. She looked at Ayden, and said, "Spread your wings, only slightly out from your body, and leap next to the horse. I want you to continue to do this, back and forth. To the horse and back to where you started until I tell you to stop." Zetia informed Ayden.

"And, while you are doing this, I will tell you what I know," Zetia stated.

She pulled up a chair as she watched Ayden practice. "The mine is the exact copper I told you about when we talked about Deborah's gift from Finch. It is a secret, and cannot be made known to those outside of this sanctuary. Most people have no idea of its value and the items made with it are created by the people who live here."

"When I sell a piece, the majority of the profit goes to the artisan. Even the people who live here do not know the importance of this copper. In this way, when they leave, they will not accidentally tell someone about its properties. They just assume it is a fine metal from these mines." Zetia explained.

"This is a perfect example of how not telling the whole truth is more about protection rather than deception," Zetia stated.

"So, you feign ignorance out in the world and around here to its true importance. Why would you even sell it if it is so important and secret," Ayden inquired.

"This copper, Ayden," Zetia leaned closer to where Ayden was standing, and then continued, "is more than a beautiful piece of metal. Its properties have life in it for the world. This copper belongs to the order of the Great Crane. Not even Choran is aware of its importance."

Zetia firmly fixed her eyes on Ayden as she spoke. "Each piece goes out into the world, both worlds, possessing a quality of keeping the sun, the moon, and the stars in communication. Without it, they would not be able to send messages across the sky."

"After the Great Crane and Great Fox decided the hummingbirds would stand with them in the sky, they needed another form of communication between all of them. Something that could quickly reach them. A subtle, non-conspicuous agent such as the copper seemed the best way to ensure communication would always be in the worlds," Zetia explained.

"The mine is one of the life forces of our worlds. Now, the copper is not the only conduit of this life force. There are other materials in other areas around the world of Eshra and your world which carry similar properties."

"The energy of these metals emits signals, so to speak. And by them being spread throughout our worlds they create a continuous flow for communication. This mine is one of the main ones where we can bring forth its power and spread it easily without bringing attention to it," Zetia continued to explain.

"You, belonging to the Great Crane and his family, are now a guardian to this knowledge. Again, it is not deception, but protection, Ayden," Zetia said with reverence.

Ayden looked at Zetia, and said, "I understand the weight of what you have spoken and I honor the decision to keep the secret of the Great Crane," Ayden said with humble respect.

Zetia nodded at her and said, "Now, it is time for you to jump up on the horse's back."

Zetia walked over to where she had Ayden first stand. She leapt with her wings barely noticeable and landed on top of the horse. She flew back to Ayden and did it again three more times.

"Ayden your wings are powerful," Zetia stated. "It only takes a small movement to make the jump upwards. And, because it is so fast, no one sees it is your wings which have propelled you," she revealed.

Ayden positioned herself like Zetia had done and leapt past the horse. She flew back and tried again. The second time she hit the horse and fell. The third try she landed on the horse, but lost her balance and caught herself with her wings in flight as she landed on the floor. The fourth attempt, she got the motion and strength of her wings in the right combination and landed on the horse perfectly.

"Good job, Ayden," Zetia said with pride.

"Now, the next thing is for you to see the power of each feather and how it works with your wings," Zetia stated as she led Ayden to the other side of the hut and out the doors where there were several bales of hay stacked in different layers.

"Each feather on your wings is a blade," Zetia explained as she lifted Ayden's wing and showed her each feather.

"Right now, they feel soft and malleable. But when you desire, from your soul, to use them in battle; they will be weapons of power. Each can slice with precision and even your spine of your wing can be used as a blade for larger objects," Zetia stated.

"Watch what I mean, Ayden," Zetia said as she stood in front of a bale and sliced it to nothing.

She walked over to another and went straight through the bale to the next to show the power of the wing's spine. "Do this all the way down to the end," Zetia commanded.

Ayden looked down the line which seemed to her to be a mile long. She sighed, as she started her wing and feather training.

Zetia walked with her and said, "Our wings are a wonder which still keeps me in awe, Ayden. When I first found out about them, I would stand sideways at the mirror and hide them and let them come out of my back over and over again. It just didn't make sense to me they could disappear into my back."

"But, then, one day, I looked at the sun. How can it disappear and the moon can come out with the stars? Or how can the stars not be seen when the sun was out, but they were still there even though we could not see them. And, I came to terms, with all of nature having a special quality that sometimes cannot be explained. We can only accept and move on and enjoy the beauty of it. Now, granted there is science behind all of it. But, to the naked eye, it seems immensely strange," Zetia schooled her.

"Why did I not know about my wings before the lockets, then?" Ayden looked at Zetia and continued,

"How come, Zetia? Why did they not show before now?" Ayden asked, as she continued to slice the bales of hay.

"Ayden, your world was one of silence about Eshra," Zetia stated. "For whatever reason, your mother chose to not tell you about Eshra and your father. Maybe she didn't know about us, maybe she did; we just don't know. But, for whatever reasons, no one told you about your wings and what to expect."

"The Great Crane, in His grace, gave you the lockets and the words of the prophecy to prepare you for what would happen when your wings emerged. And, when it did happen, you were not as frightened by it; because you had some knowledge about it beforehand."

"When you reached fourteen, your wings were mature enough to show forth from your body. Like any pubescent experience, each person blooms into the next rite of passage on their own time. Your wings would have shown no matter what before you would have turned fifteen," Zetia answered.

"The beauty of this magic, Ayden, is you have to be at the right age for it to come forth, and an enlightenment journey can help with this. But, to learn how to fly, you had to have another teach you. The Great Crane sent me to you to teach you to fly," Zetia finished.

"Here, give me your lockets," Zetia instructed her. Ayden timidly took the lockets out from under her shirt and gave them to Zetia.

"These lockets hold some magic none of us know about," Zetia said. "But, the power of giving you wings is not the magic. Look," Zetia said as she pulled a mirror out of a pouch on her waist. "You still have wings and no lockets around your neck, Ayden. Tell your wings to disappear. And, then tell them to emerge again," Zetia told Ayden.

Ayden did as she was requested; several times. She would stand one way in front of the mirror, and then stand a different way to try and see the full effect of her wings.

"Everyone thought it was the lockets giving you wings when you were all in danger," Zetia continued to explain. "No one knew you belonged to my family. Finding you, and learning you were my niece was one of the most emotional days of my life. I thank the Crane he sent me to help you. I love you, Ayden. And, I am very proud of you," Zetia said with tears in her eyes, as she handed the lockets back to Ayden.

"My brother, Ayden, you are a lot like him. When Nadab and Lydia tried to describe him to you, my heart was bursting. They gave you a good picture of his love for Eshra and its people."

"He and I were very close. And, yet he protected you from me and all of Eshra. I do not know what he knew where he felt the need to keep you a secret. Only, maybe he knew you would have been killed as a baby if anyone knew the truth about you. Because he would have seen the mark on your back when you were born, he probably knew he had to distance himself from you to save you. For whatever reason, I am thankful I have found you." Zetia said as she hugged Ayden.

"Finally, Ayden, I want you to keep it secret that you don't need the lockets to fly. For some deep unknown reason, I have this urgency for you to keep this to yourself, please." Zetia took Ayden's shoulders in her hands, and stared at her to make sure she understood the gravity of her request.

"I will, Zetia," Ayden said as she tried to comprehend all she had been told.

"I have one more lesson for you to learn before we are done for the day," Zetia stated as she walked Ayden back inside the hut. Lydia entered the building from the front door as Ayden and Zetia walked in through the back door.

"I have finished Ayden's new outfits," Lydia stated with excitement as she walked towards them.

Lydia placed three outfits on the floor for Ayden to see the whole ensemble. Each had a pair of leggings with a different color; dark brown, light tan, and a rich dark turquoise.

Each outfit had a skirt which reached to just above her knees around the back; and the front was slit and open as the two sides connected just below her hips and rose to one piece around her waist.

Two, were the same color combinations as the leggings. The third had an abstract pattern that loosely resembled small pine trees, mountains, and geometric designs in the same rich turquoise and other colors of dark orange, brown, hunter green, midnight blue and white. Each half skirt had a waist band which bunched together like a thick belt so she could just pull it up around her hips.

Three smock-like shirts were loose fitting and had the same colors as the leggings. All three could be mixed and matched the way she wanted to wear them.

Ayden shouted with excitement at how beautiful they looked. She quickly chose the turquoise leggings, the abstract patterned skirt and the brown smock to put on.

Lydia showed her how the waist belt had several hidden pockets all the way around it. The underside of the skirt in front and side held more hidden pockets and several small leather clasps to hold whatever she needed, such as a knife.

Lydia then showed her the smock where there were three pockets each with buttons like her father always wore. The last thing Lydia showed her were three matching bandanas for the outfits.

Ayden immediately took the tie-dyed blue bandana and wrapped it around her wrist.

Zetia revealed a long mirror from the east side of the storage room door for Ayden to see her new look. Ayden twirled around to get the full view of her outfit, while she looked in the mirror.

She ran to Lydia and gave her a hug, and then did the same with Zetia. "This is exactly what I wanted," Ayden told them. "They are absolutely beautiful. Thank you," she said.

"Ayden, I need to teach you one more thing before we can call it a day," Zetia said.

Lydia began to walk away and as she was leaving, she spoke, "I think I will go and talk to Deborah. Maybe she wants a new designer outfit for her birthday, too." She said with a smile and a happy glint in her eyes.

Ayden looked at Zetia, and said, "OK, I am ready."

"What you need to know about your wing weapons, is each feather can act like an individual blade," Zetia began.

"What I mean is they can leave your body and act as a throwing knife. But, if you use them like this, it takes time for them to grow back from where they came out of your wing. So, do not waste them carelessly."

"I want you to use the feathers along the inside of your wing by the edges," Zetia explained while she took Ayden's wing and showed her what she meant.

"These feathers are the least likely to cause you problems if you lose them when you fly. And, any bird loses feathers, Ayden. It is the natural course for new feathers to grow back. You do not need to fear this process," Zetia reassured her.

"And as far as your wings go, no one has ever had sterling silver wings. This is possibly a part of the magic from the lockets, or it is what you would have always had, no matter what. Or, maybe it has to do with the mark on your back, Ayden. I cannot give you a clear answer, here."

"But even though they are made of this material, it is light like a feather and works like my feathers, or like any other bird's feathers." Zetia continued to explain.

Zetia showed Ayden how to throw a feather and then proceeded to have her throw them into different strategic areas of the trees to get the feel for it.

Finally, she pulled two chairs together and said, "Come sit with me for a while, Ayden." Zetia reached down to the floor and picked up one of her feathers she had used to show Ayden how to throw.

She handed the feather to Ayden and said, "The last question you asked needs to be answered," Zetia claimed. "Why I will not be going with you to the Dead Trees and beyond."

Ayden sat next to her and waited for Zetia to speak.

"Knowing who Choran is, is not enough for you to defeat him. I need to give you history about his world," Zetia began.

"Many, many years ago, Choran's jealousy and anger fueled him to create the underworld where he resides with his followers and slaves. He has built a massive kingdom where he metes out his anger and frustration while he builds his army and his dark potions to help him succeed."

"Whoever he felt would get in his way he killed. Whatever he felt would help him he would monopolize, as in the case with the snail fern."

"His whole strategy is to gain control of Eshra and all who live here by building a force who can grow in enormous size through the use of the drug."

"What he refuses, even to this day, to see about snail fern is that it is unstable. The side effects of the drug cause all who consume it severe problems. One, it wears off in its effect quickly causing the person or animal to have to continuously drink it to stay large. Two, when it starts to wear off you become severely ill and disabled. So, having the ability to fight is out of the question. Three, continuous use causes your natural body to become disfigured. And four, to stop the effect of becoming sick, you could not stop drinking the potion," she explained.

"His desire to be the ruler of Eshra and to be honored or feared by all stops him from seeing rational reasoning. He continues to believe he has the answers to gain his desired power. And all of his ways lead to death if you go against him," Zetia informed Ayden.

"Shortly after you were born, I traveled to his kingdom. I was looking for Zayden and I knew he had the answer."

"He mocked me and toyed with my emotions; never answering my questions. We had a very big physical fight. This is when we made the pact where I would leave him alone and he would leave me alone if I never flew again. By me not freely flying the winds of Eshra, he felt he had gained superior control over me."

"He knew he could not really defeat me, at the time, because he still had an inferior potion of the snail fern where he was having difficulty staying focused. The only way I could survive against him that day was to ingest the snail fern to keep him from devouring me. "

"I knew by myself I could not continuously defeat him and he would relentlessly come after me the rest of my life. I could not see the value in that. Especially since I was the last to stand. All the others were either dead or in hiding. So, I felt the pact was the best way until the Messenger arrived to help me and all of Eshra." Zetia resolutely stated.

"What I foolishly did not realize at the time was this was his plan all along. Because you see, Ayden. We are the messengers of the Great Crane and our blood is pure where the snail fern does not affect us like all of the others. We do not become sick. We do not throw up the poison. We do become large by its properties, but we can handle all it does to our bodies."

"He needed my blood to help him perfect the use of the plant. So, one complication came from my pact with the night lord, Ayden," Zetia somberly stated.

"When our truce and pact was reached and I let my guard down by turning away from him, he sliced my shoulder with his three claws and scarred me." Zetia lifted her shirt for Ayden to see the scar on her left shoulder.

"As he laughed at his surprise attack, he said to me, 'This scar will keep you true to your word, Zetia. It carries magic, where I will know if you try to enter my underground world. Do not try to enter in secret, Zetia, because you will die.'

"So, if I were to go with you, I would put all of you in grave danger. For he would know I had entered his realm. Your greatest attack, is to go in secretly and I can't do that, so I must stay away for your safety. And, because he had my blood on his claws, he was able to cultivate a stronger snail fern plant to help him with his evil plans," Zetia sadly finished.

Ayden solemnly looked at Zetia, and said, "It's going to be fine, Zetia. We will survive, and what you have told me and taught me will carry us to victory."

Journal Thirty-Seven

Most of my questions had been answered. All except how my mom knew my dad. And, what happened to my dad.

Just like my wings and if the lockets made them sterling silver or not. I had to accept I may never know any more about my parents or my wings.

Curious though, was the power of the copper and this thing called the life force. From what Zetia said, there are several conduits throughout our two worlds.

So, of course, more questions have come to my heart. Like, does anyone in my world know about these life forces. And, what other conduits are there like the copper?

And, did Zetia know more than she said about the gift Finch gave to Deborah?

Life is just one big question mark! You think you hold the key to the answers. Then you find out the key opens more doors to questions.

I guess the lesson I was to hear, was it was OK to constantly seek answers and learn. But, accept those answers would always lead to more questions.

To stop seeking, learning, and questioning, would mean you gave up on living life to its fullest.

To seek, to learn, to question keeps you young and alive with purpose.

Chapter Thirty-Seven

Phum entered the hut, jumping through the trees as Ayden and Zetia finished their conversation. Zetia stood and smiled at Ayden, saying, "It is time for me to check on Kit, and to make sure he has had no more 'Bad Touch' incidents."

She grabbed Ayden's forearm and Ayden grabbed hers as they gave each other a look of trust and understanding. Zetia stood, smiled at Ayden and left the hut.

"Phum," Ayden called, "Would you spend some time with me?"

Phum jumped down from the trees and jumped to the chair next to Ayden and said, "It would be my honor to talk with you, Ayden."

"Phum, it truly has been my privilege to get to know you. And, to call you friend," Ayden said.

"When I saw, you use your weapon to reel the hawk in to your belt, I was just amazed at your strength and wisdom to do it that way," Ayden stated with admiration.

"You don't say much and when you do, it always holds weight. What I mean is," Ayden tried to explain, "is, you watch everything and wait until you are sure of what you feel and then speak. And, when you speak it is always with some type of wisdom," she said with certainty.

"Phum, I have a request for you. I know how valuable you have become to the Trevins." Ayden revealed. "They need you. They are an extremely emotional group who have just found a family to love. And, I know Trevin sacrificed everything to save the other seven and he is like their father."

"But Trevin and the others need you to be their sage leader. You have to do this without them feeling threatened you are taking away their power, Phum. I see you as the second father. Keep them together and safe, for me, Phum," Ayden asked him.

"I don't know what to say, Ayden." Phum said with appreciation. "I don't see myself as a father. I have always been a lone courier. And, the Trevins have survived by themselves, very well I might add, for a long time. But I do see it in a different light, now that you ask this request of me," Phum said as he studied his thoughts to respond.

"Yes, I now see what you mean," Phum said as he puffed his chest out. "The Trevins need a leader to guide them through their emotions. To help them deal with those things which make them cry. And they do cry a lot, Ayden. They are like my children who need to know they belong and can be free to express themselves. Yes, Ayden, I will be there for my young men. You can trust me, Ayden, to fulfill this task."

Phum stood, grabbed Ayden's hand, and said, "Thank you, Ayden for giving me enlightenment on my journey with you." He jumped the trees and left the building.

Ayden sat by herself and said, "Wow, that went a lot better than I ever could have imagined it to go. My Trevins will be protected by a mighty, honorable squirrel the rest of their lives. And, my Phum will never be alone again."

Ayden stood, and began to walk back to the main house. She entered through the back to the kitchen, and said to Tarhana, "I am starving, Tarhana. Zetia had me up before dawn and I have just finished training with her. What time of the day is it?" Ayden asked as she looked for something to eat.

"Oh! Child, it is only eleven thirty in the morning." Tarhana reached for the plate she had just put in the cold box, and said, "I have made fresh egg salad sandwiches, would you like to share one, or two, with me?"

Ayden nodded with joy. Egg salad was one of her absolute favorite sandwiches. And, she could not remember the last time she had one, but was sure it was long before Eshra. She sat down at the table, and looked at Tarhana as she was served by her.

An elderly woman who wore her gray hair back in a bun. Tarhana always had an apron on over her dress which draped over her ankles. Her light spirit of brightness brought joy to whomever was in her presence.

She loved to bake and cook as well as make others feel welcomed. Ayden watched Tarhana place a fresh glass of nectar water in front of her as she decided to ask her about herself.

"So, tell me how you ended up here, Tarhana?" Ayden asked as she started to eat her sandwich while she listened for her request to be answered.

"I was born into the community of the Dark Cell, Ayden," Tarhana said as her eyes became sad. "This is what the underground world in Choran's realm is called. We were all expected to be laborers for his cause. Any semblance of joy was forbidden."

"Not that you were told this, you just knew it to be true by how everyone treated each other. Fear was the only true emotion shown in the Dark Cell by the majority of us," Tarhana said with dread as she relived her life there.

"There was one other emotion that was stronger than fear, though," Tarhana declared. "And, that was anger. From Choran to those whom he trusted the most, all of them used anger to control us." she said with sorrow.

"Do you know, Ayden, how an owl eats?" Tarhana asked. Ayden nodded her head in affirmation as she continued to eat.

"Well, the regurgitated pellets Choran coughs out are called Bones. He has thousands and thousands of animals of all sorts and people captured in those pellets. He has found a way to bring those Bones back to life whenever he desires. They are bones of mindless bodies which go and fight for him," Tarhana shuddered as she spoke.

"Now, it has been many years since I have lived there, but when I was there, he had difficulty keeping the Bones regenerated if they were in the sun and moon light. They would crumble into pieces from the light. But he continuously was working at perfecting them as his tools of evil with some type of elixir powder."

"He has hundreds of workers who make his potions, especially the one with snail fern to keep him huge like a tree," Tarhana stated.

"Zetia saved me, Ayden," Tarhana said with deep respect. "No Cell person lived to an old age in Choran's world. We were considered worthless mouths to feed by him. His trusted inner court would assess the workers, and determine who was not meeting their expected quota of production."

"They would take those who were worthless and give them to Choran to eat so he could make more Bones. Then, they would no longer be worthless; nor did they eat the precious scarce food in the Dark Cell."

"He has no value for anyone, Ayden, except for what they can do for him," Tarhana said with disgust in her voice.

"I was chosen for the Bones when Zetia fought Choran. I saw the whole battle and heard all the words spoken that day," Tarhana said as she looked off in the distance of the room, as if she was reliving it.

"Before the battle, Nahrita had brought ten of us in for Choran to take his first choice of. He was angry with Nahrita for interrupting him and Zetia. We were all thrown to the side of his chamber like dirty rags. All of us huddled together in fear as we observed everything."

"Even though, Zetia allowed Choran to think he had won the battle, he really lost it. Zetia had slyly thrown ten amulets at us while she battled him. She acted like she was regaining her position every time she spoke to us about how to use the amulets. It took her several falls to give us the correct instructions."

"And, this is why she got the scar. It was her final act to slyly look at us to make sure we had blown on the amulets to bring forth the Great Fox to take on our image and for us to disappear with her in the Forest of Roots."

"She had slightly turned when Choran administered his blow to her. She threw a powdery smoke at us as she and Choran spoke their final words to each other. The smoke hid us from Choran and his followers." Tarhana finally said.

"Ayden, all of us who Zetia saved, live here," Tarhana said with joy. "We have a savior in her. Our lives have never been so full, Ayden." She said as she looked at her with tears in her eyes.

Ayden took Tarhana's hand and squeezed it as she smiled at her. "Thank you for sharing your story with me," Ayden said to her. Ayden stood up from the table, nodded at her and walked out of the kitchen.

She looked at the waterfall in the corner, and decided the hot springs was a very good idea for her aching muscles. She ran upstairs, to an empty room, and put on her suit. As she exited her room, she met Nick coming out of his.

"Hey! Nick, ya want to join me at the waterfall? Ayden asked.

"Sure, Ayden," Nick agreed. "I was just going down to the kitchen to see what looked good. I'll meet you over there after I eat, OK?" He said.

Ayden closed her eyes as she let her body soak in the continuously swirled motion from the waterfall. The way she figured, they had at least two more days at the sanctuary; and she, for one, was very thankful for it. Before she realized it, she was sleeping. Ayden woke with a start, realizing she was still in the water. She looked to her left and saw Nick on the other side of the pool.

"Were you never taught to not fall asleep in the bathtub, Ayden," he teasingly asked, as he lazily laid back in the pool, looking at her.

"I'm fine, I wasn't sleeping, really," Ayden tried to lie.

"Good, cuz I was kind of concerned the snoring coming from your direction might have been you. And, I couldn't believe someone like you could snore so loud," he mischievously stated.

"So, what have you been doing the past couple of days," Ayden quickly changed the subject to avoid being any more embarrassed."

"Oh, I have been hanging with the Trevins and Phum in the trees and at the lake. Tybin, Jerin, and I have sparred in the hut quite a bit. And, I went to the mine with Nadab," Nick triumphantly stated.

"The mine," Ayden exclaimed. "What did you go there for?" She inquired.

"Nadab wanted to see how the whole process from mining to making the copper into a finished design was done and he wanted me to go with him. The miners are extremely nice men, and were also very informative," Nick stated.

Ayden looked at Nick while he talked. She got the feeling by his easy flowing conversation he had finally found his stable ground. And, now he was comfortable with whom he had become.

She smiled as she thought about how Gethsemane, Eleea, Phum and the rest of the council had been right to include him on the enlightenment journey.

"Actually, we were coming back from the mine when I saw you come out of the hut," Nick stated. "Your choice to change your look with your new dress. Pretty bad ass, Ayden. It is totally you," Nick told her with respect.

"Thanks, Nickalli," Ayden said with mild humor. "Lydia and Zetia designed it off of my ideas, but they are the ones who made it work. I was confused about exactly what I wanted. They listened and created the whole look. And, I love it. Couldn't agree with you more that it is me," Ayden finished with pride.

Ayden looked at Nick as he sat there with his arms holding him up on the pool ledge. Wanting to talk to him, like she had the others was more difficult. She knew him before Eshra. And since he had changed so much on this journey, and because she knew him so much more intimately through their combined experiences; she didn't know if she could manipulate him anymore.

"Nick," Ayden carefully began. "Are you scared?"

"Scared of what you have to do, Ayden?" Nick asked her.

"Well, I am not so scared for me," Ayden stated. "But I am extremely scared for all of you. I don't like to see all of you going into danger." Ayden said with sorrow in her voice.

"Ayden," Nick said as he leaned forward and looked at her with deep intensity, "Do not fear. We all know what we are doing. You, Ayden, need to stop worrying about all of us. I want you to remember this, Ayden, keep your focus on what you need to do, not on us. If you focus on us, you will become vulnerable. Trust we will all take care of each other and make sure you will be able to do what you have been sent to do." Nick stated with fierce loyalty and determination.

Ayden stared at Nick almost dumbfounded. She had never heard him talk with such ferocious fortitude.

"I'm serious, Ayden," Nick continued. "You need to stay focused on Choran."

"OK, OK, I promise I will stay focused on Choran, Nick," Ayden agreed so Nick would stop being so serious with her.

Elora and Deborah came into the room from the balcony stairs as they continued to chat with each other. "Hi! Guys," Deborah said as she got into the pool next to Ayden.

"What a great day," she continued to say. "Elora, Finch, and I have had the best time in the courtyard. Zetia gave permission for me to learn from the herbalists how to make some pretty potent potions, and let me tell you, I have an arsenal now."

"Elora had to help me gather some of the plants because they told us she had the bird instinct to find them. Isn't that cute, 'A'? Bird Instinct...it just has a cool sound to it." Deborah finished.

"Of course, I can always use my knife to get whatever I want. But they wanted us to learn how to do it like it has always been done." Deborah continued.

"We got to go far into the woods and gather. And, they have berries everywhere around here. We ate till we were full." She finished while she patted her stomach.

"Happy Birthday, 'D'," Ayden quickly said when she felt she could slide into the conversation.

"Oh! Thanks, 'A'." Deborah said. "This is a birthday I will never forget. I learned so much today. And, Lydia is making me new outfits as a gift. I can't wait to see what I will be wearing." Deborah said with excitement in her voice.

Elora flew closer to the girls and said, "My heart is full of happy. Not only did I get to spend the day with Deborah and Two, I got to be important. My bird instincts were needed for Deborah to create her potions." Elora stated with authority.

"I am so thankful you guys got to spend time together," Ayden told the girls.

Before she could say her next statement, she caught Nekoh and Nip out of the corner of her eye. Ayden started to laugh at the sight. The rest of them turned to see what was so humorous, and they all laughed with her.

Nekoh was meandering through the front doors of the Home with Nip calmly riding on his neck.

"What is this," Ayden asked as the two of them sauntered over to the group.

"We have found," Nekoh began as he stood proud, "since I have to convalesce with slow movement to let my body heal, that Nip has a better view from my back than from the ground. And, I do not have to impatiently wait for her to catch up anymore." Nekoh finished with satisfaction.

Zetia entered the room and said, "Dinner will be served in about an hour, everyone. And, Deborah, Lydia and I would like to see you upstairs."

The girls quickly got out of the water, grabbed the towels Zetia held out to them, and ran upstairs. Zetia, humored by their excitement, followed behind them.

Lydia was waiting for Deborah in their bedroom. "Happy Birthday, Deborah," Lydia exclaimed as she gestured with her hand to Deborah's bed where three outfits lay.

Deborah looked at her birthday presents and said, "They are beautiful. Will you help me put them on?"

The three pants, dark green, tan, and brown, were a take on cargo pants. They each slightly bunched at the ankle where they cinched with a clasp. Right after the small poof on each leg was a pocket with a leather strap.

Farther up the leg, on the thigh, was a long open pocket. The waist secured around the body with a tie. Three shirts were designed to rest just below her hips and had one pocket on the upper part which matched each pant. The sleeves came down to her elbow with a brass clasped pocket near the outside shoulder of the sleeve. A simple under T of contrasting color graced each outfit.

Beautiful large scarves with small fringed ends, each depicting hand painted feathers across the material when placed over the shoulders looked like a full view of a bird's wingspan.

Burnt orange with little streaks of black, gray, and brown for one scarf. Dark brown with light swirls of tan, white and black on another. And the third with colors of yellow, orange, and shades of blues and greens like peacock feathers sat next to each outfit.

Lydia and Zetia helped Deborah dress in her new attire. Deborah picked the green pants, and the tan shirt with the off-white t-shirt. She picked up each scarf several times, to try and decide which one.

Deborah looked at the women and said, "I just don't know how to wear this," she finally said, perplexed.

Zetia walked over to her and said, "Let me show you how very special this scarf is. She folded it into a large triangle and tied it onto Deborah's hip. The scarf flowed down one side like a skirt to just below her knee, while the other side held the knot.

Lydia rolled in the full-length mirror from the sewing room and led Deborah to it to look at her new style. Deborah stood in front of the mirror and just stared as she touched the scarf.

"Do you like the look," Lydia nervously asked Deborah.

"Yes, yes I do, Lydia," Deborah stated in a dreamy way. "It's just I have never thought about looking like this, and I look so different. I look so beautiful I don't want to stop looking in the mirror."

Lydia and Zetia both let out a sigh of relief. "Here, let me show you the uniqueness of this scarf," Lydia said as she grabbed one of the other ones.

Lydia opened it and explained to Deborah how it could be used to gather her plants and still be on her body. Lydia took each end of the scarf in each of her hands and snapped the cloth and let it fall. The whole scarf became a table for Deborah to put her ingredients on.

Zetia explained it could adjust to any terrain and continue to hold her supplies without things rolling off. Deborah nodded her head in understanding and went back to the mirror to look at herself again.

Ayden walked over to the mirror in one of her new outfits and Deborah's mouth dropped open in complete awe.

"'A', you look beautiful," Deborah expressed as she walked around Ayden to see everything. Deborah grabbed Ayden and had her stand with her in front of the mirror. Both girls stood and stared at each other for several minutes, holding hands.

Zetia and Lydia went to stand on each side of the girls. Both with smiles showing great pride in the outfits and in the two young women.

"I hear activity downstairs," Zetia finally said. "It must be dinnertime, girls." The girls walked together down the stairs, with Lydia and Zetia behind them.

The seats were full at the table, and all eyes turned to see the girls enter. Several whispers of approval could be heard around the room.

Gethsemane broke the awe and spoke for the group with, "Girls, I have to say, I am very impressed with your new look. The two of you enter a room with stunning assurance in your walk and dress. Absolutely amazing transformation. Well done, Lydia and Zetia," he finished with great pride in his voice.

Ayden noticed there were ten more seats at the table, and she only recognized one of the ten as being Tarahna. She figured if it were ten, with her being one, then the other nine must be those whom Zetia helped to escape from Choran.

Each of them were obviously elderly with varying shades of gray hair. As soon as everyone was seated, the servers started to bring the food.

Gethsemane waited until all were served and then stood up on his perch to call
attention to what he wanted to say. "We have guests joining our dinner tonight to help all of you who will be leaving for the Dead Trees. They have knowledge of how to traverse the Dark Cell, Choran's underworld."

"Each of you have had an intimate conversation with one of the ten at some point during your stay here about how they were saved and came to live here. While we enjoy our meal, I would like our ten guests to tell you what they know about the Dark Cell." Gethsemane finished as his wing gestured to the ten to speak.

Sahl, the groundskeeper who took their horses the day they arrived, began for the group. "Thank you, Gethsemane for this opportunity and for this dinner. It is a great honor, for all of us, to be sitting with all of you and the Messenger tonight." Sahl looked at Ayden, and did a slight bow with his head.

"The purpose of this dinner is to have all of you together, and what we have to say, can be said at one time rather than several different times. The Ten, as we are sometimes known as, do not like to talk about our time in the Cell. But it is imperative for your success, to know what we know," Sahl said with determination.

"The raccoons know how to get you through the tree to open the entrance into the Cell," Sahl continued. "We were never allowed above ground; and had no knowledge of how to enter or leave. We left with Zetia through the Forest of Roots when she saved us. All we know is what life was like for those who had to live there. If you could really call it living," he said with sorrow," as he looked and nodded to another man.

"I was a worker close to the entrance, called the Front," the man stated. "My name is Baris. Ethrys and Jonis," he gestured to each of his sides where a woman and a man sat next to him, "also worked close to the entrance. Once you enter through the tree, it will take approximately twenty minutes to reach the huge doors to enter our area. To open the doors, there is a huge lever on the right side. My job in the Cell was to work with the leather and make whatever was needed for wear. Such as bridles, belts, saddles, or clothing," he stopped to give his friends an opportunity to speak.

"I am Jonis, my job was to make anything needed in woodwork. From buildings to handles for weapons, it was my responsibility to ensure each finished piece would not fall apart when used," he stated as he looked at Ethrys.

"It was my job to work with fabric," Ethrys stated. "All the clothing, bedding or household supplies in the Cell came from what we made," she stated. "There are hundreds of workers in this area past the great doors. Whatever was needed for a community to survive was made in this part of the Cell," she concluded.

"All of the workers lived together in buildings behind the work zone," Baris explained. "The Cell itself is very deep, dark, and wide, when you walk past our work stations, you cannot see the buildings where we lived. Only if you knew about them, would you know they were there," he informed them."

"The buildings where we lived," Jonis continued, "house fifty to sixty workers. There are several barracks on the other side of the work stations. When it was our shift to work, the whole building would be emptied. We labored for twelve hours a day, where no one would be in our homes. Two shifts of workers were expected to continuously keep the production line moving," Jonis solemnly stated.

"After you walk through the worker's area, which takes around ten to fifteen minutes, you reach the cottages. My name is Sari, and I maintained the fires for the cottages. What I mean is, it was my responsibility to make sure all of Choran's favorite followers had a warm dwelling with enough food and comfort for when they returned from whatever job Choran had them do," she stated.

"My job was to make what I could, from the scarce supply of resources, in food for the workers throughout the Cell and the cottage dwellers," Tarhana stated. "I oversaw all of the growers of food, the bakers, and the domesticated animals. We were not allowed to make, what I will call happy food," Tarhana sadly explained. "Only the basic survival food was to be produced; except for the cottage dwellers. With the purpose of just keeping us alive and not satisfied because we were to stay focused."

"Choran's order was, "we were not to live life, but to work for life." Tarhana sadly stated as she looked at her friends who had survived with her.

"I had to make sure those who helped me had enough supplies to carry to the workers of potions and elixirs and Cellers, near Choran's chambers," Tarhana continued. "From the cottages, it takes approximately five to six hours to reach the land of the Bones," she instructed the group who were soberly listening intently.

"I worked with Nargaut, the leader of the Cellers, and my name is Tobia," another man stated. "I worked with the Bones. There are miles and miles of bones in the Dark Cell," he gravely stated. "The regurgitated pellets from Choran are the Bones," Tobia continued to explain. "Choran can call whatever amount of Bones he desires to work for him in whatever capacity he desires. Whether it be gathering food for him or fighting for him, they do his bidding."

"The Bones came to life when workers specially trained by Choran told them to stand and fight or hunt. The Bones called by these workers were exceedingly fragile in their ability to stay useful. And would fall apart more readily than when Choran used his breath on them. If Choran blew over them, they were able to stand for longer periods of time before they fell apart." Tobia continued to explain.

"As a Celler, it was our job to make sure the Bones were transported to where Choran desired. And, when they were above ground, we had to make sure they had the dry potion on them so they would not fall apart and be useless if the sun or moon light shined on them. But the powder was far from perfect, as it did not last long in the light. Choran was working on a formula, when I left, where he could take the Bones and combine them to form creatures from their different parts. In this way, he hoped to create Bones which were more formidable and powerful for battle," Tobia educated them.

"I am Vexia, I made the snail fern elixir," a woman stated. She gestured to two men who sat on her right, and said, "Festus, and Kalim worked with me just outside of Choran's chamber. We were the potions and elixir masters. Choran kept us close to him because he always needed the elixir to maintain his enormous size and he wanted to have immediate control over his experiments of new potions and their use," Vexia said as she looked at the men who helped her while in the Cell.

"Choran has limited knowledge when it comes to herbalism," one of the men stated. "My name is Festus, and it was my job to perfect the powder for the Bones. This powder, at least when I was there, had a short life expectancy. The longer the Bones are exposed above ground, the shorter the effect lasted as the sun and moon light drastically disabled them. But, what Choran refused to see was the difficulty in making a potion to survive its purpose," he stated with sad disgust.

"My knowledge of magic and its properties concerning plants, is my specialty," the other man stated. "As Vexia has said, I am Kalim. I had to walk a very subtle line to not let Choran know what I knew. My family lineage has a very unique ability to work beyond the normal realm of mixology of plants. I was taught how to feign ignorance my whole life in the Cell by my family. We lived in constant fear we would be exposed," Kalim stated with deep regret.

"I am the last of my family, that I know about," he said with despair. Choran's anger towards us was the greatest because he felt when our potions failed it was our fault. And he ate all who I loved," Kalim said as he lowered his head and wiped a tear from his eye.

Ayden looked at the group of ten as all of them wiped tears from their eyes when Kalim had finished his statement. The weight of despair they all lived while in the Cell, had been told with such depth, she felt her throat tighten as tears began to form.

She reached for her dinner napkin to wipe her eyes and noticed everyone around her were wiping tears from their faces.

"This is the world of the Dark Cell," Sahl continued to explain. "My job was to maintain the animals and to carry supplies from the Front to the Chamber, Sahl stated.

"What is left to tell you, is three things. One, past the potion makers is Choran's
Chamber, where he resides. Two, beyond his chamber is called the Forest of Roots which leads to the surface. It runs for many miles underground; and the surface can be accessed in many different areas along the way. Choran knows all of the ways to open up the Forest of Roots to reach the surface. Whereas, only a few select others of his followers know specific limited ways to open it," Sahl explained.

"And, the third important thing you need to know, is this," Sahl stopped and looked at the journeyers with intense compassion. "You need to understand none of us chose this life, to live in the Dark Cell. We were born into it or were stolen at a very young age into it. We had no knowledge of what a different life could be like. We only knew our worth by what Choran desired of us. Yes, there was whispered talk of what it was like above ground. But our hopelessness kept us from really believing it was any different up there. Choran kept us in fear, kept us worked until all we could think about was to sleep. And kept us hungry so we stayed weak. Each worker only received food if they produced. And therefore, we were driven to make what was asked of us so we could eat."

Sahl finished his three points of instruction as he raised his glass to everyone. "We sit here, with good food and good company." Sahl expressed. "And, with great hope in our hearts the Messenger will not only free Eshra from the claws of Choran, but all who live in the Great Cell will know what the ten of us know. Freedom and love!" Saul stated as he drank.

Everyone lifted their glasses and toasted with Sahl.

"Thank you, all ten of you." Gethsemane quietly stated as he continued. "I know it was difficult for each of you to speak about your lives before the sanctuary. We are forever indebted to you for sharing what you know."

"These," he gestured to Ayden and her friends, "who go into battle have been given a gift from the ten of you. The Great Crane brought you here for all of Eshra to be saved. Now, as Tarahna says, let us commune together in spirit and enjoy each other the rest of this evening," Gethsemane finished as desert was served.

After the meal, Ayden and the rest spent time with each of the ten. Giving their personal thanks for what they sacrificed in bringing up the horrible memories of the Dark Cell.

The night's conversation had run late. And, she was thankful when everyone decided to retire for the evening.

Deborah and Ayden sat on their beds, not wanting to lay down. Ayden turned to her and said, "Well, 'D', if we ever thought our lives were complicated and bad, we were wrong after listening to the Ten," she said with sadness in her voice.

"Yes, they did live in a very difficult world, 'A'," Deborah said thoughtfully. "But, 'A', look how happy they are now. Zetia saved them and they have a life full of love and freedom, like Sahl said."

"What you need to take away from this dinner, is the valuable information they gave us from their eyes of living inside the Cell. Any general will tell you, you have to know your enemy to defeat your enemy." Deborah proclaimed.

"We need to sleep," Elora said grumpily. "Ayden, I know you. And, I know you will do whatever you need to do to make sure all of us are safe. You are the greatest weapon and Choran will regret the day he meets you. Now, let's get some sleep," Elora demanded.

The girls nodded at her and laid down in their beds. Soon Elora was snoring and the girls didn't care as they were too tired to notice.

Journal Thirty-Eight

I chose to start writing in this journal when we got to Zetia's Sanctuary. It just seemed like the right time. The peacefulness Zetia created here, took me and held me in warmth and love.

I found a place behind the Home where a little river lazily flowed into the lake and I claimed it as my spot for reflection.

I didn't want to forget anything since my parents, or parent died. And, what better way to remember details than writing it down to read in the future. And, so much has happened, ...how our lives have changed.

Truly, we have been on an enlightenment journey. Even though it was a ruse, it was real. I see everything so much more differently than six months ago.

I have gone from worrying about being beaten to worrying about protecting everyone I love.

I have a family which means more to me than my own life. Maybe, that's why the Trevins haven't been bartering with us?

Maybe, their emptiness and lack of family, even though they saw each other as family, caused them to constantly seek to fill a void. And, bartering was their way to feel loved and fill their emptiness.

Now, that they have been told by all of us, they are family, they don't have any more void. Interesting, even the Trevins have been on an enlightenment journey.

Once we leave the sanctuary, I won't write anymore journal entries. I am leaving it on my night table for when I return.

Plus, I feel life will be getting very real once we are on the move and there will be no time to stop and write down my feelings.

And, before we leave, I still have to talk to Gethsemane, Deborah, Jerin, Two, Nip, and Nekoh, and most importantly, Eleea.

Crazy, Nahrita had told Zetia, 'the Messenger was on the move' and I just used the same phrase above. I guess I am ready to meet my destiny, after all.

Chapter Thirty-Eight

Nadab looked at Nick as they both sat at the workbench designing the new weapons. "Nickalli," Nadab began. "Tell me how this journey has helped you on finding your enlightenment?"

Nick intently looked at Nadab as he started to speak. "Uncle, I have found a family. Not that I did not already have one with my parents. It's just that on the other side, I always felt out of place."

"My parents showed love and concern, but kept guarded in their speech all of the time. I guess they feared if they spoke too openly, they would accidentally reveal Eshra to someone who did not know about it."

"I was not allowed to speak of Eshra when I was in East Glacier. I do not hold this against them, really. It is just, I lived in fear I would disappoint them if I spoke of our other world while there."

Nick continued in deep thought as he spoke, "At times, it was difficult to keep everything straight because a lot of our gifts came from Eshra. I had to be careful not to blurt about how we acquired them when a customer asked detailed questions about them."

"The rule I was given, was to explain that our sources were a well-kept secret to insure no one else would have the same items for sale."

Nick looked at his uncle, smiled and said, "I was so uncomfortable there. Here I have the freedom to be me, all of me. No more fear. No more worry about saying the wrong thing. Just freedom to explore me and others and learn from all of it."

Nadab stood up, went to Nick, and hugged him. "Son, your parents are good people. A little misguided in their intentions, but good people. I do believe part of their fear with you is that they saw in you the strength of Eshra."

"What I mean is this, Eshra burns in your soul. Just as it burns in mine. The power you possess is one where one day you will become a spiritual leader. I sensed it the day you were born. Your parents feared this as they too sensed it."

"Each experience you have had will make you a great leader. It will bring you a deeper understanding of what it is to be there for others. I am so deeply proud of you, Nickalli," Nadab stated as he took Nick's shoulders in his hands and stared into his eyes.

Nick put his hands on Nadab's arms and squeezed. "Thank you, uncle," he stated. "All that you have taught me this week and, in the past, has been one of the greatest gifts I have ever received."

"I feel so very blessed to have this opportunity to be here on this journey and to be around Jerin and Tybin, as well as the rest of our family that goes to fight Choran," Nick reverently said.

Deborah found Zetia in the outer courtyard sitting on the ground with a group of black crows all around her. Zetia looked up at her and patted the ground for her to sit with them.

"Deborah, what a great time for you and I to talk together. These little guys are Uri's cousins," Zetia revealed.

"So, can they appear and disappear into other realms too?" Deborah asked as she sat down next to Zetia.

"Yes, the lineage of the ravens and crows is one of 'whisping'. All of them have the ability, like a whisper, to appear and disappear within seconds. They are highly sensitive to the needs of those whom they consider worthy of their gift," Zetia explained.

"I have always loved crows," Deborah expressed as she gently caressed the head of the crow closest to her. "From our world, they kind of remind me of raccoons. Always finding pretties and sharing them."

Unexpectedly, Deborah quickly took her hand and put it behind her back to stop the itch she felt. Immediately all of the crows whisped.

"Oh! Zetia, I am so sorry! I didn't mean to scare them like that." Deborah remorsefully stated.

Zetia chuckled as she said, "No worries, Deborah. This is just how they are. Skittish. Even I have scared them several times in the past."

"Deborah, I have wanted to talk to you for some time now. I want you to realize how truly important you are to this mission with Ayden."

"Most believe you came through the Eshra entry because you held onto Ayden. But my heart has always felt your entry was because of who you are. Your lineage, Deborah, is far deeper than anyone of us know. I sense it deep in my soul." Zetia reverently told Deborah.

"What do you mean, Zetia?" Deborah asked with a slight trepidation in her voice.

"I seriously, cannot give you a clear answer, Deborah. All I can ask of you, is to trust your heart and to trust Eshra magic. One day all will be revealed to you," Zetia confided as she stood and pulled Deborah to her in a hug.

Deborah lightly smiled as she contemplated Zetia's statements. She watched Zetia walk away as she sat back down on the ground.

"Well, that is a crazy twist of reality," Deborah whispered with bewilderment.

Deborah felt her hair brush across her face like the wind had caught it. She looked at her crossed legs as she wiped her hair from her eyes. A silver and brass charm of a fox with copper eyes lay on her lap. She picked it up and looked around to see where the bird was, as she just knew a crow had laid it in her lap.

Deborah waited patiently, barely moving to not scare her new friend. Soon, she sighed as she said out loud, "Thank you. I hope one day you and I will meet and have long talks together."

Deborah stood up, turned in a whole circle, and looked all around just in case the crow decided to whisp. She shrugged her shoulders and clipped the charm to her belt, and again, said, "Thank you, friend." Slowly, she walked back into the Home.

The tranquil environment of Zetia's Home allowed each of the traveler's time to rest, train and explore without fear. Throughout the day all of them wandered in and out of the Home and the surrounding land as they partook in the knowledge of all who lived there. Every moment held a special memory for each of Ayden's friends to help carry and strengthen them into the unknown when they once again began to travel.

The next morning, Ayden woke to Deborah and Elora singing Happy Birthday to her. Freshly cut flowers sat next to her bed, along with a tray of Tarahna's best baked goods with milk and coffee.

"This is awesome, and thanks," Ayden proclaimed as she reached for the coffee.

"Ayden, I wanted to be here to sing to you, but I have to go," Elora stated hurriedly. "Vexia is going to help me understand the properties of the snail fern I drank. Ever since Garis, I have wanted to know why it makes you throw up. So, she said she would help me. Bye, and happy birthday, Ayden." Elora said as she flew out of the room.

"Actually, I am thankful it is just you and me," Ayden stated to Deborah. "Especially since this is my birthday. Ya know, I am really happy both of our birthdays were spent here, where we have the freedom to be real and not scared," Ayden stated.

"Me too," Deborah said. "But, it's OK, 'A', to feel anxiety over where we are going. Anything worthwhile has its risks. The unknown is what scares you. But, on the other side, to decide not to risk is to give up. You give up on this, you will always regret it." Deborah stated supportively.

"Deborah, I agree with you, but I need you to know how much I love you," Ayden began as her eyes filled with tears. "I just can't say it enough; I would have been lost without you being here in Eshra with me."

" You keep me grounded. You know me more than anyone else and our friendship is the best thing to ever have happened to me," Ayden stated with deep respect.

"The fear I have is not for me, 'D'," Ayden continued as her voice started to falter.

"I never want to see you in danger again, like with the boars. I do not want you to worry about me, either. I think back to you grabbing me when we entered Eshra. It was your fear for me that made you hold on. I do not want you to do the same thing if something should happen in this battle with Choran," Ayden expressed.

Her speech became rapid as she explained, "promise me, because Nick told me I need to stay focused on Choran, and if I have to stay focused, I can't be worrying about you getting in the way, OK?" Ayden desperately asked her.

"Fine, 'A'," Deborah stated. "I promise to stay out of your way so you can stay focused. But, just remember, we all have a lot more skill than you realize. All of us have been taught by the best to use our specific skills to succeed in this journey."

"Have faith in us, 'A', we will all see victory together," Deborah finished with meaning as she grabbed Ayden's hand and squeezed it.

"Now, what is your plan for the day?" Deborah asked as she stood next to Ayden.

"I've got to talk to a few more," Ayden stopped and thought for a second and started again. "Do you find it difficult to talk about our friends? Cuz I was going to say I have to talk to a few more people, but some of them are animals so it isn't a true statement. Anyways, I have to talk with a few more souls, I guess is the easiest way to say it." Ayden finished.

"Yeah, kind of crazy how we have changed since June," Deborah agreed. "Now it is September and we have forged this huge family of friends who are nothing like people we used to know. And, to be perfectly correct, over half of them are not people. They are animals. And, I have to say I love it." Deborah said with excitement.

"So, I will leave you to do whatever," Deborah claimed. "I am going to visit Kalim. He and I had a very interesting time the other day, and I still have questions for him. See you tonight, 'A'," Deborah said as she left the room.

Ayden got dressed, sat back down, and thought about her day as she ate breakfast. Nip and Nekoh walked into the room while she contemplated who to talk with next. The two of them slept in the sunroom every night. Ever since Nekoh had gotten hurt Nip stayed close to his side.

"Hi guys," Ayden said. As they jumped onto her bed. "You two are just the two I wanted to talk to this morning."

"Happy Birthday, Ayden," Nekoh stated.

"Appy Day Ayd," Nip tried to repeat Nekoh's statement.

Ayden rubbed both of their heads and said, "Thank you."

She looked at Nekoh and began, "Nekoh I need you to promise me you will keep Deborah safe. You know how she gets, and it scares me she might do something irrational if she fears for my safety. Promise to hold on to her if she tries." Ayden asked him while she pleaded with her eyes.

"Ayden, Deborah is not the same person as the fourteen-year-old child who crossed over with you. She has grown immensely since then," Nekoh stated. "But I understand your concern, and I promise I will watch out for her," he reassured her.

"Thanks, Nekoh," Ayden said with relief. "I want you to know how special you are. To watch how you have helped Nip has been amazing to see. She has so much more confidence. And her speech is getting better, too," Ayden excitedly said.

"Also, Nekoh," Ayden continued, "I want you to know I love you. You have taught me a lot about survival. I have had a lot of fun with you in my life, and I am very thankful I know you." Ayden finished.

"I too, love you, Ayden," Nekoh stated. "Being with you and Deborah on this journey, has been the greatest gift I have ever known. The energy the two of you have and the love you two possess for all you meet. Well, it is the both of you who have taught me about life. Before, I was focused on what interested me."

"Now, I have changed. Look how I take care of Nip. I would never have done this before. My life is full because of you and Deborah. Thank you," Nekoh stated with appreciation. Nip rubbed up against Nekoh as he talked, and he leaned into her rubs.

Ayden knew both of them, especially Nip, would be OK. They had each other to be with and they, too, would never be alone. Ayden got off the bed, gave them each one last pat on the head and said, "Thanks, Nekoh. Gotta go, guys. Enjoy your morning nap on my bed."

She grabbed her journal and went down to her spot behind the Home. But, before she could open the book, Callie and Joshua strolled up to her.

"May we join you, Ayden," Joshua asked.

"Of course, you can," Ayden said as she made a better spot for them to sit next to her.

"Young One," Joshua began, "Callie and I were waiting for the right time to talk with you about all that has come to pass."

Joshua earnestly looked at Ayden and began. "After you left Sunbird, Zetia showed up. By the Crane she showed up, Ayden. From the battle with Nahrita, to your visit with the Great Crane, to coming here, and to speaking to the Ten have all been choreographed by the Great Crane," he said.

"This strategic plan has been put into place to guarantee your success, Ayden," Callie stated. "None of us could have known or planned it any better than what has already been done," she concluded.

"What we both need you to know, is you go with strong magic," Joshua explained. "Ayden, this world of Eshra only reveals this type of magic as it is needed. Go forth with the expectation you will have the resources to give you strength and the ability to use this magic. Stop wondering and worrying and go with the determination it will be there for you, to help you." Joshua earnestly expressed to Ayden.

"Thank you, both of you," Ayden said. "I understand what is expected of me and I can accept there is magic that goes with us. But it does not help me worry any less about my friends and their safety," Ayden said with sadness.

"No, we cannot take away your anguish for how you feel right now, Ayden," Joshua agreed.

"All of life, each day we walk, there is a possibility of fear and pain. It is how we choose to walk forward which defines if we will be paralyzed by it or not. I choose to believe you will not be paralyzed when the time comes to act, Ayden," Joshua stated with confidence.

Ayden nodded in agreement as she mulled over Joshua's and Callie's statements. "Again, thank you for helping me not to worry. I value both of you, and I am very thankful you are in my life," Ayden told them as she grabbed Callie's hand and Joshua's paw.

"As we are with you in our lives, Young One," Joshua said as he put his other paw on Ayden's hand, and then stood. Callie smiled and patted Ayden's hand and stood with Joshua. They both walked away in the same way they had arrived.

Ayden, again picked up her journal when Two came running through the limbs to her side. She closed her book, and looked at him. "He was so very cute and happy, now," she thought.

"Hey, Two, what are you up to?" Ayden asked.

"I have come to wish you Happy Birthday, Ayden," Two stated with excitement. And, to give you this." Two reached into his side bag and pulled out a charm of sterling silver with a raised copper design of the Great Fox, the Great Crane and a hummingbird on it. "I gave Deborah one just like this for her present. But it is opposite of yours as the animals are silver and the charm is copper," he stated with pride.

"Oh! Finch, thank you," Ayden said with tenderness. "It is beautiful," she stressed as she clasped it to her waist, and gave him a hug.

"Finch, I have been wanting to talk to you," Ayden began. "It has been one of my greatest joys having you and the Trevins in my life. The richness of love I have received from you guys has made me so very happy. And, the closeness you and Deborah have developed is something I really appreciate. She needs you, Finch," Ayden stated.

"I need her too, Ayden," Finch innocently stated. "You and Deborah have given us love we have never known before," he said as he stared at her.

"Because of you and Deborah, we have a big family, now," he expressed with joy as he opened his arms to show how big his family was now. Ayden watched as he became more animated in his expressions of love for her and Deborah.

"Finch," Ayden said as she took his paw, "I want you and the Trevins to be safe when we start to go into battle. Promise me you will keep them, yourself and Deborah safe," Ayden asked him.

"I promise, Ayden, we will go with honor to fight with you, and we will stay safe," Finch said as he bowed.

"Thank you, Finch, I just don't know what would happen to Deborah if she lost you. You mean so terribly much to her, Finch," Ayden said with deep concern.

"Ayden, both of you are family. We will always be together," Finch stated as he stood and bowed again.

"My time is up here, I have to meet the rest to eat clams, so thank you and see you later," he said as he jumped to the trees and disappeared.

Ayden decided it was of no use to write, being it was close to lunch. She stood and walked into the kitchen. Jerin was there, enjoying a bowl of chicken soup with bread.

"Ayden, how goes it," Jerin asked as he continued to eat.

"Hey! Jerin," Ayden responded back as she poured herself a bowl of soup. "It's been busy around here. Looks like all of us have been training in weird ways for our big battle. From the hut, to the copper mine, to Deborah and her new potions it's been a whirlwind," Ayden said as she slyly worked her best friend's name in as the important topic.

"Speaking of Deborah," Ayden coyly continued, "I feel a little concerned about her. She knows potions, mixing and stuff like that, but she doesn't really know battle. I mean, she never did like learning how to fight. I don't want to see her in the front of the battle, Jerin," Ayden said.

"She knows more about battle than you realize, Ayden." Jerin stated. "I have spent a lot of time talking with her. She has a keen sense of tactical maneuvering and planning."

"Yes, she has knowledge, and it is valuable. But she does not have the brute sense to follow through properly, Jerin," Ayden pleaded with him. "She reacts with fear. Just like when she almost took you out with her knife when we fought Garis."

"She has learned from that mishap, Ayden," Jerin defensively stated as he protected Deborah. "She is a young woman with tremendous character. She never forgets anything, and uses her knowledge for good. And, look at her, Ayden. The change in her, especially with her new dress, well, she is no longer a child, Ayden. She is not going to do anything irrational; I promise you that," Jerin stated emphatically.

Ayden listened with amused love for Jerin. He was smitten and he didn't even realize it, yet. She would have to tread these grounds carefully to not upset their budding relationship.

"Yes, I agree with everything you say, Jerin." Ayden tried to soothe his righteous attitude towards Deborah.

"But, look at it from my view. She is my best friend, I love her and I want to protect her, always. If I am worried about her safety, well, then I take my focus off of Choran. I just wanted to make sure you would always be there for her. And to help me keep her safe," Ayden gently said.

"Well, when you put it that way," Jerin said as he leaned into Ayden, "I will be there for her always, Ayden. And, yes, now, I do understand your concerns. I will make it my job to keep her safe, for you," he stated with tenderness.

"Thank you, Jerin," Ayden said as she patted his hand. "I love you and I know Deborah loves you too." Ayden finished.

"What do you mean Deborah loves me, Ayden," Jerin asked quizzically.

"Crap," Ayden thought. "I overplayed my hand," as she said, "Jerin, Deborah has told me she sees you as family. She never wants to be without any of us, as she sees all of us as family. And, she is very fond of you Jerin."

"I am fond of her too, Ayden. And, I too, see her as family," Jerin expressed.

"Good, then," Ayden quickly changed the subject. "I have heard whisperings your dad has a big ceremony for us tonight. So, I've got to get some things done before dinner. Catch ya later, Jerin," Ayden said as she stood and left the room before he could ask her anymore questions about Deborah.

Ayden retreated to the outer courtyard where she saw Eleea resting on the same bench Kit had taken Nekoh out on. She sat down next to him and smiled.

"Eleea, it seems like years since we first started to talk back in my world." Ayden melancholy stated. "I know it has been really busy since then, but I do miss our alone times we used to have," Ayden added.

"I have not stopped watching you, Ayden," Eleea said with tenderness. "Like a morning flower first opening its blossom to the sound of song, I have seen you bloom and shine in all your glory, Child. Just because we have not spoken to each other, privately, does not mean our souls have stopped. We will always be connected to one another through our heart and soul, Ayden," Eleea explained to her.

"I love you, Eleea," Ayden stated as she welled up with tears. "Out of everyone, except Deborah, you know the most about me. My heart soars with deep respect for you. Thank you for saving me, Eleea." Ayden stated with tears slowly rolling down her cheeks.

Eleea flew close to her and wiped her cheeks with his wing as he landed on her hand. "Ayden, The Great Crane brought us together, and the Great Crane will keep us together," he stated with reverence.

"The bond you and I carry runs deep in our souls, Child. We, no matter how far apart, will always be near each other," Eleea reassured her as he flew to a limb near her.

"I have fear, Eleea," Ayden solemnly stated. "I am so scared of the unknown. And, yes, I know everyone has spoken to me about not being afraid. But, deep, deep, in my soul, Eleea, I know." Ayden sighed as she looked at him.

"I know something major is going to happen and I will have to act alone. I don't know what, but I know I have to go by myself," she stated with confusion and fear.

"I also know you are right, Ayden," Eleea confessed. "Think back to what you told me on our journey about Joshua's prophecy. Here, let me repeat the prophecy for you,

Deep from the bowels will rise the crane.
Surrounded by dead limbs and bones.
Sing, Child. Sing with joy.
Sing with fear.
Sing to hear the stars respond."

"Sing to hear the stars respond' is the key phrase, Ayden. You will have to sing, possibly in flight, for the hummingbirds to respond," Eleea explained. "I believe this act, as seen from the whole prophecy, will have to be done by you alone."

"Do not fear, my precious Child," Eleea continued to explain. "Wherever this prophecy takes you, you will succeed. Go forth with the knowledge, and the assurance you have to do this. And then it won't seem so fearful for you," Eleea inspired her.

"Thanks, Eleea," Ayden said with some relief. "I knew if I waited to talk to you, until now, you would help me. Not to say the others haven't helped. But I needed to hear you the most," Ayden said with deep respect.

"Go spend some time at the waterfalls and relax before dinner, Ayden," Eleea said in a fatherly tone. "It will do you some good to just let your mind wander in the splendor of the sound of the water falling," he encouraged her.

"Thanks, again, Eleea. And, I will gladly take your advice; all of it," Ayden said as she jumped up and headed to her room to get her swimsuit.

Ayden slid into the pool and relished the water gently flowing over her body. Thankful no one was around; she lay in peace not having to talk. A good hour passed when she saw the familiar swirl of movement to her right. First, a blurry outline, and then the Great Crane in full majestic view.

"So, do you always enter as a blur, first," Ayden asked.

The Crane lightly chuckled, and said, *"Ayden, why is it, I am always taken off guard by you? I am the one who is supposed to surprise others. And, yet it is you who can surprise me,"* he stated.

"I don't know," Ayden responded. "Maybe it is because I am the one you need, rather than everyone else needing you. We have a different relationship, you and I. I put you off guard, because you have never experienced having to depend on a human like me," She said matter-of-factly.

"Wisely said, Ayden," the Great Crane responded. *"Yes, you may have some wisdom in this statement. I will have to ponder it for some time before I can give you a complete answer."*

"But I am here for another purpose, today," he stated. *"Ayden, a time will come, very soon, when you will know you are the messenger. When this happens, you will know when to stand and to fight. Trust your heart to take you forward,"* the Crane stated and slowly disappeared.

Ayden lay in the water, reflecting on how the Crane always disappeared. As well as being pleased she was able to talk to him in a 'normal way' before he left.

Gethsemane flew from his perch above to the edge of the pool, and startled Ayden out of her thoughts.

"Gethsemane, I didn't know you were up there," Ayden stated with surprise.

"Sorry to shock you like I did, Ayden," Gethsemane stated. "But it is me who is truly shocked. I have never, in all my years, seen the Great Crane talk to someone like he spoke to you. I have never, in all my years, had the privilege to see him speak to another like I did today," Gethsemane stated with awe in his voice.

"His appearances are a private matter for the one intended, only. He allowed me to see the both of you in conversation. I am, I am beyond honored, Ayden. To hear you make him ponder your response to him! Just simply amazing. No one I have ever known has spoken to him like you," Gethsemane stated with wonder in his voice.

"It's OK, Gethsemane," Ayden tried to soothe him from his obvious rattled state.

"It's way greater than OK, Ayden," Gethsemane expressed. "It is wonderful. If I ever doubted you were the Messenger, this meeting you just had with him confirms everything about who you are. Thank you for this great moment in my life, Ayden. I must go find Joshua, Zetia, Nadab and Callie." Gethsemane bowed to Ayden and flew off.

Ayden got out of the water, dried off and made her way back to her room. Deborah and Elora were already in the process of dressing for dinner, and she joined them.

"Do you guys know there is a big ceremony tonight," Elora stated excitedly as she continued, not waiting for an answer from the girls. "The hut has been prepared for the actual event," Elora stated. "And, it is beautiful!" She exclaimed. The whole sanctuary will be there, even Kit," Elora told them.

"I knew Nadab was ready to present the new weapons," Deborah stated.

"And, I kind of figured it would be like it was at the Great Tree," she said authoritatively.

"Yeah, I knew he was close, too," Ayden stated. "He and Nick have been to the mine, so I am sure there will be copper mixed in each weapon," she said thoughtfully.

The girls looked to make sure their dress was the way they liked it, and proceeded down the stairs to dinner. The Ten joined them, again, during the meal.

Tarhana had prepared dishes beyond the normal fair of food for this night. Prime rib, jellied cranberry mixed with chokecherry, roasted turkey, mashed potatoes with gravy, several other vegetable dishes, and desert of apple or pumpkin pie with ice cream or whipped cream graced their plates. The festive mood around the table was full of laughter and good conversations.

After the meal, Nadab stood and said, "The time has come to present each of you with your gifts. Follow me to the hut," he instructed.

Ayden was mesmerized by the path which led to the hut. Small lights lit their path with brilliant color emitting from each bulb. She was sure it was some type of magic as they weren't like normal bulbs she had ever seen before. They looked like tiny filled balloons from nature.

The hut was filled with risers of seats, all with someone in them, around three of the walls. Just like the Great Tree, the center of the room held pottery for incense to be lit when instructed. A table on the left side held the gifts to be presented.

Nadab, Lydia, Zetia, Gethsemane, Joshua, Callie, and the Ten took their seats facing the crowd. Ayden and the rest took their seats facing Nadab and the others. As soon as they sat, music began to play throughout the room. Once, again, Ayden knew it was magic as she saw no instruments.

Gethsemane flew to the armchair of Nadab's chair and stated, "This is your last night here at the sanctuary. Tomorrow, early in the morning we, the Messenger, her friends and those who sit with me will meet to discuss strategy. Then, in the afternoon, you shall depart."

Gethsemane looked at the travelers and said with deep regard, "We owe all of you a great debt. All of our hearts go with you tomorrow."

"Tonight, we celebrate each of you and I turn the events over to Nadab." Gethsemane bowed and returned to his perch.

Nadab stood and gestured to his helpers to hold the presents while he spoke to each recipient. He then moved to stand in front of his sons.

"Tybin, I took your staff and laid copper in it to form the image of the Great Crane. At the top of your staff is a small round peridot encased in more copper."

Nadab turned to the rest of the group and stated, "The olive-green peridot stone Finch gave to Deborah was a large enough stone for each of you to have a piece forged in your weapons. I believe this round smooth stone has become a stone of bonding for each of you. And, it is the gem of the Messenger from this day forward to forever."

Nadab went to Jerin next and stated, "Your journey knife is the weapon I choose to enhance. Copper has been inlaid throughout the handle, and I put the round stone at the hilt, just before the blade."

"Phum, your round stone is encased in copper directly in the middle of your buckle," Nadab showed him.

"Elora, yours is a small necklace which fits into your armor, so it does not hinder you. It will flow freely around your neck with its' beautiful copper setting, but will stay out of your way in flight," He tenderly told her.

"Eleea, your stone is in the middle of your helmet, and I added a little bit more copper to make a stronger nose piece for your beak," Nadab proudly explained.

"Nekoh, my friend," Nadab stated with deep respect. "I apologize for not making you armor at the Great Tree. This suit of copper will cover your neck and your midsection. And, your stone is on the top where the neck connects to the back of the armor.

Our little Nip," Nadab said as he addressed her. "You have the same armor as Nekoh. It seemed fitting, since you both have been inseparable, it should mimic his," Nadab said with great tenderness.

"Tari and Lok," Nadab looked at them affectionately. "Just as I neglected Nekoh, I realized I forgot you, also. Your armor is like Eleea's and Elora's, but all copper. At the center of the chest is your stone. It stands proud, just as you two have always stood with my boys," Nadab stated with profound love.

"Nickalli, I choose to take your enlightenment knife, also," Nadab explained. "The eyes of the bear are now olive-green peridot, and the copper is inlaid around the image of the bear," he said with pride.

"My beautiful Trevins," Nadab stated. Each of you have been given an enlightenment knife. Right after the hilt, on the blade is a small round peridot with copper inlaid around it. From the stone, the copper goes all the way up in one thin line to the tip of the blade."

"And, my friends," Nadab said with excitement, "Ten has his own stone on his bridle, because a shiny like him needs to fit in with his masters," Nadab said as he smiled at the Trevins.

Nadab turned to the others, saying, "All of your horses have a small peridot stone on their bridles."

"Deborah, this ring has been designed by Ayden. A slightly oblong smooth stone encased in copper. See the tiny intricate vines and leaves here, they cross over the stone and run across the side of it. When you lift this one side of the leaf, it opens the underside of the ring. A special compartment can hold whatever potion you desire, in secret," Nadab smiled as Deborah gasped in awe at his creation.

"Ayden, our Messenger," Nadab stated with tender admiration. "Deborah designed your ring. It is also encased in copper and is a smooth round stone like the full moon. Which when you closely look into it, it seems to reflect the image of the Great Crane standing in the moon. Yours has lines of copper with shooting stars on each end. And, just as Deborah's can open a secret compartment, you lift this star, and yours can house whatever you desire on the underside," Nadab stated with pride.

"Zetia," Nadab turned to her and said, "It is only befitting you too should receive a gift with the stone of the Messenger. I present to you a peridot ring with the Great Crane on it. When you lift this wing, it also has a hidden compartment," Nadab said with joy.

Zetia smiled and clasped Nadab's hands, as she tenderly looked at him and said, "I am beyond honored, Nadab."

Nadab stood back, looked at his friends and gestured to have the incense pots lit. He followed the same procedure as he had at the Great Tree. When his hands came together, the group blew on their gifts. The lightning struck the gifts with a loud clap of thunder, and the ceremony was complete.

Gethsemane, once again spoke, "Thank you to all of you for being here for this beautiful ceremony. Enjoy and laugh as snacks and drink are served. We will see all of you tomorrow afternoon when the Messenger goes on the move.

Chapter Thirty-Nine

Early the next morning, Ayden heard loud activity downstairs coming from the dining room. She woke Deborah and they both dressed quickly.

As they walked down the steps, they saw the whole table set for breakfast. The boys followed closely behind them as they entered the room. And, each took their familiar place at the table and began to eat.

Within minutes the whole table, including the Ten, was full of their friends, eating with them. Even though the mood was light, a sense of anticipation lingered in their conversations. After the meal, the dishes were removed and all sat waiting to hear from Gethsemane.

"This morning has been set aside for all of us to discuss what is the best plan to move forward to the Dead Trees. As stated, earlier, once you reach the trees the Trevins know how to get you into them. There you will have entered into the Dark Cell, and will have to become creative in keeping yourselves hidden," Gethsemane stated.

"When you leave here," Zetia began, "I can take you through a secret passage to be within a half day's ride to the Dead Trees; rather than the three days it would normally take. Once you are out of the sanctuary, remember to keep the rules you have been following on who you really are," Zetia gravely reminded them.

"There will be eyes all around the Dead Trees, watching to see who is approaching," Joshua stated. "We feel it would be best to have Tybin ride Ten to the entrance, alone."

"Dressed in the gear taken from the dead rider of Ten, he will be able to stay in disguise to open the entrance. Trevin will ride with Tybin, and whisper in his ear on how to approach the tree and unlock its' door," Joshua explained.

"Once the door is open, the rest of you can come one at a time out of hiding and enter," Gethsemane stated. "This is why you are leaving in the afternoon," he said. "We want you close to the opening in the early morning rather than at night when the Bones may be out searching. You will camp close to the entryway and as the dawn breaks, you will go in."

"We know from our life in the Cell," Sahl continued the instructions, "the entrance winds far down into the belly of that world. Ten will know the way down, trust him. He is a good horse, and is happy to be out of the clutches of Choran."

"There should be a basin with a liquid to light a walking stick for you to be able to see. I know this because, it was the potion maker's responsibility to make sure the liquid was available at all times for those who traveled to the world above," he finished.

"You will walk approximately twenty minutes before you reach the huge doors." Ethrys stated. "Here it will become tricky for all of you. Tybin, again will have to ride Ten into the entrance, alone. He will have to create a diversion to get the rest of you in without being noticed," she explained.

"Stay against the walls of the cavern whenever you can, "Jonis stated. "The workers' production areas are in the middle along the pathways, and you will be safer if you avoid the center of activity," he expressed.

"I have prepared a special smoke to help with the confusion needed to get the rest of you past the big doors," Kalim stated. "I suggest Ten will be carrying pottery bowls on him and one will accidentally fall off of the rope holding it. Tybin will have to play his part by being upset and angry. His anger will keep the workers away because of the fear they will feel if his wrath is taken out on them. The smoke will give you enough coverage to quickly pass through the huge doors," Kalim stated.

"One of the greatest risks comes when you reach the cottages," Sari said. "Choran's followers live in these buildings and they will not hesitate to kill you. Please be careful as you pass this area. Once you get past the cottages, it will take you at least six hours to reach the Cellers and the Bones," she finished.

"There will be small pockets of cottages all along the way to the Cellers," Tobia stated. "Again, stay close to the walls whenever possible. Once you reach the Cellers, it will be another area of great risk to get past them. And, again be careful," Tobia expressed his concern.

"Lastly, before you reach Choran's chamber will be the herbalists," Vexia cautioned. "Stay focused and calm as your anticipation will be heightened at being so close to him," she encouraged them.

"All of us go with you in mind and heart," Festus expressed. "We know what it will be like for you down there. Be aware, you will feel empty and forsaken. Your emotions will run high in despair. But, you have each other, and keep each other close as you proceed," he tenderly explained to them.

"Food is scarce down there," Sari explained. Tarhana and I have prepared dried protein and other nuts and fruits for each of you to carry. Enough for yourselves and for those you may happen to meet who can help you. Lydia and Nadab have designed bags," she turned to one of the bags Lydia handed her. She took the long strap and put it over her neck and situated it on her left shoulder.

"See, it rests on your hip like this," Tarhana demonstrated. "Each bag can carry, with magic, three pounds of food and not cause any of you to feel burdened by it. It secretly hides in the back of the bag and only shows itself when you open this latch," she showed them.

"I have five Great Fox amulets for each of you to carry," Zetia revealed. "They, also, rest in the bag, unseen. None of us ever know when we need to use an amulet, and it is important for all of you to have access to them. If you need the food or the amulet, just take the bag and request what you desire," she said.

"The rest of the morning into the afternoon is for all of you to pack and rest," Gethsemane instructed them. "Before you exit, Zetia will perform the procedure for all of you to receive the hummingbird tattoo. Then she will guide you to the world beyond the sanctuary," he stated as he adjourned their meeting.

Everyone went their own way as the group dispersed. Ayden approached Nadab and Lydia saying, "I have a feather from Uri, and one from Zetia I would like to somehow have them attached with a leather loop. So, they can hang on one of my hooks on the back of my outfit; on the inside where no one can see them. Can you two help me?" She asked.

Nadab smiled at her and said, "Baris, my good man can you help us with Ayden's request?"

Baris took the feathers and said, "I have a wonderful idea, Ayden."

"I forgot," she said to herself, "Baris was the leather worker in the Cell."

She obediently followed the three of them to the workshop. She watched as Baris weaved three pieces of leather together with long straps separated at the end. He took another piece of leather and formed a loop and placed it against the quiver with an inch of it hanging over.

He worked the other piece's in-between the quiver to form another braid which caught the single leather strand to keep it where he wanted. He then tied both feathers together, cinched them tight and handed them to Ayden.

"Thank you, Baris," Ayden stated. "They are beautiful," she expressed as she caressed the braid and feathers. The black feather from Uri lay nicely against the larger one from Zetia where it brilliantly showed forth its white with the outline of midnight blue.

"Uri, gave you this feather, Ayden," Baris questioned her. Ayden nodded her head in agreement.

"He does not give feathers often, Ayden" Baris informed her. "His feathers leave his body in smoke and disappear. For him to give you this has great meaning," he reverently told her. "I am thankful you came to us to secure it on you before you left. He will always be with you, Ayden," he humbly stated.

Ayden looked at Baris and then at Nadab and Lydia as she asked, "Do you know what I can do with this feather?" I mean what kind of magic does it possess?"

All three shook their heads as Nadab addressed her, "None of us know, Ayden. Just like the majority of Eshra magic, it will show itself as needed. Trust the feather was given as a promise to help you," he stated.

Ayden smiled at the three, thanked them again and left the shop. As she walked back to her room, she thought about what Zetia had said to her when she received the feather from Uri. She, too, had used the word promise. A promise of hope, a promise of tomorrow, and a promise she was the Messenger. Now Nadab had said it was a promise of help.

"Why," she thought to herself. "Why, does everything have to be in endless riddles. You don't get the answer until you are right in the middle of the stupid crisis!" she lamented.

Ayden walked past the outer courtyard and saw Kit, Nekoh and Nip sitting together. Her curiosity got the best of her and she turned to go see them.

"This is a pleasant surprise," she stated as she approached them.

"Yes, it is, Ayden," Nekoh confirmed. "Kit, here, was just telling Nip and I about his feathers. The reason he got so scared when I grabbed at them was because he, his relatives and friends lost most of their feathers to poachers. They were harvested because of the magical power they can hold if you know how to use it," he stated.

"Yes," Kit continued to explain. "Each eye sees into other parts of the world, Ayden. But it takes special understanding to unleash the power to do it. The poachers had no idea how, but it did not stop them from trying and taking our feathers."

"Most of our beautiful plumage went to Choran, because he would not stop trying to create his arsenal for attacks on the Great Crane," he finished.

"Let me give each of you a feather," he stated as he took his beak and plucked
three of them from his body.

He handed each of them a tiny feather from close to his chest, as he said, "Those idiots always thought they had to have the biggest feathers to accomplish their magic. What they did not know, is the smaller ones hold the greatest magic, and they would just throw them away. Of course, none of us told them the truth," he laughed as he spoke.

"Now, when you need to see, all you do is hold it and breath on it," he instructed them. "Tell it, while you are breathing on it, I would like to see Zetia, for example. And, it will show you her and where she is. But, for the magic to work, I have to breath on you as you hold the feather. After the first breath from me, it will always work for you when I am not around. So, the three of you stand with your feather, and as you hold them, I will breath on you," he proudly exclaimed. Kit breathed on the three recipients as they each held their precious feathers.

Kit looked at them as he spoke, "The other thing those stupid poachers didn't know, is the feather has to be given as a gift from me for it to work. Just because you desire something and take it...it does not make it yours," he finished, smiled, and walked away.

Ayden decided to take her feather and see if it would fit in her ring. She opened the secret compartment and tried to figure out how to put it inside without ruining it. She looked at Nekoh.

Nekoh said, "Ayden, tell it you want it to stay safe in there."

Ayden repeated Nekoh's words, "I want this feather to stay safe in my ring." The feather took flight and twirled its way into the ring and the ring's clasp closed behind it. Ayden smiled as she looked at Nip and Nekoh.

"Where are you guys going to put yours," she asked.

"I believe I will put it in the new pouch we received this morning," Nekoh stated. "What do you say, Nip, is this a good place for yours, too?" He asked. Both cats tugged at their newly designed pouches and put the feather in their bags.

Ayden left the sleepy cats in the courtyard to enjoy the sun's rays as she started again, for her room. Her stomach growled, and she decided the kitchen was a better idea before she went upstairs.

Deborah, Jerin, Two, and Elora were already sitting at the table enjoying a bowl of soup with bread.

"Hi, guys," Ayden stated as she entered, reached for a bowl and poured herself some soup. "I am really going to miss this place," she said with sadness in her voice.

"Agree," Deborah stated as she continued to eat. "But we get to come back whenever we want when all of this is over," she reminded everyone.

"Agree, with both of you," Elora chirped in, as she ate her bread and berries.

"This journey has been the greatest adventure I have ever been on," Two stated. "All of you have become my family. I have never known such love and acceptance as I feel with you in my life," he said with joy.

"There is way too much more I have planned for you in my life. You are my best buddy, Finch," Deborah said to him as she lifted his chin and smiled at him.

"Hey! I thought I was your best buddy," Jerin teasingly said as if he was upset.

"Well, both of you are equally my best buds," Deborah said as she tried to hide her desire to make sure Jerin didn't feel left out. "And, I include Elora in this mix of weird personalities and bodies," she stated as she stood up to leave. "But now I have to go pack, and I will see all of you this afternoon," she concluded.

"I'll go with you, 'D'," Ayden quickly stated as she cleaned her area and hurried after Deborah. Ayden slipped her arm into Deborah's as they walked to their room. "I love you, 'D'," Ayden said affectionately. "Love your optimism, your, drive, your love for me. I just love you, 'D'," Ayden exclaimed.

"You and I have to decide what to take and what to leave behind from our old backpacks. I never did see all you sneaked into your pack at the Great Tree." Ayden said with curiosity.

"I know, 'A'," Deborah agreed. "We've got to put everything on the bed and see what we have before we finally pack."

The girls entered their room and closed the door behind them to avoid anyone seeing them. Deborah grabbed her bag and dumped its contents on the bed. Ayden did the same. It was like revealing the surprises from their Christmas stocking as they looked at all they had.

The girls looked through their treasures of another flashlight, bear spray, plastic baggies, foldable shovel, candles, dental floss, hard candies, chocolate bars, a ball of twine, paper clips, rubber bands, a fishing pole with accessories and duct tape. As they looked at everything, Ayden stated, "I completely forgot we put a starter flint for fire in the bag."

Deborah turned to Ayden and said, "I want you to take what you want first, 'A'."

"OK," Ayden said. "I want the bear spray, the dental floss, the flint, the fishing pole, and the chocolate bars. The twine we can divide in two and the rubber bands and paper clips we can divide," she said as she took the items she wanted.

"Great," Deborah stated. "I think you picked the perfect things for you. But I want you to have the flashlight, the shovel and one of the candles, too," she determined. Deborah quickly organized the loot and then proceeded to divide the duct tape and twine in two. The girls placed their supplies in one of the plastic bags and then into their new bags.

Ayden was having difficulty deciding which items would fit best on her belt or the bag while Deborah sat on the bed to watch.

"A," she quietly said. "I have three vials for you. These are very important vials, 'A'. They are my birthday presents to you. I have color coded them to help you remember what they are."

"See here," Deborah showed her the waxed tops and strings, each a different color. "I did this so you wouldn't get them confused. The India blue is for illness, the 'I' in India, will remind you it is for illness. If you should ingest something that is supposed to make you sick, I mean ill, take a small portion of this powder and it will neutralize it," Deborah explained.

"The dark green vial top is for disappear," Deborah continued. Remember how Zetia made the whole pyre disappear? Well, this powder can do the same. Be very careful what you want to disappear, Ayden. This is serious stuff. Once you have it placed around your object, snap your fingers and poof it will be gone. You can't get it back, Ayden. So, be very careful when you use it," Deborah gravely instructed her.

"The last vial is red and stands for removing scent," Deborah told her. "We will be around people and, especially, animals who have a heightened sense to smell. This powder will disorient them so they can't tell your scent is near. They will just lose the scent."

"Each bottle can be attached to your belt behind your back or at your side," Deborah stated. I made sure they could be held on by the string and attach to a strap and not cause you problems when they are on your body, 'A'."

"This is why I spent so much time with Kalim, 'A'. He taught me how to use the plant properties to make these wicked potions to help us," Deborah declared. "Happy birthday, Ayden."

Ayden grabbed Deborah's arm and said, "'D', this is the perfect birthday gift. I will always treasure them, thanks."

Zetia and Lydia entered the room while the girls were organizing. "I have a special pouch for the two of you," Zetia stated. "It is the same pouch I had where I neutralized the snail fern on Nahrita and Dariat with the powder. But, both of you need to understand one thing," she said with concern.

"Do not use this powder where you will be seen or caught. Be extremely cautious and use it when there is no other choice to get out of a situation. I cannot stress it enough you have to be wise and careful in the Cell. Both of you are smart and resourceful. Depend, always, on those qualities first and not on magic," Zetia effectively said to them.

"I have nothing left to give you but my love," Lydia said as she went to hug the girls. With tears in her eyes, she continued to speak, "We, I mean, Nadab, Gethsemane, and the rest will wait here for your return. I know, in my heart, you will succeed and come back to us quickly," she said as she smiled at the girls.

"It is time," Zetia said as she gestured for the girls to exit the room. The rest of their companions were at the foot of the stairs waiting for the girls.

Zetia led them to the hut where the whole sanctuary was waiting for them. Their horses were dressed and packed, waiting for them, also. Sahl and his workers took their packs and secured them on their horses.

Zetia showed them the table in front of the room where food was prepared for all in a buffet style banquet. "This will be your last comfortable meal before you leave," Zetia stated. "We," she gestured around the room, "would like to share this meal with you in a non-formal manner. Our friends here will have the freedom to talk to you as they desire," she finished as she gave each of the travelers a plate.

Ayden enjoyed the peacefulness of the meal; thankful it wasn't stuffy and formal. Everyone was given the freedom to speak to whomever they wished. It was a refreshing change from the other dinner meals. She sat in a corner with her favorite dishes and watched all the others enjoy their time together.

Tarhana approached her with two plates, and handed her one with a piece of huckleberry pie on it. "I was told by a little bird this was your favorite pie," she said with a smile. She sat down next to Ayden and dug into her plate of pie.

"Thank you, Tarhana," Ayden said. "And, I mean thank you for everything," she continued. "I know it was difficult for all of you to relive your memories in the Cell. Your gift to us is more than all of the others we have received. Our success will be because of the ten of you."

"Ayden, my heart goes with you," Tarhana sadly confessed. "Because we have lived there, I know it will be a difficult for all of you. It is a soul-sucking environment."

"When you are in the depths of despair down there, remember, Ayden. Remember what brings you joy and what you have to look forward to when you return. Persevere, Ayden, do not ever give up. No matter how hard it may seem, no matter how dark it may become never give up," Tarahna said with deep compassion.

Ayden took her arm and said, "I promise I will remember your words, Tarhana."

"I have a small gift for you, Ayden," Tarhana reverently stated. "This spoon-fork-knife combo, may be very small; but I asked Nadab to make it for you. He and Kalim worked together to create it. My heart said you needed it, but for its true purpose I am not sure. I deeply knew it had to be in your possession," she smiled as she handed it to Ayden and then clasped her hands around Ayden's.

Ayden smiled back saying, "Thank you Tarhana."

Zetia stood in the middle of the room and called everyone to attention. "There is one more small ceremony to perform before all of you go. And, this is to give you the mark of the hummingbird so all of you will have a beacon to help you return to us."

Zetia lined up each of the group in a row. She had them open their hands, paws, or wings where she than placed a gooey substance on each area. She blew on the goo, where it disappeared and formed the outline of a hummingbird.

She stood back and said, "Now each of you will always be able to find a sanctuary wherever one is near. The hidden image will form when you are close and will become brighter until you find the opening. Raise your hand, paw, or wing and the entrance will open," she smiled at them.

Gethsemane flew to the center of the room, next to Zetia, saying, "Our time here, has given all of us hope, skills and purpose. The family all of you leave behind, will be waiting for your return. *Go, on the wings of the Great Crane and fulfill your destiny. And, bring the prophecy home to us,*" he stated.

He turned to Ayden and said, "Messenger, I humbly thank you, as all of us thank you. Because of you, we live. We live with a brighter tomorrow. We live with the heart you carry in you. Because of you, Eshra will reign in glory again. And, finally, Ayden," Gethsemane looked at her intently and finished with, "Do not forget what the Great Crane told you. Follow your heart."

Joshua stood and looked at the travelers, and said, "The prophecy will carry each of you to victory. Keep the words of it in your heart to help you see it through." He then began to repeat the prophecy:

> *"Cross to the East*
> *Send the seeker to the mighty glaciers,*
> *There his search will see the one,*
> *Upon the back deliverance comes.*
> *At rest the crane stands,*
> *Head held high,*
> *When the morning sun kisses the day*
> *The messenger enters through*
> *Prepared to take flight*
> *Riding the winds to the mountains,*
> *Where the dead tree stands,*
> *A fight ensues,*
> *The stirring sound rings*
> *Throughout the lands*
> *And, once, again the wings of the Crane,*
> *Bring the light of day."*

Joshua finished speaking and walked to the doors for the travelers to mount their horses and to begin their last leg to fulfill the prophecy of Eshra.

Chapter Forty

Zetia checked each traveler before she mounted her horse, and then turned around to face the group. "We will travel to the other side of the lake where the opening is to take you out of the sanctuary. Once you leave here, your journey will become treacherous. Stay quiet and alert at all times. The Trevins know the way, trust them," she reminded them.

"The path you were on before the sanctuary would have you entering the Dead Trees from the north. This path you are taking, now, has you entering from the east. This should buy you some protection as Nahrita will assume you will ride in from the north," Zetia instructed.

"It will take you until late evening to reach just outside the Dead Trees. Where you will be able to rest for a couple of hours before you enter the Cell when daylight approaches. Tybin, Jerin, and Nickalli have a potion to set around camp, when you rest, it will keep you shrouded, somewhat."

"Remember, nothing is guaranteed, so even with this protection stay quiet," she told them. Zetia nudged her horse with her heels and the group began their trek to the other side of the lake.

Ayden noticed, as they traveled, Ten was tethered to Jerin's horse and not being rode by the Trevins. The Trevins were in the trees with Phum, staying close to Zetia. She assumed if anyone on the outside saw raccoons riding a horse it would look too suspicious. Even though their moods were heavy, Ayden could not help but see the beauty of the lake. She hadn't even got to swim in it while they were there, and wished, now, she had.

"Where did the time go," she silently asked herself. They had been at Zetia's for almost a full week, and it seemed like it was just yesterday they entered the sanctuary.

The people and animals of the sanctuary followed the journeyers to the lake's dock. They lined up all along it and the shoreline to say their last goodbyes.

Ayden turned halfway in her saddle and raised her right hand, palm out, to them,
made a fist, and lowered it to her heart just before she would disappear into the trees. All of the observers raised their hand, wing or paw and put them on their chest in solidarity to her gesture.

Zetia guided them deeper into the trees and past the lake before she stopped. She, once again, turned to them, and said, "It has been my greatest pleasure to have been involved in this prophecy because of all of you. Each of you will always be a part of me, forever. I love you all," she said as tears welled in her eyes.

Zetia lowered her head and then lifted it as she regained her composure. *"The Great Crane rides with you, and on the winds of Eshra you will be carried to victory,"* she finished as she led her horse to each rider and hugged them.

She looked up to the trees at the Trevins, Phum, Eleea, Elora, and the ospreys and said, "My friends, guide them well, and return to us quickly."

Zetia jumped from her horse and stood in front of two large trees, spaced about five feet apart. She raised her hands, palms out, in front of her, and as she separated her hands in a circular motion down to her sides, the trees opened a doorway. Zetia stepped away from the entrance, and gestured for them to exit.

She smiled and whispered her final words, *"Remember, the Crane rides with you today."*

Ayden reached down and grabbed Zetia's arm and squeezed it as she passed by her. Their eyes locked for a brief second as Zetia squeezed Ayden's arm. "I love you, Zetia," Ayden said as she let go of Zetia's arm and went through the opening.

As soon as the last traveler was through, the door closed behind them. And, they were once again in the wilds of Eshra.

They rode in silence through fields and rolling hills for over three hours. Ayden noticed the closer they got to the Dead Trees the flowers looked sickly and sad. Actually, everything around her looked forlorn and without life. Her body shuddered with an uneasy sadness as she passed by all she saw.

Tybin held his hand up to signal for everyone to stop. He jumped off his horse and gestured for the rest to make a circle with the other horses. He led Deborah and Ayden into the circle and gestured, silently, for them to sit and stay in the circle on the blanket he laid down for them.

The ospreys took off ahead to scout the area with Two close behind them, jumping through the grass.

Nick joined the girls, offering them bread, already buttered with jam Tarahna had prepared for them while they traveled. "Eat," he quietly said, as he pulled a jug from his pack with cold milk in it, and passed it to the girls.

Ayden noticed Nick would not sit with them, but kept alert and watched in all directions as he rested his body on one of the horses. Her emotions were full of dread and she could not shake her feeling of sadness while she ate. She looked at Deborah, who was straining to hear something off in the distance.

Jerin grabbed one of the horses and took off towards the sounds. Nick readied another horse when Tybin raised his hand and said, "Stay with the girls, Nickalli, as he took his horse and stood at attention waiting for Jerin's signal to join him.

A flock of eight hawks with two eagles flew in from their right side and began to attack them. The eagles landed on the backs of two of the horses and dug their claws in, causing the horses to bolt. The hawks zeroed in on Ayden and Deborah as they soared in closer.

Nick jumped up and his claws slapped at three of them, wounding them. Nekoh came behind Nick and broke their necks as they hit the ground.

Elora and Eleea circled above the girls as their weapons pierced through the hawks. Body parts fell around the girls' heads with blood mixed with feathers spattering everywhere. Tybin took off after the horses and the eagles. The rest of the Trevins and Phum jumped onto Ten and followed Tybin.

Off in the distance screams could be heard. Deborah stood up, obviously distressed. She swiped at the birds and debris as she looked in the direction of the yelling. A blade sliced her arm, she took a bandana from her side, and quickly wrapped her arm and unlatched her knife. She firmly grasped it in her hand and started to run towards the screams.

Everything was happening so fast Ayden felt overwhelmingly confused. They were supposed to stay in the circle, and the circle was no more.

Deborah had been cut and now was running in the direction of more danger. She could hear the ospreys calls of distress, and decided she better run after Deborah.

Deborah reached Jerin who was on the ground, dazed. She picked up his upper torso, looked at his eyes, and slapped his cheek to bring him back to reality.

Jerin coughed and opened his eyes, saying, "He's got Two, Deborah, he's got Two."

"Who's got Two, Jerin," Deborah frantically screamed.

"Dariat," Jerin stated as he stood to get back on his horse which was next to him.

Deborah grabbed Jerin's arm and said, "I am going with you, and do not try to stop me."

Jerin grabbed her arm and hoisted her onto the horse behind him and took off in the direction of the ospreys' cries.

Dariat swiped at the ospreys with one of his front paws, while the other kept its pressure on Two's chest.

"You, pesky little rodent, I knew you would try to sneak up a different direction than what Nahrita believed. You are all mine," he seethed.

Not caring about the claws of the birds. Dariat focused on Two and put his whole weight on his body, crushing Two's ribs into his heart.

Two gasped for air and clawed at Dariat's face. He heard Deborah scream and lost his focus, trying to see where she was. He coughed and tried to yell at her to stay back, but couldn't complete the words due to the pressure on his chest.

Jerin leapt off his horse in mid ride and pulled his bow to his chest. He let out a loud, "NO-O-O-O-O-O," as he loosened his arrows into Dariat, while still running.

Every color he had in his arsenal landed directly into Dariat; green, blue, orange, and white flared as they struck their target. Dariat fell to the ground and broke into flaming ice blue and green pieces all around Two.

Deborah rode Jerin's horse to Two's side as Jerin reached him at the same time. She jumped off the horse and took Two in her arms, saying, "NO, TWO, no. You will be fine, I will heal you, Two." Tears rolled down her face as she caressed his fur.

Two looked at her and tried to talk, "It's, O," he coughed. "It's, Deb," and coughed again. "I love you, Deb," he whispered as he closed his eyes and expelled his last breath.

Deborah loudly wailed as she held him and rocked him in her arms.

Jerin knelt beside her and put his hand on her shoulder as he wiped tears from his eyes.

Nick jumped on his horse and took off in the direction of Ayden. Riding at full speed, he grabbed her and placed her behind him as they rode towards Deborah.

Ayden was mortified when they came into view of Deborah and Jerin. She waited for Nick to slow the horse before she jumped down.

Slowly, she walked to Deborah who was still rocking, crying and holding Two. She dropped to her knees beside Deborah and wept.

Tybin, Phum, the rest of the Trevins, Eleea, Elora, Nekoh and Nip slowly circled the girls and silently stood.

Trevin approached Deborah, put his paw on her cheek and said, "Deborah, we have to leave him and take cover. We cannot have a pyre for him as it is too dangerous. The fire will draw too much unwanted attention."

Deborah blinked as she tried to focus on Trevin. "We," she sobbed. "We have to have a funeral for him, even if," she continued to weep. "Even if it is only words to say goodbye," she cried as she leaned into Trevin's paw.

Trevin tenderly lifted her chin and said, "We will say goodbye to him, Deborah." He looked at Jerin and Tybin who nodded and then directed everyone to gather the horses and retreat to the side of the hill where they would have an advantage point to be safe and also able to watch for intruders.

Tybin, Jerin, and Nick made camp and spread the powder around three fourths of the area for protection. They walked back to Deborah who was still crying and rocking Two.

Jerin gently put his hands on Deborah's hands, looked at her, he softly smiled and brushed her tears away and took Two from her. He started to carry him to a patch of purple flowers growing near a small pool of water.

Trevin stopped him and said, "Please, he is our brother. Allow us the privilege to carry him to his final resting place."

Jerin placed Two in the Trevins' paws and followed behind them as they carried him. Trevin took Two's bandana, untied it, and handed it to Three.

Jerin watched as the Trevins positioned Two in the flowers and then went back to Deborah. He put his hands on her forearms and lifted her up. He then put his arm around her and walked her to Two.

Deborah stumbled several times as she walked with Jerin. Her tears were immense as she tried to look at Two, laying there so peaceful. Tears running freely down her face, she turned to look at everyone standing with her. She choked back her tears as she started,

"The French writer Anatole France wrote, 'Until one has loved an animal, a part of one's soul remains unawaken.'

Two awakened in all of us the need for love. He will live on in each of our souls and we will bring his dream to victory."

She stopped, fell to her knees and cried. She caressed Two as she held his charm she had given him, 'My Friend, My Hero' and, then, unlatched it from his belt.

Closing her hands around it, she leaned over him, tenderly stroked his fur around his face and kissed his forehead.

Ayden kneeled next to her. "Deborah, let me use the powder you made me to take his body so nothing can harm him again," she asked her. Deborah nodded in agreement; and Ayden looked at Trevin to see if it was OK with the Trevins.

Trevin nodded in agreement, too. She took the dark green vial from her belt and
lightly spread it around Two. She sighed, moved Deborah behind her, and snapped her fingers. Two disappeared in smoke and everyone cried again.

Ayden looked down at the purple flowers which laid on the outside of the powdered circle. She picked one and handed it to Deborah.

Deborah took it and brought it to her face and wept. Ayden went to the backside of Deborah to hug her and lightly put her head on Deborah's back.

She noticed a green glow coming from the small crater in the ground where Two had laid. She walked over to it and knelt down. Two's olive-green stone from his knife lay there.

Ayden tenderly said to Deborah, "Look, 'D', Two has left you a shiny."

Deborah looked at what Ayden was pointing at and picked up the stone. Deborah started to cry harder than before as she tightly held on to the stone.

Ayden lifted Deborah up and walked with her into the protective circle. She sat Deborah down and put her head on her chest and Jerin took a blanket and covered their shoulders.

Nick took another blanket and covered their legs. Ayden rocked Deborah to sleep while she muffled her own cries to not disturb her. As soon as all were in the circle, the boys closed it with the powder.

Nekoh moved in close to the other side of Deborah to help keep her warm. Nip crawled next to Ayden's chest and cried with her.

Eleea, Elora and Phum lay next to Ayden's side and the Trevins circled around all of them and laid down. Everyone stayed silent or slept as they watchfully looked for danger and kept their eye on Deborah.

Night fell on the group as their plans to get close to the Dead Tree entrance changed. Tybin, Nick and Jerin triple checked their small fortress to make sure all were safe.

Tybin softly spoke to the boys while they worked, saying, "Lok and Tari say Dariat was by himself with the eagles and hawks. We should be safe here, and until we get close to the Dead Trees. The Trevins, Phum, and I took out the eagles, and it looks like Eleea, Nickalli, Nekoh and Elora were able to get all of the hawks. We were lucky to keep the horses and not lose a one," Tybin finished.

"I will take first watch," Jerin stated. "Let them sleep. We will eat in the early morning hours before we travel again," he determined.

Tybin and Nick stayed close to Jerin as they rested against the hill. Their sleep was sporadic, at best, as they continuously shifted to listen for sounds of movement.

After an hour, Nick gently put his hand on Jerin's shoulder, "Let me take watch now," he said.

Jerin looked at Nick with tears in his eyes and said, "I should have gone on the scouting patrol with Lok and Tari and Two, Nickalli. Dariat had Two in his jaws when he jumped me and knocked me off my horse."

Jerin looked off in the distance saying, "I just didn't see Two take off with the ospreys. I should have been more aware of him," he said with sorrow.

Deborah woke to hear what Jerin was saying to Nick. She quietly worked her way out of Ayden's arms and went to him.

"Jerin," she said as she put her hand on his chest.

"Jerin, it is no one's fault but Dariat and Choran for Two's death. I cannot take it if you blame yourself. Please do not make me feel this pain for you too."

Deborah put her head on his chest and he wrapped his arms around her as they both silently cried together and fell asleep.

Chapter Forty-One

It was still dark out when Nick and Tybin ran their fingers around each of the traveler's bowls to cook breakfast of oatmeal and honey. Nick pulled out the rest of the bread from his pack, as well as the remainder of the milk from the jug. They gently woke each member of their group and handed them a bowl and a piece of bread.

Deborah ate a few bites, set her bowl down and grabbed her bag and knife. She walked over to the purple flowers and meticulously dug around the plant. She harvested two of them with roots intact and placed them each in a burlap pouch.

Tying twine around the top of the pouch to secure them, she looked at Nekoh and asked, "Can I put these in your apothecary bag, Nekoh?"

Nekoh gave her his bag. She gingerly placed them against the side of the bag stating, "keep these safe until I need them." She closed the bag and went back to her oatmeal.

Trevin finished eating and stood to face his comrades, "No one is to go alone on foot. In honor of Two, we will always be in twos when we leave the main party." He sat back down and acknowledged everyone's nod to him.

"Trevin," Tybin asked as he looked at him and continued, "How long until we reach the Dead Trees?"

"About an hour and a half to them, Tybin," Trevin stated.

"Then, we had better get going if we want it to still be early morning when we reach them," Tybin determined.

Everyone readied themselves for the next part of their journey. They cleaned up around the area, and prepared their horses for travel.

Elora flew to Deborah's horse and said, "Deborah I am so sorry my blade cut you. I should have been more careful in the fight," she started to cry as she finished with, "I am so sorry for you and Two."

Deborah lovingly stroked Elora's back, and said, "Elora, it is not your fault. I jumped up into your fight."

"And look," Deborah unwrapped the bandana to show Elora the cut, "It is a superficial wound. Do not be sad, Elora. We will all be OK," she stated as she finished preparing her horse.

Nekoh stopped Ayden as she was putting her packs on her horse.

"Ayden," he said, "I do not know why, but I have this very uneasy feeling about Nip. Would you take your sling out of the pack and put her in it to keep her safe with you," He asked?

Ayden looked intently at Nekoh to try and read his concern. She nodded at him and said, "Yes, Nekoh, I trust your intuition and Nip will be safe with me."

She dug through her pack and pulled out the sling and adjusted it to put Nip in it. Nip jumped into her arms as she reached for her, and Ayden slide her into her new resting place.

She hadn't realized how much she had missed Nip being so close to her, and felt a special warmth having her next to her chest. She gave Nip a kiss while she rubbed her head and mounted her horse.

Phum jumped onto Ayden's horse and looked at her closely. "Ayden. Ayden," he said again with sorrow in his voice.

Ayden tenderly lifted his chin and looked into his eyes. "Phum, do not blame yourself for Two," she quietly encouraged him.

"We cannot take responsibility for another's evil intent. Do not let evil destroy your heart by questioning yourself or blaming yourself for their choices," Ayden wisely told him.

Phum solemnly nodded at Ayden and then climbed to her neck and hugged her.

Ayden could feel his wet tears against her body as she hugged him back.

Tybin pulled out the outfit Jaeh had worn and put it on before he got on Ten. It was a leather hooded coat which covered his head enough to not recognize who he really was.

He turned to the group and said, "Trevin and I will travel alone, from now on, approximately five hundred paces ahead of you. Once we reach the Dead Trees, the only horse who can go in is Ten."

"Secure your horses far enough away to avoid their capture before you follow us. Lok and Tari will stay outside and watch the horses as well as secure our exit for us when we leave the Cell," Tybin continued to instruct them.

"We honor Trevin's wish and travel in twos forever more. Stay quiet and alert. And, know, I love each and every one of you," Tybin passionately said as he reached down to grab Trevin where he put him in front of his lap. Tybin heeled his horse and began his descent into the Dead Trees.

Nick took the lead for the rest of the group with Three in his lap to help give him directions in case they lost sight of Tybin. Ayden followed behind Nick and Deborah behind her, Jerin brought up the rear with Tybin's horse strapped to his.

The rest of the Trevins jumped on the horses to ride until they reached the trees where it would be easier for them to traverse through the limbs. Nekoh jumped in front of Deborah's lap, and Eleea, Elora, and Phum took their places in their respective saddles.

The ospreys quietly flew the winds ahead of all of them to make sure their path was free from danger. Their travel was silent as each of them listened for any foreign sounds of alarm.

Ayden's heart was troubled as she watched the scenery pass by her. The loss of Two weighed heavily on her.

"How many more will we lose?" she questioned as they road. "I don't think I can handle Deborah breaking down again. She was always the strong analytical one of the two of them. To see her as an emotional wreck was heartbreaking," she sorrowfully thought.

"To lose Two like we did," Ayden continued to think. "It was worse than losing my mother. He was nothing but innocence and beauty. Just like Lora," she silently lamented as she saw the trees ahead of her.

The sky was just beginning to turn to dawn when they reached the trees. "Deathly trees, actually," Ayden thought.

Their limbs were strikingly barren of growth and severely deformed. And what must of have once been beautiful green moss and vines, was, now, nothing but long stringy-like web hair which hung all over the limbs.

As they moved through the trees, she could not help but feel like spiders were crawling all over her as the moss touched her body.

Lok flew to Nick's shoulder, Nick nodded and Lok took off. Nick raised his hand to signal them to stop.

He jumped off his horse and led it farther into the trees to tie it up. The others followed him and did the same.

Ayden quickly went through her saddle pack and assembled what else she wanted to take with her in her backpack. Besides the bandana around her wrist, she grabbed three more. She had taken Two's bag with the food and amulets before she set the powder around him, and she put those in her bag.

Tarhana had given her a small copper set of a knife, fork, and spoon which were pierced with a hole at their ends and tied together with a leather strap, and she grabbed them and put all of them in her pack with the other things she had taken at the sanctuary to put in her bag.

After she returned from the trees where she tethered her horse, Ayden could see Tybin far up the turn of the path. He seemed to be stopped, too. She watched as he dismounted and stood in front of a single tree and put his palm on its bark.

Nick and Jerin cautioned them to silently walk along the inside of the trees and not on the worn path. Ayden took Deborah's hand, squeezed it and let go as they started to walk.

Above, the Trevins, Phum, Eleea, and Elora slowly walked or flew with them in the trees. Even Nekoh had taken to the limbs to stealthily follow them.

Suddenly, Tybin jumped back from the tree, and Ayden could see Ten move to stand in front of him while Trevin scrambled to a branch above and hid.

Men emerged from the side of the tree, carrying large cocoon pods. Two men each to a pod. Tybin immediately started to play his anger role as he directed them to take the pods to a cleared area about fifty feet away from the tree.

He leaned on Ten as he continued to direct them. They placed them in a row of twenty, and then made several more rows of twenty.

Trevin circled back and quietly said, "Keep moving until I tell you to stop." He inched his way forward, making sure everyone was following him. They got within ten feet of the opening, still hidden by the other trees, when Trevin raised his paw to stop.

A man, who obviously was the leader of the men with the pods, came from behind the tree, nodded to Tybin and stood in front of the whole group.

He lifted his hand above his head, brought it down, and the men opened their pouches from their sides, and waited.

Tybin nodded back to the man, took Ten behind the tree, and kept him out of sight.

Suddenly, a sound like a rushing tidal wave came in from the right of the men. The forceful wind accompanied with the sound blew the men's bodies back as they held onto their pouches.

Ayden looked up to the sky and saw a tremendously huge deformed bird begin its landing in front of the men. The animal towered like a brick fortress over the assembly with a dark brooding presence.

Ayden knew immediately it was Choran in all of his ugly, hateful, massive manifestation of snail fern induced body. She quickly took the vial for scent removal and spread it around the front of their path as they silently waited.

Choran's chest heaved as he coughed and looked over his cocoons. "Where is Nahrita and Dariat, Nargaut?" He spewed in anger.

"   "Sir they are nowhere to be found," Nargaut responded.

"When you find them, bind them and you send them to me," Choran roared at Nargaut.

He lifted his wings slightly away from his body and opened his gnarled beak. He drew in his breath and turned to one side of the cocoons and exhaled a continuous breath over all of the pods to the other end.

Ayden caught herself from coughing as she smelled the horrific putrid stench leave his mouth. She noticed the rest of her group were also holding their noses. The men looked like they were holding their breath as he sprayed them with his disgust.

She watched Choran turn around, walk back about five feet and turn again. Ayden could see his joints in his legs as if they were held only by a thin rubber fiber as he walked.

"His body was nothing like it should be for a bird of his beauty," Ayden thought as she remembered what Zetia had said to Nahrita, 'Nothing but a shell of a body.'

Ayden silently decided, "It was worse than a shell, he was a soulless heap of nothingness with coward-power written all over him."

Nargaut yelled, "Bones stand!" The pods began to move as they broke their casings. It sounded and looked like old dusty burlap ripping apart as they worked their way out of their prison.

Arms and legs of several types of animals and people began to take skeletal form as they stood. The workers quickly readied the powdery substance from their pouches and waited for the signal to throw it on the bones.

Ayden watched Choran walk down the seven rows of his small army. Each step he took was labored, as evidenced by him stopping several times to heave and cough.

She was amazed he was able to stand, or even walk, let alone fly with how he looked. His whole body was disfigured, looking like dried out tree trunks for his spindly legs and black unhealthy hooks for his curled claws which caused his gait to be awkward.

And his feathers all over his body were displaced as they stuck straight out like bedhead. He walked back up the line and looked at Nargaut.

Choran's eyes were just as creepy as his claws. "Just like Eleea and Zetia said," Ayden thought. 'The eyes are the lamp to the soul.' And Choran's eyes showed no light in his black holed stare."

"You know the drill," Choran barked at Nargaut. "Stand ready and fight if anyone tries to come near the entrance. When the powder wears off, destroy them and bring more to the front," he instructed. Choran lifted his feet as his wings spread, and he took off in flight, quickly leaving out of sight.

Nargaut yelled, "powder your charges!" And the men immediately spread it over the bones.

Off in the southern distance, behind Nargaut, Ayden could hear cawing and thunderous feet or hooves hitting the ground as the sounds rang towards them. She strained to see who was approaching when Uri appeared in a poof next to her and the others.

"Go Ayden," Uri stated. "We are here to secure your entrance into the Cell. This is our battle, today, not yours. Our distraction will keep eyes away from you and your friends," he said as he took flight in the direction of the oncoming noise.

Trevin dropped to Ayden's shoulder and said to all of them, "When the first hit is struck, we move quickly and enter. Tybin has the entry secure with Ten standing there to keep the door open. Do not hesitate once we start to move."

Ayden watched in utter disbelief as she saw deer, elk, antelope, moose, bears, mountain lions, badgers and birds of all sorts in the sky run and fly full force towards the bones.

Nargaut yelled, "BONES FIGHT!"

The herd of elk were the first to reach the bones. The sound of bone on antler pierced through her heart and shocked her as she jumped to quickly enter the tree.

She heard the crunch of bones under her feet as they half walked and half ran. Ayden looked around, the best she could while still moving forward, and saw remnants of bones everywhere.

Trevin jumped to the ground and showed them the side of the tree where the doorway allowed them into the Cell.

Tybin whispered as the last one entered, "Go all the way to the huge doors and wait for me there. Stay hidden against the walls," he quietly yelled.

Ayden looked at him, "No! We are to stay together," she whispered.

"I have to stay here, Ayden," Tybin stated impatiently. "I have to convince Nargaut no one entered during the fight. He needs to know I kept the entrance secure from all intruders. And he already thinks I am one of them. He'll believe me. Go!"

Ayden reluctantly nodded at Tybin and left him. Jerin put her in front of him as they wound their way down the spiral path to the bottom of the Cell. The Trevins, who had the best nighttime vision held on to each person as they quietly moved forward.

Eleea, Elora, and Phum sat on the shoulder of Nick who was in front. Nekoh stayed close to Deborah. The Trevins kept the group to the right walls after they reached the bottom. Luckily, they did not need the torch because of their friend's eyesight.

Trevin worked his way around hundreds of bone cocoons to where he found a path between the pods and the Cell wall. He continuously checked to make sure everyone was keeping up with him as he walked the dark path.

The group reached the huge doors and Trevin had them walk back a little way to stay out of the possible light when the doors opened. He then gestured for them to sit and wait for Tybin.

It seemed like they sat forever waiting. Ayden's eyes focused enough to see the outlines of everyone. She moved around the Trevins to sit next to Deborah. She grabbed her hand and lightly patted it. She was sure it was over an hour of sitting, maybe even two, before sounds of a lone horse's hooves could be heard.

Tybin rode into view and continued to the doors. He dismounted and pulled the latch to open them. He walked beside Ten as they entered into the inhabited area of the Cell.

He deftly loosed the pot on Ten's saddle just before the doors closed. The crash of the pot rang loudly throughout the hall. Workers stopped their production and looked at Tybin.

"Get back to work, all of you," Tybin yelled as the smoke surrounded him. "Any of you feel you should stop and watch, will go with me to Choran as his dinner," he angrily said to them.

Trevin moved everyone forward on the right side of Tybin and Ten, as the worker's areas were on the left. He guided them through the pathways where the barracks were and down to the cottages.

Ten steadily moved past the workers to the cottages. He stopped at the last cottage on the path. Tybin tried to heel him to keep moving, but he would not budge another step. Trevin halted the group as he watched to see what Tybin would do next. Tybin jumped down, took Ten's head in his hands and seriously looked at him, and stared for several seconds.

Ten took his hoof and stomped it three times. He gently lifted his head up and down and blew air through his nostrils as if he was trying to talk to Tybin.

Ayden let out a silent gasp as she saw a woman emerge from the cottage.

"Jaeh?" The woman said. "Jaeh, Nahrita said you were dead," she exclaimed.

Tybin slowly turned to face the woman. He had his hand on his sheath, prepared to kill if he had to.

The woman brought her hand to her mouth and let out a small scared breath. "You can't be seen here," she said. "If Nahrita sees you, she will kill you!" The woman tried to get Tybin to enter the cottage, but he wouldn't move.

"I am not alone," Tybin whispered as he dropped his hand from his sheath. "The Messenger is on the move," he said.

"You cannot be seen," the woman expressed again with fear in her voice. "I have to hide you," she softly screamed.

She grabbed Ten by his reins and said fairly loudly, "Oh! Thunder! I am so glad you finally found your way home."

She nuzzled up to the horse and rubbed her cheek against his. "Come with me, and I will put you in the stalls behind the cottage. You can rest there from your long travels," she said as she gestured for Tybin and his friends to follow her.

Trevin cautiously led his group to follow Tybin and the woman. Staying close in the shadows to not be seen.

The woman led them to a four-stall structure, pristinely cleaned with one other horse in the stall. She opened a side door, put Ten in and waved for the others to enter. She hooked a saddle blanket over the front of the opening of the empty stall attached to Ten's to divert anyone being able to see in.

She turned to the group and said with marked concern, "You are in grave danger being here. Nahrita will be home soon and I cannot guarantee your safety for long." As she moved to walk out, Tybin grabbed her arm, and she turned to him.

"We will not put you in danger for long," he said meaningfully. "It is our plan to move to the Chamber as quickly as possible. There the Messenger will deliver the destined blow to Choran," he informed her.

"You cannot leave now," the woman said. "Wait until it is nighttime when the cottages are all asleep, before you travel. I will bring you stew," she said as she hurriedly left them.

She returned within minutes holding a cast-iron pot, struggling to not spill it. Tybin grabbed it from her hands and helped her dish the stew in their bowls.

"My name is Iza," she said while she worked. "There are some who live here who believe, while others have lived too long with discouragement to believe," she stated.

Ayden watched her work, and admired her strength in a difficult situation. "She must be around the age of Jerin and Tybin," she thought.

An extremely small framed young woman, dressed in a frumpy dress and apron. Her hair was knotted in a bun at the back of her head. And by what Ayden could see, it looked dark brown, maybe red. Her hands looked weathered from hard work, but her face showed no signs of weariness. She seemed to exude the optimism of Deborah in her beautiful, round, eyes, Ayden thought.

"I will alert you when it is safe to travel," she said. "Until then, stay quiet and out of sight. My heart tells me Nahrita is close and she cannot see any of you," she stated with obvious fear. Iza turned to leave, and as she did, she triple-checked the blanket to make sure it would not fall off the hooks.

Deborah whispered in frustration to the group, "How could you even begin to know when it was night or day around here. Darkness surrounds our very presence."

Ayden nodded in agreement and said, "If we have to stay here for a few hours, it may be to our advantage to try and sleep."

Everyone took a spot along the walls and sat as they tried to stay somewhat comfortable while they rested.

After a while, Ayden looked at Tybin who was visibly troubled. She was close enough to touch his arm and asked, "What's wrong, Tybin?"

"Ayden, it was horrible having to be so mean to those workers," he said. The fear I saw in their eyes," Tybin shook his head as he shuddered. "I will never forget their fear, Ayden," he stated with deep sorrow.

"We will rescue them, Tybin," Ayden stated as she squeezed his arm.

Ayden silently said to herself, "I am past trying to figure out why Choran is so angry. It may have started with hurt, but he made a choice to perpetuate his hurt into evil anger. He's nothing but a selfish hateful being," she surmised.

Hours passed as they all stayed quiet or slept. Finally, Iza could be heard speaking to someone as she came closer to the stalls.

"See, Nahrita, Thunder has returned on his own. Let me go get him for you." She quickly untethered him, took him and led him away from the stalls.

Ayden and the others watched through the structure's slats as Nahrita reached Iza.

"Iza," Nahrita said in a cold tone, "Bring him over here." Nahrita took Ten and hit him on the side of his head.

"You, stupid horse," she angrily said to him. "It is all your fault Jaeh is dead. If you had half a brain, you could have gotten him out of Zetia's way," she said as she hit him again.

"My horse needs to rest from the hard ride," Nahrita informed Iza. "Get Thunder ready for travel to the Chamber. And get me some food," she demanded as she went back to the cottage.

Nick held Trevin back as Jerin went to Tybin's side to hold him back while Nahrita spoke. Both of them were so agitated Ayden thought for sure Nahrita would be dead in seconds.

Deborah moved to the middle of the stall and addressed both Trevin and Tybin, "We will have our due on this issue. Ten will not live in this abuse for long. Timing is everything in any battle. Wait for our chance to turn the tides in our favor," she soothingly told them.

Ayden could see both of their demeanors change while Deborah spoke. Their shoulders became less rigid as they relaxed their backs. The pain in their eyes was felt by the whole group.

"Deborah has changed," Ayden silently said to herself. "Two's death has made her a warrior," she uneasily spoke to her heart as they silently sat and waited to hear from Iza.

They listened as Nahrita mounted Ten and took off towards Choran's Chamber. For a brief second, both Trevin and Tybin showed distress at Nahrita taking Ten. All of them stood and stretched in anticipation of Iza's signal for them to leave. Jerin quickly raised his hands and gestured for them to get down and stay quiet.

"Iza," Nahrita yelled as she came back. Iza came out from the cottage and Nahrita addressed her, "Where is Thunder's original gear? This is not Jaeh's equipment," she demanded.

"Nahrita," Iza tried to calm her with a soft tone. "He never had any of Jaeh's gear left when he came home. Those who live above must have taken it. I assume he waited for his chance to escape to get back here," she cajoled Nahrita.

"When this fight is over, I will find Jaeh's gear and kill whoever took it. I will take joy in this messenger dying at my hand," Nahrita stated as she angrily heeled Ten and left again.

Chapter Forty-Two

Iza went back inside the cottage and exited again within five minutes, carrying a pack. Her clothes were no longer a dress and apron, but now she donned riding pants with leather fronts from her knee to ankle and a cotton smock with a leather hood.

Her hair was also different. No longer in a bun, it was in a curly braid on the side as it hung down in front to her waist. Ayden also noticed her beautiful olive colored skin.

She entered the stall and said, "We must go quietly. We will wait for at least thirty minutes before we move. This will give enough time for Nahrita to be far ahead of us. Stay here until I gather more horses for our travel."

Tybin grabbed her arm and said, "We cannot risk taking you. This is a mission of great danger, and we do not want to put you in harm's way."

Iza looked at him with intense strength, and said, "It is not your choice to determine my safety. None of you," she gestured around her, "know what life has been like for any of us who have lived in this fear all of our lives."

Iza put her hands on her hips and jutted her chin out as she said, "I am the only one who knows what you are going into. I am the only one who can keep you safe along the way. You do not have the right to tell me no. Not until you yourself have lived this daily terror can you say, no to me," she finished.

Tybin looked at Jerin and Nick, and then at Ayden and Deborah. He sighed and said, "No, we do not know the pain you have lived. I mean you no disrespect by saying you can't go. But, none of us know you. How can we be sure you are not leading us to our deaths," he questioned her?

"I can appreciate your concern," Iza agreed with Tybin. "But, if I wanted you dead, all I had to do was tell Nahrita you were here while we were inside the cottage."

"Give me a little honor here, you are the reason my brother, Jaeh, is dead," she revealed. "If I had revenge in my heart, all of you would already be as dead as Jaeh," Iza revealed.

"This is not about me. This is about all of the people who live in despair and fear down here. We have heard the stirrings. We know Choran is extremely nervous the Messenger will succeed."

"His fear and that of his followers have not gone unnoticed. Why do you think their anger is so intense," she questioned them? "Do you think it was just by chance Thunder stopped here," she continued to question them.

"He is an animal with instincts. He knew you could trust me. And, even if you wanted to stop me, I will go to get Thunder away from Nahrita's hate." she told them.

"Why did you not take Ten, I mean Thunder from her before she took him," Deborah questioned her. "I mean you did nothing when she hit him. You handed him over to her freely," Deborah's tone was hurt mixed with disgust in her voice.

Iza looked at Deborah and responded, "Thunder," she started and lowered her eyes as she wiped a tear. "Thunder is a beautiful animal. Down here you learn quickly to hide your emotions or die showing them."

She choked as she tried to continue to speak, "He is my friend, but even he knows the danger of showing emotions. If you saw, which I am sure you did through these slats," she said as she pointed to the stall, "then you know he did not react to her hits. He knows his time is short living down here. And, he is aware he has to play his part for the Messenger to achieve victory," Iza finished.

"Fine then," Trevin stepped into the conversation and said. "I believe her. She has true feelings for Ten. She goes with us to victory," he stated emphatically.

"There is a wagon of goods to be delivered to the workers outside the Chamber," Iza explained to them as she smiled at Trevin. "We can hide the majority of you in it, and travel with one other horse."

"You and you," Iza pointed at Tybin and Nick, "ride in the driver's seat of the wagon. The rest of you ride in the back of it. I will ride the lone horse beside you," she stated as she took the other horse out of his stall. She handed the reins to Tybin and said, "I will go fetch the wagon. Wait here until I return."

Ayden felt everyone's high sense of anticipation as they waited for her. "She's got a little of Zetia's spunk," Ayden thought. "For being so small, she wasn't afraid to stand up to Tybin. Or, for that matter, to all of us, especially Deborah's zeroed into the heart questions," she concluded.

Iza came up from behind the stalls with a hauling wagon, pulled by two horses and covered in a heavy cotton material. "Your name is," she asked of Nick as she helped him into his seat.

She next helped Ayden, Deborah, Jerin, Nekoh and Nip into the wagon, and each told her their names. Phum, Eleea and Elora gave her their names as they moved close to the girls who were already seated. The Trevins got in, and each gave their number.

When the Trevins said, "I am Trevin Three, Trevin Four, Trevin Five, Trevin Six, Trevin Seven and Trevin Eight," she looked at Tybin in disbelief.

Tybin smiled at her, and said, "Trust me, just go with the flow. And, my name is Tybin."

Iza handed Nick a shirt like hers and said, "Wear the hood up, like this," as she pulled her hood over her head and tucked her dark brown braid underneath the shirt.

"Tybin, you do the same. These hooded shirts and coats, made out of leather are a symbol of status in the Cell. No one will dare question your authority while you wear them. I and Nick wear Nahrita's, and I assume Tybin wears the one Jaeh had on him when he was killed. If you hear someone say, Hood, know they are talking to you. And if you hear Choran say 'Enforcer" then know this is your official status with him," she said.

"I do not blame any of you for Jaeh's death," Iza stated with sorrow as she looked at all of them.

"He made his decision to be groomed by Nahrita to fuel his hate and anger and use it as a source of power. Even if he would have lived, I would still choose the same path as today. He and I would have fought opposite sides. And, because he is gone, I do not have to see him die knowing I was against him," she told them. Iza gently heeled her horse and they began their trek to the Chamber of Choran.

Their travels were uneventful as they passed several cottages along the way. The hours passed with the passengers trying to stay comfortably hidden by either sleeping or resting. Ayden figured they had been traveling for at least six hours when the wagon halted.

Iza quietly said, "I know of a safe house where all of you in the back of the wagon can rest. The three of us will deliver the goods and return to this cottage when we are done. Stay inside and be careful," she stated as she dropped down to the ground from her horse.

Iza silently guided them inside the cottage. A woman who looked like an older version of Iza quickly jumped up from her chair and shut the door behind them.

"Iza," she quietly screamed. "What have you done," she cried in fear.

"Momma," Iza began. "The Messenger is on the move," she said as she guided the woman to her chair. "The prophecy is now, momma," Iza claimed.

The woman silently cried as she took Iza's hands in hers. She rocked back and forth as tears flowed down her cheeks. "I never gave up hope I would see this day," she said as she looked at Iza.

"I know, momma," Iza comforted her. "I have to go. I will return within the hour," she told her mother as she caressed her face. Iza hurriedly left to join the boys and deliver the wagon to the workers.

The woman took her apron and wiped her face as she stood and looked at her guests. She readied the pot of soup for them as they each produced their own bowl. She handed each of them a hard roll to go with the soup and gestured for them to sit at her table.

"My name is Deiha," the woman stated as she sat down with them. "When I was a little girl, I was stolen by Choran's Enforcers. My family lived in Oshyama, far away from here. Choran needed young women to breed an army for him, and the Enforcers killed my parents," she stated with sorrow.

"I gave birth to two children," she continued, as she looked past them as if she was remembering. "I taught my children all I remembered about our land and customs. Jaeh was thirty when he died," she said with sadness.

"Iza was a late birth in my life. I tried very hard to stay hidden so I could not conceive again. But, Iza was determined to become a soul of the Cell. She is just as beautiful as she is fierce," Deiha told them as she smiled with sadness.

"I proved to be resourceful as a cottage worker. Everyone wanted me to be their servant. I can make anything taste good; no matter how little the resources. It has kept me alive, even with my stories of a different life above ground," Deiha explained to them.

"Most see me as a silly old lady with very little sense. Even Jaeh viewed me this way. He took Iza from me when she was twelve. She is seventeen, now," Deiha said as she smiled, again.

"Jaeh felt I was a bad influence on Iza. So, he moved her far, far away from me. We only got to see each other when Iza would sneak into the wagon and risk her safety to come to this area. Since she left me, I have seen her only three times; today being the third," Deiha sadly stated.

"This cottage belonged to Jaeh, here is where he grew up. He kept me as his servant so he could control me from freely speaking to others. He sent Iza to be a servant at Nahrita's cottage, so she could keep Iza silent and controlled. With all of the heightened fear over the Messenger, and everyone preparing for battle, I have not been given a new master for this cottage," Deiha explained.

Ayden watched Deiha as she told about her life in the Cell. Her heart ached for the woman who knew nothing but sorrow. Her greatest joy was her daughter, and even she was taken from this woman. Ayden looked at Deborah who had tears rolling down her face.

Deborah grabbed the woman's hand and said, "It will get better, Deiha, I promise you we will get you to safety." Deborah stood up and reached down to the woman and hugged her.

"Thank you, child," Deiha said as she patted Deborah. "But my only concern is Iza. She must get to safety and leave this place. She deserves a better life than what she has only known here," she said with determination.

"Now, which one of the men with Iza is the Messenger," she asked excitedly.

Ayden stood and turned her back to the woman and showed her the mark. Deiha gasped as she stood and went to Ayden.

She gently ran her hand down her back, and said, "Before me is the One who I have spoken about for fifty years while living here in the Cell. You have kept me with hope every day. Each morning I sing to the hummingbirds who cannot see me. I never gave way to despair. I knew the promise would come," she said with awe.

Ayden turned around to face her and said, "Even if you did not see them, the hummingbirds heard your song, Deiha. The Great Crane and the Great Fox know your suffering and your trust you have in them. I want you to leave the Cell before the fight takes place," Ayden soothingly told her.

Ayden reached into her bag and pulled out an amulet. "I want you to see your daughter one more time before you leave. After you see her, you are to blow on this and let the Great Fox shape shift for you."

Ayden gestured to Trevin Three to come over to her and said, "Three will guide you out of the Cell to Zetia's. You will always be safe there," she said as she nodded and smiled at Three.

"Three," Ayden said, "I trust you to stay with Deiha. We will meet the two of you when we are done here. Stay with her and protect her, Three," she said as she kissed his forehead.

Ayden felt a little uneasy, and didn't want to look at Trevin. She had made a decision without his approval, first. She turned to look at him to see his reaction when he jumped into her arms.

"Ayden," Trevin said as he took her face in his paws and looked into her eyes. "You are a good leader. To get Deiha to safety will make our job easier. Iza will not have to worry about her when things start moving fast. It is a very wise decision to have Three get her out of here," he finished.

Iza opened the door and led Tybin and Nick into the cottage. The boys were given food and all was re-explained to them about Deiha's life and Ayden's final decision for Deiha.

"You are the Messenger," Iza surprisingly questioned Ayden.

Ayden looked at Iza, smiled and turned to show her the mark.

Iza stood and stared at Ayden's back, mystified. "My mother has recited this prophecy to me to where I hear it when I rest in sleep," she said. "It is a very proud day for me today."

She went around to Ayden's front, saying, "Messenger, I will serve you with honor." She bowed to Ayden as she spoke.

Ayden lifted Iza's chin up and said, "Iza, you stand with me. You do not serve me. Today you are a free woman."

Deiha began to cry huge tears as Iza went to her side to comfort her.

"Momma, it is a good decision to get you out of here," Iza said. "Go get one of Jaeh's hoods and his pants so you can ride without fear" she instructed her.

Deiha did as she was told, and returned dressed in the Enforcer outfit. Ayden explained how she was to breath on the amulet, and Deiha again followed the orders.

Iza had Three and Deiha stand at the door of the cottage and brought a horse from the stall for them to ride.

Deborah stood with them and handed Deiha Two's bag Ayden had given her before they entered the Dead Trees. She looked at Three, gently rubbed his head, and said, "Three, you can tell her how important this bag is and how to use it while you travel," she smiled at them and went back into the cottage and sat.

Ayden went to Deborah and hugged her. Deborah had tears in her eyes as she looked at Ayden, smiled, and grabbed her arm in their handshake. Ayden knew by the shake that Deborah's decision to give up the bag was her way of saying I accept he is gone.

Jerin moved to Deborah's back and wrapped his arms around her. Deborah leaned into Jerin's chest and wept. He looked at Ayden, smiled and nodded as he comforted her.

Ayden felt relief in watching Jerin take care of Deborah. She knew she did not need to worry anymore about Deborah's safety. Jerin would guarantee for her that Deborah stayed out of danger.

Trevin Three ran back into the cottage and hugged each of the Trevins. He looked at Trevin, took his arm and Trevin grabbed Three's arm in the same manner as Deborah and Ayden had so many times before and said, "I will see you on the other side, my friend."

He hugged him for an extra-long time and then went to the rest of the group and hugged them, too. He then ran back to Deiha, turned and waved goodbye to all of them.

Iza entered the cottage and shut the door after she sent Deiha and Three on their way. "It is almost daytime in the Cell," she told them. "It is best we wait until night to move forward."

Tybin stood up and said, "I question this decision. We saw Choran at dawn breathing over the Bones. It would seem a better plan to sneak into his chamber while he is at the Front and wait to attack him from inside his chamber," he stated.

Trevin stood up and stated, "From what we have been told, Nargaut is the leader of the Cellers and is responsible for the Bones. We do not want to be on the move if he is close by. I agree with Tybin," he said as he turned to Iza.

"Nargaut will also be at the Front with Choran at dawn." Iza looked at them and said, "I agree with what you say, but it is still best to move at night. We are very close to his chambers, and you only have to pass the Cellers and the herbalists to get to him."

"This way, we will reach him by early morning when he leaves to the Front. Nargaut has been staying at the Front these past days because of the dawn ritual. It would have been too great of a burden on him to come all the way back here, and still be able to do Choran's bidding," Iza said to them.

"Most of the Cellers are at the Front with him," she continued to explain. "A small portion of them stay by the Chamber to get Choran's food when they are ordered to go above ground."

"How do you know this for sure," Deborah questioned Iza.

"Living in the darkness of the Cell, does not mean our minds and speech are also in darkness," Iza said as she looked at Deborah with kindness.

"All of us know what is happening down here. From seeing the Bones being carried to the Front by the thousands, to the workers having to produce far more than they used to have to make, to whispered fears overheard by all of us; we know what is going on where we live," Iza stated.

Deborah nodded to Iza, and said, "I feel it is wise for us to listen to Iza. She knows the Cell way better than any of us do. But, for our protection, until we move, I think it best we stay in the stalls. Just in case Nahrita should happen to come here," Deborah warned the group.

Everyone nodded in agreement and looked around them to make sure nothing of theirs was left in the cottage.

Iza made each of them depart one at a time in case another Dark Cell resident should see them. She took one last look at all of them in the stall and said, "I will come and get you when it is time. There is clean water for you to drink in the bucket." She nodded to them and left.

Iza walked back into the cottage and looked at the image of her mother and said, "You need to get out of Jaeh's clothes."

She hesitated for a second and then said, "Do I need to tell you how you should dress?"

"Treat me no different than you would treat your mother," the shifter said to Iza. "I have all her memories and mannerisms and know how to act and respond in her absence," she said as she smiled at Iza and left to change her clothes.

Iza half smiled at the shifter and nodded. She looked around the room to make sure nothing was out of place, and then sat down at the table.

Tears rolled down her face as she replayed all that had happened in the last ten hours of her life.

"I am a free woman," she said out loud as she laid her head back on the chair and fell asleep.

Chapter Forty-Three

Ayden woke to the Trevins practicing the handshake on each other. She smiled as she watched their innocence.

She nudged Deborah, who had laid her head on Ayden's shoulder, and whispered, "Look at the Trevins." Deborah looked at them and then at Ayden and smiled. She caught Nick's eyes as he too smiled at the playfulness of their friends.

Iza entered the stall with fox Deiha behind her. She took the steaming pot of oatmeal from the woman and set it down.

Filling each bowl, she said, "This is a hardy meal before we leave. It should take us about an hour, more or less, to get to the Chamber. I am not sure of our exact time, because we have to travel along the walls and not on the path," she explained.

"We have night vision," Trevin stated. "Four will take the lead with you, Iza. And the rest of us will each take one person and be their eyes as we travel. Nekoh, too, has night vision and can carry Phum on his back. Eleea and Elora can ride the shoulders of whomever they wish," he concluded.

Everyone double checked their packs, filled their bladders with the bucket water, and prepared to exit the stall.

Iza looked at them and made one final comment before she let them leave. "Do not forget Choran also has the gift of night vision," she warned them as she guided them out.

The walking the wall was not as difficult as Ayden expected it to be. Their trek was slow, as it was dark, but the bones were fewer and not right against their pathway where they had to climb over them continuously.

They walked for thirty or forty minutes and continued to notice fewer and fewer pods. The smells of the herbalists cooking their potions wafted into their nostrils, even though they were far enough away to not see them. The flickering of their fires was the first sign they were approaching the potion makers.

Ayden began to feel the same foreboding she had felt at Zetia's about something major was going to happen.

Iza stopped the group before they were on top of the potion makers. They sat in a semi-circle waiting for instructions.

Ayden looked ahead to her left and grabbed Tybin's arm and pointed. There was Ten strapped to a latch hanging off the side of a door.

Ten jerked his head and snorted. He raised his head up and down several times and loosed the strap wrapped in the latch. The strap fell to the ground and he slowly walked backwards away from the maker's hut.

After several feet, Ten turned around and walked straight to the hidden group. He nuzzled Iza and then proceeded to the rest and nuzzled every one of them.

A boy came out of the hut, looked for the horse around the lit area and then looked down the way, where he saw him. He started to walk towards them, and Ayden and the rest got into position to bolt.

Iza stood and took a couple of steps towards the boy. The boy saw her and started to run, but quickly stopped and walked as he loudly said, "Thunder you cannot run off like that."

He grabbed Iza's arm and took her farther into the shadows and said, "I knew you would come. It is dangerous for you to be here," he said with fear in his voice.

Iza led him back to the group and he let out a soft gasp. Iza put her hand on his shoulder, saying, "Raxton, the Messenger is on the move. We have to get into the Chamber, unseen," she told him.

Raxton looked at the group as she spoke, and finally said, "I can get you in with the help of Thunder." He positioned Thunder in front of all of them and stood behind the horse to address them.

"Nahrita has been bound by Choran, she sits and awaits his judgement in the Chamber," he whispered to them. "He is about ten to thirty minutes from leaving to the Front. The snail fern has taken longer than usual to cook down and he is angry. But once he leaves, we can enter," he told them.

Tybin looked at Iza and said, "We cannot continue to bring people into the fold and put them in danger, Iza."

"Raxton is only three years younger than me," Iza stated. "He and I grew up together under my mother's roof. His mother died when he was one years old. Raxton knows the lore just as deeply as I. He goes with us because he is the only one with knowledge on how to get in. And, he knows the risk," she said as she tenderly looked at him.

"Again, Tybin I remind you," Iza passionately said, "Do not doubt our stand if you have never lived each moment of your life in fear and dread in the Cell. Raxton is just as honorable as I am," she finished.

Tybin looked at Iza, nodded, and then looked at Raxton and said, "What do you know?"

"Your greatest surprise attack is to get into his cave. The cave goes far back and will hide you. I have been in the cave before. When he would leave, as a younger me, I used to go in it to see what he had in there."

"Iza," he turned and looked at her. "Iza used to scold me for my 'foolish peril' as she would call it. I know the marks in the wall to climb to get into it," he said with proud authority.

"Our biggest threat is Nahrita, she can see everything," Raxton continued to explain. "For her to be able to alert Choran, would be her freedom from death. We will have to disable her without killing her," Raxton stated as he visibly took his hand to his chin and thought.

"A sleeping potion is our best plan," Iza stated. "Raxton you could take her food to eat and drink and by now she is very hungry and will take it without thinking."

"She will see it as a nice gesture from you. You will have to go in by yourself, on Thunder, and when you start to leave the chamber and the doors are reopened for you to come out, we can go in," she stated.

"My master has been friendly with the maker who uses a sleeping potion in small amounts to make Choran sleep. They slip it on the body of whatever he is going to eat and then deliver it to him. They don't know I know, but I can get some of it."

Raxton held his finger up for them to stay, and left quickly with Ten. He pretended to tie Ten up again and slipped around the back of the hut and disappeared.

Within minutes he returned and whispered into Ten's ear. The horse waited for Raxton to enter the hut and then, again, backed down the pathway and turned. He walked back to the group and Raxton peered out the door of the hut, and said with exasperation, "Thunder, you must stay here." He walked back to them and said, "I have it."

"We will continue to the doors and wait in the shadows for you, Raxton," Iza said as she gently shooed him away. Iza led her wards closer to the doors, as she stayed along the walls to avoid detection. They got approximately five feet from the door when Iza had them crouch down to stay out of sight of the workers.

Raxton came up on their left, walking with Ten, whose back was carrying a double side pack filled with goods to take into the Chamber. Raxton acted nonchalant as he sauntered up to the doors and opened them.

Nahrita was in the far-left corner of the Chamber. Her legs were tightly bound together, and her arms hung above her, tied to an iron ring on each side.

Raxton approached her and emotionally said, "Nahrita, while Choran is gone, you need to eat and drink."

Nahrita opened her eyes and looked at Raxton. She tried to sit up taller as she looked at him. "I do not need your unrealistic kindness, Raxton. What angle are you playing," she asked him as she harshly leered at him.

"No, play, Nahrita," Raxton stated as he took her prepared food off of Ten. "You are weak, and your mind has had too much time with hate in your heart. You are still one of us, and you do not deserve to die like this," he stated as he lifted a warm drink to her lips.

"Drink this broth; it is full of protein. Solid food would not be good for you right now," he said with wisdom.

Nahrita took a couple of small sips, turned her mouth away and said, "If he returns and sees you, he will eat you before he eats me," Nahrita stated.

"That is the risk I choose, Nahrita," he said while he made her drink more.

Nahrita took a few more sips and then said, "Enough, Raxton, I wish no more of your drink. Leave me to my fate."

Raxton stood, nodded at Nahrita and placed everything back on Ten. He began to slowly walk back to the doors, hoping he could hear her in a deep sleep.

He turned to look at her, as she watched him. He felt extremely uncomfortable and wondered if he had screwed up the potion versus liquid portions of his drink. He pretended Ten had loosed the packs and he acted like he was tightening all the ends before he continued.

Nahrita asked him, "What is your problem, Raxton. Why do you hesitate to leave?"

Raxton turned to her and said, "My problem is my concern for you, Nahrita. I do not like to see you suffer in this way. It is difficult for me to leave you," he coyly told her.

Nahrita yawned, and said, "Go, Raxton, your interest in me is useless." Her body slumped as she closed her eyes.

Raxton slapped Ten's butt and made him go halfway through the doors and then told Ten to wait for him.

Iza deftly moved everyone into the Chamber. She kept them along the right of the room to avoid Nahrita's eyes. And, to get them close to the walls which would guide them up to Choran's cave.

Raxton crawled to Iza, and whispered to the group, "The first foothold is right here," he showed them the indentation of where to start their climb.

He ducked behind Tybin, and said, "I will stay down here in case I have to divert any trouble. If I am gone any longer from my master, they will come looking for me. I can't risk all of you being seen because of my absence." He crawled back to the entrance and led Ten out of the doors.

Trevin started the ascent to the cave, followed by Tybin and Iza, then Deborah who had strapped Nekoh to her back to make it easier on him. The other Trevins mixed themselves in between their friends as they helped them secure each foothold before they took the next step.

Nick followed Deborah with Phum on his shoulder and Ayden followed him. Jerin, as always, brought up the rear. Eleea and Elora flew to the top and watched them climb.

Tybin reached the flat ledge and held his hand out to help each member and directed them to move back into the cave to stay hidden from the entrance.

As he reached for Ayden's hand, he slipped on the edge where the rock was unstable. Debris started to avalanche down the side of the fortress and he began to fall.

Ayden grasped Tybin's arm as he passed her. She lifted her wings away from her body, and thrust her way up to the far end of the ledge and saved both of them from falling.

Nahrita yelled at the same time Ayden took flight, "Stop," she screamed.

Jerin turned to leap back down the wall when Trevin One, Four, and Five bolted down with ease to the floor. They ran over to Nahrita, took a boulder from the pile she was sitting on and looked at her for a second.

Nahrita swung her head back and forth as she saw what the Trevins were planning to do. The three of them lifted the rock and climbed above her head and let it drop, knocking her out. They quickly ran back up the wall, and Jerin followed behind them.

The group walked deep into the cave. Ayden felt the long dangling roots brush up against her face and had the same reaction as she had when they entered the Dead Trees.
She shuddered as the roots mixed with years of dead moss brushed her skin like spider webs.

Tybin, Nick and Jerin made the girls and the Trevins sit farther in the cave, away from the entrance. Eleea stood guard with the boys and directed Elora to stay with the girls.

Nekoh went to Ayden and said, "Keep Nip in her sling, Ayden. She is too little to fight with us."

He put his nose to Nip's as she sat halfway out of her resting place, and then, he nudged Ayden with affection. He walked to the front and laid down behind Jerin.

It seemed like an eternity as they waited for evidence of Choran returning. Deborah took Ayden's hand and held on to it in silence. Ayden closed her eyes and focused on all of the sounds around her.

She sat on the back of her legs, ready to jump if she had to move quickly. She heard the Trevins and Phum loosen their blades and get into position to fight.

The heavy, quiet breathing Ayden sensed from the boys in front of her made her feel sad they were the first line of attack. She did not want to see them harmed, and felt strongly she should be in front of them.

Ayden kept where she was, remembering the Crane's words: "You will know when to fight…Trust your heart to move you forward."

Suddenly, a strong gust of wind blew across their bodies. Choran's wings flapped as he landed on his perch outside of the cave. He coughed for almost a full minute until he finally caught his breath.

Workers, who heard him return, entered the Chamber carrying snail fern in large jugs. They took the containers and emptied the contents into a large bowl on the floor below his perch.

Choran flew down to the elixir and sloppily drank it, making slurping sounds and grunts. He lifted his head and raised his wings out from his body as he fanned them.

Nahrita woke as the air hit her from his wings. "Choran," she screamed. "The Chamber has been breached," she said as she tried to catch her breath. "The intruders and the Messenger are in your cave," she yelled.

Tybin and the rest of them, froze as they heard Nahrita give away their secret. They all stood and waited to hear Choran's reaction.

"Nahrita, do you think I am a fool," Choran questioned her.

"I am the prince of night. I see and smell all that is around me. When I entered, I knew we had unwanted visitors in my cave," he said with a halfhearted chuckle.

"Timing is everything, Nahrita. If you would have kept your mouth shut, I would have been able to surprise attack them. Now, they know I know they are here," Choran angrily told her as he flew back up to his perch.

Jerin and Tybin readied their weapons as they pushed the rest of their friends back farther in the cave and stood in front of them. Everyone's gifted armor began to form over their bodies as they listened and waited.

"Iza," Choran revealed. "You were always a fool like your mother. Yes, I smell you back there. I should have never let Jaeh talk me out of killing both of you."

"But you are young enough to still taste good when I eat you," Choran laughed until he coughed uncontrollably.

Choran spread his wings out and repositioned himself on his perch. "The messenger has wings like me," he stated with amusement.

"Do tell messenger, do you think your wings can beat me down. Or maybe you have wings so you can quickly fly away before I kill you," he smirked as he spoke.

Nick and Jerin quickly turned to Ayden as she shook her head at them and put her finger to her mouth. She knew Choran was trying to provoke her, and she needed all of them to stay silent to frustrate him.

"What! No answer to my questions," Choran taunted her.

"It will be my greatest victory to watch you in agony as I eat the six raccoons, the two birds, the squirrel, the two cats, and then your five friends before I eat you," he laughed until his whole body rose up and down as he immensely enjoyed his words spoken to Ayden.

"Have you not seen enough death, child," he questioned her through his coughing. "Your mother, father, Lora...it could have ended with them."

"If only you would have stayed in your world. Now, by your hand, all of your friends shall die," he said as he tried to unnerve her.

Ayden could sense her friends all around her become more and more agitated. She lifted her hand to them, as she moved to the front of Tybin, Nick, Eleea and Jerin. She gestured, again, for all of them to stay silent as she stood her ground.

"That's right child," Choran chided her. "Move to the front of your friends and try to protect them," he laughed.

"Ehyah, or the Great Crane as you know him, put his misguided trust in you and your friends to save him," Choran said with disgust.

"He can't be saved, messenger! No one leaves Hollow when I send them there," he cackled.

"I am not only the prince of the night and day," Choran informed Ayden. "I am the prince of Hollow. I rule all of Eshra and your world, *mes-s-s-s-enger,*" he claimed with arrogance.

Ayden moved closer to the entrance and in front of her friends as she turned one more time before she reached the opening. She looked at her friends, and said, "I love each and every one of you. Do not follow me. This is not a request. It is an order," she seriously told them as she looked at them.

She turned around, lifted her chin with her head held high and walked to the entrance. "Face me Choran," Ayden demanded. "Or are you too afraid to see the Messenger," she taunted him.

Choran lifted his wings as he laughed and turned around on his perch.

Nick started to move forward when Eleea flew to his shoulder and Jerin and Tybin held each one of his arms to keep him back.

"This is her time, Nickalli," Eleea whispered in his ear.

Nick looked at Eleea, then at Jerin and Tybin and shook his head as tears welled up in his eyes. "No," he whispered, "It can't end this way," as he tried to continue to move to Ayden's side.

Tybin and Jerin held on to him tightly and would not let him go after her.

Ayden watched Choran turn, and as he did, she released her wings farther out from her back. She stood tall as her wings draped the curves of her body. Even though it was dark in the Chamber, her wings shimmered with light emitting from them.

Instantaneously, she flew at Choran and attacked him, slicing him with her winged blades. He fell from his perch to the ground and she was on top of him, using her wings to disorient him and cut him.

Nahrita screamed as the rest ran from the depths of the cave to the edge of the ledge to see what was happening.

Ayden jumped off of Choran and flew far enough away from him to not be harmed by him. "Do you really believe I am afraid of you," she said with repulsion.

Choran stood up and began to circle the outer end of the Chamber as he coughed and heaved in anger.

Not taking his eyes off of Ayden, he yelled, "Nahrita, if you wish to live! Call your men to arms and kill her friends. But do not touch her, she is mine," he yelled.

Ayden circled with him in the opposite direction to keep her distance from him.

Nahrita let out a spine chilling, guttural call from her throat.

As the sound rang throughout the chamber Choran laughed with an eerie demented snort.

The chamber doors flung open as men entered the room. Two men ran over to Nahrita and cut away her bondage.

Four others gathered pods and placed them two by two, until they had five rows of Bones. Raxton also entered with Ten and stayed at the entrance of the Chamber.

The two wolves from the fight with Zetia at their camp fell through the ceiling, where the roots opened up a door, and landed with snarled teeth by Nahrita's sides. Three hawks flew in the same way as the wolves.

Nahrita yelled, "Do not touch her, she is Choran's." She turned to the Cellers who were standing at the entrance and they ran and waited beside the pods. "The rest die at your will!" She commanded.

Choran walked his circle behind the pods and blew his breath across them. Never taking his eyes off of Ayden.

Phum jumped up and took his blade from his buckle and threw it into the base of Choran's perch on the floor. He took the other side of the buckle blade and threw it into the roof entrance of the cave.

He tested it to make sure it was taunt and took a piece of his leather from his belt and swung it over the steel string and zip lined down to the floor.

Tybin turned to Iza, and said, "Stay here in the cave." He grabbed Phum's line and followed Phum down. Jerin did the same. They waited at the bottom for their enemies to make a move.

The Trevins could not resist the zip line. Each of them slid down it with excitement. After all of them were down, Phum retracted the blades into his buckle.

Nick watched from the entrance to see what would happen when the Bones took shape. He kept vigilance on Ayden as he waited, making sure she would not be harmed by Choran.

Eleea and Elora stood ready as they both watched the hawks. Deborah quietly kept her hand under her scarf as she loosened a pouch from her belt and held onto it in her hand.

Her other hand held her knife as she, too waited to respond to the inevitable attacks on her and her friends. Nekoh half laid, half stood as his muscles tightened for him to quickly jump into the action.

Nahrita yelled, "Bones! Fight!" And, the pods began to open.

Choran's eyes pierced the darkness of his chamber as he looked at Ayden with hatred. "Maybe, I will kill your friends first, before I finish you," he said with vengeance.

"You will never touch my friends when they leave here," Ayden said with confidence, never taking her eyes off of him.

As she spoke, the brightness from her wings began to illuminate enough dim light in the room for everyone to be able to see and not have to fight in pure darkness. The two of them continued to circle the room as they each spoke their mind games.

"I use to feel sorry for you, Choran," Ayden said.

"Sorry! Sorry!" Choran bellowed. "You offend me messenger," he said as he raised his wings in anger. "You are not worthy to pity me! You are a mere human with no power in this world," he lashed out at her.

"What do you consider power," Ayden asked him. "Fear? Pain? Death? Is this your power, Choran?"

"All you ever wanted in this world was to be respected and honored. But because you were lazy, you took what you considered your entitled right for your perceived power by force rather than earn it by work and honor. You found ways to copycat magic to make yourself feel important. Knowing you could never earn the true respect of owning Eshra magic," Ayden revealed his heart to him.

Choran roared with anger as he raised his wings away from his body to take flight.

Ayden sensed Choran preparing to fly to his ledge. She took off before him, as Choran flew to reach his cave. She landed in front of him and blocked him from entering.

"Who do you think you are, foolish girl," Choran said with immense anger as he landed on the branch outside of his cave.

"I am the Messenger of Eshra," Ayden stated, as her wings began to glow like the full rays of the sun. She stood firmly and kept him blocked from his cave.

The Cellers quickly threw powder over the bones to stop Ayden's light from affecting them.

"You will live forever in Hollow with Ehyah! This is the message you bring to Eshra!" Choran bellowed as he lunged for her.

Nick, who had to go to the back of the cave when Ayden landed, ran through the roots and moss towards Ayden. "I cannot lose you, Ayden," he yelled as he ran.

Iza ran in front of Nick and reached Ayden first. She threw herself in Ayden's path and Choran threw her off of the ledge with his wing. As she began to fall, her leg caught the jutted edge of a limb, causing a huge gash.

Raxton watched from the open doors and saw her falling. He heeled Ten, and Ten raced to reach her. Luckily, Raxton was able to grab her before she hit the ground. He tightly held onto Iza as he maneuvered Ten back to the chamber doors. Quickly Raxton took his belt off and secured it around Iza's leg to stop the bleeding.

Nick's whole body changed, as he ran through the cave, transforming into a huge grizzly bear with his gifted armor. Moving in front of Ayden, he dropped his full weight onto Choran's chest. They both fell off of the ledge, and began to fall through the air to the ground.

Ayden darted after Nick and lifted him off of Choran and flew him to the far wall near the Forest of Roots.

Choran hit the ground with a thunderous crash. He weakly worked his way to stand and yelled, "Nahrita! You, stupid woman what are you waiting for!" He looked at his dish under his perch and flew to drink the rest of its contents.

The Trevins raced after him and threw the hay that laid on the floor all around his chamber into the bowl. The straw soaked up the elixir and Choran slapped his wings in anger at the Trevins. His left wing caught all of them and threw them against the right wall of his chambers.

Nahrita yelled, again, "Bones Fight, Now!"

The Bones began to move towards Jerin and Tybin. The boys separated to distract them from a clear target. They jumped half way up the walls, and propelled their bodies to get behind the Bones.

Jerin loosed his arrows into the first Bones which looked like a very large human, where it froze in ice and shattered. The second Bones, looked like a large cat, when Jerin's arrow caught it in mid-pounce, causing it to suspend its walk where its body looked like a statue in midair before it came crashing down to the ground.

The wolves, knowing the boys' weapons, approached each of them from behind and tackled them.

Nick ran to Tybin, who was the closest to him and swung at the wolf with his claw, throwing him and several of the Bones far into the forest. The wolf hit one of the protruding roots, which impaled him, leaving him to dangle there as his body became lifeless. All of the Bones Nick lashed at, shattered and fell apart.

Deborah, who no one had paid any attention to, had climbed down from the cave and ran to help Jerin. She strategically threw her foraging knife at the wolf on top of Jerin and as it hit its target, the wolf was thrown into the base of Choran's perch.

The gnarled roots on the stand grew out of the knife and encased the wolf into his wooden tomb.

Deborah ran to the tomb, began to pull her knife out of the wood and was tackled by Nahrita. The two of them struggled for several minutes, trying to gain the upper hand. They continuously rolled around the ground trying to stay on top of one another.

Jerin sprang to aid Deborah, but was thrown into the air by a claw that consisted of large bear Bones. He had to quickly duck from the blades of Eleea and Elora as they fought off the hawks.

As he was falling, another Bones of a dog, possibly a wolf, grabbed him and tried to break his arm with its' jaws. Jerin reached into his arrows with his free hand and stabbed the Bones with the fire arrow. The flames ignited the body as Jerin pushed himself away.

Tybin started to spring towards Jerin when he noticed another bear Bones closest to the flames began to fall apart and drop to the ground.

He yelled at Jerin, "Use more of the flame arrows, they can't stand in the light." Jerin quickly shot arrows throughout the Bones and all of them fell as the light ignited around them.

Deborah held Nahrita's hair at the base of her head and pulled with all her strength. Nahrita's head snapped back in pain.

Deborah took the pouch, she had kept in her hand from the start of the battle, and opened it with her teeth and dumped the cayenne contents into Nahrita's mouth. Nahrita coughed, trying to catch her breath from the dry ingredients as her lungs filled with more of the powder. She loosened her grip on Deborah who jumped up and grabbed her knife out of the tomb and bolted to the wall nearest Jerin.

The men who helped Nahrita, and the Cellers who helped the Bones, all ran from the room and watched from outside the door while the battle was in full fierce contact. Raxton acted like he was as scared as them, but kept Ten in their way so they could not reenter.

He refused to let Iza get down from Ten, whispering to her, "We have to let them do battle with their magic. We do not have their skills."

Ayden kept her focus on Choran during the whole battle her friends were fighting on the ground. The two of them kept up their dance of circling the room.

Nahrita crawled her way to Choran's bowl of snail fern, as she reached it, she grabbed the straw and sucked on it.

Her body began to grow as she stood to attack. Again, she let out a low guttural call. Bighorn sheep, coyotes, and two moose drooped through the roof behind Choran.

Nahrita yelled instructions, as she coughed to regain composure, to the new group of fighters, "Do not touch the Messenger! Kill all the rest!"

Nick, still in bear form, stood on his hind legs and roared. Nekoh climbed onto Nick's shoulders as they moved forward to attack the moose.

When they reached the first moose, Nekoh jumped onto its back and dug his teeth into its neck. The moose thrashed his body to try and loose Nekoh's hold on him.

Two of the Trevins climbed up the legs of the moose and ran past Nekoh's hold to its head. They both took their knives and thrust them into the moose's eyes.

The moose reared his head back snorting in pain and the Trevin's held on with all their might. Nekoh readjusted his teeth and found the carotid artery and blood spurted everywhere. All three of them jumped off the moose and looked for their next fight.

Tybin twirled his staff in front of him with a whirring sound as it gained speed. He quickly jumped into the middle of the three coyotes and chopped two of them to pieces before they could even leap in defense.

The third coyote lunged at Tybin's upper right arm as he sunk his teeth deep into the tissue and began to thrash his head forcefully back and forth. Tybin screamed as he dropped his staff from the pain.

Nekoh quickly pounced on the back of the animal while his teeth connected into its neck. The animal loosened its hold on Tybin and tried to get away from Nekoh, while Jerin's arrow hit the animal as it froze and fell to the ground.

Tybin went to pick up his staff, but his right hand and arm lay limp, unable to grasp anything. He readjusted and picked his staff up with his left hand as he kept his right arm close to his chest.

The bighorn sheep lowered their heads as they each lifted one of their feet and scratched the ground; warning those around to stay clear of them. The fierce sound all six of them made as they flanked each other, with their horns in front of them, seemed impenetrable.

Jerin, Tybin, and Nick circled the sheep, looking for their best advantage point to separate them.

Nahrita watched from the distance, near the chamber doors. She caught a glimpse of Deborah hiding by the pile of rocks where she had been imprisoned earlier. She slyly walked closer to Deborah, keeping her eyes on the fight in front of her.

Eleea and Elora eliminated all three hawks and took to attack the next moose with their wings slicing as quickly as they could. They both struggled with each slice to get past the heavy-laden fur on its body.

Phum jumped onto the moose's back and ran to its head and took his knives and pushed them deep into the moose's eyes. The moose fell to its knees and the Trevins jumped on him and sliced his throat with their knives.

Ayden and Choran continued to circle each other as they watched each fight explode in front of them.

The last three coyotes jumped onto the downed moose and attacked the Trevins and Phum. Deborah stood up from her hiding position and threw her knife.

It struck the farthest coyote and lifted it off of her friends. The coyote writhed in pain from the force of the blade cutting into its chest. The other two coyotes ran away and regrouped to attack again. Phum and the Trevins watched them to see what they would do next.

Nahrita ran into action as Deborah threw her knife, knowing Deborah was now vulnerable. She grabbed Deborah by her hair and dangled her in front of her. Deborah's legs swayed like a rag doll as Nahrita, in amazon form, addressed her. "Because of you Jaeh is dead," she screamed.

Ayden desperately wanted to take her eyes off of Choran to go and aid Deborah. But all she could hear was Nick telling her to not lose focus. Her heart screamed with fear for her friend as she tried to stay calm. "Trust Eshra's magic," rang through her soul as she kept her eyes on Choran.

"No," Deborah stated. "Jaeh is dead because of his choice and your choice to follow evil, Nahrita," Deborah exclaimed.

"You have no one to blame but yourself. Look into your soul, Nahrita. Your anger fuels your decisions. And any decision fueled by anger only ends in defeat."

"Whether you want to realize it or not: Anger is always defeat of a purposeful soul. Anger is death. You and Jaeh died long ago with anger and hatred," Deborah declared to Nahrita.

Nahrita growled with a roar as she shook Deborah. "You have no idea what you talk about," she cried out. "By my hand you will know what death feels like. Then, where will be your wisdom on anger and my soul." Nahrita screeched.

Nahrita reached with her free hand to choke Deborah and as she did, Deborah took her hand out from her pocket. She quickly blew the substance she held in the palm of her hand into Nahrita's face.

Nahrita screamed as she recognized the all too familiar smell of the powder. She dropped Deborah as she heaved and coughed, trying to regain her position.

Deborah quickly ran away from Nahrita and watched from the chamber doors where Nekoh was standing. Nahrita fell to the ground as her body began to expel the snail fern.

Deborah and Nekoh looked at each other, nodded, and ran to help the Trevins and Phum with the last two coyotes. The animals were so engrossed in trying to keep the small animals off of them, they did not see Nekoh and Deborah approach them.

Deborah pulled her foraging knife out of the already downed one and positioned herself for her next throw. Nekoh circled behind her and pounced onto the one farthest away and sunk his teeth into the animal's neck. Deborah threw her knife and the last coyote flew into the rock pile and was entombed in the stone.

The boys were still in the same stance, assessing how to attack the sheep. With no others to battle, the rest of their friends stood with them. The sheep continued to paw the ground with their hooves as they snorted.

Tybin slowly twirled his staff back and forth with his left hand, acting like he was relaxing and playing with it. Phum picked up on Tybin's strategy and started to twirl his knives nonchalantly attached to his belt.

Eleea flew to Nick's shoulder and Elora flew to Deborah's while they slowly lifted their wings up and down and began to hum a soft tune. Trevin pulled out his flute and joined in by matching the birds' musical notes.

The rest of the Trevins began to sway in unison back and forth to the music. Nick and Jerin slowly pulled back and made their way to opposite ends of their friends.

The sheep stopped pawing the ground in confusion. They each lifted their heads and tried to discern what their enemies were doing.

As they lifted their heads, Jerin and Nick flanked them and attacked the outside two. The rest of the group ran into the middle of the sheep and began to attack. Tybin's staff reached one of the sheep's neck and sliced it open from ear to ear.

Deborah ran after Jerin's foe and jumped onto the back of the animal. She took her knife and forcefully stabbed at the sheep's neck. Jerin followed with his arrows and the animal fell into a shattered mess of body parts.

Nick drew his arm back, clawed at the sheep he flanked and connected with bloody stripes along the sheep's back and side. The animal turned and butted Nick away from him.

Nick fell back from the force of the sheep's horns. Tybin reached Nick and got in front of him to protect him from the hooves of the sheep. The ram backed away from Tybin and repositioned his stance.

Nick crawled out from under Tybin and roared as he stood on his hind legs. Nick leapt over Tybin and landed on the back of the ram.

The bighorn fell on the ground and Nick sank his teeth into its neck and tore its fur and skin from off its body. The animal lay there with blood, bone, and tissue sprawling out of his body.

The Trevins clamored up the next ram and used their weapons to disorient him. Phum jumped around them and took his left blade and wrapped the wire around the ram's neck. He then took his right blade and went the opposite direction around its neck. He took both ends and pulled backwards on the animal's back.

The Trevins stopped jabbing the ram and ran behind Phum and held onto him as they all pulled backwards together. The animal choked as it tried to get air in its lungs. Deborah came around its side and sliced its throat with her knife.

The last bighorn's eyes were loosely held on in their sockets from the onslaught of Eleea's and Elora's wings. It staggered to regain its stance and fell from the pain and lack of ability to see. Nekoh pounced on him, bit down on its neck and blood spurted everywhere as it lost any chance to live.

Choran roared with anger as he saw all the animals lay in defeat. He heaved his chest five times until his upper body looked like it would explode. He worked his way around his part of the circle and blew his breath out towards the Forest of Roots. He turned back to glare at Ayden.

"Little girl," Choran seethed. "What will you do while you are in Hollow? He questioned her. "Will you look for your true daddy?" He taunted her. "Or will you cry with Ehyah because your daddy can't be found," he laughed with glee at making her question her life.

Ayden saw the thousands of Bones walking towards them from deep in the Forest of Roots. She yelled at Tybin and Nekoh who were by her side, waiting to attack Choran, saying, "Get everyone behind me by the chamber doors."

Jerin turned to see where Ayden's eyes were looking. He raced to his friends to help Tybin and Nekoh get them behind Ayden.

All of them stood in gripped fear as the sound of the Bones moving forward echoed in the chamber. What they thought was a victory against Choran, the animals, and Nahrita, was only a small feat compared to the Bones approaching them.

"Choran, you know nothing about tears of sorrow or tears of love," Ayden said to him. "Those who stand behind me are the greatest gift I have ever known."

"I do not lament over what could have been or who I could have known because of life's events. The most important thing I know is the here and now of their love and friendship. It has kept me real and full of life. Each of them knows how much I love them and trust them. They are my world, and I would do anything to protect them," she passionately said.

Choran heaved with joyous laughter as he stared at Ayden with his deathly eyes. "You live a stupid life, messenger. None of you will live past this day." Choran lifted his wings and lunged at Ayden.

Ayden flew back, looked at her friends, smiled, and took her wings and fanned them out.

Choran opened his enormous mouth to devour her, and as he did, she released twenty-seven blades from her wings.

Deborah screamed as she began to run to Ayden who was swallowed by Choran. The others ran with her to try and reach Ayden.

Suddenly, they all felt a jolt in their bodies as Ayden's feathers hit them. They swirled in an upward motion as their bodies lifted and shot them into a spiral tunnel.

All of them struggled to catch their breath as their bodies flew through a strange blackness. None of them could grasp their surroundings as they each tried to grab something to gain some bearing. What seemed like forever in an alternate space, actually took only seconds for them as they fell to the ground.

Deborah was the first to stand, and look around her. She made a complete circle as she said, "I know where we are. We are at Zetia's lake," she cried with relief.

She looked at everyone who landed with her, including the ospreys, and the horses from the Front, to make sure they were OK.

Then she started to call, "Ayden! Ayden, where are you," she asked. Deborah became frantic as she kept calling for Ayden.

Nick landed near the edge of the lake and saw his reflection of a bear in the water as he heard Deborah's screams. He jumped up and began to yell with Deborah for Ayden to show herself.

Tybin went to Nick, and Jerin went to Deborah. Both of them held on to them and solemnly said together, "She is not with us."

Chapter Forty-Four

Deborah fell to her knees and moaned as she rocked back and forth. "I can't lose her too," she cried. Jerin knelt with her, and tried to comfort her.

Nick sat silent as tears fell down his cheeks. The Trevins came to him and patted him as they cried with him.

Elora was inconsolable as she cried into Eleea's feathers.

Nekoh lay next to Deborah, dumbfounded by all that had just happened.

Tybin and Phum rounded up Ten, Raxton, Iza, Trevin Three, and Deiha and explained to them where they were.

Zetia flew in and landed next to Tybin with Joshua, Callie, Nadab, Lydia and Gethsemane following quickly behind her.

"What happened, Tybin," Zetia worriedly asked.

Tybin looked at her, saying, "I think it best we all meet at the main house to tell our story."

Zetia nodded in agreement and gestured to Nadab and Lydia to help get Deborah and Nick to the house.

Tybin and Jerin rounded up the horses from the Front and acknowledged the ospreys as they headed to the Home.

When they reached the Home, Tarhana set about gathering their war-torn clothes and others handed them washcloths to clean their bodies. New clothes caressed their skin as all of them were assessed for wounds.

Sahl looked at Tybin's arm and shoulder and wrapped them tightly against his body. Tarhana and Deiha attended to Iza's wound, cleaning it, sewing it shut and putting a salve dressing on it.

Once all the wounds were accounted for, everyone sat at the table where Tybin and Jerin proceeded to tell them everything which took place after they left Zetia's. They stopped after they explained about Two, as everyone was crying.

Zetia stood, went to Deborah, who had not stopped crying since they returned, and hugged her. She looked at Tarhana and said, "Bring her a special drink, Tarhana."

Tarhana quickly left and returned with a hot clear liquid. Zetia made Deborah drink it, saying, "Deborah this will help you sleep, peacefully."

She lifted Deborah up from her chair and put her on the couch by the fire. She held the cup while Deborah took a few more sips and, then slumped in Zetia's arms. Zetia laid her head on a pillow and placed a blanket over her and went back to the table to listen.

Tybin continued to tell the rest of the story. He finished with forlornly saying, "What are we going to do without Ayden?"

"The prophecy from Joshua states the messenger will have to go to the bowels," Gethsemane stated in deep thought.

"It would seem the Hollow could be considered the bowels of Choran," Callie continued Gethsemane's train of thought.

"But she is dead!" Nick said with sadness. "He ate her and she is gone," Nick cried out.

"What did Choran say about the Great Crane, Nickalli," Eleea tenderly said. "He did not talk about him as if he were dead. He talked about him as alive and not able to escape from the Hollow."

"True," Joshua said as he expressed his thoughts. "Ayden has to sing to release both of them. For the hummingbirds to come to them, she has to sing."

"But she will not be able to fly for months," Zetia stated. "She will need to fly out of the bowels and she can't until her feathers grow back."

"From what I have seen, she has lost at least twenty-seven feathers. By my count, I see twenty-seven feathers each of you, now, possess from her sacrifice to save you. We have to get to her to help her," she said with urgency.

"How, Zetia? How?" Phum asked perplexed. "You cannot ask us to go in the same way to save Ayden. None of us would survive. Choran would be looking for us, now. And, we do not even know if she is truly alive to be saved," he said.

"She is alive," Nadab confirmed. "I would have known if she were dead. I knew Two was gone before you told us the story. Each gift I make has a life source attached to its owner. I felt Two's leave his gift and go back to the life source of Eshra. She is alive," he stated, again.

"Then, how do we reach her," Jerin asked. "None of us know how to get to the Hollow. And, I doubt any of us could go the way she did and live to tell about it. She is the Messenger. She is the prophecy. She was our answer." he stated with despair in his voice.

"And, what do we do to help her?" Tybin stated. "I mean, what do we need to know on how to help her. All of us have to learn from someone what it will take to be there for her." he stated emphatically.

Out of the shadows a small voice said, "I know where to find the one who can give you the answers you desire. But the journey will not be an easy one."

Everyone's head spun around at the same time in the direction of the voice. A bird in full plume, his feathers glistening in glorious color as he walked, emerged from the corner of the waterfall.

Kit stood in front of the group and bowed to them.

"What do you know, Kit?" Zetia tenderly asked him.

"I know of one," Kit began.

"The one called the peacock spider. He spins his web with joy and dance. The web of fate is his speech of chance. For he knows the ways of the worlds and where each path begins and each path ends. Go to him and seek what you must mend. He will give you sight."

Kit's feathers waved in beautiful rhythm behind his body in a rippled motion as he said, "I will take you to the spider."

...this is only the beginning.

Epilogue

Ayden caught her breath as she was consumed by Choran. His odor filled every part of her senses and seemed to suck the life out of her.

She knew she was falling deeper and deeper into darkness as she tried to grab ahold of anything to stop her descent. Soon, the horrific fumes from his gut overpowered her and her mind went blank as she passed out from the smell.

When she finally woke, she tried desperately to focus, but total blackness disoriented her further. Ayden felt around her body to see what she was laying on.

It wasn't rock as there was a softness to it. And it wasn't solid ground as there was an unevenness to it. Kind of like the pods they had climbed over in the Cell.

Suddenly, she felt a wet tongue licking her face. She grabbed at it, and heard. "Ayd, Ayd, it's OK, Ayd."

"Nip," she cried. "Nip, I sent you to Zetia with the rest of them. You were not to be with me in this hell," Ayden said as tears formed in her eyes while she grabbed Nip in her arms.

"Ayd, need me," Nip stated. "Dug claws, grrrrr tight," she said as she continued to lick Ayden's face.

Ayden put her head into Nip's fur and cried.

When Ayden finally focused her eyes, she noticed her wings were flickering enough light for her to see a vast wilderness of nothingness. All around her were broken down huts of all sizes. Trees and shrubs like the Dead Trees dotted the horizon where huge mountains were off in the distance.

"Nip," Ayden said. "I promise I will get you out of here." Ayden lifted her body to stand, brushed herself off, and looked around to determine her next move.

****

Author Bio

Born September 10, 1957 in Great Falls, Montanan. Raised in a world where my Native side was only touched upon when I visited Trenton, North Dakota to see relatives live the simple life with outhouses and no running water.

I come from the Turtle Mountain Band of Chippewa Indians. Falcon is the namesake of my family. I am Metis.

Deep in my spirit the call of the indigenous people would rise in my soul and ground me as I created. From abstract jewelry known as Found Art to writing fiction, I found my voice in a world where lines are blurred and the soul cries out to be found.

My childhood was not one of dignity and respect...but one of survival. The survival anthem to stand tall and rejoice in who you are and in who you have become. It rang loud throughout my years of growth as I stumbled with mistakes and doubt. Each misstep was a stone I firmly placed to climb higher to make my stand.

Instilled into my two beautiful children, Joshua and Trevor, was the determination to be better...to be stronger...to show we can survive with dignity and respect as our testimony.

We live in Great Falls and teach kids through video game design camps with our business Add-A-Tudez Entertainment Company. We teach what we live: How to overcome and shine as a light of encouragement to others. (check out our story by SONY Playstation on Youtube: My Road to Greatness: Josh Hughes.)

Truly, I stand tall because of what I experienced and witnessed as a child. It is the Native spirit of perseverance and of remembering we belong to the Earth. Deeply rooted in this is the belief of a God who carries us as we trek across this land to make our mark in a world of diversity and beauty.

Made in the USA
Columbia, SC
05 March 2020